# GOLIATH

# GOLIATH

## Paul Geddes

St. Martin's Press
New York

*Library of Congress Cataloging-in-Publication Data*

Geddes, Paul.
     Goliath / by Paul Geddes.
         p.   cm.
     ISBN 0-312-01436-8 : $17.95
     I. Title.
     PR6057.E24G6   1988                              87-29933
     823'.914—dc19                                       CIP

First Published in Great Britain by The Bodley Head.

First U.S. Edition

10  9  8  7  6  5  4  3  2  1

# GOLIATH

# I

To understand all the events of that autumn, one must go back to something at the beginning of the year.

As the first real snow of winter fell, there was a killing in Wimpole Street. At six-thirty in the evening, Max Bevelmann, a medical practitioner with a variety of exotic qualifications, director of the Enriched Consciousness Institute and similar ventures, left his consulting rooms. He entered his Rolls which stood at the kerb, divinely immune from the harassments of wardens, the ignominy of the clamp. Lowering the window beside him, Bevelmann craned his head out into a whitening world to monitor the traffic behind. Then he eased forward through the vacant space left by a car that had driven off moments before.

The explosion caused by the bomb beneath the front wheels of the Rolls astonishingly left his head intact. Deposited with macabre neatness on the area steps of a house on the opposite side of Wimpole Street, it lay upright, to enrich the consciousness of the caretaker there and anyone else who happened to look. The remainder of the body disintegrated, became a miscellany of items for men with plastic bags to tease from the crevices of twisted metal. For this task they had to wait some time. The force of the explosion had lifted the shell of the car on to the railings of a clinic a few doors away from Bevelmann's rooms; it was morning before the crane brought in by the police finally winched it free.

The investigation into the origin of the bomb moved

5

uncertainly at first. Bevelmann had plenty of ill-wishers. But none, it seemed, stood to profit from his death, while any who might have been tempted to repay past injuries were able to establish their innocence. Only when the police began to take account of faint indications that the bomb might not have been intended for Bevelmann at all, might instead have fallen off another car to which it had been insecurely fitted and become lodged under the Rolls, was progress made.

From a list of visitors to the clinic and other consulting rooms near Bevelmann's who might at the critical time have used the parking space in front of the Rolls, emerged the name of Señor Felipe Baroja, a Basque politician. The Foreign Office was consulted: it replied that Baroja was a former leader of ETA's military wing who had decided the struggle for complete independence of the Basque provinces of Spain was no longer justified and had spoken out against continuing a terrorist campaign. In doing so, Baroja had earned the bitter enmity of colleagues in ETA who suspected him of collusion with the central government in Madrid.

In-fighting between Basques became the preferred theory for the explosion that had killed Bevelmann. The Ambassador in Madrid was asked to consult the Spanish government. His report left no room for further doubt. Baroja, whose visit to London had been for a consultation about a serious heart condition, was certainly a marked man: one attempt on his life by extremist Basques had already been made in Spain and others were feared. He was expected to return to London in October for an operation. Because of his central role in secret negotiations with others in ETA considering the abandonment of armed struggle, the Spanish government had expressed the hope that maximum security protection would be given during his second visit.

Appropriate noises were therefore made by the Foreign Office to the Home Office and the Commissioner for the Metropolitan Police was directed to make sure his Special

6

Branch had its finger entirely out during the coming months.

An uneasy calm descended. After a colourful exploration of Bevelmann's professional and private life, the newspapers, like the public at large, ignorant of the Baroja angle, lost interest in the killing. Memories faded. Even the caretaker of the house opposite Bevelmann's empty consulting rooms finally ceased to avert her eyes when, climbing the area steps, she reached the point where Bevelmann's head had lain reddening the snow.

It was Fender who, one night in October, first caught the echo of that earlier killing. Gazing at another twisted shell of a car, precariously at rest on the portico of a house, he had a sudden sense of re-enactment. The image of Bevelmann's Rolls, caught by the television news camera before it was lifted from the clinic railings, flickered in his mind. The temptation to play with the idea of some connection, unlikely though that seemed, was momentarily strong.

Then the person by his side spoke. Turning to listen, Fender let the other image go. The idea was, after all, absurd . . .

# II

TWICE Antrim had made discreet reconnaissance among the others. He had already been introduced to the majority of those in the age group that mattered; it was the remainder he had needed to study. When he returned to the drawing room, to sit watching Rylance exercise easy charm on the wife of the local Chief Constable, his earlier impression had been confirmed. In this gathering he was unique.

Not that he could be confident of recognizing every senior official who swam in Whitehall's shifting waters. Permanent Secretaries he knew well enough and most of the Deputy Secretaries too; he had met them when he had done the rounds of Departments to introduce himself after his appointment as Director of the Central Crimes Bureau. But his memory for faces was no longer infallible. Moreover, in Rylance's sprawling empire, the Ministry of Defence, there were certainly some he had never seen.

But if they had been lurking amongst the assorted dinner jackets and evening dresses of this weekend junket of Rylance's, he would have known. Coming from a different world, first the Army, then Intelligence, had given him a nose for them. On occasions such as this, officials gave off an *odour*. It arose from a compound of unease and austere watchfulness, from an inability to surrender themselves to uninhibited luxury when the source of it all was a Minister. The eyes were alert for others of their kind whose presence required evaluation, the smiles transitory as vague thoughts of the Public Accounts Committee floated through their minds. And there was always the danger that spouses,

8

plucked from suburban frugality for a night of splendour, were losing their heads in the pink champagne.

He had needed to give only the briefest of glances at those in the ballroom which Rylance had built onto the rear of the house. They represented a separate segment of the party, imported from the square mile round Harrods for the birthday of Camilla, Rylance's nineteen-year-old daughter by his previous marriage. No senior official would be at play amongst *them*. The others in the house, leaving aside Rylance's Parliamentary Secretary, the Lord Lieutenant of the county and the Chief Constable with their respective wives, divided into three groups — the local hunt, members of Rylance's constituency association and businessmen he had known in the days of building his fortune out of computer software. Only one struck Antrim as difficult to place, a man with a Zapata moustache and disenchanted eyes; the front of his dress shirt was frilled. He could surely be ruled out as well, Antrim had decided. So that was that. He really was the only official present.

A movement was beginning in the direction of the adjoining room. Beyond a buffet, a uniformed platoon of the Rylances' inside staff could be seen. Antrim drained his glass and followed others in. The question that awaited answer was *why* he was unique. Rylance's invitation for him to join a party to the races and then to stay overnight had hardly been justified by the extent of past acquaintance. There had been no corruption cases in Defence of sufficient importance for Antrim to need to brief him personally, nor did any threaten as far as he knew. Apart from a conversation about the Bureau's functions at the wedding of a niece of Antrim's who had turned out to be Rylance's goddaughter, they had had no dealings. And the wedding had been too long ago for there to be a plausible connection.

He could think of only one explanation: Rylance's move from Defence to the Home Office was imminent and he was starting to acquaint himself with those he would be controlling. When Pagett, the Secretary to the Cabinet, delicately easing one leg across another and raising the trouser crease with thumb and forefinger in his customary signal of an intimacy to come, had spoken of it, Antrim had gained the impression that nothing would happen before Christmas. But perhaps the plan had been advanced.

The Chief Constable's wife was making polite noises about the appearance of the buffet. A surfeit of flowers had been strewn round the dishes. Elaborate things had been done with the salads. He supposed the dazzle, the tendency to overkill, to be something Evelyn Rylance had brought with her from the parties of her earlier life in Beverly Hills. Not that he had sensed vulgarity when she had received him for lunch in the morning, or later, watching her organize the departure for the races. Slim enough to be a model, well but not over-dressed, with hair massed in auburn curls that were carefully untidy, speaking to everyone with the same brisk intensity laced with laconic smiles, she had played the part of the ideal hostess, a formidable contender in the stakes to be champion of Whitehall's American wives.

Rylance himself had not arrived until halfway through the races. He had been kept in the Ministry by some crisis in the Middle East necessitating the mobilization of a contingency force. After talking to the Service Chiefs, he had stayed to record as many television and radio interviews as sweating Information Officers could drum up for a Saturday lunchtime. To Antrim his greeting had been an enquiry about the state of the betting. But as he had moved away to speak to others, he had said, as though of an agenda already agreed, 'We'll have our private talk tonight.'

With loaded plate, Antrim paused at the entrance to the picture gallery in which tables had been laid. All of them seemed to be occupied by members of the ballroom gang. Gazing about for another harbour, he found at his elbow the man with the Zapata moustache. He was nodding towards the conservatory at the end of the gallery.

It was almost empty. They seated themselves among

languorous flowers and humid greenery; a fountain played into a stone-lined pool. When their wine had been brought, the man said, 'I don't believe we've met. My name's Warrilow, Hector Warrilow.'

The name was faintly familiar: the political editor of some monthly that had folded, an occasional writer in the Sundays. But there was something else too. A casual remark made once by Pagett was fretting at his mind but he couldn't quite recall it. He was saved by Warrilow speaking again. 'I write Jeffrey's speeches.'

Of course, he remembered now: Rylance's auto-cue, Pagett had said, does it quite well.

'And you?' Warrilow asked.

'Antrim. I'm Director of the Central Crimes Bureau.'

'Ah, master of that mysterious outfit in Somerset Square!'

'Not mysterious at all. There's a plate at the entrance. Our names and pittances are all in the Civil Service list. What do you find mysterious?'

'I suppose one can never quite credit that, even in today's world, corruption in the public service is really big enough to take up all your time. One imagines you're Up to Something Else.' Warrilow detached skin from a chicken wing. 'And then, there's your status: civil servants dealing with crime. That must make for problems with the police, surely?' His gaze lifted; for a few seconds those dead eyes were animated. A typical ploy of a journalist encountered on a social occasion, Antrim thought sourly—putting a question to which he knew the answer perfectly well, in the hope it would provoke a scrap of copy for the future.

'Read the Horsley Report which recommended the setting up of the Bureau. You'll see why there had to be something independent of the police.'

'But although you investigate you don't prosecute.'

'That's for the police to do. The Bureau tells them where to look for evidence. We each understand what the other's job is.'

Warrilow shook his head, simulating bafflement. The

11

trick was not to be provoked, instead to serve into Warrilow's court without delay. 'Tell me about writing speeches for politicians. Do you find it rewarding?'

'I only write for Jeffrey of course—he asked me to help when he heard he was getting Defence on which he didn't have too many thoughts of his own when he began. The answer is, in his case, yes, I do.' He was already sounding a little defensive. 'Having one's lines immortalized in that chocolatey voice is curiously satisfying. You begin to think you're hearing yourself as you *ought* to be.'

'I once met a man who wrote gags for Bob Hope,' Antrim said. 'But I suppose that's a little different.'

Warrilow took it well, even smiled. But they sat in silence for a while. Since they had blazed the trail to the conservatory, it had been filling up, mostly with members of the local hunt. A foursome appeared in the doorway. They were from the birthday party. Camilla Rylance was leading. In a bare-shouldered dress, her blonde hair drawn back at the neck, she looked more attractive than at the races. Notwithstanding traces of puppy fat and a careless walk, she was undoubtedly beddable.

Bringing up the rear of the foursome was a youth in an ancient dinner jacket and a stiff-fronted shirt. His razor edge collar had left weals on the sides of his throat. The youth's eyes were very bright and his shoulders see-sawed to some private music as he walked. Occasionally he bowed to tables on his route.

'A little chemical help I think,' Warrilow said.

'Perhaps.'

'I went into the lavatory by the ballroom half an hour ago. There were two of them standing by the washbasin. One said, "Sorry, do you want to come here?" They moved to one side and went on snorting as though that was the most normal thing to go to a lavatory for. I washed my hands and went out.' He shrugged. 'I suppose it was cocaine. You have to warm heroin, don't you?'

He nodded neutrally. He suspected that Warrilow was once more fishing for a reaction. The foursome was making

12

a lot of noise at the table it had chosen at the end of the conservatory. They seemed extraordinarily callow. Yet, as he gazed at the sheen of Camilla's skin, thought how his fingers would begin by delicately tracing the shoulder line, he felt a twinge of envy.

'It doesn't trouble your official conscience . . .?' Warrilow said.

'Fortunately, it's paid to concern itself with other things.' He looked again at the youth and wondered how the Chief Constable would have handled it, had he been in the lavatory instead of Warrilow. Judiciously no doubt, not judicially.

Warrilow had reached out to pluck a petal from the hydrangea beside their table. He held it up to the light. He had obviously been drinking a good deal before they sat down. 'Of course, it's hardly the most desirable thing to be going on under the roof of a Home Secretary.'

He was not trying out a speculation, he plainly knew what was planned. So Rylance had even let his speechwriter in on the move. So much for the aura of secrecy Pagett had created. 'You see that as his next post, do you?' Antrim said.

Warrilow's smile implied that he was not to be fooled by such disingenuousness. 'Jeffrey has to decide which way to jump over this new GOLIATH weapon first. In the spring he seemed convinced we had to have it. Then he set up this enquiry which has produced these bloody leakages to the press. However, once he *has* decided and it's gone through Cabinet, he'll be into the Home Office like a shot. The PM can't wait to get your present master out to grass. But you must know all this of course.'

Clearly Warrilow was well-informed. Boorish and needling though he might be, if he was on the inside track to this extent, it might pay to cultivate him in days to come. 'Do you think he's changing his mind about buying GOLIATH from the Americans?' Antrim asked.

'Could be. He's certainly less enthusiastic than he was. The enquiry committee will go whichever way he wants to push them. But I expect Evelyn will decide in the end.'

He didn't seem to be joking. 'You mean she's influential in a thing like this?'

'Definitely. Jeffrey's political career is *her* career. She makes the decisions with him whenever she can. Over GOLIATH she's seen the amount of opposition that's been building up in the country, and not just from CND. It scares people. I think Evelyn's worried that going on with buying it could damage him politically for a long time. In which case, you may take it she'll be against. Never underestimate Evelyn's influence.

It sounded a useful piece of intelligence. 'Will you stay with him when he moves from Defence?'

'He wants me to. I think I shall find home affairs more attractive—less technology to mug up. And law and order are very reliable for getting the pulses skipping, especially at Party Conferences.' Warrilow flicked the hydrangea petal away and sat back with a satisfied gesture. 'The move will be good in more than one way. Jeffrey needs to widen his appeal, acquire a little more of the common touch. The Home Office needn't be a bed of nails if you give the punters what they want.'

Camilla's party were already on their feet again, returning to the buffet for seconds. The hyperactive youth had acquired a pair of serving tongs from somewhere. He was making elaborate efforts to draw down the zip of Camilla's dress as she walked ahead of him. Warrilow said, 'She's going to be quite something in a year or two.'

'Did her mother and Rylance divorce?'

'No, Diana Rylance died of leukaemia. Nice, gentle creature—much too withdrawn for a politician's wife. From the point of view of Jeffrey's career, Evelyn is streets ahead. She works at it. When Jeffrey joined the Cabinet her own car was a Porsche. It went the next day. In its place is a white Jaguar XJS with Union Jack transfers on the door panels. Flashy, you may say; but effective. It gets her noticed. Evelyn intends to be the first ex-air hostess to rule the roost at No. 10.' When Antrim raised his eyebrows,

Warrilow went on, 'You know that's how she began in the States, don't you?' There was amused malice in his voice.

'A lot of things could go wrong on the way.'

'Agreed. But Jeffrey's the right age. He's able. He hasn't made a mess of anything he's been given. He may get jeered at by my fellow hacks on the Sundays as a *Novus Homo* but that isn't going to matter when the crunch comes. It may even do him some good. Just because he likes scarlet linings in his suits and wears the odd gold chain doesn't mean he can't run things better than the old gang. I would say that for the younger generation and a lot of others too Jeffrey is the acceptable face of commercial success. Now that Ropner has thrown in his hand and gone off to that curious United Nations job, my money's on Jeffrey for No. 10 within five years. He wants to get there very much. And if he ever shows signs of resting on his oars Evelyn will apply the goad.'

Antrim drained his glass and thought about Evelyn Rylance. One could envy Rylance possession of that elegant driving force. Her ambition and energy apart, he wondered what she was really like. Sexually adept, no doubt, in a cold-blooded way. If the risk were not too great, it would be interesting to discover if he could sample her. But he suspected that he might then become aware of a core more steel-like than his own. Vulnerability, an openness to pain, was what he looked for increasingly as the years went by. Clearly she had lost that a long time ago.

'Presumably she stopped being an air hostess when she married her first husband.'

'Yes, that was Sam Giordano, the film producer. They had a couple of daughters and then she opened a boutique in Beverly Hills. It became *the* place for Hollywood people to buy imported fashion jewellery. She also moved into Giordano's production company. Before they divorced I gather she'd established herself as an almost equal partner.'

'Then Rylance came along . . .'

'He'd known them both quite a while. He told me that he used to stay with them on his trips to the States when he was still in software. Giordano had some interest in that area. The divorce was an amicable affair as these things go. Perhaps Giordano thought it would be nice to be able to take his own decisions again. And Evelyn, having come to the conclusion that she was never going to get him into the White House, reckoned that an English politician on the way up and with enough money to maintain her lifestyle wasn't too bad an exchange.' It was obvious that Warrilow was not over-fond of Evelyn.

A servant arrived to invite them to return to the buffet. There seemed to be enough puddings and sweets to last a fair-sized hotel a fortnight. A lot of them were of the sculptural kind; the centre piece was a swan in ice. They stayed to eat standing. Rylance was visible in the drawing room beyond. He was seated on the arm of a chair, chatting up two elderly females, probably from his constituency committee. After a few minutes he rose and advanced towards the buffet. His smile contrived to convey to anyone he passed en route, both extreme approachability and a delicate warning that now was not a convenient moment.

He placed a hand on Antrim's shoulder. 'I hope you'll forgive all this scramble. We'd planned a separate dinner in here, leaving the young to pig it with a buffet next to the ballroom. But Evelyn decided this morning that the staff simply couldn't cope with the double act. Has it been too ghastly?'

He didn't wait for a response before turning to Warrilow. 'I looked through your notes on the way down, Hector. Admirable as ever. I do just wonder about the Agincourt bit. Can I really get away with that?'

'I think so.'

'Not too strong a whiff of Laurence Olivier . . .?'

Once more he failed to wait for an answer, turning back to Antrim, the hand still on his shoulder. 'Shall we have our few words? Let's go to the library.'

They sat in blue leather armchairs with a bottle of Remy Martin between them. While a servant poured their coffee, Antrim watched Rylance clipping a cigar. He had rounded

16

his lips ready to receive it; they were heavy, disagreeably moist. Yet, despite the lips, the high colour and the slackness beneath the chin, the effect conveyed by his features was not unattractive. It was the eyes that redeemed them. Framed by lashes that were unusually long, they had a lustre and depth of expression that startled. Compelling was the word the newspaper profile writers preferred. Had Rylance been a woman, they would have said beautiful and been right.

When the door closed behind the servant, Rylance said, 'What I need your help on, Antrim, is a private matter.'

So he was not just wanting to familiarize himself with one of his future dominions against the day when he became Home Secretary. An alarm bell sounded in Antrim's head.

'As you may know, I have two stepdaughters through my present wife. They grew up in America but came over to England later. Jacqueline, the elder, is in the process of getting divorced from a member of the Bar who's gone off with someone else. At the moment she's in Majorca, trying to sort herself out. Lauren who is twenty-two stayed with us for a few months then went to live with a friend who works in television—a woman. Lauren has now disappeared. The man she's gone with is a Basque. I'd have no objection to that in the ordinary way. But he happens to be a terrorist. I want your help in finding her.'

'*My help?*'

'That of your department.'

He searched for temporizing words. 'You've considered normal methods . . .'

'Such as?'

'A private detective agency.'

'We've tried one. There are reasons why we prefer not to go further along that road.'

'Perhaps the police—'

'I don't wish them to be involved. Not knowingly.'

Antrim shifted in his chair. 'I should like to help, of course. The difficulty is that it would be rather a long way outside the Bureau's charter. Our responsibility—'

17

Rylance said smoothly, 'The Home Secretary is aware of course I'm consulting you. Since you and I will be seeing a good deal more of each other I should be grateful if you would find a way of doing this.' He paused, smiling. 'You *had* heard I'm taking over the Home Office . . .?'

'I understood there was a possibility—'

'As soon as I've been able to resolve a particular problem of weapons policy the move will take place. As you can imagine, I should find my position as Home Secretary intolerable if this business of Lauren and the Spaniard had not also been cleared up. The relationship would get to the press sooner or later. I don't have to spell out what they would make of it.'

He was not bothering to use any finesse in putting the pressure on. What the consultation with the Home Secretary had amounted to was dubious: almost certainly not about actually using the Bureau's resources. This was going to be just between Rylance and Antrim himself. Antrim watched the Remy Martin being poured into his glass and had the sensation he had entered a trap. 'You believe that if you can locate Lauren you'll be able to persuade her to break with the Basque?'

'I have no influence with her. But her mother certainly does. She's confident she will make her see reason.'

'Do you believe they're still in this country?'

'Probably not.' Rylance pursed his lips and looked into his glass for a moment. 'Let me tell you the story from the beginning. My wife and I first heard about the relationship in the early summer. All we knew then was that Lauren had met a Spaniard who was supposed to be studying politics here. We weren't in any way worried. However Lauren started expressing some very radical views soon after, talking of the Basque separatists and the IRA having ideals in common. I decided to make enquiries about the man whose name is Luis Fernandes. I discovered he was a secret member of ETA's military wing, a terrorist. My wife confronted Lauren with the news and said she ought to break with Fernandes. She refused to accept what my wife told her. The next thing we discovered was that she had left the house of the friend she lived with in Pimlico and gone off with Fernandes.

'The private detective my wife employed to try to locate them got nowhere. It's true we made things difficult for him. He wasn't allowed to reveal to anyone that we were employing him or to give the impression there was concern about Lauren's whereabouts. Nor did I feel we could tell him what I knew about Fernandes' background since I'd got the information through my Department. We've now paid the detective off. I believe we're not going to locate them unless official resources are brought to bear.'

'Surely the police—'

'Naturally I've considered them. But I should not feel confident about the security of any enquiries I asked them to make. At present they're investigating a tiresome series of leakages from my office which relate to the weapons policy issue I mentioned. Although the enquiry was supposed to be conducted with maximum secrecy I found that within forty-eight hours the press had been tipped off about it. However, I have another reason why I prefer one of your officers to carry out the enquiry. If Lauren is to be traced, it's most likely to be through her friends. I can't think she hasn't revealed to at least one of them where she is. From what you once told me about the staffing of your department, the sort of people you employ are more likely than the average police officer to get them to talk freely. Of course, I would expect your man to use some suitable story so that a hue and cry isn't suspected. My name must be kept out of it. I assume he would be able to get help from the police and other official agencies without revealing anything. For example, Fernandes' movements as an alien must have been the subject of some record.'

It was plain that he had thought it through. Enquiries by the Bureau in the official world would not strike anybody as likely to have originated with a request from Rylance; he would be getting access to machinery, at home and abroad, that no private detective could use and, moreover, through a secure cut-out. The fact remained there was no flavour of corruption to provide an excuse for intervention. Rylance had no right to expect help from any government agency in looking for the girl. If it got to the Opposition or the press that official resources were being used, there would be an almighty row. On the other hand, there wasn't any reason why it should get out. The enquiry could be limited to one or two people in the Bureau.

Rylance was watching him through his cigar smoke. Faintly in the background Antrim could hear the thump of the group playing in the ballroom. He said slowly, 'And you are simply asking that we find Lauren? Nothing more?'

'Nothing more. I would not want your people to approach her or disclose themselves in any way. We just need to know where she is so that my wife can make a further attempt to get her to see reason. She might still refuse I suppose. But Evelyn can be very persuasive. In any case, it has to be tried.'

There was no way of escaping without giving a direct refusal. That would put paid to any hope of reasonable relations with Rylance in the future. He had to take the risk and hitch his waggon to Rylance's star. After all, if Warrilow was right, that was where it ought to be.

'I'll do what I can to help,' he said. 'We may not succeed of course.'

Rylance smiled, nodding his head slightly. 'I felt sure I could rely on you.' He seemed to be offering congratulations rather than thanks.

'Shall I send an officer round on Monday to get more details?'

'I'd rather he saw my wife—she will be more helpful than I can be.' Rylance took a pad from his pocket and scribbled on it. 'This is her private telephone at our house in Chester Square. Tell him to ring her there—no one else will answer.' He drained his glass and stood up. 'Let's join the others.' It was as though he considered the problem solved already. At the door he began to say something about how they might spend the following morning when a

20

bleeping sound came from his left wrist. He pressed a button at the side of his watch. 'Forgive me, an interview with my Opposition shadow is coming up on the box. I must see it in case there's anything I need to answer in time for the Sundays.' He eased Antrim through the door and turned. His thoughts were already with the television set in the corner of the room.

A corridor door to the garden stood ajar. Antrim stepped outside. The night had turned mild, almost summer-like. On this side of the house the paths were lit by lamps concealed beneath bushes. Ahead of him, a couple from the ballroom party were moving hand in hand towards a summer house. The girl walked with a lazy grace. Her back was bare and he saw her flesh glimmer as she passed one of the hidden lamps. The man's free hand was stroking her cheek. As they disappeared inside the summer house, desire asserted itself once more. He thought of himself approaching to listen, waiting for the crucial moment to burst in and see in the girl's eyes a certain subtle mingling of fear and lust. He was trembling a little. Aside from the Bureau, that precise image and its pursuit sometimes seemed all that mattered now, an obsession driving him forward onto a tightrope that stretched more dangerously with each day. Ahead lay crisis, perhaps humiliation. Yet the prospect only exhilarated.

He tried to push the thoughts away. Turning the corner of the house, he found himself on the main drive. Beneath his shoes the gravel crunched with a satisfying evenness; freshly raked that morning no doubt. The flower beds beyond, seen earlier in the day, had born witness to the same unremitting attention. When he went to his bedroom he would experience a similar sensation to now, a mixture of melancholy and jealousy, as his gaze moved from bed linen to silk-lined walls, from the spun-crystal lamp beside the bed to the oak side-table bearing the bowl of old roses, the bottle of mineral water and the cut-glass tumbler. Rylance's wealth had created something he had once had in his own grasp and then lost. During his marriage to Juliet, with injections from her trust fund, he had fashioned a perfect small country house out of a draughty ruin, had entertained with almost equal style, had even begun to think of abandoning the Bureau to behave like a gentleman farmer. But he had reckoned without Juliet deciding, as she moved into resentful middle age, to take umbrage at his *affaires*. She had divorced him, taken instead an Irishman met at a point-to-point who was more willing to forego adultery in exchange for such comfortable board and keep. So he had lost the house, filched by Juliet's lawyers in a settlement that left him the flat in Harley Street, the Aston Martin and precious little else. From the windows of the flat, watching the consultants step sprily from their limousines to greet the latest batch of punters from Kuwait and Bahrein, he would sometimes wonder if the houses they were creating with all that loot were as perfect as his had been.

In the distance he heard voices; someone called out that Charles had fallen down the ha ha. He could see a gleam of shirt fronts moving on the edge of the formal garden. A girl sang a few bars of a song he didn't know. He was beginning to feel old and irrelevant which was surely ridiculous in his mid-forties. Before the shirt fronts could reach him, he went back to the house in search of a drink.

From an armchair in the drawing room, too near to be ignored as he passed. Warrilow called his name. 'Business disposed of?'

It was getting on his nerves, being treated by Warrilow as though they were equals. 'Yes.'

'Not a corruption case in the Ministry to add to the other horrors? Are you putting your ferrets in?' He was blatantly fishing.

'Nothing like that.'

'Jeffrey hasn't reappeared. I'd hoped for a few humble words myself.'

'He stayed to watch his Opposition spokesman on TV.'

'Ah.' Warrilow settled back in his armchair. He was on his way to getting completely drunk, the outward corners of the eyes more downturned than ever. 'He never stops. That's what gives him the edge over the others. He's going to make No. 10 all right.' He looked up at Antrim lazily. 'I hope you were able to help.'

His expression was sardonic. It occurred to Antrim to wonder if Warrilow had really guessed what Rylance had been talking about. Perhaps he was in the secret. That would be disturbing. He took cover, so far as he could. 'Just advice,' he said. 'Nothing more.'

# III

MANSELL heard the door of his office swing open, far enough to jar the filing cabinet that stood behind. Without raising his eyes, he knew with absolute certainty who his visitor was. Eighteen months of Antrim as Director of the Bureau left no room for doubt.

Over the extra gin he now prescribed himself before lunch, Mansell sometimes dwelt on the passing of courtesy. Long gone the days of Lorimount, the Bureau's first Director, telephoning to enquire if he would find it convenient to step along for a few words. He had never appreciated at the time the gentle stroking applied by Lorimount when introducing Mansell to visitors: my head of Personnel . . . vital job in a Department of this kind . . . always like to get his view. Soft soap of course; moreover it had to be acknowledged that in Lorimount's last years, a failing nerve and anxiety to postpone the moment of decision had meant getting a view from virtually everyone, down to the office cleaners. Yet those emollient touches had eased the daily grind. Now, with Antrim's elevation, all that had vanished, along with men raising hats in greeting and women being graceful when offered seats on the Underground.

Stubbornly he went on reading papers until Antrim spoke his name. Then he lifted his head and fashioned a sort of smile. 'Good weekend?'

'Pleasant enough.'

Antrim seated himself and took out a cheroot. In his double-breasted waistcoat and high-collared shirt with its repellent mauve stripes, he seemed to Mansell the anti-thesis of what an official should look like. Of course, he had come from Intelligence. Perhaps in that grey world, dandy-ism was the consolation for being faceless.

'Rylance's wife is always written up as very attractive. Is she?'

Antrim flicked at a speck of fluff on his sleeve. 'I wasn't over-impressed. I preferred what I saw of Rylance's daughter from his first marriage. Still very young—but she has something.'

Mansell watched Antrim's eyes following the smoke from his cheroot and knew he was thinking about the Something. At the time his marriage was foundering, it had seemed he could think of nothing else. He had cut a swathe through the secretaries, then lifted his sights to Antonia Strachan who had had the misfortune to be working alongside him on a case. She had just escaped making a mess of her life, but only just. Since his appointment as Director of the Bureau, the goatishness had not been so evident. Perhaps he had external arrangements to satisfy tastes that by some accounts had become both specialized and alarming. But the disagreeable possibility remained that on Mansell's desk one day would appear instructions to transfer to Antrim's private office in some nebulous capacity a tasty morsel glimpsed at a typewriter or in the gold fish bowl of the Registry. Returning home to Twickenham and reaching for the whisky bottle that night, he would have to announce: now I have become Antrim's ponce.

He left his desk and seated himself in the armchair opposite Antrim. 'Who else was there from Whitehall?'

'Just Yates, his Parliamentary Secretary. No officials.'

When Mansell raised his eyebrows, Antrim went on, 'Rylance invited me because he wanted to discuss something away from his office, an enquiry he needs carrying out. He felt we would handle it more discreetly than anyone else. It's rather personal.'

'Does that mean it isn't official?'

'In a way. But it could have serious official implications.

I've no doubt we have to help. In any case Rylance's goodwill is going to be important to us in the future.'

There was clearly an inner meaning to the reference to Rylance's goodwill but he courted a rebuff if he enquired what it was. Antrim was about to embark, not for the first time, on something that would take him outside the Bureau's charter. He sighed silently.

'I need a good officer to work full-time on it,' Antrim said. 'I've decided to use Egerton. Perhaps you'll arrange to make him available.'

At moments like this, with not even a pretence of consultation by Antrim, he had learned to show no annoyance. 'Any special reason?'

'He seems bright. And he has the sort of social background I want. He should go down all right with Rylance and the other people he'll have to meet.'

Mansell smiled agreeably, searching his mind for ways of making Antrim uneasy. 'I can understand your being tempted to take a risk with him.'

'Risk?'

'I was thinking of his newness. It's less than eighteen months since we recruited him. You'll remember we took him on in rather a hurry. Because his experience matched what we needed on the Beynon case, you decided we wouldn't wait for all the usual enquiries into his background.'

'*I* decided?'

'Yes.'

'When?'

'After the selection board meeting, you said we should rely on the personal referees he'd provided together with the very favourable employer's report. Apart from confirming his academic qualifications we didn't go any further into his background.'

Antrim raised a hand, brushing it all aside. 'He's given no cause for worry since, has he?'

'No.'

'Well, then . . .?'

'It's simply that we still don't know him particularly well—he hasn't been given enough exposure. This is obviously a delicate case. Can we be sure he's right for it?'

'I see no reason why he shouldn't be. After all, when Antonia Strachan went to Rome with Ludo Fender, Egerton took on a good deal of her work. His performance was perfectly adequate.'

'Bryant was keeping an eye on the section.'

'The fact is, he was satisfactory.'

It was time to switch horses. 'The other thing that occurs to me is that the Beynon case is virtually ready to be handed over to the police. It's very intricate financial stuff. No one else has the facts at his finger tips.'

'He can't have been doing the case totally on his own.'

'The detailed work had been almost all his. I gather it's so complicated, it will take the best part of a week briefing the police.'

Antrim was silent. Knees crossed, he had begun to move a foot up and down. He was either accepting the need to think again or working up to his refusal-to-be-thwarted act. Mansell began. 'If I might make a suggestion—Gilmour who's back from sick leave would—' But Antrim was already speaking again.

'Antonia will have to work up the financial detail herself. If she needs help, put somebody in, Gilmour if you like. It's Egerton I want. Apart from his other qualities, I remember an American connection in his c.v. It could be helpful.'

Mansell rose and went to call up Egerton's record on his VDU screen. He had not really expected to win, had only gone through the motions of arguing in the interests of self respect. Irritatingly he couldn't now remember what the American connection had been.

Antrim crossed to watch the screen with him, grunted with satisfaction when it told its tale. Resigning from the merchant bankers who had been his employers since he had come down from Oxford, Egerton had spent the nine months before joining the Bureau in the United States. Mansell now recalled him describing it at his selection board. There had been a cousin in New York, the younger son of a peer who had made a success in American advertising and settled down there. Egerton had gone out to stay with him. He had thought he might join the cousin's company. But it hadn't worked out.

Antrim said, 'There's an American angle to the enquiry. The experience could give him an edge.'

'It doesn't seem to have amounted to much.'

'That doesn't worry me.'

Mansell switched off the VDU and sat down. 'How long is this enquiry likely to take? For staff planning purposes, I'd like to be given some idea what it amounts to.'

Antrim was already moving towards the door. He said over his shoulder, 'Sorry Andrew, it's really very delicate. You'll just have to accept Egerton's off strength for as long as Rylance needs him.' He paused by the mirror above the filing cabinet. He was inspecting grey hairs sprouting among the gold. 'I'd better see him over lunch since I've appointments for the rest of the morning. Tell him to contact Baxter to find out what time I want him at the club.' He didn't close the door behind him.

Mansell sat and stared silently through the gap. When his secretary appeared and began to shut the door, he said, 'That man . . .'

She nodded, knowing the play backwards by now. Going to the cupboard under the bookcase she took out the bottle of gin. 'Don't take it so personally.'

She was irritatingly sensible of course. 'Get yourself a glass,' he said.

The great silver egg that was the roast meat trolley had arrived at the table. As Antrim turned to examine the joint, Egerton let his eyes wander to the long windows of the dining room. A few leaves from the plane tree in the corner of the courtyard outside had floated down to the white painted tables and chairs. It was still just warm enough to sit outside in comfort. At a table near the fountain in the courtyard's centre, a family party were

28

having drinks before their lunch, parents and two daughters. The father couldn't be anything other than a retired soldier. The daughters were still schoolgirls; they looked about them hopefully for handsome youths and saw none.

The atmosphere was quieter, duller, than Egerton had expected of Antrim's choice of club. The little he had seen and heard of him since arriving in the Bureau suggested a taste for more modish surroundings. But perhaps the choice hadn't reflected inclination but had been part of a game of displaying *gravitas*, reassuring those in Whitehall with whom he dealt that ostentatious clothes and a taste for fast cars didn't mean a basic unreliability.

It would be interesting to know at what point he had decided he should begin sending that signal out. Long before he became Director presumably. Perhaps as early as Egerton's own age he had laid in this membership, like a case of good wine maturing for the future, to be produced at the right time as an emblem of taste and sound judgement. If he wanted to emulate Antrim, he ought to be thinking of doing the same, collecting credentials like this to add to the other cards of identity.

The silver egg moved on. Sipping claret Antrim said, 'So that is what I want you to do. I take it you see no difficulty in handing over your present work straight away.'

He knew enough about Antrim to understand he should see nothing of the kind. 'I'm sure in a couple of days—'

'No, not a couple of days, I want you to start this afternoon.'

'My section head—'

'Antonia Strachan will have been told by Personnel this morning that you're off all other work. She'll have someone else posted in if necessary.'

'May I talk to her about this?'

'I suppose you may need to take advice occasionally . . . All right, you can talk to her. But to no one else. And you report only to me. Understood?'

Egerton nodded. He was still trying to come to terms with the surprise of having been chosen for this task.

Hardly any of his colleagues in the Bureau had as exiguous a track record. In the Beynon case he felt he had performed well enough, albeit with Antonia Strachan always at his elbow. But he had reconciled himself to several years of working for others before being let loose on as delicate an enquiry as this. 'When I ask the police and other departments for help, you say I must conceal I'm interested in the girl. There's to be no exception to that?'

'None. You ask about Fernandes. Never her.'

'He'll seem an unlikely target for the Bureau.'

'If you're challenged, you'll have to think of something that makes him likely, won't you?'

The curtness of the response shook him out of his mild euphoria. Antrim went on, 'You'll also need a good cover story for use when you're talking to the girl's friends and other people who might know where she's gone. They mustn't know you work for the Bureau or that there's any search on. Settle the story with Antonia Strachan.'

Someone en route to a round table in the centre of the room which seemed to be for unaccompanied lunchers paused and talked to Antrim about some meeting they had attended together. He eavesdropped for a while but gave up trying to understand in the face of jargon so heavily laced with nicknames. Presumably this was how Antrim spent most lunch times, exchanging Whitehall gossip over prime cuts and claret. He had been greeted by the head waiter as someone special; the waitress who served their vegetables had asked tenderly after his health. To be cossetted in this handsome room for an hour or so each day seemed agreeable consolation for whatever the burdens of office might be.

The man who had paused made some wry parting comment and went to his seat. Antrim glanced at his watch and summoned the cheese trolley. Over Stilton his gaze wandered, mostly in the direction of the women in the room. Now that he had delivered his instructions, small talk with Egerton evidently had no appeal. He raised only one topic before their meal ended, asking if Egerton had met anyone from California during his stay in America.

'I don't remember doing so.'

'Mrs Rylance is a Californian. It's important that you get on with her. Some of the girl's friends you'll need to talk to will probably be American as well.' He snapped a cheese biscuit between his fingers. 'Didn't you travel about the States while you were there?'

'No.'

'Why was that?'

'I didn't have the opportunity.'

'In *nine months*?' Antrim's eyebrows were raised.

He felt himself going cold. 'I was unwell for part of the time.'

'So where *did* you go apart from New York?'

'Minnesota.'

For a second or two there seemed a danger that Antrim might go on with the questioning, but then he glanced again at his watch. 'We'll have to miss coffee. I've a meeting.' He rose.

Following in Antrim's wake as they left the room, Egerton fought back the tension. His skin crawled in the old way, though not, thank God, for the same reasons. The probing about the States had been a moment of truth somehow evaded ever since his recruitment. Next time, there might be no escape.

# IV

'TODAY?'

Antonia Strachan raised her arms towards the ceiling in a gesture that mingled outrage with imprecation. She lay back in her chair. 'I don't believe it.'

Egerton said, 'I think Personnel were supposed to have told you this morning. He made the point that you'd get someone else posted in, if necessary.'

'Golden Boy's promises have a way of evaporating when put to the test.' She sat forward again, shaking her head. 'Forget what I just said.'

He smiled. 'I didn't know he was called that.'

'I happened to meet a woman last summer who'd known him when he worked in Intelligence. Apparently that was his name there.'

'About the Beynon case. I could stay on in the evenings—'

She was shaking her head again but in resignation this time. 'Don't worry, we'll manage. I'm glad he's given you the job. I'm sure you'll do it well. Just be careful though.'

He was uncertain how to interpret the cautionary words. 'It doesn't sound dangerous. Not unless I fall foul of the Basque boyfriend. But I'm under strict orders not to make actual contact anyway.'

'I meant that it's . . . unusual. If it had to be justified . . .' She let the words trail. 'He no doubt had his reasons for taking it on. But don't go out on a limb. You might get sawn off with it.'

'By whom?'

She shrugged. 'Just see that the moves you make always have his approval. Preferably in writing.'

The telephone rang and she turned to answer it. Strands of black hair had fallen across one cheek; she shook them back with a movement familiar to him. She was unquestionably beautiful. Working as her subordinate, he recognized the fact, albeit with a certain detachment. He didn't know her age but noting the faint lines at the corners of the eyes and on the throat he guessed the middle thirties. At first he had supposed her lacking in warmth. But he had come to see that cool, sometimes mocking manner as a way of facing a world that had perhaps been rough. He knew she lived alone because when he had first been posted to her section he had visited her flat in Little Venice for a meal. He had heard that she had been married but the husband had died in an accident years ago. It seemed inconceivable that someone else had not by now passed muster and been invited to know her undefended.

Her eyes had caught him studying her while she talked into the receiver. He glanced away. She was examining him with a faint smile when he looked again as she put the phone down. He had the sensation she had glimpsed his thoughts and had been amused. She said, 'Well, that was it—Personnel telling me you're needed for "special duties". I suppose you want to go on using your own office?'

'It would be convenient when I have to consult you. He told me I should do that.'

Her eyebrows rose. 'How flattering. Well, let me have the Beynon file before you get immersed in this other thing. We'll have to go over it together some time. No doubt I'll end up briefing the police myself. Good luck with Rylance's wife. According to the press, she's quite something.' Her look was faintly derisive.

He made three calls before he got an answer from Evelyn Rylance's line. At first he thought a man had answered, the register of the voice was so low. The tones were laconic but pleasant enough. She'd expected his call but had been at some political lunch that had gone on and on. He agreed to present himself at the house in Chester Square at six thirty.

It was nearly five o'clock. If he left the Bureau straightaway, there would be time to buy something for his evening meal, drop it in at his flat and shower before he called on her. Cutting through Soho Square on his way to the Italian grocer in Old Compton Street, he saw the slight figure approaching and knew it was Gail a fraction of a second before she recognized him. She ran the last few yards, holding her arms out. They kissed. He held her close, glad and sad at the same time, but mostly glad because at least it meant she was still around.

Two years had not done the things he feared, although she had lost weight and had stopped taking trouble with her hair; now it was an urchin cut that seemed an insult to the romantic qualities of her features.

He best remembered the hair when it had been shoulderlength, although as often as not swept up in a loose golden swirl, from which strands escaped to spill distractingly against one cheek. Then the face—all soft planes and a mouth shaped as though anticipating a smile—had been as vulnerable as now. But the expression had been unhaunted. He had never imagined her then as threatened, only needing to be cherished.

Today her clothing struck him as a grim complement to the urchin cut. Below what looked like a navvy's blue jacket were jeans that ended in thick woollen socks and sneakers. The sneakers were heavily soiled. Perhaps after all she hadn't been dressed so very differently the first time he had seen her, wheeling a bicycle out of college all those aeons ago. But then the effect would have been no more than jokey, lacking real significance.

He looked into her eyes. They were the identical grey of Antrim's, he noticed. But unlike Antrim's, there was still laughter behind them. It was that silent laughter as much as her beauty that had captivated him once. Seeing it again was like having a hand gently squeeze his heart.

She kept her forearms resting on his shoulders. 'When

34

did you get back? I bet you've been back *ages*! Why didn't you write? Only one mingy postcard . . .!'

'I meant to write again.'

'Tell me about New York.'

Some time he would have to admit how long he had been back, find an excuse for not having tried to make contact with her or Julian or any of the others. When he first returned to London, it had seemed the safest thing— postponing the moment of seeing them until he felt sure he couldn't be sucked back into that world. After he had been taken on by the Bureau, there had been another reason for putting it off. He had become someone who had joined The Other Side. He had imagined the expressions on their faces when he told them, sensed the chill that would follow. They would see it as a kind of betrayal.

She wasn't waiting for him to reply to her questions. 'You look marvellous, you must have had a super time. How could you *make* yourself come back? Have you gone into that dreary bank again?'

'No, I'm working for the government.' He held up the black briefcase with the official crest on the flap and grinned apologetically.

'You! A civil servant?'

'Yes.'

At least she stopped herself laughing, simply shook her head incredulously.

'And you,' he asked. 'What are you doing?'

'Oh, well,' she said, 'bits and pieces. The last thing was unpacking china at Harrods. But it got rather a bore.'

'How's Julian?'

She stared into his face for a moment, then looked away as though noticing someone across the square. 'You don't know?'

'Know what?'

'He died a year ago.'

He stared back at her, appalled. 'How?'

'Jamie was away for a week or two and Julian bought from somebody he didn't really know, a man he met when

35

he was filming in France. Apparently the stuff had been cut with something lethal. He died trying to get to the phone after he'd injected. I'd gone to buy some food. It all happened inside twenty minutes.' She was being very controlled.

He put his cheek against hers and wished that he could have drawn the pain into himself. 'I am so sorry.'

She compressed her lips and smiled. 'After that I wasn't too good for a while. Ma got to hear about it of course. She and Leo arrived the day I had to get out of the flat Julian had rented and more or less dumped me in the back of his car.'

He managed to remember that Leo was her stepfather; he had married her mother the year Gail had come down from Oxford.

'Leo said I had to go for a cure to a place in Devon. I felt too depressed to argue, so that's where I went. They search your room every day to see if you've smuggled anything in. After a fortnight I just left. Ma had hysterics when she discovered. They stopped my allowance then. I suppose it's not surprising.'

'Where are you living?'

'I've got a room in Notting Hill that Jamie found for me. The house is owned by a very nice Indian from Gujerat. His wife comes up with food sometimes because they think I don't eat enough.'

'I suppose you see Jamie quite a bit. How is he?'

'Getting rich.' She laughed. 'But just the same. We're both just the same.' She took one of his hands and squeezed it between hers. Looking down he winced to see where her nails were bitten back to.

'But *you've* changed,' she said.

He shrugged.

'Have you stopped?'

'Yes.'

'Completely?'

'Yes.'

She was shaking her head slowly. 'How was it?'

'Easier than I expected. Much easier.'

She went on shaking her head. He tried to imagine what she was thinking: he's gone over; soon he won't even understand any more. 'There's a lot to tell you,' he said. 'Come and see my new flat one night.'

'Where is it?'

'Prince of Wales Drive, it looks out over Battersea Park. When I wake up I see ducks on the lake.'

She was impressed. 'All alone?'

'Not quite. I have a neighbour called Gwen. The way the flats have been sub-divided in the past means that we have a common lobby where she stands her pot plants. When her lover from the fire brigade isn't around she keeps her door open to monitor my private life.' He turned her face towards him. 'So will you come?'

He thought for a moment she was going to make some excuse. Eventually she said, 'That would be nice,' but still seemed doubtful. He told himself she was thinking, now Julian's dead, he's going to be a bore again, just as he was at Oxford.

They fixed on the following night. Looking at his watch he realized there was no time now to get the *pasta*; it would be scrambled eggs again for supper. 'I'll have to go, there's somebody I'm supposed to interview tonight.' He chose the words carefully, not wanting her to think he was off enjoying himself in his new world.

She danced a little on her toes as though cold then stood still with hunched shoulders, pulling herself together. 'Right. See you tomorrow.'

As she turned away, he asked, 'Where are you off to?'

She waved vaguely in the direction of Shaftesbury Avenue. 'Meeting one or two people.'

It wasn't like her to be vague. He wondered what that meant. Perhaps she was pushing now. With her allowance cut off and only occasional jobs, that might be the only way she could be sure of scoring. In one of those alleys near Foyles or further down, towards Cambridge Circus, dependent on where the police had last been spotted, he imagined her slipping packets to people who had come up with the cash an hour or so ago.

She looked back at him, lifting a hand briefly. He felt suddenly hopeless, thinking of the risk she might be running in a few moments. If he was right, it meant Jamie was giving her more smack than she needed for herself. Knowing him, that wasn't so unlikely, although he must be aware of the danger to himself if she was caught.

She certainly wouldn't have a shortage of customers. After the first time, they'd know they were on to a good thing. Because, unless he'd changed since Oxford, Jamie would only be supplying the best. Nothing cut, no Chinese. Just pure white Thai.

# V

TWILIGHT heavy with autumn dampness was falling when he arrived at Chester Square. He parked the Mini next to a bright red Golf. Climbing out, he caught the smell of woodsmoke from a fire of still-smouldering twigs in the central gardens. A policeman, presumably on protection duty, stolidly watched him mount the steps of the Rylances' house.

His finger had not reached the bell push when the door opened; he was almost pushed backwards by a girl of eighteen or nineteen in a brown leather skirt and shaggy jersey. The ring of car keys she had been holding tinkled on the steps.

He bent and handed them to her.

'Terribly sorry,' she said.

Egerton smiled. 'I've an appointment with Mrs Rylance.'

The girl's eyes had fixed on the official briefcase. It seemed to disconcert her. 'Oh, gosh, Chief Superintendent Clayton? But I thought you were coming tomorrow!'

Being taken for a policeman was a new experience. Perhaps his time in the Bureau had already stamped him with the look of a lackey of law enforcement. He shook his head. 'My name's Egerton, Mark Egerton.'

She wasn't stopping to listen, her agitation was too great. 'You see, I was going to *telephone* beforehand. It's *very* difficult here. Couldn't we—' She broke off, glancing back into the house.

The accent was unalloyed Sloane. So Rylance's other

39

American stepdaughter could be ruled out. This was presumably Camilla, daughter of his first marriage. She was a pale, almost ash blonde with a pushed forward mouth and freckles disarmingly sprinkled on the cheeks and forehead. She needed to lose a few pounds but there was nothing else wrong at all. He began, 'You misunderstand, I'm not—'

A woman was approaching from the other side of the hall. He recognized her immediately from Antrim's description. Slender, graceful in movement, she had an air of cool purposefulness. Under the light of the hall chandelier her hair was the colour of chestnut leaves about to fall. 'Mr Egerton?'

'Yes.'

'Evelyn Rylance.' She held out a hand. 'Come in.' As on the telephone, he was struck by how deep the voice was. She was in full fig for some evening function, wearing a dark blue sheath dress that left one shoulder bare. Her eyes moved past him to the girl. 'I thought you'd gone out.'

Camilla had reddened. She said, 'I was going just as he arrived.' She glanced quickly up at Egerton. 'Perhaps we'll meet again . . . ' Ducking her head in an embarrassed way she hurried down the steps to the red Golf.

Evelyn Rylance closed the door. Turning back to Egerton, she appraised him. 'You're younger than I expected.' She turned on a sudden, brilliant smile. She wanted him to be affected by it and he was. 'But, then, your Director—is that what you call him? He's pretty young, isn't he?'

'Forty-seven, I think.'

'And you?'

'Twenty-six.'

She gave a light nod of the head. It might have meant approval or simply that her own calculations had been confirmed. Diamond drop earrings danced against her throat. The skin was completely taut and smooth; yet she could hardly be younger than Antrim.

She led him to a room with a bar in one corner. He asked for a glass of Perrier. She opened a bottle of vegetable juice for herself and moved towards the door again. 'We'll talk upstairs. In an hour I have to go to a very boring dinner. I need some air to set me up.'

For a moment he thought she meant they were adjourning to a roof terrace. But on the first floor she opened another door. The room was difficult to categorize. In origin plainly a large dressing room, one half of it was still being used as that; the other half was furnished as an office with desk, typewriter and telephone. Beside the desk was a small table on which stood a black box with metal circles on its face. Through another doorway he could see paraphernalia for keeping her face and figure the way they were: exercise bicycle, rowing machine, a bar suspended from the ceiling.

Evelyn seated herself in a chair next to the black box. He sat down opposite her and took his folder out of the briefcase. She had clicked a switch on the box and begun passing a filament embedded in a piece of card in front of the two metal circles. It was clear that he was supposed to stay quiet for a while.

Now that he could study them unobserved, her features seemed as perfect as the skin. Yet there *was* something amiss; after a moment or two, he realized what it was. She had had a nose job and the surgeon had been a little too keen to reverse the effect of what had been there before. A quarter of a centimetre needed to go back before she would look entirely real.

Without turning from the box, she said. 'Understand about ions?'

He had to ask her to repeat it.

'Ions. Active ions get eliminated from the atmosphere in big cities, they're wiped out. Without negative ions your battery's flat. Some people take speed to give them a lift. Ions are the natural way. This is a micro air processor. It filters out pollutants and produces the negative ions.' Apparently satisfied by her check with the filament, she sat back. 'There ought to be one of these in every office. Tell your Mr Antrim to get you fitted up.'

The Californian accent which had been subdued on the telephone was quiet strong now, the voice agreeably throaty. Although there was only a table lamp alight she put on a pair of dark glasses. 'What's your first name?'

'Mark.'

'So *you've* been slated to find Lauren.'

'I'll do my best.'

'I hope so. Because I have to be able to talk to her. She's in the process of ruining her own life and maybe my husband's. To say nothing of mine.' Unexpectedly she produced the brief, brittle smile again. 'By that typewriter there, Mark, you'll see an envelope. I've typed out for you a list of names. They're people I know are friends of Lauren. She could have given any of them some hint of where she is. You'll also find I've included the report of the private investigator we used.'

He opened the envelope. The detective's report was five pages long. There was a fair amount of padding, no doubt directed to justifying the size of the bill that had originally been attached to it. The theme delicately woven through the report was that if it hadn't been for the restraints under which he'd laboured at Evelyn Rylance's insistence, he would have brought home the bacon. It was signed 'William Carter Ingalls' in writing that made it plain his ego was surviving the reverse; typed underneath the signature were words which also headed each sheet of the notepaper, 'Certified Private Investigator and Security Consultant'. It wasn't clear who had certified him.

'Was Mr Ingalls recommended to you?'

'He was used by my ex-husband, Sam Giordano, when we suspected a British producer was two-timing us over a deal. He got results for us then. But maybe he's no good any more.'

She had made it sound as though the deal had been as much her business as Giordano's. Although Antrim had spoken of her first husband as having been a film producer, he hadn't suggested she had also been in the business. Perhaps she had counted for something in Hollywood and

42

in the film world generally. He wondered how it compared with being the wife of the Secretary of State for Defence.

He glanced quickly through the list of names and addresses, then at the photograph of Lauren clipped to it. She was a dark-haired, serious-looking girl with heavier features than her mother but a nicer smile; she was holding a spaniel in her arms. Evelyn Rylance said, 'That shot's a year or two old. But she hasn't changed—that's the way she looks.'

'When was the last time you saw her?'

'One day in the middle of July. I talked to her about Fernandes, that he was a terrorist and she'd make a mess of everything if she didn't give him up. She wouldn't listen. She wasn't living with him then, she was staying with her friend, Lisa Husak, the address is in the list I've given you. We had one or two phone conversations after that, I was trying to make her see reason. Then she telephoned me at the end of July. She said she was going away with Fernandes and it would be no good trying to find her because we wouldn't.' She reached for her vegetable juice. 'She was always a rebel. But I never thought she would go this far.'

That somebody of Lauren's age had dug her toes in over the man she had chosen for a lover didn't seem to warrant all that much surprise. But it obviously wasn't politic to say so. 'So you got no hint where they might be planning to go . . .'

'No. It could be Spain I suppose since that's his country.'

His spirits drooped. He could picture himself combing the Basque provinces until the end of time. 'You've no photograph of Fernandes I suppose . . .'

'I never set eyes on the man.'

He looked down at her list again. 'Have you spoken to any of these people yourself?'

'What for?'

'In case they had news.'

'One or two telephoned me early on to ask if I knew where they could contact her. I said that she'd gone on a

43

trip and I didn't know when she'd be back.'

'Perhaps if you had asked Lisa Husak for example—'

She interrupted him. 'Listen, I'm not going round asking people if they can tell me where my daughter is. Certainly not Lisa Husak who works in television and would probably tell somebody there was a story worth following up.'

It was obvious she had a temper that flared easily. But he had to allow for the fact that she must be anxious. 'At the time she went, was she in any sort of employment?'

'She'd been teaching at a school for young kids, Hazlewood School—it's somewhere in Chelsea. The boys wear funny caps and long socks. You'll see from Ingalls' report that he talked to one of the teachers there. She didn't contribute anything.'

'Her father, Mr Giordano, you've checked she hasn't written to him?'

'I called him in Beverly Hills some weeks ago. He'd heard nothing. He came up with the idea of using Ingalls to find her.'

'And your other daughter?'

He saw her compress her lips. 'Jacqueline. She's in Majorca. She had a messy divorce not long ago. There's some sort of artistic community round the place where she's staying—Jacqueline is the cultured member of the family.' The dark glasses made it impossible to see her expression but he was pretty confident it was sardonic.

'Were they close—Lauren and Jacqueline?'

'At one time. But not after Jacqueline married. He's a tax lawyer. Lauren called him a Fascist but she likes to sound progressive.'

'Now the marriage has broken up, they could be on close terms again perhaps?'

'I wrote to Jacqueline. She wrote back saying she had no news. Because Jacqueline can be tricky I got Ingalls to check through a Spanish agency that Lauren and Fernandes weren't there with her'.

He persisted. 'Lauren might have told her where she is but asked her to say nothing.' When he sensed she

44

was thinking about it, he went on, 'Would you like that possibility explored?'

She was silent for a while. Eventually she said, 'Maybe you ought to check the idea out. I'll talk to my husband about it.'

He had chalked up a brownie point. 'That leaves one other member of the family, your stepdaughter.'

Evelyn shook her head. 'You can forget Camilla, they never got on. Lauren would never have told her where she was going with Fernandes. I don't want Camilla approached or let in on the fact these enquiries are being made. She'd spill everything to those crazy friends of hers.' She took off the dark glasses. 'What was she talking to you about earlier?'

'She'd got the idea I must be a police officer, a Chief Superintendent Clayton.'

'What did you say?'

'Simply that I had an appointment with you. I didn't mention what we were going to discuss.'

She looked pleased. 'If you should see her again let her go on assuming it was something to do with the leakages.'

'I'm afraid I don't understand.'

'That's what Clayton's due to call about. Some papers from my husband's department have been getting to the press—secret papers. The *Globe* have printed the details. Clayton wants to look at the arrangements my husband has for the papers he brings home to work on. Apparently he also wants to talk to me about the study where the papers are kept and whether the servants can get in when we're not around. If he thinks I'm some sort of hophead who doesn't know how to control what goes on in this house, Mr Clayton's going to get his balls chewed off.'

It seemed he was well out of the business of the leakage enquiry. He put the envelope and his own notes in the briefcase. 'I think that's all I need at the moment. I'll go and work out my programme.'

'Telephone me on this number when you have any news. My husband will want to see you himself when he has time.

45

You'd better write your office and private numbers on that pad so that we can get you.'

She smiled pleasantly enough but it was plain she reckoned he was their personal property now. As he stood up she went on, 'You've got it clear, have you? No one is to know we're employing you or that there's a search on. No one. Don't let's have any mistakes about that.'

'I understand.'

She smiled again as though she realized her manner might be becoming counterproductive. 'I'm sorry. I come on rather strong when I'm worried. I have to get to Lauren somehow and make her see reason.'

He nodded. 'Of course.' She stayed where she was so presumably the ionizing still had a way to go. His fingers were on the door handle when she called out, 'There'll be something good in this for you, Mark. As long as you move fast.'

He had switched on the ignition in the Mini when he became aware that someone was tapping his side window. Lowering it he saw Camilla. She was protecting her hair from rain that had begun to fall by holding a magazine over her head. 'Hullo,' she said.

He nodded. 'Hullo again.'

'I saw you just as I got back.' It was probably true; but it crossed his mind that she might have been sitting in the red Golf all the time, waiting to way-lay him.

'I'm awfully sorry to bother you, but could I get in for a sec?'

He could hardly refuse. Leaning across he opened the passenger door for her.

She scrambled in. 'I wanted to talk to you earlier. But since you'd come to see Evelyn ...' She placed the magazine in her lap as though about to read it and stared down at the cover. 'The fact is I think I've got a clue about how the leakages might have happened. I wanted to tell you, but not when Evelyn was around.'

He began to regret acceptance of Evelyn Rylance's airy dictat that if he met Camilla again he was to let her go on

46

thinking that the leakages were his bag. It hadn't occurred to him that she would once more cross his path, certainly not this evening. 'Wouldn't you like to keep all this for Superintendent Clayton?'

'But Evelyn will be there then. Please let me explain.'

He resigned himself to listening.

'When Pa brings a box of papers home from the department he works on them in his study. It's on the first floor at the back of the house. The door's kept locked when he's not there so that none of the servants can get in and empty wastepaper baskets and things like that. There's also a safe he puts papers in at night.

'My bedroom is above his study. A few evenings ago I was in front of the window changing before going out to a party. When I was practically starkers I looked up and realized that somebody was watching me with a pair of binoculars from one of the flats in the block behind the house. I nipped smartly back and didn't think anything more about it until yesterday when Pa announced that the policeman who's in charge of the leakage enquiries wanted to come and check on the security of papers when they were in the house. Then I remembered Pa's desk is right in the window.'

'You think somebody has been able to get to the window?'

'No, that's impossible. But isn't it true that telephoto lenses on cameras can be so fantastic nowadays that papers on Pa's desk could be photographed from the apartment block behind?'

'It's possible. But I haven't looked to see how far away the block is.'

She turned more towards him, encouraged by his response. There was something touching about her enthusiasm for her idea. 'What I thought was that if the papers that got to the *Globe* were amongst any of those Pa brought home to work on, that could be the answer—somebody like the man with the binoculars in one of the upper floor flats working with a telephoto lens.'

47

'I see.'

'So you don't think I'm talking nonsense?'

'No. Could you identify the flat in which you saw this man?'

She shook her head. 'I backed away so quickly I didn't register it.'

'Tell me why you didn't feel you could talk about this when your stepmother's around.'

When she grimaced, he went on, 'You could have told your father, couldn't you?'

'Yes.'

'Why didn't you?'

'I suppose this will sound terribly weedy.' She sighed. 'When Pa took over Defence, a little cove from the department's security set-up came to the house to look at the study. He had a safe put in and new locks on the door. He also decided there had to be net curtains to prevent overlooking from the flats. So they were put up and he came round to see them in place. But Evelyn *loathes* net curtains, she's all for wide-open living.' She paused and shrugged. 'At least she says she is. Anyway, as soon as this security chap had gone she had the curtains pushed right back. The result is that in the ordinary way, unless it's getting dark and Pa doesn't for some reason put his desk lamp on, it must be possible to get a view of anything on his desk.'

'You're saying that while you don't actually *know*, this could be the answer to the leakages, but you don't want your father or your stepmother to be told you suggested it?'

'Particularly not Evelyn. She's built up this image of being super-efficient, which she is in a way, of being the absolutely perfect wife. She'd *kill* me if she thought I'd ratted on her. On the other hand Pa is very upset about the leakages and it won't do him any good at all if they go on.'

'But if what you've just told me can't be used to explain to your father how they can be stopped in future, what do you suggest is done?'

'I've thought about that. There's a space against the wall by the window where the desk could go and still give

48

plenty of light. Nobody in the flats could see it then. If you told Pa that it had been discovered that net curtains no longer give enough protection and that the desk has to be moved, he'd agree and not suspect anything.'

It was a neat answer to the problem although he was rather sorry to think Evelyn would escape being fingered as less perfect than the image she had cultivated. A way of unloading the story was taking shape in his mind. He would telephone Bellamy in Special Branch, whom he'd met over a case that had involved corruption in the Department of Trade and the export of embargoed equipment, and ask him to pass on a message to Clayton. A source whose information could not be quoted to the Rylances had reported the net curtains were not being used and that long-distance photography of Rylance's desk from the apartment block was possibly taking place. Moving the desk would probably be advisable. If Clayton asked for access to the source, Bellamy would have to tell him the answer was a lemon.

'All right,' he said. 'Leave it to me. I'll make sure your idea's explored and that neither your father nor Mrs Rylance knows that any of this comes from you. Moving the desk is a good idea anyway. Actually I didn't talk to Mrs Rylance about the details of the enquiry today but I'll see Chief Superintendent Clayton gets the facts. To avoid embarrassment you'd better not mention our talk if you meet him when he calls at the house.'

'Super,' she said. 'Absolutely super.' She showed not the smallest interest in what he and Evelyn had really been discussing. 'I'm so glad I caught you. I couldn't see how I was going to handle it and not land myself in the shit.'

She paused, hesitating. 'Would you think it an appalling cheek to ask you to tell me if you decide my idea is probably right—about the photography?'

'I'm not sure I could do that.'

'Won't you try? I wouldn't breathe a word.'

He could hardly tell her he wasn't likely to know himself. And, after all, he needed to do no more than ask Bellamy some time to find out if Clayton had found the report useful. He took the magazine from her and wrote on a corner of the cover. 'That's the telephone number of my flat, you'll get me there in the evenings, usually after seven o'clock. Give me a ring in a few days and I may have some news.'

She studied the number closely as though she feared it might fade away and she had to memorize it without delay. 'Super,' she said again. She was a little gauche, he thought; but there was something touching about her.

As he drove away, she stood on the pavement waving, the magazine once more held over her head. In his driving mirror he saw the policeman salute when she turned to go up the steps of the house and she gave him a wave as well. In her brown leather skirt and white jersey she looked almost edible, a chocolate éclair of a girl.

# VI

ONCE only had Egerton visited Antrim's office. It had been on his first day in the Bureau, now no more than a confused series of impressions, like the shifting patterns of a kaleidoscope.

He could recall walking along this corridor with Mansell, the Head of Personnel, entering this ante room. When the double doors had opened, he had gone in and listened to five minutes pep talk from Antrim on what was expected of him. Hovering outside, like a small fruit fly, had been Baxter, Antrim's Private Secretary. That was all he remembered of the visit.

This morning as he entered, there was Baxter again, a diminutive, all-seeing *concièrge*, just visible behind the piles of papers and files that covered his desk. Do not ignore or underestimate Baxter, people said. Don't let that pink-cheeked appearance, that shy smile, deceive you. Baxter the Minder will drop you in it as soon as look at you. Also, remember Baxter's ambition is limitless. Best to think of him as Antrim writ small; but growing.

'Yes?' said Baxter. He was reading, a faint smile on his face as though some elegance of syntax or inwardness of meaning had charmed him. He hadn't looked up at all. Perhaps he was now so powerful he no longer needed to vary the politeness of his response according to the status of the traffic.

'The Director wanted me to report about a case he asked me to take on yesterday.'

Baxter lifted his head, quite affably. 'Oh, yes, your lunch

51

at his club . . .' He exuded omniscience, a total confidence that nothing new of any importance could be happening without his knowledge.

'Is he free?' Egerton asked.

'I'm afraid not. The Assistant Directors are in there talking about next year's estimates.' Baxter's eyes returned to his reading matter. 'If you'll let me know what you wanted to tell him, I'll see that he hears when he's free.'

Instinct told him that the omniscience was not in fact entire. 'It's all right, I'll wait.'

Baxter allowed him a less affable look. 'Just trying to save you time. He may be quite a while.' He turned a page. 'If you're going to hang on, there's a copy of *The Times* over there.' He was pointing to the far corner of the ante room where visitors were corralled before he let them through the gate.

Twenty minutes passed before the double doors opened. Egerton watched them file out, the Assistant Directors, that body of superior beings of whom he still knew only one or two. They stood exchanging cryptic glances, the occasional joke. He thought he detected a hint of discreet disaffection. Perhaps that was the mood in which most of the meetings in Antrim's room dispersed.

Mansell had seen Egerton and nodded a greeting. He was talking to Kendick, the Legal Adviser: Kendick with the crooked shoulder and pebble glasses and the air of being resigned to catastrophe, if not by lunch time, certainly before another day dawned. Off and on during the early stages of the Beynon enquiry, Kendick had told Egerton disaster was imminent, that by his failure to grasp that what mattered was not discovering the facts but the seemly strands of admissible evidence he courted a terrible retribution—if not from the Attorney General then before the bar of Parliament itself. Somehow Egerton had brought the ship almost into port, fact and evidence stacked neatly side by side on its decks and even Kendick had relaxed enough to address him by a Christian name, although admittedly not the right one.

The Assistant Directors trickled out into the corridor. Baxter who had been foraging among them for briefs for some meeting Antrim was due to attend next week vanished through the double doors. Further time passed. He had read even the Nature Notes before Baxter nodded to him over the threshold of the sanctum.

Antrim was relaxing after his budget meeting. He lay back in his swivel chair, feet resting in a half-open drawer of the desk. He looked pleased with himself. Perhaps the Assistant Directors had been enjoyably flogged, told to get more work out of less staff and to use fewer paper clips in the process. He waved Egerton to a seat. 'So how did it go?'

'She produced a list of Lauren's friends and the private detective's report. I said I'd let her know as soon as there was any progress.'

'No ideas of her own where they might have gone?'

'None, apart from Spain.'

Antrim raised an eyebrow. 'You got on with her, I hope?'

He avoided a direct answer although on the whole he had. 'I have the impression she won't be very understanding if we can't find the girl.'

'Then you'd better not fail.'

Antrim's tone was flippant; but Egerton registered the shift back of the pronoun. 'If she and Fernandes *are* in Spain, perhaps lying low because he doesn't want to attract the attention of the Spanish police, it could prove impossible.'

'No reason to think that yet. Have you got all your enquiries out to departments about Fernandes' movements?'

'I've asked the Home Office and the Security Service for anything they have. I'm having air line passenger lists checked for around the time they might have left the country.'

'But you've tied your enquiry to Fernandes alone . . .'

'Yes.'

'What about the Yard?'

'Someone there is ringing me back later this morning.'

Egerton watched Antrim lighting one of his small cigars.

'I'd like your approval for the cover story I'll use when I talk to Lauren's friends.'

'What is it?'

'I shall take the line that I deal in antiques. A few months ago Lauren met me at a party and heard what I did. She gave me a couple of Japanese *inros* to sell for her on the basis that since I had good contacts in the oriental art world I'd get her a fair price. I've now got the cash in hand and want to pay it over but have discovered she's gone away.'

'Will you use your own name?'

'Yes. If pressed I'll also give my address in Battersea. Then people can look me up in the telephone directory and see that I exist.'

Antrim inspected the tip of the cigar. 'What are *inros*?'

'Small cases that used to be carried at the waist in Japan. At one time they contained a man's personal seal and ink. They're usually lacquered. They can be very beautiful.'

Antrim waved away the aesthetics. 'Do you know anything about them?'

'Enough. My father started to collect them when he was Military Attaché in Tokyo. I still have one but my mother had to sell the rest when he died.'

'I suppose it's as good a story as any. Let's hope the private detective didn't use anything like it, since he'll have seen most of the same people.' Antrim yawned and glanced at his watch; at almost the same moment Baxter's face appeared round the door in mute enquiry. 'Ring and tell him I'll be ten minutes late,' Antrim said. 'I'm not going to break my neck for some Treasury *babu*.'

Rising to his feet he stretched and sighed. The hang of the jacket from the shoulders told the same expensive story as the silk shirt and crocodile skin shoes. Rumour had it that after being divorced by his wife he had been hard-pressed to maintain his customary living standards. Promotion to be Director of the Bureau had saved the day apparently; but even a salary at that level could hardly be too much for these tastes.

54

'I understand Rylance wants to see me as well. She said they'd contact me when he was ready.'

Antrim was gathering up papers to put in his briefcase. 'Make sure you talk to me beforehand. You're still working for this office. I don't want that forgotten.' He glanced at himself in the mirror beside the door. Satisfied, he went out through the ante room with Baxter prancing beside him to deliver some last minute message about his meeting.

Back in Egerton's own room, the phone was ringing. It was Bellamy, calling him back from the Yard.

'What's new?' Bellamy asked.

'I've a snippet that may be useful although not to you personally. Do you know a Superintendent Clayton who's concerned with the leakages from the MOD?'

'That would be Detective Chief Superintendent Clayton, may the Lord preserve him,' Bellamy said portentously, 'He's in charge of the Serious Crimes Squad.'

'Do you mean that leakage is a serious crime?'

'Mass murder, piracy on the high seas, leakages— there's nothing between them,' Bellamy said. 'What do you want from Clayton?'

'Nothing. I hoped you'd pass on to him some information I picked up last night. The source, who is well placed to know, says that if the documents that have been leaked to the *Globe* lately were amongst any that Rylance has been taking home to work on, there's a very good chance they were photographed with a telephoto lens while they were sitting on the Minister's desk in his study. The reason is that there's a block of flats that overlooks the house and although there are net curtains in the study they're usually drawn *back*. Furthermore a man has been seen watching the house with binoculars from the flats.'

Bellamy laughed. 'Who's your source—the window cleaner?'

'Never mind. Just tell Clayton my source *knows* it could have happened like that. But when he's talking to Rylance and his wife he mustn't let on he's aware the net curtains aren't being used properly. And he shouldn't be surprised

55

to find them in position if he makes an appointment to visit the house to look for himself.'

Egerton could sense Bellamy working up to another crack about the source; somehow he managed to resist it. 'All right, I've got that. Any more?'

'Should he decide that what my source says could be a true bill, Clayton might like to consider telling the Minister that there are cameras these days against which net curtains are no protection and the desk has got to be moved out of a line of sight from the flats. That'll get over the problem of not being frank with him about what he knows.'

'I don't think Clayton enjoys being told how to handle his cases. Are there such cameras?'

'I've no idea. But I'm offering him the thought free of charge.'

'Do you know what he's going to say?' Bellamy said. 'Tell your friend in the Bureau to ante-up with his something-something source and let me get on with the job properly.'

'If he does, you can tell him to forget it because this is all he's getting.'

When Bellamy uttered a resigned grunt, he went on, 'Now that I've made your day, perhaps I can ask you for something. I'm interested in a man called Fernandes, Luis Fernandes, a Basque. I don't have a London address for him but he was here doing some sort of research into British politics until the end of July. I believe he may then have taken off with a girl friend. You presumably have a nice fat file on him because he happens to be a terrorist when he's at home in Spain.'

'What do you want to know about him?'

'Anything you've got. But most of all where he's gone to. If it's thought he's back in Spain and the Spanish police might have a line on him I'd be very grateful for anything you can give me from that quarter.'

Bellamy was silent, presumably making notes. Eventually he said, 'Fred Rivers, the chap who deals with Basques, is off for a couple of days. But I'll make some enquiries.'

'I'd appreciate it if you could do it fairly quickly.'

Before he rang off, Bellamy said, 'About the leakages: don't be surprised if you get a call from Clayton saying he intends to go higher if you won't introduce him to your source.'

Afterwards he wondered for a while how he would handle it if Clayton *did* act up. But there was no point in getting worried about hypothetical problems. He took out Evelyn Rylance's list. It was very short, even bearing in mind that Lauren hadn't been living in England more than a year or two. Perhaps Evelyn Rylance hadn't had much idea where and with whom Lauren spent most of her time. Seven of the people on the list lived in central London; that left a woman in Cornwall and a married couple who ran a school for handicapped children in Fife. The sensible course was obviously to take the London group first and begin with Lisa Husak since Ingalls' report showed he had not been able to meet her. A call to her home number produced no reply and he rang the switchboards of all the television companies he could trace. Half an hour later, his spirits dampened by denials from every quarter of anybody named Husak being employed, he tried the other London numbers of people on the list and raised not a single reply. One of them, an Angela Montague on a City exchange, seemed perpetually engaged. It began to look as though he would only make progress in the evenings when they returned from work or whatever they got up to in the daytime.

He told himself that physical reconnaissance could hardly be less productive than being mocked by ringing tones that went on and on; Lisa Husak's house might well be split into apartments in which case he stood a chance of learning where she worked from one of the occupants. He put on his coat and took a bus to Pimlico.

Hope began to fade as he gazed at the house from across the street. It was surely too small to be divided, a Victorian clerk's house that gentrification had provided with a colour-washed façade and brass door furniture. But crossing the street he noticed two bells beside the door. He rang the one marked Husak, expecting and getting nothing, then tried the other: Victor Crispin, said the card alongside the bell in a neat italic hand. A voice answered through the door porter almost at once; when he stated his business he was unhesitatingly invited in. At least he'd found somebody to talk to.

Crispin occupied the upper floor of the house. A slight figure in jeans and a skin-tight tee-shirt, he stood beaming at the head of the stairs as though Egerton was the answer to some sort of prayer. '*Hullo*,' he said, 'What do you say to a cup of coffee?'

In the room where he left Egerton while he went to make the coffee was the evidence of what he had so eagerly abandoned, a typewriter surrounded by paper and assorted books standing on a table near a window. A publisher's letter lying open amongst the debris of screwed up notes on the floor offered a clue to the warmth of his reception. Crispin was in gaol with his typewriter: a commissioned book on Trends in the Development of Community Theatre was unspooling at interminable length. No diversion was likely to be too inconvenient, no conversation too inane if they stopped him getting on with it.

Crispin arrived back with the coffee cups and a barrel of muesli biscuits. Making room for the tray, he picked up a bowl of flowers and almost deposited it on a book shelf before abruptly abandoning the idea.

'That would never do for Fred, would it?' he said. He spoke in a way that implied Fred was well known to Egerton and the prohibition must have occurred to him no less forcibly.

He received the cover story about *inros* with a flattering interest and spoke warmly of Lauren; but the extent of his knowledge proved minimal. He had met her twice only. The first time had been when he and Fred had been invited to drinks by Lisa; the second while Fred was visiting his mother in Bexhill and Crispin had joined the two of them and Lauren's friend, Luis, for a restaurant meal one night in July. He had never been told Luis's surname. Lauren had been introduced as Lauren Giordano; it was plain he didn't know of the connection with Rylance.

Luis, it seemed, had powerful shoulders and jet black hair curling tightly into the neck. Crispin mentioned them with a faraway look; Egerton wondered how the absent Fred had reacted to such unbridled admiration when he got back from filial duties in Bexhill. The restaurant where they had eaten had been a Basque-run place in Camden Town. Halfway through their meal they had been joined by someone Crispin gathered was Luis's brother; he had been addressed as Garcia.

Crispin's gossip was entertaining but it wasn't leading anywhere useful. He didn't even have much idea when Lauren had actually left the flat downstairs. He thought it was shortly after Lisa had had her apartment taken apart by burglars.

'When does Lisa usually get back from wherever she works?' Egerton asked. 'I'll try phoning her.'

Crispin folded his arms and looked sympathetic. 'Not much point I'm afraid.' He had a way of pushing his fingers within the sleeves of the tee-shirt and stroking his skin affectionately. 'She's away in Singapore making an epic about World War II with the film company she joined when she left BBC television. They've been at it for weeks. The postcard she sent me the other day said she expected to be away for another fortnight.'

The absence of Husak in any of the television companies was now explained. But that was no comfort.

'Why don't you try the restaurant?' Crispin suggested. 'If you think she's gone away with Luis, it's worth asking there. He obviously knew the owner very well—I'm not sure they weren't related. He might have some news of Luis or the brother.'

The chance seemed slight. But he had nothing better to do for the moment. 'Could you tell me the name?'

'El Portalón. It's off Camden High Street. I remember it being a few minutes from the Underground station.'

He was rising to leave when Crispin held up a hand apologetically. He had thought of something else to postpone the moment of getting back to community theatre. He went to a drawer and returned with something wrapped in tissue paper. It was an *inro*. Someone had given it to Fred ages ago. 'I don't imagine it's much good,' Crispin said hopefully.

The decoration on the *inro* showed a fat owl perched on a branch and looked as if it might be eighteenth century. 'Actually it could be rather valuable.' Egerton said. He glanced at Crispin's expression and knew he had to do better for him. 'As a gift, it's perhaps a *bit* ambiguous.'

Crispin was wrapping it up again. 'How do you mean— ambiguous?'

'The owl's the symbol of ingratitude. Perhaps the giver didn't know that.'

'I *see*,' Crispin said. He stretched the vowel a very long way. 'Fancy that.' He stopped wrapping and placed the *inro* on the table, owl side uppermost. From the head of the stairs he called after Egerton as he left. 'Lovely to see you.' He looked braced enough to face even the typewriter.

It was after twelve o'clock. Lunch at El Portalón, together with a little probing, seemed as good an idea as any. He took the Underground to Camden Town.

El Portalón had once been a butcher's shop, the glazed tiles and lettering were still visible each side of its windows. The extent to which it scorned the vanities of most Spanish restaurants outside Spain was at first sight forbidding. The tables were paper-covered, the chairs the metal and plastic kind advertised to stack in piles of fifty. At the back of the main room, a smaller one was visible, past a dusty velvet curtain that didn't meet the floor; apart from a large television set it seemed to be as spartan as the rest of the place. A Relais Routiers sign might have restored a little hope but the only announcement to the curious, apart from

60

the name above the door, was a card in the window advertising a coach that ran to San Sebastian once a fortnight.

Egerton seated himself at a table with a single artificial rose and ordered what proved to be rabbit stew. Most of his fellow lunchers were plainly Spanish. Those arriving after him were greeted with varying mixtures of formality and familiarity by a man who seemed to be the proprietor. He wore a suit that was too large and a white shirt buttoned high above his Adam's apple. There was no tie with the shirt and he was not a careful shaver; yet he had an air, a certain distinction. Moving between the tables to conduct grave conversations, he would occasionally turn to bark in the direction of the kitchen in a language that bore no relation to Spanish or any other tongue Egerton knew. To question him without likelihood of interruption was going to have to wait until business slackened.

Egerton had finished his second cup of coffee before the moment seemed ripe. He raised a hand. Dexterously adjusting chair angles on the way, the man approached and looked solicitous.

'I wonder if you can help me about someone who is well known to you. The name is Fernandes.'

The man smiled. 'It is quite a common name.'

'There are two brothers, Luis and Garcia. One of them has a girlfriend who is American. They were eating here in the summer. Have you seen them lately?'

The man paused, considering, 'Not lately.'

'How long ago?'

The man's lips rounded as he drew breath; his expression told of looking down great corridors of time. 'I cannot remember—many many weeks.'

'Do you know where either could be contacted?'

The man shook his head in sorrow. 'Is there some message you might leave perhaps?' Before Egerton could reply, a demand for a bill from a nearby table drew him away. When he returned, he flourished a pen and pad. 'If you would give me your name and telephone number,

61

perhaps one of them will come in. Or perhaps another friend will have news.'

It sounded fairly hopeless but there was nothing to lose. He gave the details then added a five pound note to the amount of his bill. 'Will you look after the waiter, please?'

The man inclined his head as if to say he had known from the start he was dealing with a true gentleman. At the door he called out, 'I shall not forget.'

In a phone booth in the Underground station he took out Evelyn's list again. Two of the London numbers answered this time. On the first, he got no further than Angela Montague's secretary; but when he mentioned Lauren's name there was a pause while she consulted elsewhere. Eventually she gave him an appointment with Ms Montague for four o'clock the next day.

On the other line the voice of a cleaning lady told him that if it was important to talk to Miss Sally Kirkwood before the evening he ought to try her number at the American Embassy. Things were looking up; he checked Ingalls' report to confirm his impression that, like Lisa Husak, she had also been uncontactable when he carried out his enquiries, then dialled the Embassy.

Ms Kirkwood had a pleasant voice but the going was sticky for a while. She listened to his story of the *inro* cash burning a hole in his pocket in total silence then asked him how he had discovered her name. When he told her it had been as a result of contacting Evelyn Rylance, the answer didn't seem to make things easier. Gradually he thawed her out. She wouldn't say whether she knew where Lauren was but she did agree to meet him for a drink at six o'clock near the Embassy.

He paused in the phone box to review the position. Gail would be coming at seven thirty and so far he had bought no food for their meal. If he picked something up from Harrods he would then be only a few minutes walk from the school where Lauren had worked. Although Ingalls had already been over the ground there, he ought to make sure he'd missed nothing.

Rain that had been threatening during the morning had become a relentless downpour as he arrived at Hazlewood School. Although it was barely a quarter to four, small figures in coloured socks and blazers were already darting past him into the maws of cars double-parked outside. Fortunately the staff were still there. After two fruitless encounters he found himself in classroom 4, gently dripping on a wooden bench and taking tea with Flora, by common consent the teacher who had been closest to Lauren.

She was in her forties and on the heavy side, with the intimidating qualities of the pure in heart. She accepted his story about the *inro* with an eager concern that pricked his conscience and went on to mention Ingalls' previous canter over the ground as the sort of coincidence that life's rich tapestry innocently provided. Ingalls, she told him, worked in a bank and Lauren had mentioned to him at a party that a flat was coming up that might suit him. He'd lost the bit of paper on which he had noted down the details and her mother hadn't been able to help. Not a bad story, Egerton reflected; less interesting than his own and perhaps on that account better.

'So you've absolutely no idea where she might have gone,' he said.

'Not really. I imagine she's somewhere with her boy-friend, Luis—they'd planned it for ages.'

He tried looking surprised. 'Luis Fernandes? I didn't know they were that close!'

Flora smiled, hugging to herself knowledge unshared, then relented. 'Oh, yes! Twin souls.' She rolled her eyes towards heaven.

'What brought them together?'

'I'm not sure. Lauren had so many interests. Protecting the environment, peace—all that.'

'Peace?' he repeated.

'Gosh, yes! To achieve something really big for peace, she said, would be the most satisfying thing in the world.' She sighed. 'I wish I could have seen more of her, she was a tremendous person. We got together when we worked for

63

the Save the Seals campaign. But she was only here for two terms.'

That was all she could tell him. He tried to imagine Lauren and Luis Fernandes together; while she was busy saving the seal, he would presumably be planning ways of blowing up Spanish policemen or whatever his speciality in ETA was. It seemed an odd combination.

He left Flora and launched himself once more into the rain. There were no taxis to be had. He rode the Underground, stacked with other steaming bodies, his trousers clinging to his legs. By the time he reached the Audley in Mount Street where Sally Kirkwood had agreed to meet him, he had had enough of his first day looking for Lauren Giordano.

Sally Kirkwood arrived in a yellow oilskin coat, shaking a flowered umbrella boldly over the occupants of nearby tables as she advanced into the bar. Her large saucer spectacles gave her an intense expression. He thought she might turn out to be another Flora but the attack with which she downed her vodka Martini pointed to a brisker life style. As on the telephone, she began with a disconcerting degree of reserve. Not until the third Martini did things really improve; his mention of his own visit to New York seemed to be what finally lowered her guard. When she produced a pack of Marlboros and offered him one, he knew she was taking him on board. She snapped her lighter for them both.

'I was afraid you might turn out to be some sort of detective employed by her mother to find her. I wouldn't like to be a part of that.'

He wondered if Ingalls would have passed the test if he had ever managed to meet her.

'You knew Lauren pretty well . . .'

'I didn't see a lot of her but I felt I did. We flew back together on the same plane from New York earlier in the year. She'd been staying with her father, Sam Giordano. You know who I mean?'

'Yes.'

64

'Apparently she hadn't seen him for a while and decided to make the trip on the spur of the moment. Odd really, because Lauren's interests are definitely not Hollywood.'

'I gather she was keen on ecology and that sort of thing?'

'Non-violence is really what she cares about most. She's gone away with a man who feels the same way. She's a very concerned person.'

He frowned. 'You say she's gone off with somebody who believes in non-violence?'

'Yes, Luis Fernandes.'

'Have you met him?'

'No, but she talked to me about him a lot, about what he wants for his people. He's a Basque, very proud.'

'Basques don't have a particularly non-violent reputation,' he said cautiously.

'Violence would never be acceptable to Lauren. She might be ruthless in other ways if she thought what she was doing was for a good cause. But the means would still matter to her.'

Either Lauren was in for a major shock one day or she had gone to a lot of trouble to fool friends like Flora and Sally Kirkwood about Fernandes' attitude to life. Egerton glanced at the clock over the bar. If he was going to be back in Prince of Wales Drive before Gail showed up, he needed to hurry things along. 'Can you think of any way that I can get this money to her?'

She pushed her lips forward playing with her glass which was empty again. 'I know what I'd do.' She half-rose, eyeing his Perrier bottle. 'Are you staying on that stuff?'

He took the glass from between her fingers and made her sit down again. She certainly wasn't another Flora, after three Martinis she didn't look even mildly flushed.

When he came back from the bar, she had taken her spectacles off and was polishing them with the end of the silk scarf she had worn on her head. Her eyes were big and solemn. He guessed that under a brittle manner she was very alone. 'So what *would* you do,' he asked.

'I'd contact her sister, Jacqueline. Lauren told me she'd

gone to stay in a village in Majorca called Deya. I don't know the address but you could probably get that out of their mother. The reason is something Lauren said when we had lunch a few days before she took off. That was when she told me she was going. Something had happened between her mother and herself. She wouldn't say what, but I had the impression that it was the trip to see her father in the States that had triggered it. She talked about having taken the biggest decision in her life.'

'Presumably she meant going away with Fernandes?'

'No, I'm sure she wasn't talking about that. She said it was the sort of decision about which one feels both ashamed and proud. I tried to get her to explain but she wouldn't. She just said with a little smile, "This is between me and David." '

'David? Not Luis?'

'No, David.'

'But who is David?'

'I've no idea.' She lit another cigarette. 'Anyway, what I was going to say is that when I asked how I'd be able to contact her, she said that she'd write but couldn't tell anybody for a while where she'd be. I said, "Do you mean nobody at all's going to know?" And she replied, "Well, maybe Jacqueline might have an idea." '

It was his first real step forward. Moreover it confirmed his feeling from the beginning that the possibility that Jacqueline knew something ought to be checked.

'You mentioned her trip to her father in the States perhaps had a link with her decision to go away with Fernandes. Could it mean they've gone there?'

She was shaking her head. 'No, I bet they're in Spain. She told me Luis was planning to go later this year anyway. By now she's probably become more Spanish than the Spanish.' She burped behind her hand. 'Or Basque than the Basques.'

Her glass was empty again. She looked into its depths as though weighing the thought of yet another refill. Then she seemed to decide that the evening could be faced after all and reached for the umbrella. 'Give me your number, I'll call you if I hear from Lauren or think of anything else.' He wrote it down on a page of her diary. She thrust it into her handbag. 'St John's Wood, here we come.' she said.

When they parted he stood for a moment, watching her move waywardly along Mount Street towards Park Lane. The heels of her shoes were on the high side to be coping with the consequences of four Martinis. He wondered if he ought to have walked her to the bus stop. But then he saw her free arm shoot out. With surprising speed she ran across the street and vanished into the black hole of a taxi.

# VII

ALTHOUGH it was well after seven o'clock, the snarls in the rush hour traffic which the rain had brought with it had still not unravelled. Egerton's bus ground its way in shuddering spasms down Park Lane and Sloane Street. The whole of central London seemed congealed for the night. By the Guards' barracks he finally abandoned riding and began to foot it to Prince of Wales Drive, sure that Gail would be waiting, soaked and forlorn at the entrance to his apartment block.

But there was no sign of her. He climbed the stairs, wondering if she had forgotten the day or simply given up. In the shared lobby to their two flats, he found Gwen hovering among her pot plants. He recognized the signs at once: she had been lying in wait. 'I heard your bell ring. When I found it was a friend I felt you wouldn't want me to leave her standing in the rain.' It was her hoarse-whisper voice, her stage aside. Confidentiality was not the object, just the appearance of it.

He swallowed irritation. 'Absolutely right.' After all he ought to be grateful. It was the steady erosion of privacy whenever she took charge of his life that got to him. The mistake, made at the very beginning, had been to leave the spare key with her. But someone had to deal with visitations from the gas and electricity boards, from the builder trying to cure the damp rot in the kitchen and from the only man in England who knew how to fix the Japanese cooker he'd bought with the flat. Gwen, the ever-present, churning out woollies for the boutiques on her knitting machine, was indispensable to his domestic economy.

Gail was on the sofa, her legs drawn up beneath her. She was reading his copy of *Time Out*. He saw with pleasure that the jeans and donkey jacket had been abandoned for a skirt and blouse: she had decided to be feminine for the evening. Even the urchin cut seemed less harsh. Under the lamplight, the pale down along the cheekbone was infinitely tender. When he kissed her, he smelled a scent familiar from long ago, recalling happiness and misery in more or less equal parts.

He poured a drink for her, changed his clothes and went to cook the chops. She followed him into the kitchen and peeled the potatoes. 'I know your secret,' she said.

'Which one?'

'Where you work. When I picked up a magazine from the table there was a pay slip underneath with the name of your department at the top.'

He remembered meaning to put it away before Gwen had a chance to look round.

'The Central Crimes Bureau!' She made it sound the most bizarre thing in the world. 'So you're really a policeman!'

'No, I'm not.'

'Then what?'

'An ordinary official. Mostly the job's investigating corruption in government, looking for snouts in the public money trough, that sort of thing. The police do the prosecuting when it's possible—which it often isn't.'

'Whatever made you join?'

'When I got back from the States I answered an advertisement. It sounded interesting. The man who used to be my boss at the bank wrote me up in a nice way. And apparently it was thought my experience could be useful. So they took me on.'

She was looking into an eye of one of the potatoes, as though imagining it all going on within. 'They didn't mind?'

'Mind what?'

'I thought they were stuffy in the civil service about drugs.'

'I'd stopped long before I joined.'

'They didn't ask if you'd ever been on them?'

'No.'

She dropped the potato into the saucepan with the others and lit a jet on the stove. 'I suppose they wouldn't like it if they knew?'

He shrugged and reached for his Perrier. She was looking at his glass. 'Do you just drink that now?'

'I have wine occasionally. But no spirits. It's part of the new me.'

'*Verboten?*'

'I'm not even supposed to have wine.'

She rolled her eyes.

'It's quite bearable,' he said. 'Honestly.' He turned the grill up on the chops. 'Could you mix vinaigrette for the avocados?'

She sighed, then moved to the cupboard and located ingredients in the intuitive way he associated with her. 'How did you do it?'

'I went to a clinic in New York my cousin knew about. Then to a place in Minnesota.'

'Was that the real reason you went to America?'

'No, I only made my mind up when I was there.'

'And you've never wanted to since . . .?'

'No.'

She was staring, perhaps not quite believing him yet. 'Clever you.'

'It didn't feel clever. Just necessary.'

She picked up the potato peeler and turned in on its point on the draining board as though driving home a screw. 'It didn't work for me when I was in the place in Devon.'

'You have to want to do it.'

She poked him suddenly with the peeler. 'You are so *pi!*' She was laughing in an exasperated way.

When they were eating she reverted to what the Bureau might do if they found out. Her probing was making him

70

jumpy. 'I hope they'd simply accept it isn't relevant now. Anyway they're not likely to know.'

'Somebody might tell them.'

'It would have to be somebody who knew at Oxford. Like you or Jamie.' He just stopped himself adding Julian's name.

She nodded. 'I suppose you don't have to worry really.'

But that wasn't quite true. Increasingly since his conversation with Antrim yesterday, he had reflected how it could seep back to the Bureau through casual gossip. Gail even, although she had loved him before Julian came along, perhaps still did a bit, might be careless just when the ears were flapping of somebody who fed the Drugs Squad at the Yard with information.

As they drank the wine he had bought, his spirits became lighter. She talked about the jobs she had done since Julian's death, made him laugh with imitations of the people she had worked with, and of some of the customers she had served; they didn't get on to the way the jobs had ended.

'Tell me about Jamie,' he said.

It seemed that he was riding high. A grand apartment, a Porsche, a bungalow built for his mother outside Glasgow. Even before Egerton had left for America, the talent developed at Oxford for supplying what people asked for, with the maximum of charm and the minimum of fuss, had been getting him noticed about London. For those in need of his special sort of music, he was the perfect impressario, civilized, discreet, ungreedy. Even, to complicate it all, kind.

He shook his head at the end of her recital. Impossible to identify his exact feelings about Jamie—Jamie who had saved his life one summer's afternoon in their first year at Oxford—who had also helped him begin destroying it . . .

'One day he'll get caught,' he said.

'Not Jamie.'

He started collecting their empty plates. 'Now that you

71

don't get an allowance from home, how are you paying for the stuff?'

'Jamie doesn't seem to mind when I can't. He also lets me have a bit over.'

'You mean you're pushing . . .'

She reddened. 'Occasionally.'

'That's why he gives you the extra . . .?'

'I suppose so.'

'But you're *doing it on the street*?'

'Yes, sometimes.'

'Don't you realize the risks?'

'I'm terribly careful.'

'They're bound to spot you sooner or later. They use cameras in upstairs rooms as well as people on the ground.'

She shrugged. 'If they get me, they get me.' He couldn't make out whether she really was indifferent or was just pretending to be, but the words chilled him.

He fetched the acacia honey ice cream which had been the main reason he had gone to Harrods and watched her taste the first mouthful. Her eyes widened. 'You remembered.' She shook her head and leaned across to link her fingers in his. 'You couldn't know how often I think of that summer. If I'm really low I go back there and imagine it all again.'

He felt a spurt of happiness that she'd said it and a little hope. But perhaps she was simply trying to please him.

The telephone was ringing. He squeezed her hand and went to answer it. A man asked his name and then rang off without even the hint of an apology. He returned to the table. She smiled and went on eating the ice cream. The moment had died. He might never discover if she had meant the words.

Later they sat, chastely gazing at the news on the box. She began to bite at the quick beside a thumb nail. He guessed she was going back over their conversation in the kitchen; the thought that he had escaped the habit both fascinated and nagged at her. She said, as though the earlier conversation hadn't ended, 'Do you know what I couldn't face? Losing the works, not just the fix, the whole works. Never being able to go to the drawer and see them waiting for me, my very own works. Being able to think, in a few hours I'm going to find a spot for you and you'll make the prick and then—whoosh, we're home again.'

He couldn't let her get away with jazzing it up. 'If you're saying it's really the ritual you want, the Japanese tea ceremony's supposed to be very good. And it doesn't actually kill you.'

She didn't smile. He could see she was still thinking about the works, about the impossibility of life without their consolation. Once he had played with the idea of keeping his own works, but for a different reason. They would have been in their cardboard box with a blood-stained handkerchief and a note on which would have been written the exact time and place in Manhattan they had last been used. The box was to be his talisman against the devils of the future, a reminder of that moment when he stood shaking over the bowl while he tried to fill the syringe and people shuffled past to the urinal beyond. That was what he had planned on the way to the clinic, the truth he would preserve to confront the black dogs whenever they came again. Later in Minnesota, he had winced at the theatricality of the notion. And by then the syringe and the blood-stained handkerchief had long since disappeared.

The television news was ending with a report on famine in Central Africa. Gail's attention veered away from her thoughts and became trapped by the pictures. Intrepidly the camera zoomed in on the sunken eyes and shrivelled limbs on the hospital mattresses, waited patiently for the scarecrow cattle to stagger and fall. Great pictures, an editor somewhere had said.

Gail put her head against his shoulder and shut out the screen. A faintly disagreeable odour rose from her skin, breaking through the surface of the scent. He kissed her hair, more in guilt at his awareness and hatred of the odour than anything else. If she wanted to stay the night, he couldn't turn her away. But that meant she would need to

73

fix before they finally parted and the thought of her doing it while she was with him was more than he could bear. Her handbag was open beside her. Unsuccessfully he tried to peer inside to discover if she was carrying a syringe.

Presumably she hadn't had the thought because she suddenly lifted her head and stood up, saying she must go, the nice little Gujerati landlord would have to let her in because she had lost her latch key.

When he dropped her at the house, a gaunt peeling affair in a terrace on the north side of Notting Hill, she said, 'Next time it's going to be a party. We'll go on the town. I don't think you're having fun any more. We've got to stop you getting *old.*'

She kissed him quickly, just away from his mouth, ran up the steps and pressed a bell. When a light appeared behind the transom, she didn't look round again but raised her fists above her head, imitating a boxer's salute to victory. He had a sudden terrible premonition that one day she would be gone like Julian and this gesture of empty triumph would be etched on his mind for ever.

On a chair in the sitting room when he returned to his flat he found a rain-spattered copy of the *Mail.* Presumably Gail had brought it with her. He didn't feel in a mood to wash the dishes. Pouring himself the rest of the wine he settled down with the paper.

On the Show Page a name caught his eye. Sam Giordano, fresh from producing a block-buster in the States, was in London for talks en route to Rome where his new production was about to start. The reporter who had interviewed him in his suite at Claridges had asked if he had any plans to see his former wife, now married to the Secretary of State for Defence. Well, Giordano had said, Evelyn and I have remained very good friends and I'm a great admirer of Jeffrey who used to stay at my house in Beverly Hills in the old days whenever he had business on the West Coast. I expect we'll get together. Of course my daughters are over here in Europe and I expect to see them too. Although we're in different parts of the world now, we all feel very close.

# VIII

THINKING about it afterwards, he wondered how he could have doubted that the man who stepped out of the green Vauxhall as he left his flat the next morning was following him. He had first glimpsed him when turning to watch a line of ducks which had forsaken the lake to stare at wild life in Prince of Wales Drive; the man was locking the car door, a stocky figure in blouson and navy slacks. That he hurried to catch the same bus was unremarkable: commuters, avoiding the expense of inner London parking, often left their cars for the day along the edge of Battersea Park. Only when his figure remained visible in the distance as Egerton was walking the last few hundred yards to the Bureau building in Somerset Square did the coincidence seem interesting. Egerton turned sharply into the mews behind the Square and slipped into the unmarked entrance to the Bureau's garage. From the darkness beside the ramp he watched. The other also turned into the mews. He was walking quickly but showed no signs of being disconcerted by Egerton's disappearance. At the end of the mews, without apparent hesitation, he again turned, right this time, away from the Square. He didn't reappear. It was an odd event; but to conclude that the man had been tailing him seemed excessive. Pressing the button for the security guard to let him in, he forgot the incident.

He sat idle in his office for a while, wondering how best to arrange the day. Apart from Sally Kirkwood's conviction that Jacqueline was more likely than anyone to know Lauren's whereabouts, the other interesting thing to emerge from their conversation had been her suggestion of a link between Lauren's visit to her father in the States and the disappearance with Fernandes. Since Sam Giordano was in London, it seemed a possible pointer to pursuing the idea with him: Giordano might recall some conversation with her that hadn't seemed significant before. But to tackle him without Evelyn Rylance having given her approval was obviously undesirable. Giordano had told the *Mail* reporter he expected to see her and Rylance during his visit. In that event she might prefer to tell him herself what Sally Kirkwood had said.

Her private number at Chester Square remained unanswered when he rang. It was barely nine forty. She hadn't spoken of going away, had if anything implied the contrary. Perhaps she was out jogging in Chester Square gardens after a breakfast of negative ions and a preliminary work-out on the exercise bicycle. He decided to keep ringing at intervals.

He filled in with trying the remaining numbers on her list of Lauren's friends. More of the London numbers answered this time. They listened to his story with mild interest but expressed themselves as having nothing to contribute on the subject of Lauren's whereabouts. There were references to having already said this to a man who seemed to think Lauren had found a flat for him. None of them offered to take down his name in case they got news.

He moved on to the two numbers he had for people outside the London area. The male member of the couple who ran the school for handicapped children told him that if he wanted to unload a cheque he could find a good home for it. The woman in Cornwall talked about Lauren's sterling character at great length. But she too had nothing useful to suggest.

At midday, having made his fourth unsuccessful call to Evelyn's number, he decided to ring through on the ordinary house line. A servant answered and at least solved one riddle: Evelyn was away in Brussels for two days. Apparently she was a member of a party of Ministers' wives

76

who had gone to learn about the glories of the European Community from the wife of a UK Commissioner there.

Egerton cursed. By the time she returned Giordano might have left for Rome. It seemed foolish to let slip the opportunity of seeing him. Obviously he knew the Rylances had employed an investigator to look for Lauren since he himself had suggested Ingalls for the role. There need be no mention of the Bureau; Egerton could simply say he had taken over from Ingalls.

He looked up Claridges' number, half-dialled, then decided to play safe and take advice from Antonia first. But when he tried her door he found it locked. Her secretary reported she was out until the late afternoon. He went back to his desk and told himself he was paid to use his initiative sometimes.

A female voice with an accent rather like Evelyn's came on the line when he got through to Giordano's suite. Mr Giordano was in conference somewhere and she didn't know when the hell he'd be back. She didn't sound like a secretary, not the conventional kind anyway. She asked him in a bored voice what he was calling about. He told her.

A little interest flickered in her voice. 'What about Lauren?' she said.

'I'm making some enquiries. Mr Giordano knows about them. There's one point on which I'd like to consult him.'

'Are you one of Ingalls' people?'

'No, I'm not. But it *is* the same enquiry.'

She grunted and said he could ring back at five o'clock when Mr Giordano might be available. He looked at his diary: the appointment with Angela Montague was for four o'clock so it seemed to fit reasonably well. Before she rang off she asked him what had happened with Ingalls. He told her nothing had happened, that was why he was on the job. 'That goddam girl,' she said.

Angela Montague's office was perched high in a block of pigmented concrete off London Wall. Red sandstone was

77

probably what the architect's water colour sketch had promised, but it had turned out the colour of stale bacon. Egerton waited in a hessian-walled room where girls sat fiddling with VDUs or speaking into telephones. After a while he deduced from the answers they were giving to callers that Angela ran an investment advice service through advertisements in the press; one had appeared the day before which no doubt explained why he had not been able to get through on his first attempts.

When he was finally shown into the presence, he paused uncertainly. With a grey flannel suit, Missoni tie and short beard, Ms Montague seemed to be pushing back the gender frontier pretty far. He allowed himself to be seated in a black leather chair and to be handed a cup of coffee from an espresso machine. Montague said with pencil poised, 'Delighted to meet a friend of Lauren's. Before I ask how much you have in mind to invest, would you care to tell me what holdings you have at present?'

The misunderstanding was laid at the door of the secretary Egerton had spoken to the previous afternoon. Montague tried, not very hard, to conceal his irritation. They were off to an unpromising start. 'I really can't discuss the affairs of a client, as I explained on the telephone to someone else who telephoned about Miss Giordano not long ago.'

It was becoming steadily more unproductive, trailing along in Ingalls' footprints. 'I don't want you to do that. I simply want to be put in a position to pay her some money.'

The magic word softened Montague a little. 'Quite frankly I don't know where she is at present. She promised to provide an address but so far I haven't heard.'

'You knew she was going away . . .'

'Oh, yes, she came and told me.' His gaze ranged over Egerton's suit and shirt. He began to display a faint geniality. Perhaps he was thinking that, after all, Egerton might turn into an investor one day. He said he'd met Lauren at a party soon after she came to England since when he'd handled all her financial affairs. Two months ago she'd told him she was going abroad and wanted an account in a Swiss bank in Geneva to which all her investment income was to be paid in future. He'd arranged it for her.

'So she's in Switzerland?'

'I doubt it. I gathered she was planning to go to Spain eventually but was likely to be somewhere else for a while. The point of the Geneva bank was that she needed the money out of England in a place which could be reached easily from anywhere in Europe.'

'You can't give me the name of the bank?'

'I'm not authorized to do that I'm afraid. If you care to let me have a cheque for the funds you're holding I'll see they're transferred to her account there.'

He clearly wasn't going to be shifted from that. Egerton stood up. 'Thank you. I'll hang on to the cash a bit longer, I think.' At the door he said, 'Do your clients find it a bit confusing when they meet you?'

'Very few do. My service is largely intended for people who can't travel to London.'

'But the name—'

'Many women nowadays prefer to take financial advice from one of their own sex. All my staff are women. They deal with the calls and correspondence.'

It had to be said. 'But *you're* a man.'

Montague opened the door. He had consulted a half-hunter on the way to it as a sign that they were now in extra time. 'I aim to give my clients the best of all worlds,' he said.

Out in London Wall again, Egerton went to look for a call box. When he got through to Claridges, the same woman answered from Giordano's suite. It was obvious that she'd forgotten all about his earlier call. Her voice became remote, she was relaying his words to someone in the background. When she addressed him again it was to say he could come if he was snappy.

Although the air outside was mild, a fire had been lit in the foyer at Claridges. In a reception room beyond, Egerton could see men and women sunk in the *accidie* between afternoon tea and the first drink. On one side, a piano and other musical instruments pointed to a trio having been lately active. A waiter moved silently to and fro, adjusting empty chairs.

The woman who admitted him to Giordano's suite was in her late forties, not unlike Evelyn Rylance to look at except that her colouring was blonde and she lacked the other's tigerish quality. She was dressed in a white towelling robe and wearing high-heeled mules. Leading him into a drawing room she poured him a Perrier from the forest of bottles on a side table. While she fixed a freshener to her own drink she made laconic enquiries about the weather in the streets, the best place for cashmere cardigans and the precise location of Annabel's. By the time that was over it seemed he had passed a test of sorts because she took him by the hand. Leading him to a television set she said, 'Tell me what the hell this is.'

'It's cricket,' he said, 'being played in Australia.'

'It *is*!?' She shook her head, marvelling, and called over her shoulder in the direction of a door behind them. 'Sam, I'm *watching cricket*!'

There was no audible response. She went on frowning at the set for perhaps ten seconds before her interest evaporated. Switching it off she drained her glass and handed it to Egerton for a refill. It was as though they had known each other for years although not quite as equals.

As he was pouring her whisky she asked, 'Is that suit custom built?'

'No.'

'Sam's ordering six suits tomorrow from some little guy in Savile Row he's known for years. He says it's the hand stitching that makes the difference. What do you *know* about that—something the machines still can't do!' As with the cricket she seemed in the instant to be deeply interested. Then she was away again, walking the room, prospecting for something else that might really grip her this time. Trying a radio beside the television set she located some forties jazz. As she stood back to listen, the door to which she had addressed her announcement about cricket opened and Giordano appeared.

He was naked, a stocky tanned figure going bald on top but with grizzled hair forming a flourishing mat down the thorax and abdomen. He paused, glancing from one to the other with parrot-bright eyes, then allowed his attention to be caught by the jazz. Extending sideways a hand holding a bath towel, he advanced with a little run as though towards a camera, not quite up on his toes, the eyes half-closed. He raised his eyebrows at the woman.

'Don't ask me,' the woman said, turning away.

'Lana Turner.'

'Jesus,' she said.

Giordano winked at Egerton. 'My greatest fan.' He exuded a mixture of geniality and powerful menace. The woman fetched him a drink while he seated himself in an armchair with the towel wrapped tightly round his waist. 'So you've taken over looking for Lauren?'

'Yes.'

'Well, it looks as though you couldn't do worse than that wimp Ingalls.' He looked at the woman. 'When are we going, Joanie?'

'They're sending a car at eight.'

He turned back. 'My social secretary, Egerton.' He winked again.

'Like hell,' Joan said, 'I've had enough of taking your goddam messages. Tell the hotel to do it.' She went back to the television set.

Giordano yawned. 'So what do you want, Egerton? We haven't much time.'

'A friend of Lauren's I spoke to yesterday felt sure there was some sort of connection between Lauren's stay with you and her going off with Fernandes.'

Giordano lifted one of his legs to rest the ankle on the knee of the other. He began to search for hard skin under the foot. 'Is that so?'

'It struck me that perhaps she'd met somebody at your

81

house who could be the key. Or that you might remember putting some idea to her, making a suggestion that she might have acted on.'

Joan called out. 'Lauren wouldn't buy suggestions from Sam, that's for sure.'

'And I'll tell you why,' Giordano said. 'I'm not serious. I don't wear stickers on my tits about the end of civilized life as we know it. I don't bleed for whales.'

'Seals,' Joan said.

'Whales, seals, sharks—they're all in the same bag. Lauren wants nobody to touch nothing. She's making the world safe for Jaws.'

The telephone rang. Giordano looked at Joan. When she didn't stir, he padded across the room to take the call. He stayed standing as he talked, his responses alternating between outraged disbelief and heavy menace. Finally he said, 'Well, you tell him, pussy cat, that if he doesn't come up with the money by the day after I check in at the Excelsior in Rome, I'm going personally to break his goddam hands.'

He returned to his armchair, leaving two damp patches on the carpet beside the telephone, where his feet had been. 'Women lawyers. I have to pull my punches in case they get hysterical. You think I'm too soft?' He scratched his chest, looking enquiringly at Egerton but went on without waiting for an answer. 'This friend of Lauren's—what exactly did she say? Had Lauren talked to her about her stay in my house?'

'I suppose so but she didn't know anything specific about it. It was just a feeling that seeing you, staying with you, had made Lauren's mind up to do something big.'

'Big?'

'Yes.'

'She said that?'

'Yes.'

Giordano studied his face for a few moments; he seemed to be trying to make a calculation about Egerton. Then he stood up and drew the towel meditatively between his legs, dealing with a few precious spots still damp. 'But that's all . . .?'

'Except that Lauren mentioned some person named David who may be connected with it. Does that mean anything?'

Giordano was frowning in concentration. Then he shrugged. 'None of this stuff makes sense. She met no Davids in my house. And nothing I said to her gave her a reason for taking off.' He stood up. 'I have to get dressed, Egerton. Did you tell my ex-wife you were coming to see me?'

'No, I tried to contact her this morning but she's away visiting the European Community headquarters in Brussels.'

Joan had looked round at the mention of Evelyn. Her eye caught Giordano's and he winked at her. 'Evelyn sounds like a real politico these days.' He moved towards the door. 'When we were together, Egerton, Washington was the place she always wanted to be, with all those crooks shooting their mouths off. Remember that TV film of Jackie O. showing people the White House? She liked that.' He produced a wolfish grin then threw the towel magisterially over one shoulder. 'You find Lauren, Egerton. Like her mother, I got a few things to say to her. Such as I don't expect a daughter of mine to go off with a goddam Communist.'

Egerton turned to say goodbye to Joan. She raised her glass to him. 'Come and teach me cricket some time.' It seemed he had made a bigger hit there than he had supposed.

Giordano had the door open. He looked up and down the corridor in the hope of scandalizing some passing citizen but there was nobody about. 'When I was a kid C. Aubrey Smith once drove his car over my foot. Then he blamed me for scratching his fender. So I don't go for people who play cricket.' After the door closed Egerton could hear Joan's voice raised. She was asking Giordano what that bullshit was about C. Aubrey Smith.

Down in the foyer the scene had changed. Somnolence

had lifted. People were moving purposefully, demanding attention at the porter's desk. Evening had brought its urgencies, new challenges for the senses. In the street outside a party of four in evening dress were climbing into a chauffered Bentley. The doorman turned to glance at Egerton, but only for a second. They both knew there wasn't another Bentley further up the street, riding gently at anchor for him. No glittering challenge waited out there. He was a man who lived in Battersea now, with a mortgage and rates and service charge to pay before he started eating. He was someone who didn't even have a flexible friend in his pocket to take the waiting out of wanting, because there were still too many debts to be paid off from the days of wine and roses and the other thing.

He wondered idly where Giordano and Joan would be spending the evening. Even that vaguely threatening and unpredictable company would have the edge on scrambled eggs back at Prince of Wales Drive. Gail had been right: he wasn't having any fun. When the clinic took away the habit, something else had gone with it, a feeling of expectation, a sense that out there limitless experience was waiting to be tasted. He didn't ask for euphoria, perpetual sunbursts; just a lift to the heart now and then. Since he had joined the Bureau, existence had been like a film shot in black and white. If he didn't pull out of this mood he'd become like all those defeated faces he saw as he rode the 137 each day. Staying late to read files and improve his promotion chances, pounding the track in Battersea Park to keep the flab at bay and making occasional duty visits at weekends to sister and godchild weren't adding up to a life.

He crossed Berkeley Square. The last of the marquees erected in the gardens for a charity function the night before were being removed. According to a poster, it had been something to do with the protection of wildlife. If Lauren Giordano had still been around, perhaps she would have gone, with a reluctant Fernandes in tow: making the world safe for Jaws.

Something about the way Giordano had talked about Lauren and her visit to him had a hollow ring. There was knowledge that he hadn't cared to reveal. Sally Kirkwood had been right in sensing that the visit had changed things for Lauren. But whatever Giordano might be holding back, he could swear he was genuinely ignorant about her whereabouts.

He had arrived at Piccadilly. Standing opposite the Ritz, waiting for the lights to change, he glanced down at a blonde in a coupé that had drawn up beside him. Her head was turned towards the driver as she talked, one arm resting on his shoulders. He was about thirty, lean-featured with thick black hair that needed a trim; if it hadn't been for a certain rattiness he would have qualified as handsome. As the lights changed and the car swung left down Piccadilly, the blonde sat back. In her expression Egerton saw that oddly seductive combination of naivety and determination already familiar from their meeting at the house in Chester Square. It was Camilla Rylance.

Walking from the delicatessen with the eggs for supper, Egerton paused briefly by the Mini for the ritual morning and evening check: aerial still intact, no fresh messages scratched on the bonnet, all four wheels in place. Another day when the Indians had stayed up in the hills.

As he felt for his key in front of the entrance to the apartment block, he was vaguely conscious that two figures had disembarked from a car parked a few places in front of the Mini and were approaching. Someone said, 'Mr Egerton?'

Turning, left hand still deep in his trouser pocket, he inclined his head slightly. The alteration of plane made the blow aimed at a point behind his ear less than accurate; so that, although blackness descended, some remnant of stupefied consciousness remained. Hands were reaching under his arms, turning him fully about, carrying him to where other hands reached out to take possession of him. His face was plunged into ribbed material that smelled of

85

cigarette smoke and dust. An engine started and he knew he was in a car.

He felt his limbs begin to stir; it was as though they were conducting their own uncoordinated protest. Dazed as he was, he knew that wasn't wise and tried to control them. Someone became displeased. His hair was gripped, pulled down so that his chin was touching his chest and this time the blow was perfect. Down he went, down it seemed through the seat and floor of the car, through everything, down into total obliteration.

When he returned to consciousness, he at first had no memory of the attack. It was as though he had simply slipped out of time for a while. He became aware by degrees that he was sitting up, his head against wooden palings. Through a mist he saw, beyond a line of parked cars, a familiar sight, the façade of his own apartment block. He had been dumped more or less on his doorstep.

The mist, he was relieved to discover, was not in his own vision; it had drifted across from the lake in Battersea Park to settle on the line of buildings that stretched towards Albert Bridge. A drum beat had started in his head. When he touched the skin behind his right ear, it was puffed and sticky. He held out his wrist until he could glimpse his watch face in the light of the street lamps: twenty past ten. After seeing Camilla, he had caught his bus and gone straight to the delicatessen; he had stayed chatting there for perhaps twenty minutes. That meant he must have spent at least an hour, either with the people who had attacked him or stacked against the palings. Few walked on this side of Prince of Wales Drive at night. Any who had seen him unconscious had presumably decided he was drunk and better left to sleep it off.

Struggling to his feet, he went through his pockets. To his surprise his cheque book was still there; so were his wallet, bank card and keys. Puzzled, he checked again. The envelope containing the list of Lauren's friends supplied by Evelyn Rylance seemed more crumpled than before but that could have happened in his pocket; the list itself remained inside. He could find only one sign that the attackers had searched him. The compartment of the wallet in which he kept his Bureau pass and a few photographs had had its contents taken out and replaced; the snapshot of Gail and himself, taken on Magdalen Bridge the summer of the year they had met, was on top instead of his Bureau pass.

Half an hour later, with the lump behind his ear bathed and most of the filth removed from his clothing, he could think of nothing useful to be done about the attack, at least not at this time of night. Aspirin was already dulling the headache; the idea of calling at a hospital and letting some bored houseman prod the wound was unattractive. He ought, of course, to telephone the police. But that would bring an even more bored constable round to take a statement. He hadn't got the number of the car into which he had been bundled nor could he give even the sketchiest description of his attackers. Since he was simply going to end up as another mugging statistic in the Incident Book, he might as well leave it until the morning when he could call at the local station on his way to the Bureau.

He was in bed when he remembered how the day had begun, with the man who had followed him onto his bus. Obviously the mugging had a connection. What it was he had no idea. But after all, he had become a part of the evening's urgencies. The challenge had still to reveal itself. But somebody out there was *interested*.

# IX

HE was shaving next morning when he heard the telephone. The time was barely seven thirty. He could think of no one who would call him so early in the ordinary way. Wiping soap from his chin, he prepared for crisis.

The voice was a man's, pleasantly authoritative.

'Jeffrey Rylance here. I believe my wife mentioned I wanted to hear how you were getting on.'

For a second he wondered if somebody was playing a practical joke. He had not imagined Rylance putting through a personal call to him, certainly not at this time of day. Rylance went on, 'I suggest you come to my room at the House of Commons this evening. Make it six forty-five. If I'm not there my secretary will look after you. Can you manage that?'

'Certainly.'

'I prefer you not to say you're an official when you call. I'll tell my secretary to expect someone of your name and that you're a constituent. When you arrive at the House, that's the line to take with the police on the door.'

Delivered in that brown velvet voice, the words did not sound hectoring, merely firm. The assumption conveyed was that clear instructions were all their relationship needed.

Back in the bathroom, he reflected on a suddenly urgent priority: to chase Bellamy at Special Branch for anything he had been able to discover about Luis Fernandes' movements. A report of the results of his own enquiries would sound pretty thin. Apart from the question mark over Lauren's trip to her father in the summer, all he would have to offer was Montague's disclosure of having opened a bank account in Geneva, plus his own conviction, reinforced by what Sally Kirkwood had said, that if anybody knew where Lauren now was, it was her sister Jacqueline.

Bellamy proved elusive. According to his office, he was out for an unspecified period and couldn't be contacted. Several people had gone sick in the Special Protection squad where Bellamy had once served; he'd been taken off his normal duties to nursemaid an Arab Emir round London. The only thing left, it seemed, was to contact whoever was actually running the Basque desk. He went to Antonia's room to borrow her directory for the Branch. She was writing a minute in a file.

'Did you get my note?' he asked.

She nodded. 'You should have waited until Rylance's wife got back. But in your shoes I'd probably have done the same.' She gave him a smile. 'Anyway, how *was* life at Claridges?'

'Very civilized.'

'And Sam Giordano?'

'Not so civilized.'

'Did he have anything worthwhile to offer?'

'Not really. I rather suspect he's holding something back about Lauren's visit to him. But I'm equally certain he doesn't know where she is now.'

He sat down. 'Rylance called me at my flat before breakfast this morning. His staff must have a tough time if that's the way he functions normally. Anyway he wants a report on the state of play. I'm going to his room at the House of Commons tonight.'

'Well, well,' she said. She turned sideways from the desk towards the window. 'And you've told master about this?'

'I called on him as soon as I got to the office.'

'How did he react?'

'He was put out that Rylance hadn't fixed the meeting through him. Also that he'll be away tomorrow and won't know at once what transpires. He's working in the office on

Saturday morning and I have to come in and report.'

She was looking through the window, smiling. 'I expect he found it all *very* irritating.'

Nothing in her expression or manner hinted that there had been the *affaire* between her and Antrim that office gossip alleged. Apparently it had happened when Antrim was in the throes of being divorced by his wife. The *affaire* had ended when a Canadian policeman named Muir had appeared on the scene. He had wanted her to marry him and go back to Canada, but she had never gone. No one knew why. Behind that detached, often ironical expression was something mysterious that had defied the probing of admirers and the merely inquisitive alike.

'I need something hard from Special Branch about Fernandes if I'm to convince Rylance I'm really trying. Unfortunately—'

She interrupted him, snapping her fingers. 'I meant to tell you—Bellamy was trying to get you first thing this morning. I took the call since you weren't in. He's on some protection job but hopes to be able to telephone you soon after twelve thirty. I gather you've given them a shock in Special Branch.'

'What sort of shock?'

'He didn't say.' She glanced at her wristwatch and rose, shutting the file. 'Good luck with Rylance. I hope you won't find him in too bad a temper because of the piece in the *Globe*.' Seeing his puzzlement, she went on, 'You'd better read it beforehand. Apparently they've another secret paper from his office.'

He was almost at the door when she exclaimed. 'Your *head*—whatever happened?'

He hadn't thought the lump would be visible through his hair. He told her the story.

'Have you reported it?'

'I called at the local police station on my way in this morning. They were very polite and said there was A Lot of It About.'

'But it doesn't make sense if nothing was taken.'

'I know, I'm still trying to work it out.' He didn't care to admit how barren his thoughts had been. He was about to tell her about the man who had followed him the previous morning, when she looked at her watch again and swore.

'I must go, the man who's lunching me gets very scratchy if he's kept waiting.' She picked up her handbag. 'We ought to think a bit more about the mugging. Could it be backwash from the Beynon case? We know he hates your guts. You'd better be careful.' She didn't smile as she went out of the door.

In the Press Room he looked up the *Globe*'s story. It was on the front page. There was also a leader, full of high-mindedness about the *Globe*'s Duty to Inform a public panting for its guidance. But the story was a genuinely impressive scoop. It seemed to be based on the summary conclusions of the Committee Rylance had set up to consider alternatives in defence weaponry if GOLIATH were to be dropped. The Committee had said that to achieve a comparable level of protection over the next ten years without GOLIATH would be difficult. It *could* be secured by a further investment in existing weapons but involving much higher cost to the defence budget. On the other hand if that course was adopted British manu-facturers would benefit as would the level of unemploy-ment. Some fairly detailed figures were quoted in the story.

Presumably the *Globe* was not among the papers de-livered to Rylance at Chester Square otherwise he would surely have sounded tetchier on the telephone. But by evening he would no doubt have been through enough fall-out from the article to be spitting blood. That made it even more vital to have something encouraging to offer on the search for Lauren.

Back in his own office, he wrote up his meetings with Montague and Giordano, reminding himself of Antonia's aversion to purple prose; since he was supposed to refer to her for advice, he could hardly refrain—not that he wanted to—from showing her his file notes. Off and on, his mind turned to her lunch appointment. He felt idly curious about the man who got scratchy if she kept him waiting. Some chalk-striped admirer, impatiently devouring olives in the American bar at the Savoy? Or an aged uncle, grumpily pacing the hall of the Ladies' entrance to his club?

Bellamy came through at a quarter to one. He was speaking from a call box and sounded in a hurry. 'We ought to meet.'

'Fine—as soon as you like.'

'I'm free until one forty-five when I have to be back with my Emir again. Could you join me for a sandwich at St Stephen's Tavern, across the road from Parliament?'

'I hope you've some news for me.'

'I've more than that,' Bellamy said.

Egerton watched him thread his way through the crowd in the bar, a stubby figure in a blue hopsack suit that seemed to fit too snugly to have an automatic tucked away beneath it. He was a determined mover, swift to tap the shoulders of those who didn't shift from his path sharply enough. The word from rugby football fanciers in the Bureau was that the police had never had a better stand-off half.

Egerton handed him his beer. 'How's your Emir?'

'Very civil.'

'Where did you go with him—the Foreign Office?'

'No, this morning was strictly business: Harrods. We bought twenty-five videos.' Bellamy downed slightly under half his pint with no evident movement of the throat. 'I'd forgotten what this lark was like. Let's get something to eat.'

With their sandwiches they beat a path towards the corner of the room. 'Luis Fernandes,' Bellamy said, 'You wanted to know his whereabouts.'

'Yes.'

'The answer is, we've no idea and we couldn't have cared less until you asked. All I can tell you is that he flew out of Heathrow on an Air France flight to Paris on the 27th of July.'

'Accompanied?'

92

'Can't say. In fact there's hardly anything we *can* say about him and for a very good reason. According to our information he's not a terrorist.'

'*Not?*'

'No. When he first came here we asked the Spanish police what his form was. They told us that although he'd been a member of ETA at one time, he'd definitely moved away from involvement in terrorist activity when the present Spanish government won the elections. He now claims to be committed to pursuing Basque aims by peaceful constitutional means. That's what the Spanish told us and appeared to believe themselves.' Bellamy lifted a corner of his sandwich. He wrinkled his nose before deciding it was just fuel after all. 'Luis has a brother however, Garcia, who is a different kettle of fish. Nobody questions that *he's* a terrorist. In the ordinary way he wouldn't be allowed to land in this country. He came in on a false passport earlier this year and although we'd already had warning from the Spanish police, at their request he wasn't stopped. He was going to see Luis while he was here according to their information and they believed there was a fair chance that as a result of the meeting Garcia who is still very close to his brother would be persuaded to join the non-violent Basque movement which Luis supports. If that happened it would have been a major blow to one of the most dangerous ETA terrorist groups. Are you with me so far?'

'Yes.'

'Well, it didn't work. Garcia is still the leader of a murder squad that operates from a base in French Basque country—that's down in the south-west corner of France. So Luis didn't pull off the trick as the Spaniards hoped. But did he really *try* to? According to *you*, Luis is a terrorist himself, after all. Fred Rivers on the Basque desk wants to know why you say that. Did Garcia convert Luis back again? Or have the Spanish had it wrong all the time?'

Egerton hesitated, fumbling for prevarications that

would not sound uncooperative. 'I can't tell you the answer, I'm afraid.'

'But what's your source?'

'I can't tell you that either. The information came from somebody reliable, somebody who had the means to discover the facts.'

'Spanish?'

'No, British.'

'This is a human source then?'

'Yes.'

'How can you be sure he didn't mix the two brothers up?'

'In his position he isn't likely to have made that mistake. It was definitely Luis he was talking about.'

Bellamy grimaced and turned to elbow his way to the bar with their empty glasses. When he came back, he said, 'I'm told that to date we've been working on the assumption that the Spanish police have good coverage of the situation and also that they've been frank with us. If they haven't, that's worrying.'

'I see that.'

'There's a lot of current aggro about Basques. According to one report Garcia Fernandes is back in this country. It's thought he may be planning some sort of terrorist operation here, God knows what, perhaps he's going to blow up the Spanish Embassy—Fred Rivers seems to have an idea but won't tell me any details. What he *did* tell me was that if you have anything reliable to contribute, he needs to know—now.'

'I'm seeing the person concerned tonight.'

'Good, then I'll tell Fred you'll be ringing him direct.'

Bellamy raised his glass, celebrating the fact that he was out from under; looking about him, he appraised the talent, nodded briefly to someone he recognized, offered scandalous intelligence about a Member of Parliament loudly demanding service at the bar. 'By the way,' he said, 'you've made a Friend: Detective Chief Superintendent Clayton, no less.'

It took a second or two before the connection came back

to him: the leakages to the *Globe*, Camilla Rylance's story of the man with the binoculars. 'The long distance photography idea was right . . .?'

'It's got a lot going for it. The morning you phoned me, Clayton sent somebody around the block of flats behind the Rylance house to find out what could be seen. It would be possible to get a good camera shot on a desk in Rylance's study window from several of the flats. What's more the net curtains were drawn *back*. However when Clayton kept an appointment he had with Mrs Rylance that afternoon, they'd been drawn *across*.' Bellamy grinned at the infinite duplicity of man and woman kind.

'What did he do?'

'Had the desk moved away from the window so that it couldn't be overlooked. He didn't say why and it seems she didn't ask either, which is interesting. He's now checking on the occupants of the flats. The porter of the block says that one of them has girls up there to use as photographic models. He gives out that he does it professionally but the porter believes it's just for kicks. Clayton's waiting to be sure his checks on the other people don't throw up any better bets. Then he'll interview this guy, using the visits by the girls as a bit of leverage. Anyway I was to tell you—thanks.'

To be viewed with favour by a Detective Chief Superintendent couldn't be bad. But that wouldn't last if the steer turned out in the end to be wrong. 'When I saw the fresh leakage in today's *Globe* it struck me that the photography theory might not hold water after all. I guessed Clayton would have had the desk moved pretty quickly. But according to the *Globe* the document they've now seen has only just been submitted to Rylance.'

Bellamy shook his head. 'I slipped into the Yard before coming here and happened to meet Clayton. I told him I was seeing you and asked if the new leakage made a difference. It doesn't. What the *Globe* have got isn't the Report that's just been submitted but a draft of the conclusions which the Chairman of the Committee let

Rylance have some time ago so that he'd know what was in the wind. One or two discrepancies make this definite. Clayton's satisfied that although the *Globe* has run three stories about GOLIATH, in a sort of historical progression as though they had got each separately, there was almost certainly just *one* leakage.'

He glanced at his watch and then at their glasses. 'One for the road, I think.' He had a rugby man's hollow legs. When he came back with his fresh pint, he went on, 'The stories as I understand it were, first, Rylance's decision to set up a committee to review the proposal to buy GOLIATH and consider if there were feasible alternatives; second, the personal minute from the Chief of the Defence Staff hinting at top brass resignations if GOLIATH was cancelled; and third, today's piece on the committee's conclusions. The papers that formed the basis for all these stories were worked on by Rylance at his house a week or so before the first leakage appeared. All the photographer needed was patience and a bit of luck to get the lot at one time.' Bellamy raised his glass. 'Of course, this assumes they *are* genuine leakages.'

'You've just said they are.'

'The *contents* are genuine. But the question you have to ask is—do the leakages perhaps suit Rylance? The first story will have done him no harm with the public and quite a few in his own Party. It quoted him as saying that no fresh nuclear option like GOLIATH should be pursued if a practicable alternative could be found. In other words, look at me, I don't forget that nuclear weapons are terrible and that the Great British Public don't want any more than are absolutely necessary. Even this latest story could be useful if he's preparing to come down against GOLIATH. Of course he'll take stick over breaches of security in his department. But that may be a price he's willing to pay in the interests of softening his image. It's the sort of game these chaps play, isn't it? After all, he's expecting to become Home Secretary soon. Perhaps he doesn't want to go there looking too hawkish.'

The remark about Rylance's imminent move from Defence was a genuine aside, he obviously assumed that the news had reached Egerton. But if it had been whispered in the Bureau, it had not been in his hearing. Antrim's concern to be obliging to Rylance over trying to locate Lauren suddenly became easier to understand.

They came out of the pub into watery sunlight. Bellamy said, 'Don't be too long coming back about this Basque business. Rivers is an awkward bugger when he's roused.'

Turning quickly he crossed over Bridge Street. As he moved along the railings outside the Houses of Parliament, he broke into an easy trot. A ragged column of tourists, bear-led by a guide, was surging along the pavement in the opposite direction, but he didn't pause, brushing them aside like a setter going through bracken.

# X

VISITORS to the Public Gallery were being herded out when he arrived for his appointment with Rylance. A man with a beard and a proprietorial air, presumably an MP, stood pressing the flesh of each in turn, dispensing farewell charm. A coach was drawn up waiting to take them back to the real world.

Negotiating a rabbit warren of corridors with the aid of an attendant, Egerton reached a small ante room. A secretary was reading a novel beside a typewriter. She acknowledged he was expected. Rylance was apparently with the Prime Minister however; this made the time of his return a plaything of fate. She sat him down with a newspaper.

An odd sort of calm prevailed. He sensed he had reached the end of one run in the rabbit warren; behind these walls were other runs, other beings, almost certainly making noise. But here was the stillness of a capsule. Half an hour passed with a single diversion, a girl who appeared silently from the corridor. She perched herself beside the secretary's typewriter for whispered gossip and swung her legs interestingly.

He had abandoned the newspaper by the time the door was flung wide and Rylance entered. He tossed a folder of papers in front of the secretary. 'Forty balls-aching minutes and I don't know if he agrees even now.'

She gave him the standard secretarial smile of sympathy which conveyed that it had no doubt been hell but she knew he'd get over it. Rising, notebook in hand, she said, 'Private

98

Office were on about the *Globe* story. The head of Security wonders if you want to see him again tonight.'

'God forbid.'

Impassively she drew a line through an entry in the notebook then pointed behind him. 'Mr Egerton.'

He wheeled sharply. Although he was carrying too much weight, his movements were very rapid; he took in Egerton's appearance with a single dispassionate glance. 'Right.' Making his way into a room beyond the secretary's table, he sat down on a sofa, reached for a cigar and pointed towards the chair. The secretary shut the door behind them.

'Been with the Bureau long?'

'Just over eighteen months.'

'What were you doing before?'

'I worked in a merchant bank—Hogarths.'

Rylance seemed encouraged. 'Impressive people.' He was beginning to unwind after the frustrating interview with the Prime Minister. 'What made you leave them?'

'I felt banking wasn't for me.'

He raised his eyebrows: the answer had lacked appeal. No doubt a move from merchant banking into public bureaucracy struck him as eccentric if not bizarre. Leaning back with a grunt he rested his head on the edge of the sofa and closed his eyes. The eyelashes were extraordinarily long and thick; they might almost have had mascara on them. Beneath his chin, the flesh swelled like a chicken's breast. 'Well, let's hear how you're getting on.'

Egerton took a deep breath. 'I've no lead so far to where Lauren is living. What I *have* discovered is that a bank account was opened for her in Geneva at the time she went away.'

'Which bank?'

'The person who arranged it won't reveal that.'

'Who is he?'

He told him. Rylance's eyes remained closed. 'Presumably the identity of the bank is on a file in his office?'

'Yes.'

99

'Well, can't you get at it? I imagine you're equipped in the Bureau to carry out a little operation of that sort, aren't you?'

He cleared his throat. Nothing Antrim had said had prepared him for quite such a buccaneering approach. He said carefully, 'Having regard to Swiss banking practice I doubt if it would do us any good if we *knew* the bank. We'd never persuade them to reveal Lauren's address. And I'm fairly sure Montague doesn't have that in his files. She told him she would write with it later but she hadn't done so at the time I saw him.'

It seemed for a moment as if Rylance might be going to persist with a demand for a quiet little burglary. But then he sighed. 'All right. What have you got on Fernandes' movements?'

'According to the police he left London on the 27th of July on a flight to Paris. They can't say if he had anyone with him.'

'And . . .?'

'That's all.'

Rylance opened his eyes. 'All? Surely you've got other channels through which you can discover where Fernandes went from there? Aren't you and the police in touch with *foreign* police services? What about INTERPOL and that sort of thing?'

They had reached the crunch. 'Unfortunately Fernandes doesn't seem to have been viewed as being of criminal or security interest. According to the Special Branch they were told by the Spanish police that he wasn't a terrorist. His brother Garcia is. But not Luis. Could you tell me where you got the information that he's also a terrorist?'

Rylance was looking at the tip of his cigar. 'The security people I expect. I can't really remember.'

'Was it in a written report?'

'No, oral.' He shrugged. 'I suppose that whoever told me was mixing the two brothers up.' He seemed oddly uninterested in what had happened. 'I expect I got my Private Office to make the enquiry and a mistake occurred somewhere along the line. Anyway that's water under the bridge. Whether he's a terrorist or not, it's still important for us to know where he and Lauren are.'

'But if he's *not* a terrorist, surely your principal anxiety is removed?'

'Not really. It doesn't mean it's desirable for the relationship to become permanent. From what Lauren told us, it's clear that Fernandes is, at best, very radical in his views. My wife is extremely anxious. Having to appear unconcerned while getting absolutely no news of Lauren's whereabouts has been a great strain for her. I don't want that to go on for months on end.'

It was difficult to see why appearing unconcerned was going to remain necessary in the future. The only likely explanation seemed to be that her vanity was so great she couldn't bear the thought of the world learning that her daughter had gone away with, in the words of Sam Giordano, a goddam Communist. And Fernandes probably wasn't even that.

In any case, the basis for himself being involved in looking for Lauren seemed to have been removed. The Rylances ought to go back to William Carter Ingalls, unsatisfactory though they'd found him. But he could scarcely take that line without reference to Antrim who might decide that now he'd started the job he'd better finish it.

Rylance said, 'I hear from my wife you think it would be worthwhile checking with Lauren's sister.'

'Yes. One of Lauren's friends also believes that Jacqueline is the most likely person to know where Lauren is.'

'Which friend was this?'

'Sally Kirkwood. She works at the American Embassy.'

Rylance was chewing his lip. 'Lauren and Jacqueline did seem very close at one time, I've wondered myself if they might have stayed in touch without telling my wife. Not that I know either of them very well.' He threw the cigar into a metal waste bucket as though suddenly bored with it. 'Do you believe you could find a way of exploring this without revealing that you're working under our instructions?' Like Evelyn, he clearly saw Egerton as a hired hand for the duration of the search.

'It's possible.' He groped for a diplomatic form of words to reserve his position. 'Of course it would depend on the view my Director takes about going on with the investigation. In the light of what now seem to be the true facts about Luis Fernandes' security status.'

Rylance was staring at him; he opened his mouth as if to say a great deal then changed his mind. He smiled. 'I fancy your Director will see the logic of your going on. If he's in doubt perhaps you'll ask him to speak to me.' He took out a pocket diary and copied something from it on to a scrap pad. 'That is Jacqueline's address in Deya. There's no telephone apparently. As far as I know she is living alone. You may find her in a . . . rather erratic condition.' He grimaced. 'I should be grateful if you would get off quickly. I have reasons for wanting a result out of this enquiry by the end of the month.'

Rylance rose to his feet. He stared grimly at the Pugin paper on the walls for a moment, then crossed to his desk and began glancing at the papers on it as though in search of distraction. He was displaying a sudden tension. At last he said, 'Well, is there anything else?'

'Very little I'm afraid. I called on Mr Giordano last night since I'd noticed he was staying at Claridges. I thought he might possibly be able to help.'

Rylance frowned. 'Did my wife suggest you should see him?'

'No. When I was talking to Sally Kirkwood she told me she felt something happened when Lauren was visiting her father earlier in the year which had a link with her going away with Fernandes. Since Mr Giordano was supposed to be in London for only a day or two I thought it would be sensible to follow it up with him straight away. I tried to reach your wife beforehand but I understand she's in Brussels. I hope that was all right.'

'Did he say anything useful?'

'He could think of nothing that fitted Sally Kirkwood's theory.'

Rylance went on frowning. Then he shrugged and looked at his watch; it was a clear signal that he was closing the interview. Egerton rose. 'Did Lauren ever speak of a person named David?'

Rylance shook his head. 'Not to me. Why?'

'He seems to have played a part in her life during the summer. He doesn't appear on the list of friends your wife gave me. But he could have something to contribute about her whereabouts.'

'I'll ask my wife. If it means anything to her, she'll get in touch with you.' He moved to the door. 'I should like a report on progress in another week's time. Please tell your Director that.' He held out a limp hand.

In the ante room the secretary was reading her novel again. She took Egerton back through the rabbit warren. At the exit onto Millbank he found himself caught up in a cluster of visitors also leaving. Once more somebody was shaking their hands in turn. Before he could escape, his own was grasped. The man grasping it gave him a winning smile. 'So glad you could come. Now you'll know we're not as bad as we sound.'

A girl was standing in the entrance to his apartment block and for a moment he thought it was Gail. But when she turned her head to greet him he realized it was the wife of the lawyer who lived in the flat above. He felt an absurdly sharp stab of disappointment. When they had parted the other evening he had not meant to leave the prospect of their next meeting quite so open-ended; not now Julian was dead. He suddenly wanted to see her, very much.

Turning, he got into the Mini and drove to the house in Notting Hill where he had dropped her. A small, bright-eyed Indian in overalls opened the door; he was holding a paint brush wrapped in a rag to stop it dripping. When Egerton asked for Gail, he shook his head regretfully: she was out.

'You don't have any idea where, I suppose?'

The Indian shook his head again. 'Nice dress. So maybe party.'

There was a pub on the other side of the street. He felt a strong impulse to break the rules and go inside for a scotch. But he gritted his teeth and drove back to Prince of Wales Drive.

The phone was ringing as he opened the door of the flat and for a second his hopes rose. But it was Camilla Rylance. She began with a rush of words as though nervous of his reaction to her call, spoke of trying to get him twice before, apologized for bothering him when he must be very busy. He sensed she was trying to judge his mood all the time she was speaking. Eventually she got to the point. 'I wondered if you'd seen the article in today's *Globe*?'

'Yes.'

'I suppose everybody's running round in circles. I haven't seen my father today but he must be absolutely choked.'

Preoccupied though Rylance had seemed once or twice, it hadn't struck Egerton that the leakage was weighing very heavily on his mind. But at Rylance's level there were presumably a dozen things demanding attention at any time. If he allowed himself to be hypnotized by one of them, he'd never get through the work.

Camilla was saying, 'It's really about that I rang. I wonder if I could possibly see you? I've spotted the man with the binoculars again. Of course the desk's been moved. But it shows he's still keeping watch.'

He was getting bored with the leakage saga and even more with maintaining the pretence that he was in some way connected with the people carrying out the investigation. 'I see. Well, thanks for letting me know.'

'Can you tell me anything about how the enquiry's going?'

'It's a bit early to say. But Superintendent Clayton was very glad to get the information you gave me.'

'Oh good,' she said vaguely. She hesitated. 'I expect I'm

being an awful bore . . . but I would love to talk to you if you can spare the time. Only for a few minutes. Perhaps we could have a drink somewhere?' Her voice trailed away.

The tentativeness of her appeal was hard to resist. He was conscious moreover that he quite liked the idea of seeing her again; her remembered image had become touching and a little seductive. 'All right,' he said. 'What about tomorrow?'

Her voice lifted in a surge of relief. 'Super.' They settled on the bar at Trader Vic's.

Just before she ended the call, she said, 'This is terribly sweet of you, Mark. I can call you Mark, can't I?'

# XI

WAITING for her in Trader Vic's, a pineapple juice at his side, he stared at the whisky bottles behind the bar. If it's only the drink you feel you're missing they'd said—fine, you're lucky. Think about other things to take your mind off it.

He lifted his gaze conscientiously. Suspended from a roof of imitation bamboo and plaited straw was a canoe; more Polynesian artefacts of a miscellaneous character loomed from different corners of the room. He studied them all. Concentrating on other things was painless as long as it didn't include the day so far. That had been a write-off.

It had begun with a call from Rivers in Special Branch, at first reasonably genial but rapidly cooling. 'Bellamy told me that the report about Luis Fernandes being a terrorist came from you.'

'Yes.'

'There's a big push on over Basques at the moment. Could I get something straight about your source? You say he's reliable and in a good position to know facts of this sort.'

'I did say that.'

'So he's into Basque politics . . . ?'

'Not really.'

'Then what?'

'I'm afraid I can't say more.' He had hesitated then before deciding to come out with what seemed inescapable. 'As a matter of fact I don't now rate the report as reliable.'

There was silence at the other end. 'I'm sorry,' he said, 'but that's the way it looks now.'

'You mean you were talking about the brother, not Luis—that your source mixed them up?'

'That's one explanation. I'm not sure it's the right one.'

'What else could it be?'

He sensed Rivers's impatience growing. 'The situation's rather complicated. As I said, I'm sorry, I suggest you forget all about it.'

'You're withdrawing the report . . .'

'I didn't put it in the form of a report. But, yes, I am.'

Rivers had said, after another pause, 'I don't think we've met, Egerton. I'm told you're fairly new in the Bureau. In our business we don't call sources reliable unless we've bloody good reasons for doing so. Not if we want to be thought professional.' Then he had put down the phone.

The afternoon had brought an even less agreeable encounter, this time face to face. A superintendent from the Yard had visited Antonia to be briefed on the Beynon case and she had asked Egerton to join them. He had been chilly from the start. Except when he had a question to ask, he had listened to Egerton's account of his investigation with eyes that never left a point above the door. Early in the meeting, he had fastened on an issue of protocol, wanting to know why Egerton had made a direct contact with Pasquier of the Sûreté in Paris, instead of first going through the Yard's liaison channel. When it emerged that Pasquier had pushed the boat out to the extent of making special enquiries for Egerton into Beynon's property investment activities in Paris, the atmosphere had become even more strained. That might not have mattered if the superintendent hadn't been able to go on to pick holes in the investigation. But he had pointed out a line of enquiry that remained with its end hanging loose. He would need to check it out before applying for any of the search warrants. Arguably it was something best done by the Yard anyway. But they all knew that Egerton had missed the trick.

He gazed gloomily into his pineapple juice. Camilla was now twenty minutes late. About him, men and women drank livelier fluids and talked properously. He learned about the new season's grouse, the price of Rollers in Brussels and the current temperature range in Acapulco. Someone had left an evening paper on the bar. He opened it. On the front page was a photograph of Rylance in full throat at some public meeting earlier in the year. The eyes flashed, the gaze was lifted towards the horizon, even the jaw was unfleshy shot from beneath. Today he had apparently not looked so good; he had been taking stick in the House of Commons for the latest leakage. Under the headline STORM OVER LEAKED REPORT were the details of the Opposition's attack over the *Globe*'s latest coup garnished with references to general mayhem in the security burrows of Whitehall.

At last he saw Camilla at the entrance to the bar, wearing her distracted look, waving with relief when she recognized him. He listened to a complicated explanation for her lateness that involved a hairdresser and a traffic warden. She had on a short grey jersey dress with hooped black tights that would have been death to legs less slim. He observed that she had inherited the remarkable eyelashes he had noticed on Rylance the day before; fringing these dark blue eyes they came into their own. Her breasts brushed lightly against his arm as she settled on the next bar stool. He decided that, after all, the day was not a complete write-off.

She asked, without having to look, for the most expensive drink on the card. While it was being mixed, he saw her eyes move to the headline in his newspaper. 'How does it feel, having a father who's always in the public eye?' he asked.

She shrugged and took a cigarette from her bag. 'I'm used to it. Before he went into politics Pa was always being written up as a whizz in the computer world and he loves publicity. Ma didn't enjoy it much.'

'Were you still at school when she died?'

'Yes. Nobody let on to me how ill she was until just before the end. I blamed Pa for ages. When he remarried I wouldn't speak to either of them to begin with. Evelyn eventually persuaded me that all I was doing was cutting off my nose. Evelyn's *very* persuasive.'

'How do you get on with your stepsisters?'

'Jacqueline married soon after she came over from America so I haven't seen much of her. She's a culture bug. Lauren's rather intense in a different way. I imagine she thinks I'm just too frivolous for words. Anyway, I don't see her either these days because she's pushed off with a Spanish boyfriend, God knows where. Evelyn won't talk about it.'

They had drifted into the subject so easily, there didn't seem any reason not to explore further. 'Doesn't she write?' he asked.

'She wouldn't write to me. I don't know whether Evelyn's heard. I shouldn't be surprised if they've gone to America. Her father is a film producer there and Lauren was apparently his pet when she was younger.'

Clearly she had nothing useful to offer on Lauren's movements; she even seemed to be unaware that Giordano had been in London.

When her drink arrived, she said, 'I expect you want to hear about the chap with the binoculars.'

He summoned up an appearance of lively interest while she launched into an account of her second sighting; this time she had remembered to note the flat from which he was watching and also the time. 'It was about nine in the morning. I'd just got up and went to have my bath. Then I nipped back into the bedroom to find some stuff I use to dewhisker my legs. There he was, bang up against his window. Incidentally Pa was in his study making some early morning calls before going off to the Department.'

It could have been the morning when he'd been a recipient of one of them, he thought. He let his eyes drop. She had crossed her legs to show a fair amount of thigh; dewhiskered or not, it appeared exceptionally inviting.

'I hope you can tell me a bit about the investigation,' she said. 'I'm dying to know if you think I'm right.'

'As I told you, I'm not really involved in the actual enquiry.'

'But you must have heard *something*.' Her hand was on his arm. 'What does Superintendent Clayton *say*?'

She wasn't going to give up. He reached for his glass to give himself time to think. There seemed no great harm in telling her what he had learned from Bellamy. She was, after all, the source of the lead. He looked at her solemnly. 'You understand this is very confidential.'

'I promise not to breathe a word.'

He gave her the bare bones. She watched him intently as he spoke, drinking in the words. At the end she said, 'So he thinks I'm right.'

'It's possible.'

She was childishly pleased. A momentary fear gripped him that she might retail the facts to some Hooray Henry like the one he'd seen her with in the car in Piccadilly; then it would turn up in a gossip column. 'Look,' he said, 'I've no authority to tell you any of this. If you pass it to somebody else—'

She was shaking her head earnestly. 'I absolutely won't. You can trust me.'

He had to accept her word; and in fact she seemed perfectly serious about it. She reached across him to stub out her cigarette. 'It's been terribly sweet of you,' she said. Under the light scent she was wearing, there seemed to be the smell of sun about her although there had been no glimmer of it all day. He experienced a sudden sharp hunger such as he had hardly known in recent months, a desire to go on breathing the odour of her skin and to taste the essence of her. He wondered if she would be willing to spend the evening with him. He was in no shape financially to pay for the sort of junket she would probably expect. But he could ring the bank tomorrow before the cheques went through the works; some jacking-up of his overdraft must be possible.

She had finished her drink and was reaching for her handbag so there was no time to be lost. 'Would you let me take you to dinner?'

Her eyes widened. 'Tonight?'

'We could eat here or go on somewhere else. Just as you like.'

She became uneasy as it sunk in. 'That's terribly nice. Really I can't think of anything I'd like better.' She put her hand on his arm again. Vague sentences of disengagement were being assembled. 'The awful thing is—I've actually arranged to meet someone quite soon ... and then we're going on ... I'm so sorry ... terribly sweet of you to suggest it.'

The invitation had been a *gaffe*, he realized, never for one moment had she contemplated their relationship moving off the plane on which she had established it during their meeting at Chester Square. That spontaneous manner, that appealing vulnerability, they were not exactly part of an act; but she was conscious enough of their effect to use them for her purposes. He shook his head, smiling. 'Another time perhaps.'

'Yes, of course, I'd love that.' She glanced at her watch. 'Do you mind *terribly* if I *fly*? I seem to have been late for everything today.'

He saw her into a taxi then made his way to the 137 stop opposite the Hilton entrance. A bus was disappearing as he reached it. He might as well accept that this really wasn't his day. All that remained to crown it would be to get himself mugged again. Nobody hostile seemed to be awaiting him at the entrance to his block. Seeing Gwen appear in their lobby as soon as he opened the door to it produced a momentary twinge of apprehension. But her news was mundane: the builders had called again to look at the damp rot in the kitchen; they'd said they'd be back in a week or so. He smiled with relief. Gwen's hair was in rollers which meant either that it was Bingo night or her admirer from the London Fire Service was expected for a little spontaneous combustion. Before she could put him in the picture, his telephone began to ring and he made his escape.

It was Gail's voice. He felt a sudden glow. 'What are you doing?' she asked.

III

'Nothing.'

'Perfect, we're coming to collect you.'

'Who are "we"?'

'It's a secret. There's a new club opening in Beak Street. We're taking you. It's your Coming Out party.' She coughed theatrically. 'Let me read that again. It's your Coming Back to Life party.'

This time the voice had a lift to it which had been absent the evening she had visited him for supper. Some of the gaiety and zest he remembered from the summer they had met seemed to have returned. To be with her in those days had been like walking on a volcano's rim with no time to glance down into the crater. Caution began to pluck at him.

'I'm not sure I can manage it.'

'Why?'

'Cash is very tight at the moment.'

'You don't have to worry—it's a freebie. Eats as well as drinks.'

'I'm also going abroad for my department probably, tomorrow or the next day. There are things I need to do.'

It sounded totally wet. 'Don't be so *old*,' she said. 'They'll get done. What you need is some *fun*.'

His reluctance was only half-hearted. 'All right,' he said, 'I'm on.'

Within seconds of replacing the receiver, he heard Gwen's knock. Cursing under his breath, he went to see what she wanted this time. She was holding his laundry box. 'Going out?' she asked. Obviously she had been listening in the lobby while he talked to Gail. He nodded, fumbling for money to pay her.

'The girl I let in the other evening?'

He went on nodding. There was no point in prevarication. No part of his domestic habits remained unknown to her. She had probably even deduced by now what he did in the Bureau. All that remained to be charted was his sexual bent on which she must feel he had provided disappointingly inadequate data since moving in. Her expression was indulgent. He could imagine her thinking: looks like he's normal after all.

Gail arrived half an hour later than her forecast. With alarm he saw that the other person climbing the stairs behind her was Jamie. Gail was wearing a long satin skirt and a cobwebby top; either her exotic bird phase was over or she had decided that this was not the evening for a Spectacular. Jamie seemed to have become a dandy. That scruffy, thrown-together appearance of his Oxford days had been gradually fading from the time he came down and settled in London. Now it had totally vanished. The suit was a dazzling white with shoes to match. Beneath the suit was a pleated silk shirt the colour of Victoria plums. Odd bits of jewellery were visible here and there. None of it seemed tiresomely affected because his manner was unchanged, a heavy-lidded amiability that declined to accept anything as remotely serious.

He still looked as fit as in his football-playing days. If he had started drugging since he had certainly found the right balance. But it was difficult to imagine he ever would. At Oxford his great success had been in combining the role of universal provider with that of non-participator. All he had ever done was smoke a little hash at times when it would have seemed stuffy to refuse. Floating to Oxford on the wings of charm and quick-wittedness from the Glasgow suburb where his mother taught in the local school, he had decided, early on, that he didn't want a degree or even a Blue, just the reputation for being the indispensable organiser of revels. It had made him money of course but not very much in those days. All he'd had to show for it had been an old Aston Martin. The bonanza hadn't started until he came to London.

While he fixed their drinks, they wandered about the flat. Rude comments were offered on the curtains and the age of the lavatory fittings. When he showed them the outsize bed bought as part of the deal with the previous owner they rolled their eyes and collapsed upon it.

They continued to make mild fun of him but he was

aware of affection in their voices. The misgiving he had felt on seeing Jamie faded, to be replaced by a slow surge of elation. He went to the kitchen and poured himself a glass of wine in place of the Perrier he had opened. He had almost forgotten how, when they were both on form, life ceased to be dreary and even the commonplace became incandescent.

Returning to the sitting room, he raised his glass to them and grinned. 'So what's the name of this new club?'

# XII

DIDO'S. It came back as the first thing of all when he opened his eyes to morning light: Dido's. His brain locked on it, turned the word into a recurring cry while he lay inert, unwilling to start the hammers inside his skull by moving. Nobody had explained why the club had that name. A negress in a sheath of sequins had been in frequent evidence. She had greeted with a kiss Jamie and others who had been admitted to her magic circle, sometimes giving a great shout of triumphant affection. No doubt she had been Dido. Aeneas had never appeared; somewhere out of sight he had been counting the bottles of champagne as they left the kitchen perhaps.

The night was returning in disconnected frames which towards the end had only the vaguest form. As he entered the club he had been conscious of an old feeling, a kindling of anticipation. Then, as Jamie disappeared into a group in the far corner and Gail became engulfed by faces reaching forward to kiss or whisper, the feeling gave way to a chill. Involuntarily he was becoming distanced from his surroundings. It was not that their predictability now bored him, the strobes and lasers, the metallic paper on the walls, the perspex floor lit from beneath; he could still experience the tug of this night world of scent and sweat, of hectic or calculating eyes. But the figures that eddied about him belonged to a sealed-off section of his life. When a few smiled in recognition, he greeted them self-consciously, spoke about his American visit as though it had ended only yesterday and moved on before the questions could become too probing. The terms on which acquaintance could be renewed had changed irretrievably. Somewhere, in New York or Minnesota, he had lost the sense of belonging here.

He was trying to locate Gail when he saw a face recently familiar although at first he had difficulty in placing it. It belonged to a youngish man in dinner jacket and red bow tie who was holding court at the bar. He had the air of knowing, or expecting to know, all; while he talked his eyes ranged the room as if it were a landscape. It was the driver of the sports car in which Egerton had seen Camilla the evening of his call on Sam Giordano at Claridges. This was perhaps the date she had been hurrying away from Trader Vic's to join. He studied the people clustered round the man but couldn't see her.

When he found Gail, he asked if she recognized him. She glanced across. 'Simon Bowe.'

'Who is he?'

'A gossip writer on one of the give-away magazines.'

'He looks very pleased with himself.'

'Madly ambitious—on the way up according to Jamie. He never misses any of these things.' She glanced across again. 'Is it really him you're interested in, or the blonde?'

When he looked once more in Bowe's direction, he saw that Camilla had materialized by his side. She had changed out of the jersey dress into a little black jacket and what looked like silver jodhpurs.

'Does she turn you on?'

'She's quite attractive.'

Gail was appraising her. 'I imagine you ending up with somebody like that. Cuddly and fertile.' Then she had pulled a face at him and called out to someone who had just arrived.

He lifted his head gingerly so that he could look at Gail as she slept. She lay neatly in the centre of the bed, one hand beneath the pillow on which they both had their heads. Her lips were parted as though at the prospect of something agreeable. Seeing her like this, he could almost dismiss his fear that she was going downhill. And yet, when he looked closer, there was an underlying pallor, an unevenness to her skin that was wrong. At the club he had thought of her as a tropical fish, darting and shimmering through the crowd, always elusive. When she returned to his side, she was tender as though she had discovered him afresh and only he mattered. Her energy had been breath-taking. But he was sure she had fixed when she went to the powder room.

That must have been about nine hours ago. It wouldn't be long before she needed the next one. If he let her sleep on he wouldn't see the signs of her wanting it before he left for the Bureau.

Gently he raised the sheet away from her body. Her top was bare but she was still wearing briefs. So, presumably, Nothing had Happened when they finally dropped into bed. Recollection of events after they had arrived back from Dido's offered no guidance on that score; but he had drunk so much wine, there and later, that it hardly seemed he would have been in a competent state anyway. Jamie, as ever, had been the most pulled-together at the end of the evening, a little more heavy-lidded perhaps but with all his muscles functioning to order. Almost the last frame on the memory track was of him, fiddling through stations on the radio, the jacket of the white suit folded on the sofa beside him. At what stage he had given that up and joined Gail and himself in the Emperor bed was unknowable. But there he was, beyond Gail, dead to the world yet faintly smiling.

It was five minutes to eight: time to pull himself together, preparatory to reporting to Antrim at the Bureau. Slipping out of the bed he went to the bathroom to shower and shave. Torn Alka Seltzer packaging lay on the floor. Neither Jamie nor Gail was likely to have bothered to look for that sort of thing so presumably *he* had taken the tablets. He was in fact steadier in the head than he had expected. He began to see the night as a test from which he had emerged successfully. The past had reached up and fallen back again without him.

Neither Gail nor Jamie had stirred when he returned to the bedroom for his clothes. Jamie lay very neatly, still with the faint smile on his face. It gave him the look of a man who knew he was sleeping and found it good. He was turned away from Gail so that no part of his body would touch hers. That was a characteristic, the avoidance of physical contact, except on those few occasions he would disappear with a boy or girl who had shaken him out of his neutrality. When it was over he would be uncommunicative about what had occurred. The other person would also be silent, bewildered to have become so soon a footnote.

He was back in the kitchen, making toast and waiting for the kettle to boil, when he was aware of a movement behind him. It was Jamie, now completely dressed. Apart from the stubble on his chin he looked unchanged from the previous evening, the suit uncreased, the shoes still close enough to white.

'We seem to have stayed over,' he said.

'How do you feel?'

'Fine.'

'Is Gail still asleep?'

'I think so.'

He reached past Jamie for the tea. 'There's something I want to say before she wakes up. She's got to finish with smack. Now. I know she's tried once and failed. She's got to try again. I don't want her to end up like Julian.'

Jamie gazed through the window. A rubbish collection truck had double-parked beside his Porsche. 'She'd never get stuff like *that* from me.'

'It's still poisoning her. She says you're giving her more than she needs anyway. You realize she's dealing, I suppose?'

'I knew she needed money. If I'd offered cash she wouldn't have taken it.'

'But the *risk*! She'll be arrested sooner or later. It's a risk for you as well.'

'I'll live with that. Anyway I know she wouldn't talk if it happened.' Jamie turned and smiled, wanting to be rid of dismal speculation. 'You're getting bloody serious in your old age.'

He persisted doggedly. 'If I can persuade her to go somewhere for treatment, will you help?'

'In what way?'

'She *has* to stay with the treatment this time. I'll try to make her. But she might ask you to slip stuff to her without my knowing.'

'What do I do then?'

'You've got to refuse.'

Jamie took out a cigarette. 'You're in love with her still, aren't you?'

'Never mind. Do you promise?'

He was smiling again. 'All right.'

As always, he was being amiably biddable, ready to fit in with whatever seemed broadly reasonable by his own lights. His degree of detachment might have been repellent in another. In Jamie it was a neutral fact that needed to be overcome; when it was, his resource as a friend and ally amounted to no small thing. Never less than when pulling one away from a bloody end in an Oxford river.

Egerton heard Gail's voice calling from the bedroom; she was asking where everybody was. He took her a mug of tea and sat on the bed. She lay, smiling faintly at him.

'I wasn't going to wake you,' he said.

'Why are you dressed already—it's Saturday isn't it?'

'I have to go to the office. But I want to talk some time. Will you still be around this afternoon? Can you wait until I've finished at the Bureau?'

She was chewing her lip. 'No, I can't stay. I've promised to see some people. Tomorrow perhaps?'

He shook his head. 'I'll have left on my trip—assuming my boss doesn't veto it. Are you absolutely sure you can't manage it today?'

'I really can't.' She went on chewing her lip. She wasn't going to tell him any more; but he could guess what she'd be doing.

'What's your trip?' she asked.

'To Majorca. I have to interview somebody in a place called Deya.'

'Lucky old you.' She sat up, wrapping the sheet tightly over her breasts as though against the cold. He thought he could see tension working at the corners of her mouth but it might have been his imagination searching for tell-tale signs. 'So what are we due to talk about?'

'You.'

She looked at him mockingly. 'Are you planning to take me in hand?'

'Perhaps.'

'The blonde you lusted after last night would be *much* more rewarding.'

'I want you to start to cut down on the smack while I'm away.'

She groaned.

'It's getting to you.'

'It isn't.'

'I know it is.'

She lay back and closed her eyes. She wanted to be rid of him, to escape. He told himself that she was thinking he'd turned into a Born Again bore. He said, 'I'm not going to let up on you.'

'You shouldn't try to make people's decisions for them.'

'It's going to be your decision. Eventually.'

'Why should that happen?'

'It's the only way you'll get me off your back.'

She opened her eyes to stare silently at the ceiling. He leaned over and kissed her gently on the lips. At first she made no response. Then her hands reached up and she was holding his head tightly against her.

'I love you,' he said. 'That could be inconvenient. You may as well face the fact because it won't go away.'

Back in the kitchen as he was preparing to leave he said, 'Don't let her fix here, Jamie. If she has to do it, I don't want it to happen here. Ever.'

While Egerton was speaking, Antrim had begun to unwrap

120

the package that stood in the centre of his blotter. A piece of highly coloured marble emerged; it was set on an ebony base to which was attached a metal plate with an inscription. The marble had no form that was immediately recognizable. Antrim studied the inscription impassively. 'You're telling me the Secretary of State simply invented his story of having been told Luis Fernandes was a terrorist?'

'I can't be sure but I think it's likely.'

'Why should he do that?'

'It provided a justification for asking your help in finding Lauren. He knew you were bound to refuse him otherwise.'

Antrim bent to open a side drawer of his desk. He dropped the marble object inside with a grimace. 'Why do you dismiss his explanation that one of his staff put a query to the security people and in the process Luis Fernandes was mixed up with his brother?'

'Somehow it didn't ring true.'

Antrim was staring at him. There was an uncomfortable silence. Antrim said, 'I hope you're not going to persuade me I made a mistake when I selected you for this enquiry, Egerton.'

He looked down. 'I just felt you ought to know how it looked to me, in case you consider we're no longer justified in going on with the search.'

'You want to abandon it half-way through . . .'

'I'm not saying that. But can we justify—'

'Leave the justifying to me. *I* decide what this department does. And because the Secretary of State for Defence made a mistake—' Antrim paused '—for whatever reason, doesn't convince me we should back out of what we've agreed to do.' He was screwing into a tight ball the tissue paper that had been wrapped round the piece of marble. 'Do you want me to take you off the enquiry?'

Egerton gritted his teeth. 'No, sir.'

There was another silence. Eventually Antrim said, 'Very well, perhaps we can get down to what needs to be done now. Since Rylance accepts that the sister may very well

121

be the only person who knows Lauren's whereabouts, you'd better go and see her. It shouldn't take more than forty-eight hours. The cover story you've been using won't be any use of course.'

'I realize that.'

'You're quite confident, are you, that Montague wasn't lying when he said he didn't have an address for Lauren?'

Earlier in their talk he had let Antrim know of Rylance's assumption that a little burglary of Montague's office would be considered part of the package if it was likely to produce results. Antrim had raised his eyebrows and gone to look out of the window, presumably to brood on the implications of that from a future Home Secretary. 'How very interesting,' he had said.

'I'm sure he wasn't lying.'

Antrim sighed and sat back in his swivel chair. 'All right. Telephone me from Deya as soon as you've formed a view on whether the sister knows anything. I'll need to keep Rylance in the picture. Tell Baxter I want him as you go out.'

When Egerton reached the door, he said, 'Just remember, for the future, Egerton, I'm running this department.' He enjoyed showing the whip.

Baxter was stirring sugar into a cup of coffee. Having to come in on a Saturday morning because Antrim had decided to work didn't seem to be irking him. He placed a saucer with several biscuits on it over the cup to keep it warm; but what went on inside the inner room was his real nourishment. 'Did he open that package while you were in there?' he asked.

'Yes.'

'What was in it?'

'A lump of marble.'

Baxter produced his all-knowing smile. 'Parting gift from the Head of the Pakistan Anti-Corruption Office. We'd rather hoped for mangoes.' He picked up pad and pencil. 'Progress on your front?'

'Not much.'

'I gather you're up in the stratosphere, high wire stuff. Try not to fall off, won't you?' He disappeared through the double doors.

Antonia had asked to be told the outcome of the talk with Antrim. He telephoned her at her flat. When he had finished, she sighed. 'So you're still on the case.'

'Just.'

'When do you leave for Majorca?'

'Tomorrow. I'd made a provisional booking before I reported.'

'You presumably guessed what he was going to say . . .'

'Not entirely. But I could see he'd find it very uncomfortable to tell Rylance we weren't going to help any more.'

'Are you unhappy about it?'

'No. Having started the thing, I'd like to see if I can find her. As he said, it's his business whether we ought to be doing it.'

She made a non-committal noise. 'Well, Jacqueline may have the answer. I hope you get her talking.'

'I'm taking a tape recorder and a Minox.' He laughed. 'Do you recommend a weapon?'

She didn't laugh back. 'I might,' she said, 'if you could tell me what that mugging meant.'

# XIII

From the balcony outside his bedroom he could see bodies already stretched beside the swimming pool, oiled and motionless. To his right the village of Deya clung to its hillside, half in shadow, half bathed in a sun that seemed undimmed by the onset of autumn. The scent of gardenias rose to his nostrils from the hotel gardens below. This time yesterday he had stepped off a 137 bus into a steady drizzle and the remains of somebody's hamburger. Even if failure lay ahead, there were worse ways of spending an October morning than this; and all on the Queen too. To consolidate the festive feeling, he went down to reception and bought a postcard to send to Gail.

When he had posted it, he strolled in the gardens for a while. Whatever Rylance had meant when he had talked of Jacqueline's condition being erratic, it seemed sensible to give her scope to get a grip on the day. By the time he finally set out for the address Rylance had provided, the perfumed languor of the garden and the gleam of brown flesh gliding through the pool had given him the sensation of embarking on an adventure.

The street proved to be little more than an intermittently paved track. It led steeply downwards from the village in the direction of the sea. On one side, across a small stream, there were groves of lemon trees and small vegetable plots. Village cottages ran along the other side except where, as the track began to peter out, two or three villas had been built.

Jacqueline's house was the last of the cottages. Fresh

paint, a new door, a certain uniformity about the window boxes, set it apart from the rest; it had obviously been done up for letting. Precariously parked on a steep slope of grass beside the front wall was a dusty MG Metro with a cracked side window.

He strolled past, glancing into those windows that were unshuttered for signs of life, but there were none. By the first of the villas he halted and looked back. A small boy seated on a wooden bridge across the stream called to him. 'Señor.' The boy was pointing down the street in the direction of the sea; he grinned. Placing his hands flat on the boards of the bridge, he arched his back in an ecstasy of knowledge. By some mysterious process he had exactly gauged Egerton's purpose.

Egerton hesitated. His vague plan had been to call at the cottage pretending he had heard it was to let, not to appear to be looking for Jacqueline. But the boy was pointing again. 'Señor ... playa.' Nothing was going to alter the conclusion he had already reached. Egerton gave him a wave and went on down the track.

By the time he reached the beach, the track had given way to a stony path. He had supposed he would find a stretch of sand or shingle with coloured umbrellas and more bodies like those beside the hotel pool. Instead he entered a rocky inlet. Beside fishing boats drawn up in the shade of a cliff men were mending nets. A few children, obviously locals, played on the edge of the sea. Nobody at all lay on the beach.

Turning away he saw to his rear a primitive-looking bar constructed of timber. A verandah ran along its front with two or three tables and empty chairs on it. Seated at the bar with her back to the sea was a woman. Her head was lowered over a glass of wine so that, apart from the sapphire blue beach dress, he could see little more than the hair caught up in a loose *chignon*. It was exactly the colour of Evelyn Rylance's.

He took a bar stool a little distance from her and ordered a drink. As the barman served it the woman turned to look at Egerton over the rim of her sunglasses. With one hand she moved her almost empty glass to and fro along the bar top. 'You wouldn't have a cigarette, would you?' she asked. The voice was lighter than her mother's, the Californian accent less noticeable; a year or two married to the barrister had perhaps clipped the vowels. She was very tanned and wore no make-up.

He bought a packet of cigarettes from the barman. When he had lit one for her she exhaled smoke as though she had waited a very long time for it. 'Perhaps you'll join me in a drink,' he said.

While her glass was being refilled, she said, 'See? A friend.' The barman smiled and made an enigmatic movement with his head. It wasn't clear he had understood her. She twisted abruptly back to Egerton. 'So who *are* you, friend?'

He told her his name and that he was on a short visit to write an article about Deya, a quick job for an airline magazine.

'I'll tell you *all* about Deya,' she said. 'But it won't be any use for the magazine. Deya is the pits, take it from me.'

She drew cigarette smoke down to the lower reaches of her stomach. She was only half-drunk but anxious to get on with the job. He picked up his cue. 'So what exactly is wrong with Deya?'

She talked laconically about the place, leaning towards him in a pretence of making the conversation private from the barman, while occasionally glancing back in the hope she wasn't succeeding. What was wrong seemed to boil down not so much to Deya itself as the expectations that had drawn her there. Some Wordsworthian vision mysteriously acquired years before at Berkeley had filled her imagination. She had rented the cottage unseen for six months through a travel agent in London and had arrived anticipating a blue skies version of Grasmere with Vodka Martinis thrown in to enliven the dull bits. Somehow the culture scene had failed to deliver. Or perhaps it had simply rejected her.

When she had finished the glass of wine he had paid for he watched for a while to see what she would do. Eventually she took off the sunglasses to search the corners of her handbag for *pesetas*. It went on too long to be just an act. He understood the remark to the barman about friends now. She was apparently without cash. And her credit with the barman was no good either.

He ordered more wine. She began to tell him about her divorce. There were problems in getting the alimony through, her lawyer had produced fancy excuses. But he was in cahoots with the louse she had married. Probably they went to the same school together. All lawyers were bastards anyway. Very faintly he caught an echo of Sam Giordano.

Occasionally she glanced towards the point where the path he had followed joined the beach. He had the impression she was expecting another companion, albeit without much hope. At such moments he was able to study her features. They were as good as Evelyn's, almost identical except for the cheekbones which were higher. They gave her a faintly feral expression, a dangerous sort of beauty.

So far, all had gone his way. He guessed that, with hardly any prompting, she would move on to talk about her family. But her speech was becoming slower and less distinct: before long she would stop making sense. As he hesitated over ordering her more wine, she seemed alerted to his misgiving and stood up, holding on to the bar to stop herself swaying. 'I have to go,' she said, 'Somebody coming . . . mustn't be late.' The words were an effort. 'You coming?' He sensed it was an appeal of sorts.

One of her sandals had fallen onto the verandah. She spent a while trying to put her foot in it without bending down. He stooped to help her; the toes were grimy and scratched. Finally they set off up the path. She began with a show of determination to make it unaided but when he took her arm she rested against him, her head pressed to his shoulder.

At the gate of her cottage she looked round uncertainly

but whoever she had expected (if it had been more than a hope), was not there. By now however it didn't seem to matter too much. He was sure she would collapse onto her bed as soon as she got inside. As she fumbled in her bag for a key he said, 'I wonder if you'd care to have dinner with me.'

She didn't look up from her search of the bag. Inside it he could see a variety of pill containers.

'Tonight perhaps?'

She delayed answering until the key was found then grunted in triumph. 'Fine! Let's do that, Mark.' She said it defiantly to some unseen presence. He told her he'd pick her up at around seven thirty. 'It *is* Mark, isn't it?' she called out.

He walked back to the hotel. Seven thirty meant that she would have nearly seven hours to sleep off the wine, assuming her visitor didn't turn up after all and start her drinking again. Depending on her condition when he collected her, he would either give her one stand-up drink in the hotel bar or steer her straight into the restaurant. The challenge then would be to keep her wanting and able to talk.

When evening came, the heat had become sultry. Although the cottage was less than five minutes walk it seemed wise to take the car he had hired at Palma airport. Parking it alongside the Metro with the cracked window he saw with misgiving that no lights were visible in the house. She could hardly be still sleeping off the morning session; but she might easily have forgotten their date and gone out. The door yielded to his touch however. When he called into the darkness behind, she answered in reassuringly lucid tones.

He followed the voice through a darkened sitting room and french windows on to a small terrace that ran along the back of the cottage. The only light came from a small lamp. In its beam he could just make out Jacqueline's face and shoulders. She waved at him with a cigarette. '*Salud.*'

On the table by which she was seated were a practically

full wine bottle and two glasses. He could make out little else in the gloom but she seemed to be wearing a long evening dress of silk or chiffon, the collar severely high at the front. When she reached forward to pour his wine he smelled her scent; it was sharp and metropolitan, the antithesis of the gardenias in the hotel grounds. She was hepped up but he had the feeling it was from pills not wine.

She seemed to want to stay and talk their way through the bottle. He began to worry about getting her moving. Not that it was disagreeable sitting in the relative cool of the terrace with the lamplight tracing the line of her cheek and neck, sometimes catching the richness in her hair. The garden beyond was drowned in darkness. He had a pleasant sense of displacement, of the world gone away.

She talked unrancorously at first. She was knowledgeable about the flowers he could smell but not see and spoke about the herbs that grew wild on the hillside behind. But before long she was back to people, this time not the slobs in the cultural colony but the island's indigenous inhabitants. The greatest of the demons was her landlord, a Palma wide boy, a bimbo. Her cigarette end glowed and danced as she gestured bitterly. 'Georges Sand was damned right about this place. They're all bimbos.' She had turned her head to stare into the darkness and in the general direction of the village. She made no attempt to lower her voice. 'Bimbos.' She wanted everything to be bad. There was a taut fragility behind the sentences and sometimes when she paused he had the sensation that she had disconnected from her surroundings.

Somehow he got her away from current discontents. Before coming to Deya she had stayed for a while in a friend's villa in Sardinia. That seemed to have been a happier time. She might decide to settle there once the alimony had been sorted out properly and the louse was paying on time. Or then again, it might be Nice. Or Lugano. But not here. She was pretending she retained some sense of direction, a capability for choice. But really she was rudderless. Divorce hadn't simply removed the louse, it had taken from her the sense of a structure to her life. Intention had oozed away leaving only fantasy and whim.

He drained his glass and leaned forward as she reached for the bottle of wine again. 'Why don't we go and eat?'

She rose jerkily, touching her hair, then took his arm. They were at last on their way.

He decided in the car that they would go straight to the hotel restaurant. She was high but making sense most of the time. With food inside her and careful control of any more bottles, all might be well.

Falling momentarily behind her as they crossed the reception hall of the hotel, his attention was suddenly riveted on her body. Illuminated by the lamp ahead, in the corridor to the restaurant, was an arresting fact: beneath the virtual transparency of her dress, she was wearing nothing at all. As the head waiter led them to a table, Egerton saw the heads at first lifting casually and then becoming very still as the eyes focused.

She was moving with a pretended confidence, her gaze straight ahead as she concentrated on remaining steady. The manner she had assumed at first made him think she had planned the display, either out of bravado or to make these fuddy-duddy tourists on middle-brow packages sit up and take notice. Yet when they were finally seated, he became aware of the bewilderment in her eyes, a flicker of unease at the corner of the mouth. His annoyance slowly gave way to resignation. He realized that she had no idea what they had been looking at, only sensed that the stares were hostile.

There was no point in telling her. At least no further peepshow would be offered until they left the table again; and since it was late, most of the others in the restaurant would then have departed. When he smiled reassuringly, she smiled back with an almost desperate gratitude. He felt guilt that a few moments before his only wish was to be able to disown her; reaching for the menu he began to read out the dishes.

He had almost relaxed when he saw the manager bearing down on their table with the air of an undertaker. Somebody had alerted him to the occurrence of scandal. Bending low over Egerton, he offered whispered observations. 'Certain rules . . . consideration for other guests . . . service in your room of course . . .'

Jacqueline had caught the drift halfway through the sermon. He saw her mood lurch through embarrassed realization into belligerence; the manager was going to receive the George Sand treatment, strength five. Retreat even at the cost of humiliation seemed the wisest course. 'Come on,' he said, and took her by the hand.

They left the restaurant in a silence appropriate to high theatrical tragedy. The manager brought up the rear, his eyes cast down, away from sin. Jacqueline led the way to his car, moving now with grim defiance, calling the manager names between her teeth as she passed the reception desk. When Egerton began suggesting another restaurant after a trip back to the cottage for further covering, she rejected the idea fiercely. They would eat there; in the refrigerator was chicken and she would toss a salad to have with it. It would be better than anything else in this dump. She was not to be argued out of it. The suspicion grew within him that she might not be *persona grata* in Deya's other restaurants.

Standing beside her in her kitchen while she sliced tomatoes viciously, he managed at last to direct her thoughts towards her family. She spoke neutrally and without naming them of Giordano and Evelyn, affectionately of Lauren. She didn't mention Rylance or Camilla at all. 'Do you ever see your sister?' he asked.

'She visited a couple of months back.'

'From London?'

'No, she's not there now.' He couldn't gauge if it was deliberate reticence that made her stop.

She worked with surprising deftness making the salad and dividing up the meagre amount of chicken that had come out of the refrigerator. It seemed she could function well enough in short bursts. When they had carried the food and a fresh bottle of wine through to the sitting room, she looked down at the dress as though suddenly reminded.

'To hell with that bimbo,' she said. She sat down and reached across to touch his glass with her own. 'I like you Matt.'

'Mark,' he said. He looked about him. 'How much longer are you planning to stay here?'

'I don't know, maybe to the turn of the year. That's when the lease runs out.'

'It could be rather lonely. You ought to have your sister come to stay again.'

She shrugged.

'Does she look like you?'

'Not really. Would you like to see a photograph? She sent one the other day.' Her fondness for Lauren was obvious. Reaching behind her she opened a drawer in a small desk. From an envelope on top of a pile of straw place mats, she extracted a Polaroid snapshot and handed it to him. He saw a folded sheet of notepaper was still inside the envelope.

Lauren was seated on what looked like a sea wall. Evelyn Rylance had been right in telling him the old photograph she had provided was still a good likeness. In this latest snapshot, Lauren looked hardly changed, just a little more assured. The man seated beside her was presumably Fernandes. He was much as Egerton had imagined him, thickset with sombre eyes but handsome in a rough-cut way.

'Is that a friend with her or someone closer?'

'I guess they'll marry soon.'

'What does he do?'

She slipped the photograph back in the envelope and closed the drawer. 'He's going into politics in Spain. He's a Basque.'

He pressed on, trying to make his voice sound casual. 'Is that where the picture was taken?'

'No, they haven't got there yet.' He sensed the constraint

as she spoke the words. She was holding back and however drunk she became she was unlikely to be tempted to say more. He needed to get at the letter that was with the photograph.

The chicken had been barely enough for even one person of normal appetite. Nothing else seemed to be on offer after they had finished the salad. Hunger gnawed at him. He decided that the wine was the only way of quietening the pangs inside.

Half and hour later he was still sober but only just. Jacqueline seemed to have reached a plateau of muzzy contentment. Seated beside him she was making a pretence of reading his palm. Nothing much she said made sense. Her face was very close. He kissed the back of her neck and felt her fingers tighten about his wrist to hold it against her body. When he gently turned her head so that he could kiss her throat, the grip slackened and she sighed as though some final residue of tension had left her.

After a while she picked up her glass and left him. When she returned, she stood in the doorway, empty glass in her hand, gazing at him silently. Her hair had been combed out and she had applied fresh lipstick. She had drunk too much to be wholly desirable; but someone could well say the same about him. When he raised his eyebrows she said, 'Let's work something out to put in that article.'

He contrived to force himself awake three or four times during the night. Each time he was looking for enough light from the window to feel confident of reaching the desk in the sitting room without blundering into furniture. Not that there seemed a real danger that Jacqueline would hear him. After they had made love, she had reached for her handbag and taken another couple of pills. By the time he had finally crept out of bed, she was lying on her stomach, her breathing heavy, a little trickle from the corner of her mouth moistening the pillow. He fetched the Minox from his jacket pocket and went to the sitting room.

Taking the letter from the drawer he switched on the

desk lamp. The writing was untidy and hurried but easy enough to read.

Hotel Constantine
Nice.
Tuesday

Dearest Jake,

I have to give somebody my world exclusive . . .! We decided today it really is a Thing so—we plan to marry as soon as we get to Spain in December and L. has introduced me to his parents. You are positively the first and only person to be told.

Enclosed is picture taken by passing American tourist from La Jolla (where else?) of happy couple before eating 200 franc celebration lunch. Am God knows how many kilos heavier than when I left London but relying on L.'s assurance that Basques like their women *sturdy*!

We leave this hotel at the end of the week and move to an apartment L. has rented. I'm not telling you where, then if Evelyn turns up in Deya you really won't know. You can always contact me in an emergency through L. He and his friends use the Basque Club at 115, Rue de L'Hôtel des Postes for their meetings and he collects his mail from there most days.

I hope you're feeling happier. Also that Rat QC is now coming through with the alimony regularly. I worry about you, Jake. If things got very tight, I could have some funds transferred from my account in Geneva. Don't forget that.

Must now go and collect laundry. No more news except you can tell David, I *think* he's won! In three more weeks we'll know. Keep him safe!

Love, darling,
Lauren

The desk lamp could have been brighter but he took three shots each of the letter and the photograph and hoped for

134

the best. The final stage of his search for Lauren seemed intoxicatingly near. On the face of it, all that was left to do was go to Nice, pick up Luis when he emerged from one of his visits to the Basque Club and tail him home. He put the letter and the photograph away again and tried the other drawers of the desk. There was more correspondence but this was from friends and the solicitor in London. Before he switched off the desk light he glanced at the books beside it. Three volumes of poetry and a biography of Robert Graves lay next to a Harold Robbins paperback. The Robbins had a page corner turned down. When the air at the mountain top proves inhospitable, he thought, you have to join the caravans in the valley.

He returned to the bedroom and dressed. It was barely six thirty. The pangs of hunger he had felt the previous evening were back, sharpened by a sense of triumph. In the kitchen he located the remnants of a stale loaf and wolfed it with a layer of apricot preserve. There was nothing else whatever that was edible. When he took a glass of orange juice and placed it beside Jacqueline's head, she still hadn't stirred from the position in which he had left her. It seemed pointless to disturb her dreams. Alongside the orange juice he left a scribbled note, announcing that he was going back to the hotel to work on the article but would look in to say goodbye later in the morning. Before he left he opened her handbag in case it might yield another letter from Lauren but there was none. Apart from tablets and some cosmetics the bag was almost empty, the only money a few small coins. It was impossible to believe that everything she had was going on white wine and pills; her solicitor must surely be extracting enough from Rat QC to keep her from these straits. But if so it was being siphoned off.

Back at the hotel, he was the only person about, apart from cleaning women and the odd floor waiter. On his bedside telephone he ordered a double breakfast and lay back to think about Lauren's letter to Jacqueline. It had been nearly a fortnight old but it seemed certain that she and Fernandes would still be in Nice. He could hardly wait to get a plane out of Majorca. But he would need to get Antrim's chop on it first.

It was nearly eleven before the hotel exchange got his call through to the Bureau. Antrim was in a meeting. Baxter wanted to take a message.

'I think he'll wish to come out for this.'

He had to say it three different ways before Baxter gave in.

Antrim's voice was already expectant when he came on the line. 'You've found her?'

'Almost.' He told him the story. 'If you approve I'll leave here today. I've a provisional booking on a Madrid flight this afternoon. I ought to be in Nice by tomorrow.'

'Right.' It was the first occasion Egerton had heard geniality in Antrim's tones. 'Rylance will be very pleased. Keep at it.'

He was back in favour, for the time being anyway.

He returned to Jacqueline's cottage with a bunch of roses. Food for the kitchen might also have been a good idea but he decided she'd find that eccentric. A light motor cycle, almost new, stood near the open front door. He found her seated on the terrace; she was dressed in shorts and a bikini top. In the chair beside her a dark, good-looking youth of nineteen or twenty sat smoking a cigarette. He was a local, presumably the owner of the motor cycle; possibly the mysterious David who kept cropping up, as well.

Jacqueline raised an arm. 'Hi.' She pushed a chair towards Egerton. 'How does the article look?'

'Pretty good.'

'Will I be in it?'

'Oh yes,' he said.

She gestured towards the youth. 'Meet Pepe.'

So it wasn't David. He shook the youth's hand.

'Pepe wants to go to Madrid and be an actor. I suppose you don't have any contacts there?'

'I'm afraid not.'

'He's driving his mama up the wall because he won't work any more as a waiter. He just keeps asking his family

136

for money to get him to Madrid. He keeps asking *me*. You're a bastard, aren't you, Pepe?' her hand was stroking his thigh.

The youth stretched with languid grace. It seemed doubtful whether he had understood all the words but he seemed to have sensed the general line. His air was a curious mixture of nonchalance and watchfulness.

'Do you speak English?' Egerton asked.

'A little. Little, little.' The youth laughed as though he had been witty. He lacked any sort of charm but his looks were undoubtedly handsome. He wore an expensive wrist-watch. Perhaps this was where the alimony was going.

Egerton turned back to Jacqueline. She had accepted the roses with suitable noises but he noticed she wasn't offering him a drink from the bottle of wine she and the youth were sharing. 'My plane leaves this afternoon. Is there anything I can do for you when I eventually get back to London?'

'You could shoot my lawyer.'

'I hope things work out.'

She shrugged and picked up her glass. He wasn't of interest any more.

When he went out of the garden gate, the small boy who had spoken to him the day before was back on his perch on the bridge. This time he was mending a bicycle inner tube.

Egerton nodded and the boy smiled at him in the same way. He looked as though he knew everything and perhaps he did. But all he said was 'Goodbye, *señor*.'

# XIV

ON the plane to Nice, he pictured the last round, the final stake-out. From the tall windows of his bedroom in a hotel, small but immensely comfortable, across the way from the Basque club, he would keep watch. Because he would have chosen a room only one floor up, there would be no problem about the dash to street level when Fernandes was sighted; or about trailing him back to the apartment where he and Lauren were holed up. When staying indoors became oppressive, he would find a table at a pavement café which would provide an equally convenient view.

Reality proved as unrelenting as ever. No hotel, commanding a view of the courtyard through which the club was approached existed in the Rue de l'Hôtel des Postes. Even access to the apartment block immediately opposite, supposing that could have been arranged, would yield no joy. At the vital spot, the Rue de l'Hôtel des Postes opened out into the Place Wilson, with a garden and children's playground occupying the length of a block; the foliage of the trees in the garden would effectively conceal the courtyard entrance from even the highest apartment. To maintain any long-term coverage, short of brazenly sitting on the stones of the courtyard itself, he had no choice but to alternate his time between two cafés on the corner where the Rue Gubernatis stretched northwards from Place Wilson and a bench in the children's playground. In the late afternoon of his arrival, after taking the film from the Minox to be developed, he seated himself amongst the infant hordes. Gloomily reviewing his plans, he was suddenly aware of an ominous blotching on the bench beside him. Looking up at what, an hour before, had been a brilliant sky, he realized that he still hadn't allowed for the worst.

By dawn next day, a grey hissing downpour made mockery of the idea of taking up his vigil. When, during a brief respite, he ventured on to streaming pavements to collect the developed film and prints, he found tables and chairs at the cafés stacked away as though for winter, the gardens of the Place Wilson a desolation of dashed flowers.

Eating his evening meal in the hotel he had found in the next street, he pinned his hopes on *Nice Matin*'s robust assurance that tomorrow the *orage* would have yielded to *cieux eclaircis*. He studied the prints of Lauren's letter to Jacqueline in case it had more to tell him. But there was nothing, just the curious riddle of the final paragraph. The David whom Lauren had mentioned enigmatically to Sally Kirkwood seemed to have turned up in Majorca although there had been no sign of him at Jacqueline's. Perhaps he was hiding up in some other part of the village. But if so, why? From what? After a while he decided it was an insoluble conundrum. And anyway, it didn't seem relevant to his search for Lauren.

The next morning he saw with relief that they had got it right, those confident French forecasters, so different from the havering each-wayers at home: the *cieux* could hardly be clearer and, opposite his window, the roofs were already drying in the sun. Half and hour later he had his first coffee of the watch at a specially unstacked table on the pavement beside the brighter of the two cafés. But, as the day wore on, he began to doubt the practicability of his task. It was not only that the combination of fatigue and boredom from constantly watching in the same direction was an increasing strain. His regular appearance in one of three places excited more interest than he had forseen; and while tips ensured that cordiality outweighed the curiosity of the café waiters, he feared it might not be long before someone in the children's playground fingered him to the police as a child molester waiting to pounce.

When darkness fell, without a glimpse of anyone who resembled the photograph of Fernandes, he decided another plan was needed. Boldness was going to be unavoidable. He would call at the club the following day and ask for help in identifying an unknown Basque who had lent him money in a nearby bar when his notecase was stolen. The Basque had said the money could be left for him at the club; but now he had forgotten the Basque's name. He would then describe Fernandes as he looked in the photograph. If the story produced an address or a statement of when he was next expected at the club, he was practically home and dry. If it didn't and his enquiry was reported to Fernandes that might be unfortunate. But some risk had to be taken.

The following day, reckoning that the club would not be in effective operation much before noon, he spent a while in the alleys of the Old Town, absorbing the odours of new bread and old refuse. Returning to the Place Wilson via the Rue Foncet, he was brought to an abrupt halt. Standing near the entrance to the courtyard was a group of four men. Two were middle-aged, wearing dark suits and berets set very squarely on their heads. The others were younger and more casually dressed. Hand-shaking was in progress, preparatory to a parting.

Given the location and those berets, it seemed at least possible that they had just emerged from the club. Moreover, although one of the younger men was nearly bald, the other had the right build for Fernandes and hair curling into his neck in the way that Victor Crispin had found so thrilling. He felt hope surge inside. It was difficult to accept that his luck had revived in so handsome a fashion; yet, as the man broke away from the others and wheeled, his profile showed him to be a more than reasonable fit for the figure in the snapshot.

The man walked to the end of the block and turned north into the Rue Gubernatis. His disappearance from sight galvanized Egerton. If he proved not be to Fernandes, following would have cost only a little wasted time and energy. He walked quickly to the end of the Place Wilson and saw that his quarry had changed to the left-hand pavement and was strolling almost aimlessly as though to kill time. Finally he halted at a restaurant and went inside. After a couple of minutes Egerton followed.

It was barely twelve thirty and few of the dozen or so tables were taken. The room had a pleasantly faded and unfashionable appearance; black and white photographs of Nice in quieter times lined the walls. The man sat alone on a red velvet banquette, beneath one of the photographs. Taking a seat at the table immediately alongside, Egerton watched while he sipped a cognac and talked with an air of polite melancholy to a waitress. He seemed to be waiting for someone.

Egerton ordered and opened the copy of *The Times* he had bought earlier. In a side column on the front page there was a new GOLIATH story but not about leakages this time. A march of peace organizations opposed to the purchase of GOLIATH had taken place in London. Something had gone amiss in the liaison between the march's organizers and the police, with the result that traffic had been immobilized in the West End for several hours. There was a photograph alongside the story, taken somewhere in the Mall, of Rylance in the back of an official limousine, looking very put out.

The empty tables were filling. Most of the arrivals were elderly men and women; the greetings exchanged with the waitresses were at once formal and intimate. Some nodded in the direction of the next table. With each acknowledgement the man half-rose in his seat and bowed courteously. The unwelcome thought began to harden in Egerton's mind that here was an ordinary local business man, a Niçois who happened to look rather like Fernandes.

But suddenly the other was upright and for the first time smiling. Hurrying through the door of the restaurant to accept and return his kiss, without a shadow of doubt, was

Lauren Giordano. She took her seat between them on the banquette. Although lacking the fine-boned features and auburn hair shared by Evelyn and Jacqueline, she was more attractive than the photographs had suggested. She looked about her. Catching Egerton's eye she smiled quickly before her gaze travelled on; it was the smile of someone who still believed the world could be a good place and wanted others to feel the same.

It was impossible to hear her conversation with Fernandes, their heads were too close together: no one could doubt they were in love. Egerton ate slowly, trying to avoid getting too far ahead of them but they seemed set on lingering over their meal. Almost an hour passed. Toying with his second portion of cheese, he gazed at the photograph on the wall in front of him. It would have been taken, he supposed, towards the end of the nineteenth century: women were scrubbing laundry on the stones beside the river that ran through the town. One of the women had the look of Gwen about her. He felt a twinge that he had not sent her a postcard. At this distance her contribution to his domestic existence gave off a rosier glow. He decided he must take her a gift.

Fingers rested lightly on his arm and pressed. Startled, he turned. Lauren had leaned towards him, smiling. 'Would you mind if I looked at your *Times*?'

She studied the front page and made some remark to Fernandes. 'You can keep it if you like,' Egerton said.

She thanked him. 'Are you from London?'

'Yes.'

'Did you get caught in the great snarl-up?' She was pointing to the item about the anti-GOLIATH march.

He explained that he'd flown in two days before it happened. Pointing to the photograph of Rylance he said, to see how she would respond, 'Portrait of a cross politician . . .' She smiled but said nothing, her eyes returning to the news story. For all her apparent openness, she was quite good at dissembling, he decided.

He supposed that would be the end of the exchange but

she went on to ask him which part of London he lived in. Fernandes said nothing but his smile was indulgent. The opportunity to keep them talking was too good to let slip. As they finished eating, he invited them to take brandy. It was hardly consistent with Evelyn Rylance's instruction to have no contact with Lauren. But she had not allowed for circumstances in which Lauren might approach *him*; now that had happened, there seemed little point in holding back, provided she wasn't alerted to his role.

They exchanged names. Fernandes gave his in full, Lauren only her christian name. She embarked on more questions about London, mostly light-hearted but with a touch of wistfulness. She might have been some exile encountered in a remote, forgotten place. Mundane facts about the strike on the Underground and the new programme at Covent Garden she greeted with relish. Once or twice Fernandes added his own questions, but Egerton suspected they had been invented simply to please *her*. For the most part he sat quiet, admiring each tiny movement, each shifting plane of her features.

'What do you do?' Lauren asked. 'I mean—what's your work?'

He had forgotten that he might face that question. He picked up his glass of wine to give himself more time to think of an innocent-sounding answer. 'I'm in estate agency, my firm's planning to open an office here. I came to look into the possibilities.'

He sensed that some train of thought had started in her mind.

'Are you going back to London soon?'

'Tomorrow or the next day.'

Her eyes turned towards Fernandes spelling out a question. He remained silent but gently smiling. She said to him, 'Do you suppose he could perhaps deliver your letter? It would be a way round . . . the problem. Don't you think?'

Fernandes looked into his brandy. 'I don't want to inconvenience Mr Egerton.'

'A letter . . .?' Egerton asked.

Fernandes shrugged. 'It's for a friend in London. There is some family business on which I have written—very personal. Unfortunately letters to her can go astray. Someone in the apartment block, the porter perhaps, is unfriendly. I do not wish to risk the post. But it may be out of your way.'

'What address?'

'She lives in Crawford Street, Marylebone. It is near the High Street.'

'But I go quite close every day.' He wasn't even having to tell a lie. 'It would be no trouble if you feel it would help.'

He waited for Fernandes to make up his mind, not wanting to seem more eager than courtesy demanded. If, as seemed likely, Fernandes hadn't got the letter in his pocket now, it would surely be natural to invite him back to their apartment for a drink. That would remove the hazard of having to tail them after this lunch. Moreover, Bellamy had spoken of Garcia Fernandes perhaps being back in England for a terrorist operation. Luis's letter might be intended for him. If so, it would amount to a useful extra bonus from his trip to Nice. One in the eye for the sarcastic Rivers too.

'If you are really quite sure . . .?' Fernandes said.

Lauren looked triumphant. She squeezed Fernandes' hand: she had solved a problem for him. Turning to Egerton she said, 'Why don't you come to dinner tonight? Then Luis can give you the letter. Are you free . . .?'

'Absolutely free,' he said.

The address they had provided was up the hill from the town, almost into Cimiez. Halfway along a cul-de-sac, Egerton's taxi driver pointed to a cement-faced block of flats, less grand than most of its neighbours. There were balconies looking out to sea, bright with pot plants and sunblinds. The board in the entrance hall said that 'Fernandes' was on the highest floor of all. He rode the elevator, big with expectation of a sunset view across the Baie des Anges.

But the apartment skulked at the back of the block. The balcony on which Lauren led him gave on to a strip of

144

scrubby hillside and the foundations of apartments higher up. A second-hand glory from the sun was reflected in the window panes above.

Rising from a basket chair beside which Fernandes stood, was an untidy, middle-aged man, his forehead crowned by a thicket of grey hair that looked as though it would see off the attack of any normal comb. He was dressed in voluminous shorts and sandals that revealed plump brown toes. 'Arthur Boyd, our neighbour,' Lauren said, indicating the balcony of the adjoining apartment. The man extended a hand. His eyes were very sharp.

Drinking cassis, they sat on the balcony while the orange glow deepened in the windows behind. A smell of flowers and cool foliage drifted into their nostrils. On the Boulevard de Cimiez a few hundred metres away the noise of traffic died to a murmur. The view might be a write-off but the place still had the edge on Prince of Wales Drive.

It appeared that Boyd was a writer which accounted perhaps for the ferociously unkempt appearance; every year he came to the adjoining apartment for a month or two to work on his books. At other times he lived in Epping with a wife who was a gynaecologist and their Shi Tsu dog. He showed a marked reluctance to talk about his writing; obviously for him, it was like stockbroking or the manufacture of condoms, not a trade to be worn as a badge. But on other subjects he was articulate. Resting one foot on the knee of the other leg and wriggling the plump toes he showed himself to be well-informed, whenever his views were sought.

Dinner was *bouillabaisse*. Lauren's campaign for the seal hadn't apparently widened to cover other forms of marine life. Dipping his bread vigorously, Boyd uttered knowledgeable praise. Lauren accepted it with an unforced pleasure that was engaging. There was nothing brittle or blasé about her; a capacity for simple pleasure had survived whatever childhood had been like with Giordano and Evelyn. It softened a manner that would otherwise have been over-intense.

Fernandes talked very little, preferring to watch and listen. When Egerton asked him where in Spain he came from, he said with a dismissive gesture, 'You would not have heard of the place. It's in Vizcaya—a Basque province.'

'You're a Basque yourself . . .?'

'Yes.'

There seemed no reason not to press on boldly. 'Do you support the Basque nationalist movement?'

Fernandes smiled politely. 'Of course.'

'. . . To the extent of wanting independence from Spain?'

'Not full independence, no.' Fernandes hesitated. He was plainly wondering whether the occasion called for more than a superficial response. 'I should like to see a proper acknowledgement of our identity and culture by Madrid. I can remember when, in my village, if you were heard using even a few words of the Basque language you were taken away to the police station.'

'But that was under Franco,' Boyd said.

'Old attitudes die hard.'

'Even with your present government?'

Fernandes shrugged. 'Whatever government you have in Madrid it will always say it is worried about the integrity of the State. Ministers eventually become obsessed by what they see as threats to it. People in Madrid say "Give the Basques an inch and the Catalans will take a mile." Of course there is an element of truth in that. But what most Basques ask for is no more than the restoration of the rights we had as a separate people—our *fueros*. Restoration *in reality*, not just on paper.'

'You might then become a State within a State.'

'Perhaps.'

'But do you expect to achieve that?' Egerton asked.

'I *expect* nothing. God will decide.' He used the word casually as if he had been referring to someone living, albeit very senior. 'We must simply carry on the struggle.'

Lauren was watching Fernandes in a way that was both admiring and protective. Egerton said cautiously, 'But there seem to be fundamentally different views on the means.'

'One follows one's conscience,' Fernandes said. 'God speaks through that.' It was an evasion and intended as such.

Lauren said gently, 'But never through killing.' She had looked down at her plate. Fernandes waited until her eyes lifted again. He spread his hands wide in some message and smiled. She smiled back.

Lauren was in the kitchen making coffee when the telephone rang. The call was for Fernandes and he disappeared to answer it. 'Do you know anything about Basque politics?' Egerton asked Boyd.

'A little. I've met one of the nationalists who gave up the armed struggle when the present government took office in Madrid, a man named Barillo. He used to live in Nice until a year or two back. We got into conversation in a café one day.' Boyd loosened the belt straps on his antique shorts. 'Luis has also talked to me about his aims after he's had a few drinks. He's going into politics when he returns to Spain.'

'I was surprised to see there's a Basque club here. I thought the Spanish Basque emigrés were over on the west coast.'

'That's where the bombers hole up when the Spanish police flush them out. After Barillo decided that violence ought to be dropped and ETA should reach an accommodation with Madrid, he moved away from Bayonne where he was living and came here. It was a way of distancing himself from the terrorist wing of ETA. His supporters came with him and established the club. Luis is a great admirer of Barillo. The club was probably one of the things that drew him and Lauren to Nice. The organization Barillo set up here is still very active amongst Basques living abroad.'

'What exactly do the initials ETA stand for?'

'I can't remember the words but they mean Basque Homeland and Freedom.'

147

'Does Luis support ETA?'

'Not the military wing. He may have done once. But like Barillo he's now fundamentally opposed to violence. He genuinely believes in a Spanish entity. But it has to accommodate all the ways in which the Basques insist on being different.'

There was a chill in the air now. Lauren closed the balcony doors while they drank coffee. She played a tape of thirteenth century *cantigas* Fernandes had bought that afternoon. Sometimes alone, sometimes accompanied by a harp, a woman sang. The sounds reached out to them like the call of distant bells: it was as though each syllable had been rinsed by the crisp air of the uplands before it descended to fill the silences far below.

They listened with their eyes closed or fixed on the ceiling. When Egerton glanced across at the others their appearance was relaxed. Yet in both Fernandes and Lauren he could sense a tension. About Fernandes there was always a look of vigilance, as though he was prepared for something to happen elsewhere. Lauren's manner was different: she was alert for any shift in Fernandes' mood, any threat to his wellbeing.

By the time he rose to leave, the letter was still unmentioned. He wondered if some remark he had made or his questions to Fernandes about Basque affairs had caused misgivings about entrusting him with it. But in the hallway Fernandes took from his pocket an envelope and handed it over. 'Are you sure this will not inconvenience you?'

'Quite sure.'

It was addressed to Señora Castillo at 11d, Hoddershall Mansions, Crawford Street, London W1. In the top right-hand corner of the envelope, in polite reminder of Egerton's commitment, Fernandes had written 'For Personal Delivery Only.'

'If Señora Castillo is out when you call, would you please place the letter under the door of the apartment, not in the mail box? It is on the first floor of the block at the front. The entrance doors are open in daytime.'

148

'Of course.'

'One further request if you will be so kind: it is important for me to know that you have been able to deliver the letter safely. Would you telephone me when you have done that? Perhaps this will cover the cost . . .' He had begun taking a banknote from his wallet until Egerton made him stop. Lauren was copying down the telephone number for Egerton; she handed it to him and then stood, her head against Fernandes' shoulder, fingers linked with his. The chances of Evelyn Rylance or anyone else succeeding in breaking up their relationship seemed very slim.

The following morning he waited until he could be reasonably confident Antrim would be in his office before he called to give him the news. Antrim was making sounds close to enthusiasm as he took down the address and telephone number.

'Would you like me to fly back today?'

Antrim hesitated. 'No, stay where you are until I've spoken to Rylance. I don't suppose there's anything more for you to do but we'd better see. I'll get back to you, probably tomorrow morning. Enjoy yourself in the meantime.' He was being uncharacteristically expansive.

Outside the hotel, the day had the clarity of crystal. Coffee smells mingled with the perfume of passing women as he walked beneath the arcades of the Place Massena. He was free as the air, at liberty to do whatever he wanted. Yet, now the euphoria of success was past, he found he had no appetite for pleasing himself. Meeting Lauren and Fernandes, observing their relationship, having their trust placed in him over the letter, had changed the character of the search from an abstract challenge to something tiresomely complicated by human feelings. He had wormed his way into their sanctuary simply to play them false, Lauren by betraying her whereabouts to the Rylances, Fernandes by letting him think the letter's contents would be seen by no one except Señora Castillo. Lauren could tell her mother to go to hell, of course, when she showed up in Nice. But the elaborate steps she had taken to avoid the confrontation were proof of how much she would hate it.

About Fernandes, there had been an authority, a moral tone, that made deceiving him seem just as squalid. Even if Boyd had read the signs wrongly and Fernandes retained an association with terrorism which went beyond remaining on close terms with his brother, he somehow deserved better than to have his hospitality abused. He was conscious of a vague resentment against Antrim for having given him this task; an illogical sense of having been exploited grew inside him.

Trying to shake off the mood, he embarked on a desultory exploration of the town, ate well, drank good wine, studied women; but nothing pleased. By the evening he was conscious only of a sour weariness. Entering a cinema he found himself watching pornography and realized that that was to be the flavour of the day, feeling exploited.

Relief came the next day before he had finished breakfast. It was announced by Baxter speaking with careful condescension. 'I believe you're waiting for instructions, Egerton.'

'Yes.'

'I'm to tell you that you can fly back as soon as you like. Or, rather, as soon as possible.'

'Right.'

'How does the *Côte* look?'

He gazed down from his bedroom window. Outside a lingerie boutique, a cat slept in a shaft of sunlight. It was going to be another fine day. His mood began to lift. 'Quite good. In fact, marvellous.' He enjoyed the thought of making Baxter envious.

He booked a seat on the afternoon plane to Heathrow, regretting, now that departure was no more than hours away, that he had made so little of the previous day. In pursuit of lost opportunity he visited galleries, walked in the Roman Arena, then took a taxi back to the beach and lay gazing at the sky in a last farewell to summer.

He arrived at the airport bare minutes before the final

150

check-in time shown on his ticket; but hurrying through the entrance hall he saw from the indicator board that the plane from London on which he would be making the return trip had landed less than a quarter of an hour beforehand. Handing in his luggage he went to the airport shops in search of gifts for the women in his life, Gail and Gwen. When he emerged, the London passengers were beginning to appear from passport control. He stayed to watch, seized with the thought that he might glimpse Evelyn Rylance among them, on her way to browbeat Lauren.

The crocodile diminished to a trickle. She was hardly the sort of person who would be trailing in the rear but he lingered until a new surge of passengers appeared with an air of vivacity that ruled out an Anglo Saxon flight. It was just as well she hadn't been there, he reflected: she might have caught sight of him and embarked on an interrogation long enough to make him miss his own plane.

As he turned to make his way to the departure lounge, he glanced briefly through the airport doors to where cars were picking up passengers from the new flight arrival. A squat man carrying an overnight bag stood in profile for a second or two. He wore jacket and trousers of black leather with an open necked white shirt; around a gorilla throat was a gold chain. An older man in a broad-brimmed hat and a cashmere top coat was greeting him. As they turned away from Egerton, a uniformed chauffeur held open the rear door of a limousine with smoked glass windows. They climbed inside. At this distance it was impossible to be sure. But the squat man with the gorilla throat had certainly had the look of Sam Giordano.

# XV

THERE was a note from his secretary when he opened his diary after reporting back to Antrim. Gail had telephoned the day before he left Nice and asked when he would return. She'd been told there was no news and had rung off without leaving a message. He wondered if her call had been a SOS. Half of him hoped it might have been. He reached for the telephone directory then remembered she had no phone of her own; there was probably one in the house but it would be in the name of the Gujerati landlord and he didn't know that.

Jamie was the only certain source of news. To his surprise he found that he was listed and rang the number but there was no reply. That could mean he was away on one of his trips. If he couldn't raise Jamie by the evening he would have to call at Gail's when he left the office for the day.

His door opened. Antonia Strachan was looking round the side of it with an expression of enquiry. He should have stopped by her room before now to give her his news.

'I hear you got your girl.'

'How did you know?'

'Baxter told me last night. Congratulations. What's she like?'

'I think she's rather nice. So was Fernandes for that matter. If Evelyn Rylance has turned up there I hope they show her the door. In fact I'm sure they will.'

She seated herself on the corner of his desk. 'I hear you're getting a week's leave as a sort of prize.'

He grimaced. 'I'm sorry, I thought I'd be back with you today. When I said so, it was made clear that I was not expected to look a gift horse in the mouth. I'm to go off tonight after I've written up my notes.'

The look on her face was ironical. 'Our leader is bucked I imagine.'

'He did give that impression.'

'Onwards and upwards to his "K",' she said. 'That's what he's thinking.' She slid abruptly from the desk and pulled up a chair. 'You didn't hear me say that. So tell me how you found them.'

He told her. She had her head resting against the back of the chair as she talked. At the end she turned it towards him; soft black hair fell across her cheek as she nodded, 'So that's that . . .'

'Pretty well. I'm told Rylance wants to see me sometime, presumably to hear the details. But he's just off to a conference in Washington and won't be back for a week or so. Baxter's supposed to fix a date for when I return from leave.' He opened the folder in front of him. 'Before I forget . . . I was told to ask you to have Fernandes' letter to Señora Castillo fiddled open and, assuming it's about Basque business, a copy sent over to Rivers in Special Branch. Then somebody can push it under the Señora's door.'

'What explanation do I give to Rivers for our having intercepted it?'

'Antrim said you'd think of something.'

She compressed her lips. He watched her tapping the letter against the palm of her hand and wondered again about the *affaire* she was supposed to have had with Antrim. 'You *will* see it's delivered afterwards . . .' he said. When she raised her eyebrows at his tone, he went on, 'It's simply that meeting Fernandes, hearing him talk—' He broke off. 'Well, I don't care to let him down to the extent of not even delivering the bloody letter. I'd like to be able to ring him and say I've arranged it.'

He was being wet about both Lauren and Fernandes; he

153

could imagine her pausing, as she wrote his next annual report, at the column headed Moisture Content or whatever the approved phrase was.

She gave no hint of what she was thinking. 'How are you going to spend your leave?'

He gazed out of the window. 'There's something I must that he couldn't see her expression.

She looked politely interested. He felt obliged to go on. 'I have a friend with a problem that needs sorting out.'

'What sort of problem?'

It was almost certainly unwise to have embarked on this. But he had to talk about Gail to somebody and she was the most level-headed person he knew. 'It's a girl who's been injecting heroin for rather a long time. If I could get her away from London for a while, I might talk her into having treatment. The trick is going to be to make her *want* to get off it. The last time it was tried, she walked out of the clinic.'

'How close are you?'

'Close?'

'I mean—are you in love with her?'

'I was when we were at university. Then she met someone else, an actor. They lived together when she came down from Oxford. Unfortunately he was also on heroin. I discovered the other day that he died about a year ago.'

'Sad,' she said.

He wondered what she really felt but she had turned so that he couldn't see her expression.

'I'd thought of having her to stay in my flat for a while but London's hopeless for anyone who's trying to stop, there are too many pressures. Somehow I must get her away.'

'Do you still love her?'

He knew that she was no longer looking away from him. It was the first time he had squarely faced it. 'I never really stopped I suppose. It was one of the reasons I had for going to America the year before I joined the Bureau. Yes, I do still love her. Very much.'

She was brooding. 'It's possible I can help. My mother's house in Shropshire is empty. Since my father died last winter she's been staying with her sister in New Mexico. I visit the house to keep an eye on things but I'm not going this weekend. You can have the key if you like. It's eight miles from the nearest real village and nobody is likely to call round offering heroin. As far as I know, incest is the only local diversion.'

'You wouldn't mind my taking her there for a week?'

'You'd be doing a favour by airing the place for me.'

Now the opportunity was there, he wondered if he would actually succeed in persuading Gail to go. At present he didn't even know where she was. But he didn't want to sound lukewarm. 'That's marvellous,' he said.

When she was leaving him, she hesitated by the door. 'You were both taking drugs at Oxford, were you?'

He felt a surge of relief that she had asked. 'Yes.'

'Heroin?'

'Yes.'

'But *you* stopped . . .'

'Eventually.'

'And never went back to it . . .' Her tone was matter of fact, perhaps too much so.

'Never.'

It was his opportunity to get it all out in the open. But before he could go on, she nodded briskly as though she had as much of the story as she wanted. 'Let me know if you want the key.'

He watched the door close behind her. He hadn't told her about the man in black leather at Nice airport who had looked like Giordano or of the questions it had raised in his mind. She would probably have said it wasn't his business, and she would have been right.

For an hour or two he argued himself into a mood of optimism about getting Gail to leave London for the week. If necessary he would pack her bag and simply bundle her into the car. Late afternoon brought news that killed the plan stone dead. He had finally got a response from Jamie's

155

number. When he asked about Gail, Jamie sounded surprised. 'Haven't you heard?'

'Heard what? Is she all right?'

'I imagine so. She was when I saw her the night before she left.'

'Left for where?'

'Barbados.'

He stared at his blotter only half-listening to the explanation. Some sprig had come into a million from his family trust on reaching twenty-five. He had chartered an aircraft and flown a party to Barbados to celebrate. Gail had been invited along. The gossip columnists were making the usual meal of the affair. The sprig's name meant nothing. 'How did she meet him?' he asked.

'I introduced them—that night at Dido's.'

His heart had begun to sink. 'I gather she tried to get me at the office. Do you know why?'

'She told me she didn't want you to misunderstand her reason for going. It just seemed a marvellous chance of some sun.'

He wondered if Jamie had invented that to make him feel better. 'This is somebody you supply, I suppose.'

There was a pause at the other end. It had been an indiscreet thing to say on an open line but to apologize now could make it worse. 'Just a chap I know.' Jamie's voice was faintly aggrieved. It was the closest he ever came to sounding angry.

He went to look for Antonia and told her he wouldn't be borrowing the house. She didn't ask why. 'So you'll stay in London?'

'No, I'll probably visit my sister. Her son's my godchild. I haven't seen him for months. He's a fiend but I'm fond of him.'

She went back to the file she'd been reading. 'Don't forget to leave your number. Other fiends may need to contact you. We're still short on evidence for the Beynon prosecution.'

He inclined his head and left her. If it wasn't intended as

156

a crack that he'd left the case only half-wrapped up, it came pretty close.

For nearly four days that world went away. Together with the evening sun it dropped behind the horizon as he stood at his bedroom window, suitcase still unpacked, and watched the fiend operating a ray gun against a cow that had strayed into the orchard. The next morning he cut the grass, fetched Joanna's provisions order from Cirencester, mended her steam iron and resumed the godfather role. It was less demanding than on previous occasions. In the months since his last encounter with Marcus, there had been a shift from mass destruction to conservation. Lauren Giordano might not have gone for the style however. The garden shed was now a combined laboratory, clinic and concentration camp. Tea chests, jam jars, matchboxes, each with its occupant, covered the floor and potting bench. The prisoners were paraded once or twice a day, put through an exercise programme and returned to confinement with rations that were varied and experimental. Those who failed to respond vivaciously to the regimen were released, the others were doomed to languish in custody. The prize inmate was a mouse of exceptional beauty.

Away from the shed Marcus's attentions were focused on the river inlet at the foot of the orchard. He had built a dam of mud and branches; twigs, felled by notional lumberjacks working further up the river swirled into sight, to spin for a few aimless moments before drifting against the dam wall. Concentration on these events, at first reluctant, eventually became unforced, even absorbing. Once, lying full-length to catch the drama of six logs, roped together, hurtling into the pool, he turned his head and saw a buck rabbit watching with the same intentness. The Bureau ceased to have a reality. He thought now of Rylance and Lauren and Fernandes as figures in a show that had closed long ago.

But he was wrong. That evening, after he had left Marcus at last in bed with the mouse in its plastic box to see him through the night, he settled by the fire to read a newspaper while Joanna hunted hens in the long grass. At the bottom of the overseas news page was a story date-lined Nice.

## MORE 'DIRTY WAR' DEATHS?

The bodies of Luis Fernandes, whose brother Garcia is one of the most wanted members of ETA's extremist military wing, and Lauren Giordano, an American national who had been living with Fernandes, were discovered in a Nice apartment today. Both had been murdered.

Luis Fernandes is not believed to have been involved in terrorist activities during his stay in France although his past association with ETA is well known. The French police consider the killings are either the result of quarrels among factions within ETA or, more probably, in revenge for the recent murder of an Army colonel in Barcelona. They suspect the hand of the mysterious GAL (Anti-Terrorist Liberation Group) which is dedicated to eliminating prominent ETA figures in France.

The English author, Arthur Boyd, who lived in the next apartment heard the killings take place and was injured when he tried to intervene. He called the police on recovering consciousness by which time there was no trace of the killers.

This latest eruption of the so-called 'dirty war', (assuming police suspicions are correct) will provide additional ammunition for the French Prime Minister on his official visit to Madrid next week. It is known that he already intended to protest to the Spanish government about both Basque incursions and activities of GAL in France. There have been allegations that GAL represents clandestine counter-terrorist activity by Spain's principal intelligence service, Cesid.

He sat staring at the wall opposite, shaken by the thought of them lying dead in the apartment where he had been their guest hardly a week ago. Only now was he conscious of how much they had engaged his sympathies. It was as though he had ceased to see them as quarry and joined them in spirit against those who had been their hunters.

After supper he decided he must find out more. 'Have you ever heard of a writer called Arthur Boyd?' he asked Joanna. She had switched on the television set and was clicking through the channels.

'Yes. He writes sexy thrillers.'

'Sexy thrillers!' He saw again that ungainly, vaguely academic figure in the outsize shorts and open sandals. It was impossible to credit. 'You must be thinking of someone else.'

'No, I'm not, I've read one. His wife's a gynaecologist. They live in Epping with a Shitsu.'

'How do you know all that?'

'I read about them in a Sunday colour magazine. His wife does the sex bits. The books are very hot on technical detail.'

'The clinical approach,' he said. 'Do you suppose that really turns people on?'

She shrugged and gave him wool to hold while she balled it. 'Of course.'

He thought of Marcus upstairs with the mouse in the plastic box. She was right.

'Why are you interested in Arthur Boyd?' she asked.

'He knew two friends of mine who've just been killed. I'd like to ask him some questions.'

The next morning he left Marcus to do the logging on his own and drove to Cirencester. Research at the public library produced the telephone number of the Boyds' house in Epping. If the gynaecologist wife was at home, she could presumably tell him whether Boyd was fit enough to take calls in Nice and, if so, what the number there was. He went to a telephone box.

The answering voice was intimidatingly deep but also familiar. After a second or two he realized it belonged to Boyd himself. Apparently his injury hadn't immobilized him; he had flown back to England to consult his own doctor about it. If all proved well, he was returning to Nice at the weekend to get on with the book.

'I wonder if I might come and see you before then?' Egerton asked. 'I could drive over to Epping tomorrow if that suits.'

There was silence at the other end. He sensed Boyd's surprise. 'It's just that I'd very much like to hear what you think happened and why. The story in yesterday's paper struck me as a bit odd.'

Boyd grunted. 'That's one way of describing it.'

He agreed Egerton could visit him at noon. As he was saying goodbye, he said, 'You're not really an estate agent are you?'

He couldn't very well keep that up now. 'No, I'll explain tomorrow.'

Apart from the bandage tied at a rakish angle round his head, Boyd looked well enough when he opened the door. The results of an X Ray ordered by his doctor had come through that morning and had been satisfactory. On the rest of his body he had suffered only bruises.

He led the way to a small conservatory at the back of the house and extracted bottles of German lager from a refrigerator in the corner. A gardener was staking asters in the herbaceous border outside. There was no sight or sound of the gynaecologist wife. Presumably she was on the job somewhere, getting the technology sorted for the current work.

'Since you're not an estate agent,' Boyd said, 'What are you?'

'When we met I was being employed by Lauren's mother to locate her. I'd be grateful if you'd keep that to yourself.'

That seemed safe enough. The newspaper report hadn't connected Lauren with Rylance and from her caginess at their meeting, he felt sure she wouldn't have revealed the relationship to Boyd.

'Lauren's family didn't approve of Luis, so she'd run off with him, I take it,' Boyd said.

He nodded.

'I thought something like that had happened. So what are you after now?'

'Although the family haven't asked me to pursue this, I have the feeling there's something very strange about Lauren's death. As I told you on the telephone the story in the newspaper seemed unlikely to me. For one thing it shrugs off too easily the fact that *she* wasn't a Basque. Do *you* believe they were murdered by this anti-terrorist organization, GAL, the Spanish government are supposed to be behind?'

Boyd made a gesture of disgust. 'Total balls.'

'You're sure . . .?'

'Absolutely. Luis was a Basque nationalist all right. But whatever might have happened in the past, he wasn't a terrorist when I knew him. As I think I told you, Barillo was the man he admired most and *his* objective was a negotiated settlement of all Basque claims. It makes *slightly* more sense to imagine the extremists killed Luis because he was about to come out in opposition to their methods.'

'But you don't sound as though you believe that either . . .'

'No.'

'Then why have the French police taken the line it was a political killing?'

Boyd shrugged. 'It suits them. Blaming Spanish in-fighting saves trouble—they don't have to look for other reasons. And blaming GAL is even better. After all GAL have been getting very active in France recently. The French want Madrid to rein it in.'

'So what do *you* think was the explanation for what happened?'

'I don't know exactly. I'll tell you what I told the police. You'll have to judge for yourself from that.'

Boyd poured himself another lager. Something had happened two days before the killings which he was convinced was connected. Going on to his balcony in the evening to water the plants, he had heard Lauren talking next door. She had two visitors, and he could tell from their voices that they were American. Unusually she had closed her own balcony doors so that he couldn't catch more than a few of the words spoken but it had been a quarrel, she was being threatened. Fernandes' voice was absent. He was often out, meeting his Basque friends in the early evening and Boyd guessed he hadn't been in the apartment.

The following day Boyd had met Lauren in the entrance hall to the apartment block. She seemed very quiet. She spoke of Luis deciding that after all it would be convenient if they went to Spain now instead of in November as had been their original intention. She said they'd probably be off at the end of the week.

The killings took place the following evening. Boyd had been working at his desk when he heard a commotion. The noise had come from the next apartment. Curiosity drove him to the balcony to listen. But all he heard now was a half-shout which could have been from Fernandes, then the noise of a chair or table overturning.

He hadn't been sure what he ought to do. Since he couldn't hear any more sound, it occurred to him that Fernandes had been drinking in the apartment alone—he knew he drank heavily on occasion—and had collapsed in a stupor. Finally he opened the door of his apartment, intending to go next door and knock. At that moment he was relieved to see Lauren coming down the corridor. She gave him a little wave with her latchkey and went into the apartment. Boyd withdrew, reckoning that if Fernandes *was* out cold on the floor, she'd be able to handle it.

His memory then was of events moving very fast. Almost at once there had been more noise, a scream from Lauren that seemed to be strangled in her throat and the low murmur of a man's voice that certainly wasn't Fernandes'. Boyd went and hammered on their door.

After a pause during which there was dead silence, the door was opened by a young man. Boyd noticed he was wearing gloves. When Boyd asked what was going on, he said he was a doctor who had been called to deal with a patient who had become violent. Boyd wouldn't buy that and began pushing the door open behind the man. He just had time to see Fernandes tied and gagged in a chair before Lauren seemed to materialize from nowhere, screaming to him for help. Behind her was another man with a gun which he brought down on Lauren's head to stop her reaching the door. Boyd rushed towards Lauren and that was the last thing he remembered before he was felled himself. When he recovered consciousness, he was still in the apartment. The place was in chaos—everything had been ripped apart in a systematic search. Fernandes had either been freed or had broken away from the chair because he was lying, still gagged, near the balcony doors. He'd been shot and was in a pool of his blood. Lauren was propped up in a corner. There were curious burn marks on her face. The cause of death, Boyd learned later from the police, was a brain haemorrhage which had occurred some time after the blow on the head.

Outside the conservatory, the gardener had turned to cutting down blackened lupins. Apart from the asters, no colour remained in the border. It was a world that was spent, over. Egerton stared into his glass, remembering the expression on Lauren's face as they told her the *bouillabaisse* was fine, perfect. 'It must have been a ghastly experience for you.'

'I've dreamed about it most nights since.'

'Do you know how the burns got on her face?'

Boyd pushed his fingers through the nest of grey hair that remained exposed by the bandage. 'This is only my idea . . . I believe Lauren was still alive after the blow on the head and recovered consciousness for a while. The burns looked as though they were made by a cigarette. I believe she was being tortured when she died.'

'But why?'

'They wanted something she had. *She*, mind you, not Luis. It was whatever they searched the apartment for. That's one reason why I don't believe what happened had anything to do with Spanish politics. Besides which, the men I saw weren't Basques, or any other sort of Spaniard, they were *Niçois*, local thugs. I know the type from seeing them in the courts there when I was researching a book.'

'You told the police this . . .?'

'Of course. I even picked out from the mug book they showed me at police headquarters somebody I was pretty sure was one of the thugs. The chap who interviewed me said he belonged to a gang led by a big local crook named Raoul Baptiste. But by the next time they saw me they didn't want to know. Their line was, it could only be political. They got a bit uneasy when I persisted in talking about the visit of the Americans two days earlier. But they weren't going to be shifted from the story that suited them.'

Outside, the gardener had gathered together his tools and put them in a wheelbarrow; he was off to lunch. 'Did you happen to look out of your window when the Americans left and see the sort of car they had?'

Boyd shook his head. 'You forget, my apartment's at the back of the block.' He was watching Egerton curiously. 'What sort of car did you think it might be?'

'It doesn't make much sense at present,' he said. 'But I wondered if it was a limousine with smoked glass windows.'

# XVI

BACK at the Bureau, he found the going hard when he tried to interest Antonia in theories he had begun to form.

'You're not even sure it was Giordano you saw at Nice airport.'

'It looked like him.'

'But how did he know where Lauren was staying?'

'He may have telephoned Evelyn Rylance just after I passed the address back. She'd have had no reason to withhold it from him.'

'So he feels so keenly about her relationship with Fernandes that he goes to Nice and threatens her . . .'

'No,' he said patiently, 'He *may* have felt keenly about Fernandes but I suspect the reason he went was that when she visited him in the summer she acquired something he badly wanted to get back.'

'What sort of thing?'

'That I don't know.'

'So when she refuses to give it to him, he goes out and finds two thugs who agree to rough her up. That strikes me as pretty unlikely. Giordano may or may not have a line to the underworld where he comes from. But this was in Nice. He probably only knows the place from flying in on the way to film festivals in Cannes.'

'The man who met him off his plane seemed to be local. Not French but possibly an American living there.'

She was still looking unreceptive. 'Look,' he said, 'I accept that I can't be sure it was Giordano I saw. But I also can't forget what Sally Kirkwood said about something having happened during Lauren's trip to the States. Or my feeling that Giordano was holding back when I saw him at Claridges.'

'But are you suggesting she stole something from Giordano—papers perhaps that showed he was involved in criminal activity? That she was using them as blackmail? From all you've been told about her, from everything you *saw* of her, she doesn't sound like a person who'd go in for that.'

That of course was true. He could imagine Lauren Giordano being stubborn, even unbending when she was fighting for someone or something she cared passionately about. But she was too principled to be a thief. Nor was she the sort to get down in the gutter in order to pressure her own father. Or might she just bring herself to do it if it were for Fernandes' sake? He didn't know the answer to that. But, in any case, what could Fernandes need or fear from Giordano?

He gazed grimly at a photograph that stood on Antonia's desk. It was of a man with fair, wavy hair and a sunburned face; he seemed to be standing on an airfield. Presumably it was the husband who was said to have died in a flying accident. It occurred to him that perhaps she'd never been able to accept the fact of his death and this was the reason why she hadn't remarried. 'How much do you think I should mention of this to Rylance?'

She raised her eyebrows. 'You're still going to see him?'

'Apparently. I'd supposed he might have cancelled the appointment. But Baxter says I should assume it's still on. I'm going to Chester Square this evening.'

She pursed her lips. 'He's entitled to know what you've learned from Arthur Boyd.'

'Not more?'

'Anything else is really speculation. It's also very delicate ground. If he wants to pursue Boyd's story, it's up to him.'

'I don't think it ought to be dropped.'

'Perhaps not. But is it our business?'

He couldn't say it was. He felt she was being irritatingly casual about it, all the same. He picked up the photostat

166

she had shown him earlier. It was a copy of the letter he had brought back from Fernandes for delivery to Señora Castillo. Apparently an inner envelope had been addressed simply 'Garcia'. Pinned at the back was the translation done in the Bureau.

The letter was a long and complicated affair with allusions that were often too cryptic to grasp to the attitude of different government ministers in Madrid and recent developments in the Basque territories. The thrust of it was plain however: Luis was pleading with Garcia to call off some imminent operation; he was also claiming to know that Madrid would do a deal over Garcia's past activities but that chance would be lost if the operation went ahead.

He handed it back to Antonia. 'It makes Luis Fernandes' position pretty clear. Rylance and his wife might get some satisfaction from knowing that the man Lauren went off with was not only not a terrorist, he was trying to prevent some terrorist operation here. Can I tell him that?'

'I think you should.'

'What was Special Branch's reaction to the letter?'

'They were very pleased. They've been on tenterhooks for some Basque operation in London this autumn so they now know Garcia is holed up here for that.'

'Have they traced him?'

'Unfortunately not. The Castillo woman slipped surveillance the day they believe she delivered the letter. One of their surveillance team got caught in a lift.'

He remembered Rivers' voice on the telephone, that crack about how one should behave if one wanted to be thought professional. He could almost be sorry for him; but not quite.

Back in his room he found that most of the Beynon files had been deposited on his desk again. He turned a few pages without enthusiasm. He still felt sore at Antonia's lukewarm reaction to his suspicions about Giordano. After a while he knew he wasn't going to settle down before he had tested his theory. In the phone conversation he had listened to in the suite at Claridges, Giordano had talked of staying at the Excelsior Hotel in Rome after he left there. An hour later he found himself talking on a crackling line to someone announcing herself as Mary Jane Cord, Mr Giordano's Personal Assistant.

'Miss Cord, this is the British Department of Health,' he said.

She made a baffled noise. He went on, 'I expect you're aware from the press that the plane on which Mr Giordano flew from the United States to London a short while back carried a suspected smallpox case.'

She said she hadn't read it and wondered if she ought to tell him.

'No need just yet. But we're trying to keep track of passengers' movements and also their contacts. Did he travel directly to Rome from London?'

'Yes, he and Mrs Giordano.'

'Ah yes,' he said, 'that would be Joan Giordano.'

'Correct.'

'And have they both been living since then at the Excelsior Hotel?'

'Yes.'

'No trips outside Italy?'

He heard pages being turned. 'Only one, a visit to France for discussions about finance of the production he's working on. That was about ten days ago.'

'You went with him . . .?'

'No, Mrs Giordano and I stayed back here and did the shops. We had quite an orgy, I haven't recovered yet.' She laughed. She sounded better than Giordano deserved.

'Perhaps I'd better have details of the exact dates,' he said.

He knew before she read them out that they were going to match. It *had* been Giordano he'd seen at Nice airport; and he hadn't returned to Rome until the same day the killings had happened, albeit in the morning. His pulse was going quite fast. 'And the address where he stayed . . .?'

'I don't have that, only the telephone number.' She gave it to him. 'If you'd like me to ask Mr Giordano this evening—'

168

'That won't be necessary now, Miss Cord. You've been very helpful.'

Before he rang off, she said. 'I was on that plane to London. You've got a note of me, have you?'

He was into the spirit of it by now. 'M.J. Cord. That's right. You've saved me making a separate call.' She sounded very impressed as he said goodbye.

He got the supervisor on the Bureau exchange to check out the number he had been given. It proved to belong to a Frank Catini, living in a villa in Antibes. The case for further enquiries, he told himself, was unassailable. This was the moment to find out if Bellamy had been right in saying he'd made a friend in Chief Superintendent Clayton of the Serious Crimes Squad.

Contacting Clayton took most of the day. First he was said to be with the Commissioner, then out to lunch with a foreign liaison contact. The sergeant who answered the calls spoke of his movements in weary tones and declined all responsibility for arranging that Clayton should call back. It wasn't until the fourth attempt that Clayton came on the line. His voice had an impatient edge but warmed when he discovered who Egerton was. He asked if this meant more tit-bits from Chester Square.

'I'm afraid not. How's that going by the way?'

The photographer, it seemed, hadn't made any admissions but he still looked very interesting: one of his lenses could have produced a decent print of anything Rylance might have had on his desk before it was moved away from the window. He had become steadily more shifty as he maintained his story of not pointing the camera at anything except girls in spicy positions.

'What we need,' Clayton went on, 'is to establish a connection between him and someone on the *Globe*. Then I reckon he'd break. We're working on that. Anyway, thanks for the information.'

'Could I ask a favour in return? I have an interest in two men, both foreigners. The first is an American film producer from Beverly Hills named Sam Giordano. I haven't an exact address for him but he's quite well known. He was staying at Claridges a couple of weeks ago, and he's now moved on to the Excelsior in Rome. I'd like to know if you or the Americans have any sort of criminal record for him. I don't know the nationality of the other man but it's possible that he's American too. His name is Frank Catini and he has a villa in Antibes. Whether he lives—'

Clayton was interrupting him. 'Frank Catini—you're after Catini?'

'You know him?'

'Catini is Mafia. He was a big noise on the West Coast of America until a few years back. Then when it looked as though he was going to be nailed for tax fraud, he took off for Europe and settled in the south of France. He runs Catini Enterprises, a conglomerate he built on the Mafia money he managed to launder. But he also has drugs and gambling operations. He's got at least one going here.'

'What's the operation in England?'

'A club that opened last year, aimed at the high rollers. On the face of things it belongs to a twit who used to be in the Life Guards. In practice we know Catini's the real boss.'

'What would particularly interest me is if the American police are aware of some tie-up between Giordano and Catini.'

Clayton said, 'Pity you didn't get me this morning. I've been having lunch with Hal West, the FBI man at the Embassy. Anyway, leave it with me.'

He had half-feared Clayton would ask for something on paper, a formal request. Relieved, he said, 'It's a rather delicate case—I'd appreciate it if you'd pass the answer to me personally.'

Later in the afternoon, seeing Antonia talking to someone as he turned a corner in the Bureau, he beat a hasty retreat. At some stage she'd have to be told what he'd been doing. But it would be better to have Clayton's answers first.

* * *

170

This time it was a manservant in black coat and striped trousers who opened the door of the house in Chester Square. He looked faintly surprised to hear an appointment with Rylance being claimed. Leaving Egerton to sit on a velvet sofa he went away. After a while he returned and conducted him to what was obviously Rylance's study. He said that Rylance might spare him a few minutes shortly.

The room was next to the one in which Egerton had sat with Evelyn Rylance while she stoked up on negative ions. In front of what was plainly the vital window, were heavy velvet drapes. He went over and parted them. The net curtains were neatly in place behind. Clayton's visit had persuaded Evelyn that her sensibilities about rooms behind gauze had to yield to the demands of bumbledom, for the time being anyway. The desk was also well away from the window. Egerton looked up at the lights of the apartment block behind the house. Where windows were uncurtained, he could see clearly the detail of ornaments standing near them. The reverse view, with a downward angle would be even better.

The door opened behind him and Rylance appeared. He was halfway into evening dress, his tail coat over his arm. 'Egerton, I'm afraid that owing to various preoccupations, I overlooked that I'd arranged to see you. As it is, I'm now in rather a hurry. I have to call in at the House on my way to a dinner at the Guildhall. I'm sorry.' Slipping on the tail coat he went to a cabinet behind the door. 'However that doesn't mean I want you to go without a drink.'

He handed Egerton the tonic water he asked for with only one eyebrow slightly raised, poured himself a large brandy and sat down. 'I asked to see you to express my appreciation for your efforts in tracing my stepdaughter. It was excellent work. The tragedy that happened afterwards doesn't diminish what you did.'

The words were rapidly spoken but he raised his glass at the end. He was keen to do his stuff, even if the effect was rushed. He seemed a nicer man than had appeared in his room at the House of Commons.

171

'My wife will be sorry to have missed seeing you. She's in Nice until tomorrow, arranging for Lauren's body to be brought over.'

He wondered how hard the news had hit her. The only feeling towards Lauren she had displayed when they had talked had been exasperation. 'Was she able to speak to Lauren before it happened?'

'Yes, she telephoned her the night after we got your news. They had quite a long conversation. Although Lauren wouldn't agree to my wife visiting her in Nice, she eventually promised to come back here to spend a weekend. The next thing that happened was a call from the French police about the murder. Fortunately I took it, having just got back from a trip to Washington. My wife had gone to stay with friends in Ireland while I was away. The police found the number in Lauren's diary and rang in the hope of tracing next of kin.'

'Did your wife think Lauren sounded upset when they spoke on the telephone?'

'If she did, she didn't mention it. I believe Lauren expressed surprise she had the number and they then got into the usual argument about Fernandes.'

It seemed as good a moment as any to pass on what Fernandes' letter had established about his character. 'I have one piece of news that may be some consolation to your wife over Lauren's relationship with Fernandes. There's incontrovertible evidence now that he was opposed to all extremist activity. One of the last things he did before he died was to attempt to persuade his brother Garcia to abandon a terrorist operation he'd planned.'

'So I *was* misinformed about him . . .?' He was still sticking to his previous line.

'Yes.'

'Interesting.' But Egerton guessed he wasn't really interested; he wasn't concerned with what sort of a person Fernandes had been now that the relationship with Lauren no longer had a relevance for his political career, or amounted to an irritant in his marriage.

'There is something about the deaths I think you and

172

your wife should know. Some information that doesn't fit with what's been published.'

Rylance raised his eyebrows.

'I believe the killings had nothing to do with Basque politics.'

'But the French police—'

'The story put out by the police can't be squared with the facts. I'm not sure *why* they gave it to the press—possibly because it's convenient for domestic political reasons. But it's phony.'

'Why do you say that?'

He described what Boyd had told him. Rylance listened with a frown; for the first time since they had met, he was wearing an expression that was not in some degree calculated. At the end he shook his head in bafflement. 'Are you saying it was Lauren and not Fernandes who was the real target?'

'Yes. But they didn't plan to kill her when they went to the apartment. Their purpose was to make her give up something. I believe Lauren's killing was an accident resulting from Boyd's intervention. After they discovered she was dead they decided to kill Fernandes as well because it was too dangerous to leave him alive. But they weren't interested in him.'

'I don't understand what Lauren could have had in her possession that would have been of interest to French crooks.'

'Nothing. They were working for others. Boyd believed the answer to it all lay in the visit of the two Americans. They sent the thugs. I have no idea what was so important to them. But you'll remember that Sally Kirkwood told me she believed that something happened when Lauren visited the States in the summer that was linked with her decision to go away with Fernandes.'

Rylance went to replenish his glass. It was plain he still had difficulty grappling with Boyd's story. When he came back he said, 'Are you quite sure that Boyd isn't fantasizing? He's a thriller writer, you say. He probably lives in his imagination.'

'I learned some things this morning that persuade me he

173

could be on the right track. I may be able to discover more in a day or two. What I'd like next is to find out what the French police *really* think happened. After all, Boyd identified one of the thugs for them.'

'Is it possible to get at that?'

'I'm not sure. But there's someone in the Sûreté in Paris who's been very helpful to me in the past and may have friends in police headquarters in Nice. I'd ask his assistance, off the record of course. But I'd need my Director's approval to approach him.'

He stopped short of saying that it would also call for a request from Rylance himself. Rylance was swirling the brandy in his glass. 'What does your Director think of Boyd's story?'

'I haven't told him yet. He's away in Scotland until Monday.'

'Do you want me to speak to him?'

'That would be helpful.'

Rylance looked at his wristwatch and stood up. 'All right, I'm grateful for what you've told me. Of course I shall want to pursue this. If you get any more information from the enquiries you've already made before Monday, please telephone me. I shall need to know at once.' He was being Ministerial again.

On the way down to the hall, Egerton said, 'Did your wife happen to speak to Mr Giordano when you heard the news I'd found Lauren?'

Rylance paused, frowning. 'I don't —no, wait, I believe she may have done. He'd been in touch with her earlier about your call on him when he was staying at Claridges.' He opened the street door and gave a faint smile. 'You're not suggesting that Sam Giordano might have been one of Lauren's mysterious American visitors, I hope.' His arm was up, signalling to the driver of his official car.

It seemed for a moment he might have to admit he *was* suggesting it. But the manservant came hurrying across the hall with a message and Rylance turned away.

# XVII

AFTERWARDS he pinpointed the beginning of the sense of unease, the premonition that the ground was about to shift remorselessly beneath his feet, as coinciding with the arrival of the letter from Boyd. Postmarked Nice, it was written in a neat italic hand that seemed at odds with the ungainly figure who had greeted him in Fernandes' apartment and later at the house in Epping. He read it with his breakfast coffee.

Dear Egerton,
   When you gave me your address in case I had further thoughts about the ghastly business next door, I didn't think I'd have occasion to use it. But within a day of arriving back here, I had a visit from a curious little party. Two were Basques, the third could have been French, perhaps local, although since he insisted on speaking English throughout, I wasn't sure.
   They announced themselves as friends of Luis Fernandes and said they were enquiring into the circumstances of his death on behalf of his family. I told them the story I told you. They'd picked up quite a bit of it already — the non-Basque had some private line into police headquarters.
   Their chief concern was to discover if I could amplify what I'd said about Lauren's American visitors; they seemed to have all they needed about the two thugs who were responsible for the killings. I said that I had no idea who the Americans were or what they'd been after, but I'd gained the impression that

you might know more. They asked how they could contact you.

So this note is simply to say that they (or some London friends of theirs) may pay you a call. I don't imagine they'll give you any trouble—they were extremely courteous in a stolid sort of way. They just want to get to the bottom of what happened and why. In view of the refusal of the police to bother about the underlying facts, I can't say I blame them.

Sincerely,<br>
Arthur Boyd

A perfectly civil letter; but the touch of malice didn't escape him. Boyd had enjoyed handing over his name and address and suggesting his visitors applied there for further information. Egerton's lack of frankness had got to Boyd more than he had shown. When he had spoken vaguely of being employed by Lauren's family Boyd had pretended a lack of any further interest. In reality he had been piqued at not being let in on Egerton's speculations about who the Americans might have been. Now he was relishing the thought of Fernandes' friends putting Egerton through what might be some awkward hoops.

It might have been the unease prompted by the letter that made him suspect he was once more being shadowed when he returned to Prince of Wales Drive from the Bureau in the evening. He spent time looking down from his window, without the light on, for anyone loitering outside. A car with two occupants parked a few yards further up towards Albert Bridge engaged his attention for several minutes before he identified it as belonging to people in the adjoining block.

The hospital call drove the thoughts from his mind. The voice was female and very business-like; she made him repeat his name before she opened up.

'Mr Egerton, we have a patient who has asked you should be told she's here. A Miss Gail Henderson.'

His mouth became as dry as parchment.

'You *are* a close friend . . .?'

'Yes. Has she been in an accident?'

The woman appeared not to hear him. 'She tells us she has no near relatives.' She was waiting to see if he would contradict that.

'Is she very ill?'

'Not now. She's had a lucky escape. If she's—' she paused fractionally'—sensible from now on, she'll be all right. After treatment.'

'It was an overdose, was it?'

Once again she rode over the words as though oblivious to them. 'She should be well enough to be discharged for the weekend. We understand she has no regular doctor we can inform. She ought of course to attend an addiction clinic. I hope you'll be able to persuade her to do that. Meanwhile she must be in someone's care.'

'I'll accept responsibility of course.'

'She will be given a small supply of tablets when she leaves. Taken regularly they should alleviate the addiction symptoms for a few days. But they are *not* a substitute for treatment.'

'I understand.'

The voice became a little warmer. 'Good. Perhaps you'd visit her tomorrow between two o'clock and four. I'd like you to call in at sister's office beforehand.'

'Can't I come sooner?'

'No, tomorrow will be best. We can then make arrangements with you for her discharge the following day.'

At the office next morning, he went in search of Antonia only to be told she was away until the afternoon. When she was still not back at two o'clock, he scribbled her a note and left for the hospital.

Now the suspicion that he once more had someone following him returned more solidly. Glancing from the upper deck of his bus as it pulled away down Baker Street, he glimpsed the face of a man he felt sure he had seen as he returned to Prince of Wales Drive the previous evening. The man had stepped forward from behind a queue waiting for another bus and hailed a taxi.

When he left the bus in the Fulham Road, he waited for a few seconds, watching to see if a taxi was slowing down. There was no sign of one. He walked back to where an oil tanker was blocking traffic. An empty taxi was beginning to manoeuvre round the tanker. If the man had been inside it, he had had time to slip into one of the nearby shops.

He bought chrysanthemums and made his way into the hospital. His mouth was dry again. But she looked better than he had feared. Sitting in an armchair at the end of the ward, wrapped in a hospital dressing gown, she gave her boxer's salute of triumph as he recognized her. Her hair had been freshly washed and there was colour in her cheeks; only their hollowness seemed sinister.

He sat down beside her. 'Sorry about this,' she said.

He took one of her hands in his. 'Why didn't you send me a message before?'

She shrugged apologetically.

'Do you know how you got here?'

'Jamie brought me.'

Somehow, it was the last answer he had expected.

'The Indian who owns the house found I'd flopped on the bathroom floor. He telephoned Jamie.'

It still didn't make much sense. 'He had Jamie's number?'

'Jamie had told him when he found me the room that he was to ring if I was ill or anything.'

Jamie, the Good Samaritan, he thought ironically: if you need hospitalizing, leave it to me to get you there, it's all part of the service.

'I still can't understand why one of you didn't tell *me*.'

'I made Jamie promise not to. I didn't want you to see me until I was better. At least until I wasn't quite such a mess.'

He glanced down at the hand he was holding. The finger nails seemed to have been bitten back more than ever. 'You *are* going to stop now, aren't you?'

She was chewing her lip.

'Yes, *yes*, YES!' he said.

178

'How?'

'We'll get you back to the place in Devon. . .'

'Maybe they won't take me again because I ducked out before.'

'They will, I'll talk to them.'

She was shaking her head. 'You have to stay at least six weeks. It would cost hundreds, thousands. I can't go to Ma or Leo for the money, after what happened last time.'

'You don't have to worry. I can find it.'

She gazed at him doubtfully but didn't ask how. That was fortunate since for the moment he had no idea.

'Why should you?'

'Because I want to.'

She said. 'I began to think about stopping while you were in Majorca, about managing it on my own. I had the idea of going to live somewhere in the country, a long way from London where I wouldn't know anybody. Plenty of people, after all, just take a decision to stop. Why shouldn't I? Then the chance of the trip to Barbados came up. I thought, well, afterwards.' She looked away. 'Stupid of course.'

'Forget about that. Think about the treatment. When it's over you'll come back to my flat. We'll keep each other in a state of grace.'

She smiled wanly. He could tell the concept remained unreal to her; but he had to get her started. 'Anyhow, we're going away for the weekend, so that we can talk it through properly.'

She was beginning to look tired; her nod was the slightest of movements. He leaned closer. 'You tried to telephone me while I was away. What was it about?'

Her eyes were on his hands still holding one of hers; she placed her free hand over them. 'I wanted you to tell me not to go on the party. I knew what it would be like of course. I oughtn't to have gone. But you weren't there.'

He was afraid she was going to fall apart in front of him. He turned and held her by the shoulders until she looked into his eyes. 'I love you,' he said. 'You're going to kick the thing for your own sake. But you're also going to do it for

179

me.' He was trapping himself he knew: there'd be no escape. But the idea of escape was absurd anyway, because he had never been able to stop loving her. Now there was no longer Julian between them, the thought of losing her again was unendurable.

Outside the hospital he told a cab to take him to Jamie's address. Occasionally he looked through the rear window to see if another cab was following but saw nothing.

Jamie's apartment was in a mansion block in Portland Place. A superior sort of concierge in a black coat sat in the entrance hall with a bowl of flowers and a telephone. His name had to be telephoned through to Jamie before he was allowed into the lift.

Jamie was buttoning on a shirt as he opened the door.

'Mark.' He showed absolutely no surprise at the call, just polite pleasure. 'Come and see this pad, it's really rather grand.'

They entered a vast room that had drapes for curtains, swagged and splendid; behind the drapes security grilles dense enough to dishearten flies had been fitted across the windows. The furniture was ornate and highly polished. Here and there, suspiciously pale-looking busts in the Roman style stared out from half-moon tables of florid marble. It was as though a dealer in fake antiques had supplied a job lot. But perhaps they were actually genuine. 'You own all this stuff?' he asked.

'Yes, I bought it from the Lebanese who sold me the flat. He was leaving the country rather quickly for reasons not disclosed and wanted to get rid of everything. So I took it.' He waved an arm casually. But he was quite proud in an amused way.

A bronze and procelain clock had announced it was a quarter to five. If he was going to be back in the Bureau in time to catch Antonia, he needed to hurry. 'I've been to see Gail in hospital. I wish you'd called me.'

'I tried. There was no reply from your number the night I took her in. I remembered you'd said you were going abroad and I thought you might still be away. When I saw

180

her the next day, she made me promise not to contact you. She said she wanted to do it herself. How is she?'

'They've decided to discharge her tomorrow. I'm taking her to the country for the weekend. She's more or less agreed to go back to the place in Devon for treatment.' He hesitated. 'Do you believe she O.D.d deliberately?'

'I don't know.'

'I *have* to make her stop this time. If she ever contacts you for more stuff, you've got to say "no". Whatever she says or does, never supply any more.'

Jamie slightly changed the position of a cigarette box on the table between them. After a while he said, 'All right.'

'Jamie, if you supplied her just once more, I think I might kill you.'

He smiled. 'I said—All right.'

'I also need some help. The treatment is going to cost. You know she hasn't got the money. Neither have I. I want to borrow it from you. In the New Year I get an increase in pay—I'll start paying you back then. But I want a few hundred now and a lot more later.'

He had been prepared for hesitation, perhaps a polite enquiry about the amount of the pay increase. He watched Jamie go to a drawer and open it. When he came back he counted out five hundred in twenties.

'If you come back on Monday I can let you have more. But make it before one thirty because I'm due to take a plane trip in the afternoon.' He brushed aside thanks.

He walked Egerton down to the entrance in Portland Place and asked the black coat to find a cab. On the way out of the apartment Egerton had heard the noise of water running. Somebody in a room off the hall was taking a bath or a shower. He wondered if Jamie had been dressing, not just changing his shirt when he opened the door to admit him. He had walked past the room without giving a sign that he was conscious of the sounds. Like so many other things in his life, they remained unacknowledged. Behind that door could have been a girl, a piece of rough trade or even some innocent cousin from Glasgow, up on an Away-

Day to goggle at the apartment and return with a tale of wonder. All seemed equally likely.

Back at the Bureau, he went to Antonia's room. He stopped to listen for a moment in case she had somebody with her. There was no sound. It crossed his mind that she might still be out but the door was unlocked when he tried the handle.

She sat smoking a cigarette and staring through the window at the darkness. None of the files on her desk was open. When she glanced over her shoulder, he wasn't sure she was recognizing him since the only light was from her desk lamp.

'Sorry, am I disturbing you?'

She stubbed the cigarette out and turned back abruptly from the window. 'No. I was just reflecting I ate far too much lunch. A man in the Canadian Embassy took me to the Savoy. We have a mutual friend in Alberta.'

He sat down. 'You know Canada . . .?'

'Not really. I went there on a case with Ludo Fender who used to be an Assistant Director here until he retired. The RCMP man who helped us resigned a while ago to run a farm. He's the mutual friend.'

She gazed at the heading on the file that was uppermost in her tray but he could see she wasn't reading it. 'Have you heard of the pika rabbit?'

'No.'

'When the sun shines in Alberta, the pika rabbit cuts all the grass he needs for winter and lays it out to dry. Then he goes away. You might think he'd forgotten it. But he's always back before the weather breaks to get the grass under cover. That's the extent of my knowledge about the pika rabbit.'

She sat back with an exaggeratedly relaxed gesture, saying, 'Well . . .' There was more to it than pika rabbits, he thought, but he was never likely to be told. 'By the way,' she said, 'I heard over at the Yard today that Clayton, the head of the Serious Crimes Squad, finds you quite acceptable, considering you're a member of this department. I didn't know you had dealings with the Great Spotted Clayton.'

He cleared his throat. 'I have a confession to offer.'

He told her about his calls to Giordano's personal assistant, Mary Jane Cord and to Clayton. At the end she looked less frosty than he had expected. 'How did you get Clayton to agree to put questions to the FBI for you?'

'He owed me a favour. A lead in one of his cases that I picked up by accident and passed on through Baxter may turn out to provide the solution.'

She weighed up the new facts. 'So you know it was Giordano you saw at Nice airport and that he stayed with a local crook over the period when Lauren and Fernandes were killed.'

'Not just any old crook—a big fish who belonged to the Mafia in America and still has drugs and gambling operations running.'

She acknowledged herself impressed. 'What do you want to do?'

'If Antrim will agree when he gets back from Scotland on Monday, I want to ask Pasquier of the Sûreté if *he* can help—off the record. He may have a friend in police headquarters in Nice, someone who will come up with what they really suspect or know, about the murders.'

She looked at him with an amused expression. 'Don't you think you should be waiting for Rylance to ask for that?'

'He more or less has done. He's going to speak to Antrim.'

She nodded in a resigned way. Before she could pick up a file again, he said. 'I'm afraid I've also come to bore you with my private affairs again.'

He told her about his visit to Gail. 'I want to take her away for the weekend somewhere quiet. She has to decide—really commit herself this time—to go through with the treatment. I wondered if I could take up the offer of your mother's house? I guarantee to be back early on Monday morning.'

She made a knot in her handkerchief. 'I'll bring the keys

183

tomorrow.' As he was going out of the door she said. 'You think she does *want* to give it up this time?'

'Yes.'

'I hope you win.'

'I have to.' She knew enough now, he thought, about the way he felt, for him not to have to explain that.

Buying provisions the following lunch time to take down to the house, he again had the feeling that he was being watched. Once he turned sharply to confront a woman, small and mousy, carrying a plastic shopping bag as her badge of innocence; but her expression of bemused alarm convinced him he had made a mistake. In the evening, on his way home to Battersea, with paranoia beginning to grip again, he spent time doubling back on his tracks and waiting at corners to see if he would recognize a face.

When he started out again with a weekend bag to collect Gail from hospital, Gwen had appeared in the lobby to bend over her array of plants. She had on her lurking look.

'Going away?'

'Just for the weekend.'

'Your sister again?'

'Not this time. Somewhere in Shropshire.'

'There are storms coming from the west according to the radio forecast. I hope they won't get as far as where I'm going.'

He registered that she was prompting a question from him; moreover he now realized she was dressed for something more special than bingo. 'Where's that?'

'Portugal. It's a five day package. We're leaving tonight.'

The fireman again, he supposed: romance was gathering pace in her life. He tried to see if she was still wearing the wedding ring from the master mariner who had gone down with his ship off Land's End, but her watering can was in the way.

'Have a good time,' he told her. He had almost escaped when she said, 'You had an odd sort of visitor today.'

'How odd?'

'I heard a noise and opened the door. He was standing here in the lobby near to your flat. For a moment I thought

184

he'd come out of it. He said he was calling on behalf of the First Church of the Holy Crucifixion. There were some pamphlets in his hand but he didn't try to give me one.'

He put down the bag. 'Do you think he was a thief?'

'I did feel rather suspicious. He went off in such a hurry.'

He went to look at the lock on his door. There was no sign of forcing. Inside, with Gwen twittering at his heels, he checked the places that mattered. Nothing seemed to have been disturbed. In the lobby again, he examined the door jamb. Now he could almost persuade himself there were scratches on the paint where plastic card had been slipped in to tease back the catch.

There was no way of being certain. The man might after all have been genuinely hawking religious pamphlets. On the other hand it would have been natural for him to try Gwen first. 'You're sure he hadn't rung your bell or knocked on the door . . .'

'I'm positive.'

He looked at his watch. It was already twenty minutes past the time he had promised to be at the hospital. Before they could start the drive to Shropshire he had to take Gail to her own place to collect clothes. He picked up his bag again but as he did so he began to register that Gwen had been saying something important. 'You got what?'

'His number. When he left, I thought, well, just in case . . . so I watched from the window. He went to a yellow car across the road. I took down the registration number.'

There was no doubt, she would have made a marvellous concierge. 'Could I have it?'

She fetched the pools coupon envelope on which it had been scribbled. 'What was he like?' he asked as he slipped it into his notecase.

'Dark, medium height, ordinary sort of suit. He had a cockney accent. And bad breath.'

He shook his head. 'You've missed your vocation, Gwen. Why aren't you in the police? Or MI5?'

She smiled up at him, pink with delight. 'My late husband always said that.'

# XVIII

WAKING and going to the window, he found a garden alight with gold. Either Gwen had misheard the forecast or the weather men had got it wrong again. An Indian summer had arrived. Bees moved lazily amongst the flowers beneath as though they had all the time in the world.

He and Gail had entered the house in darkness, stumbling about in search of switches and taps specified in Antonia's note. As they drank coffee beside an ancient electric fire, they had occasionally glanced at the night through the open curtains and wondered what it held. The house, creaking in its shadowed corners, had seemed like a third presence; they had found themselves talking in low voices as though they might disturb it. When Gail had fallen asleep, almost in the middle of a sentence, he had carried her to the room where they had earlier made up their bed. She had lain with her head pressed against his cheek, fingers gripping his and tightening when he moved, as if, even in sleep, she feared he or she would float away.

He made tea and toast only to discover they had forgotten to bring butter with them. When he took a tray to her, she was gazing drowsily at the ceiling. He sat on the bed. 'I'm driving into Ludlow to buy one or two things. Sorry there's only dry toast. Will you be all right?'

She nodded. There was no trace of tension, she seemed completely relaxed. Going downstairs again and seeing her handbag on the floor where she had left it beside the fire, he told himself he needn't look, then changed his mind.

186

Apart from make up and the usual oddments, it yielded only the pills the hospital had given her. He had zipped it up and was returning it to the carpet when his fingers detected an unevenness in one corner. Fishing with her nail file at the gap behind the end of the zip, he located the package in the lining and knew he had been right to check. There was enough in the package for three, perhaps four, fixes. He flushed it down the lavatory in the lobby and went out of the house.

When he returned with butter, newspapers and a bottle of wine, she was dressed. Beside the chair in which she sat was a vase of dahlias she had gathered from the garden. The handbag hadn't been moved. He kissed her. 'How do you feel?'

'Super.'

'Honestly?'

'Honestly.' She seemed to mean it.

They were standing side by side in the kitchen, making a salad for lunch when she began to talk about the overdose. 'Did you wonder if I did it on purpose?'

'It crossed my mind.'

'I didn't. I was just being terribly careless.'

He felt like telling her that it could sometimes amount to the same thing. 'It occurred to me that something might have gone wrong in Barbados.'

'What sort of thing?'

He shrugged. 'Somebody you met . . . perhaps didn't match up. That sort of thing.'

She was smiling as she sliced the beetroot. 'You're mad. Why would I want anyone else to match up?'

They took lunch and the newspapers to the pear tree that grew outside the kitchen window; in the garage Egerton had located canvas chairs, cobwebbed but sound. When they had eaten, she handed him *The Times* while she flipped through the *Globe*. Apart from a chain saw that whined occasionally in the distance there was absolute silence. When he reached forward to brush a wasp away from her, she took his hand and slowly kissed the palm.

187

Finally she tired of reading. Dropping the paper on the grass beside her, she yawned and lay back to study the fruit above their heads. 'Your rival for the blonde you were eyeing the other night seems to have made the big time. She'll never look at you now.'

She had to explain before he realized she was talking about Camilla's companion at Dido's, Simon Bowe, 'What's happened to him?'

'He's been appointed the *Globe*'s gossip columnist. It's a plum job.'

'Isn't that a rather meteoric rise? You said he was just a writer on one of the give-away magazines.'

'So he was.'

He picked up the newspaper she had dropped. There was a box on the right-hand side of the front page in which the news was announced. Bowe was described as the man to whom all doors were open. He frowned then shook his head slowly. Suddenly he could see Camilla in a new light; himself too.

'What's wrong?' she asked.

'I think I know how one of the doors they mention happens to open.'

She grinned. She had guessed he was referring to Camilla, but not in the way he meant. If she knew how big a fool he'd made of himself, she might not think it was so funny.

The evening brought a telephone call from Antonia. She asked how they were surviving. 'Fine,' he said.

London had been like an oven, she told him. She was off to the theatre and then to supper with a friend, sex undisclosed. He wished her a pleasant evening. 'Are you winning?' she asked.

From where he stood in the hall, he could see into the kitchen. Gail was unwrapping the pasta they had brought from London. If he was going to be strictly honest he would have to admit he wasn't yet sure. 'We're going to talk later.'

'Don't let her fudge it.' There was that familiar crispness in her tone; he sensed an implication she perhaps wondered whether he was just messing about. The message was that he wasn't there to enjoy himself.

Back in the kitchen, Gail asked him who had called. 'Antonia Strachan. She wondered how things were.'

'Is she your actual boss in the Bureau?'

'I work to her, yes.'

'Efficient?'

'Yes.'

'Attractive?'

'Very.'

She dropped the pasta into the boiling water. He stood beside her and watched it uncurl. One of her hands reached out to his. It was trembling a little. He wondered if she was beginning to get the shakes.

'Have you remembered to take those tablets?' he asked.

She nodded. 'What were you saying to her you thought would be all right?'

He decided he might as well be frank. 'She knows why we came. I said we were going to talk about the treatment this weekend.'

She was silent.

'Perhaps we don't need to,' he said. 'Shall we just ring the clinic in the morning and fix when you arrive?'

She was still looking at the pasta in the saucepan. 'I haven't changed my mind, if that's what you're asking. I mean to stop. For ever. Do you believe that?'

'Yes.'

'There's just something I have to know, beforehand. To stop me making a fool of myself. Are we together now? I mean, *really* together? If I do beat it, is that what *you* want?'

He knew and supposed she did too, that at the end of it all, the struggle might have changed her so much, their relationship would simply crumble whatever they might now say or want. But the chance had to be taken.

He said, 'You know I love you, that I've always loved you.'

She was trying not to weep. He shook his head at her until she smiled. 'So it's settled.'

But she went on, 'One more thing. I'd rather you didn't come to see me while I'm there. I've got to do it on my own. I want to feel I can reach you on the phone but not to have you visiting and then going away again. I want to wait for afterwards.'

When he tried to argue her out of it, she proved immovable. Finally he gave up. 'You don't have to worry.' she said.

Sunday dawned better than ever. They took their breakfast rolls and coffee into the garden and had pears plucked from above their heads as starters. Afterwards he telephoned the clinic and fixed her arrival for the Monday. She refused to let him drive her down so it was arranged that she would go by train from Paddington. Once the call was over she seemed totally relaxed again. There had been no return of the shakes he thought he had noticed the previous evening. As he watched her energy awaken, the thought that perhaps she had managed to hide some stuff on their arrival and had been using it in the bathroom briefly numbed his happiness. But he decided that he had watched her too closely for that to have happened.

They walked in the woods that stretched to the south of the garden. She made him tell her every detail of how he had felt in the clinic in New York. She was like an explorer about to embark on an expedition, determined to find out about the terrain from someone who had gone before.

They made love in a birch grove where old leaves rustled beneath them and this year's were still up there, dancing in the sunlight. Watching through the branches the occasional wisp of cloud, he was conscious that, impatiently as he awaited the coming days, he also wanted to hold them back.

When, after the drive to London through a cloudless dawn, he put her on the train at Paddington the tension was back in her features and she was sweating a little. Most of it could have been simple foreboding at what lay ahead but he wished he was going with her. They agreed that she

190

would be the first to telephone. As the train began to move he said through the open window, 'Remember, it's Us now.'

He had half-resigned himself to driving straight from the station to Somerset Square and pleading for a space in the office garage. But it was barely ten to nine as he turned into the Bayswater Road. He decided that he had time to call at his flat, change into a clean shirt and pick up a bus.

He slotted the Mini into a space on the park side of Prince of Wales Drive. Reaching out his overnight bag, he saw a familiar figure step from a Rover parked at the entrance to his apartment block and lift an arm in greeting. After a few seconds he realized who it was: Newth, one of Mansell's people. It was to Newth he had been handed over on his first day in the Bureau, immediately after receiving Antrim's benediction. Newth had given him the Official Secrets form to sign and a card with security classifications printed on it which he was to stand on his desk. I'm your man, Newth had said, a little too breezily, if you have any problems: how to handle the press if they get through direct to you about a case, obtaining passes for other Departments, things like that; oh, and details of the squash club in the basement. I expect we'll meet a good deal. Then Newth had vanished, to be glimpsed again only in a cluster of others from Mansell's division at the bar or in the canteen. Personnel people move in packs to avoid being waylaid, older hands had told him. Best left alone. Never call them, let them call you.

'Hullo, Egerton,' Newth said. His greeting was still breezy but lacked the warmth of that first day. 'We thought you'd probably call back to dump the car.'

The shape of another person was dimly visible in the back of the Rover.

'Nice weekend?'

'Yes, thanks.'

'We'll give you a lift.'

He raised his eyebrows. 'Were you waiting for me?

'Yes.'

'Something up?'

'A tiny crisis.'

'I see.' Egerton looked at his watch. 'If you'll give me five minutes, I'm going to change into a clean shirt.'

Newth was shaking his head jovially. 'Mansell would rather you came straight away. A few problems to be sorted.'

Anxiety had started to seep into his stomach. 'What sort of problems?'

'I'd better leave it to Mansell to explain if you don't mind.' Newth reached out and took the overnight bag. 'Let me put this in the boot for you.'

Climbing into the Rover, Egerton recognized the figure in the back seat as another of Mansell's acolytes. They exchanged nods; then the other looked away, to study a perfectly ordinary privet hedge.

As they swung into the traffic approaching Chelsea Bridge, Newth nodded towards the east. There was the sun, an orange ball, riding up the river to zap the autumn mist; already the Thames had a glassy sheen.

'Look at that sun,' Newth said, 'It's going to be really hot today.'

It seemed the most ominous remark yet.

# XIX

A cardboard box lay on Mansell's blotting pad. It contained what looked like the whole contents of the desk in Egerton's flat: letters, bills, old diaries, even some cuff-links he'd mislaid. He stared at Mansell; apprehension gave way to anger. 'Why has my flat been searched?'

Mansell said carefully, 'It was a decision of the Director's. He concluded that in view of the information he had received, there was no alternative.'

'Were the police involved?'

'No.'

'So there was no search warrant . . .'

'No.'

'I understand that's illegal.'

'Would you rather the police *had* been brought in?' Mansell raised his eyebrows; he seemed entirely confident of what, on reflection, Egerton's answer would be.

'I'd like an explanation.'

Mansell slid two fingers under a folder that lay on his desk alongside the box. They reappeared with a photograph, postcard size. 'On his return from Scotland on Saturday morning, the Director found that an envelope containing this photograph had been delivered for him at his flat by someone who left no name. It shows you standing at the entrance to a block of flats in Portland Place and talking to a man. On the back has been pasted a typewritten note, unsigned, which says that if the head of the Metropolitan Police Drugs Squad is consulted, he will provide interesting information about the identity of this man. The note also says that even more interesting information will be obtained if a thorough search of your flat is made.'

Mansell held the photograph in front of Egerton. It showed Jamie standing beside him, with his hand on his arm; it must have been taken the afternoon Egerton had gone to Portland Place from seeing Gail in hospital.

Mansell said, 'The Director telephoned me. I collected the photograph and saw Lancaster of the Drugs Squad at his home during the afternoon. He said that he recognized the man with you as James Hendry Buchanan, a known dealer in heroin since coming down from Oxford a few years back. The Drugs Squad have been anxious to move against him for some time. Apparently they've had problems in establishing his sources of supply.'

He put the photograph down and sat back. 'In the circumstances you don't presumably feel too much surprise at the Director's decision.'

'My going to see Buchanan had nothing to do with *getting* drugs.'

'Why *did* you go?'

'I'd been to visit a friend in hospital. She was recovering from a heroin overdose. Buchanan was her supplier. She'd decided to give it up. I went to Buchanan and told him that. Also, if she asked him for more, not to supply her. He agreed.'

'Why should he be concerned with your wishes?'

'We were friends at Oxford, I know him very well. If he gives a promise he keeps it.'

'And the friend in hospital—did you also know her at Oxford?'

'Yes.'

'May I know her name?'

'Gail Henderson.'

'A close friend?'

'I'm very fond of her.'

'She's visited you at your flat I suppose . . .?'

'Once or twice.'

'Did you use heroin there with her?'

'No.'

'You never touch it . . .?'

His throat felt very dry; but at least the facts were going to be out in the open at last. 'I took it at one time. But I stopped. That happened before I came to the Bureau. I've never taken it since.'

'Why didn't you tell us any of this when you joined?'

'I wasn't asked.'

'Don't you think you should have disclosed the fact before now?'

'Perhaps it would have been better in view of what's happened. But it was all in the past. As I said, I don't touch heroin or any other drugs now.'

Mansell was tapping two fingers on the photograph; he seemed to be thinking. Egerton said, 'If you doubt it, you can have me medically examined. I'm willing to—'

'An examination wouldn't necessarily show you weren't still using heroin—by inhaling for example.'

'If I were, why haven't you found traces in my flat? Why hasn't Newth found any in my overnight bag which he so considerately took charge of? If you're still not convinced, perhaps you'd like to have my clothing searched?'

He silently thanked his stars that he'd had the sense to flush away the heroin as soon as he'd found it in the lining of Gail's handbag. Yet suddenly a premonition was upon him that something ghastly lay ahead. Mansell's fingers had reached under the file again. When they reappeared, they were holding a plastic packet.

'Perhaps you could explain why this was on the top of the wall cabinet in your bathroom?'

He made himself take the packet from Mansell. He wet his finger and tasted the powder inside.

'You agree that is heroin?'

He nodded, sick in the pit of his stomach. There was only one explanation: Gail had left it the morning she and Jamie had stayed behind in the flat while he went to report to Antrim. Although he had asked Jamie not to let her fix there, he had let him down. They had both let him down. Presumably she had placed the packet on the cabinet while she did it and then forgotten. If she'd remembered the next day, he would already have been on his way to Majorca.

'How do you account for it?' Mansell asked.

'I've never seen that before.'

'You mean it isn't yours?'

'Yes.'

'Then who does it belong to—Miss Henderson?'

If he said it did, he couldn't be hurting her; and no doubt she'd back him up if Mansell wanted corroboration. But, something was making him pause. He stared at the packet, frowned and tasted the powder again.

Mansell said, 'Are you going to say it's not heroin after all?'

'No.'

'Then what?'

Nothing made sense any more. 'I just don't have an explanation at present.'

Mansell sighed heavily. 'Well, if you don't wish to say more . . .' He scotchtaped the packet, placed it in a drawer of his desk then locked the drawer. 'I have to tell you that the Director, after hearing the results of the search at your flat, decided to suspend you while a full report was prepared for him, incorporating any statement you wished to make. If you want to add to what you have said I advise you to let me have your submission in writing in the course of the week. Meanwhile I suggest you go back to your flat and think things over. I shall arrange for these articles—' he placed his hand on the cardboard box '—to be returned very shortly.'

Mansell's voice had begun to sound remote. Egerton stood up. 'I want to repeat that the heroin isn't mine, that I haven't used drugs since I joined the Bureau and that I'm very opposed to anyone else using them. Miss Henderson will confirm that's my attitude. And if you want the address of the American clinic where I was treated and the name of the doctor who discharged me, you can have the details any time you like.'

Mansell said nothing, simply looked uncomfortable. It did, after all, sound pretty pathetic.

The secretary smiled at him charitably as he emerged from Mansell's office. His overnight bag was beside her desk, having presumably been parked there by Newth after his prying fingers had turned everything inside out. She handed the bag to him. The gesture had a symbolic flavour. There wasn't much doubt what would now happen: he was going to be sacked. On what they had, he could hardly blame them. The next few days would be spent assembling a formal case on which to justify the action in case, later on, he tried to make waves through an MP or a newspaper.

In the corridor he saw Antrim's driver waiting for the lift that went express to the Director's lair. The driver was carrying a brace of grouse, no doubt part of the dividend from Antrim's visit to Scotland. Until a short while ago, he had supposed that, about now, he would be taking that lift himself, en route to seek Antrim's agreement to his asking Pasquier for help in discovering what the police in Nice really believed about the killings of Lauren and Fernandes. Already the idea had become unreal.

He went in search of Antonia to tell her what had happened. Nobody knew where she was; her secretary thought she might have called in at the Yard on her way to the office. He waited about for a while, then gave up and handed the Beynon files back once more to the secretary. Mansell would presumably tell her soon enough that her establishment had gone down by one, this time permanently.

Walking out into the sunshine in Somerset Square, he crossed to the central gardens and sat on a bench hidden from any curious eyes that might be watching from the Bureau's windows. He was the only person in the gardens. Above him the sky was almost hidden by arches of gold and bronze formed from the foliage of chestnut trees. At about this time yesterday he had gazed upwards to find the sky through the dappled shade of a Shropshire wood. He had made love to Gail and begun to feel that life at last held meaning and the hope of joy. Now everything was about to fall apart. A terrible lassitude crept upon him. Somehow he had to fight it: if this was the finish for him in the Bureau, the sooner he started combing the Situations Vacant columns in *The Times* and the *Telegraph*, the better.

But something even more immediate demanded attention—the plastic packet Mansell had conjured from under his file. Perhaps it really *had* belonged to Gail. Yet he couldn't believe it. The taste and colour had been all wrong for pure heroin, the contents had been cut with coffee powder to provide a cheap sell on the streets. The idea of Jamie supplying Gail with that was nonsense. Nor would she have cut the stuff herself.

He looked at his watch. Jamie had asked him to call not later than one thirty to collect the rest of the cash he was borrowing. After that, he would have to pay it into his bank before he sent off the further cheque he had promised the clinic would be in the post that night. He went to catch a bus to Portland Place.

Jamie was dressed in a dark grey suit and his college tie; on a chair in the hall of the apartment was a Gucci bag already packed. Wherever he was going, a vaguely merchant banker look had been thought to match the occasion.

They were in the drawing room. It looked more than ever like a dubious antique dealer's set-up. Jamie took an envelope out of the desk. 'Two thousand in twenties. That all right?'

'It's going to be a while before I repay it.'

He was waving a hand. 'I'm not worried.' He watched Egerton put the envelope inside his breast pocket. 'Has she started the treatment?'

'This morning.'

'Did you drive her down?'

'No, she went by train.'

A politeness had descended upon them. Egerton gazed at a Roman bust. 'Tell me something. Has she ever to your knowledge used Chinese?'

Jamie looked surprised. 'I can't say what happened when Julian was alive. But she's never had Chinese from me.'

'The morning I left you both in my flat, did she fix?'

'No.'

'You're sure?'

'Pretty sure. Why do you ask?'

He shook his head. 'Something odd has occurred. I can't understand it at the moment.' He didn't feel like telling Jamie what had happened to him. He walked back into the hall. 'How long are you away for?'

'Difficult to say. The people I do business with are a bit unreliable about exact dates and times of appointments. Could be a week.'

At the far end of the hall, a middle-aged woman appeared briefly, passing from one room to another. 'Mother,' Jamie said, following Egerton's glance. 'Come to hold the fort while I'm away.' It could have meant anything from keeping an eye on the furnishings to handing over small packets in discreet corners of bars; but even Jamie would surely not have got Mother into dealing. If it *was* Mother.

He was almost through the door into the corridor outside when he knew he couldn't just leave without a word of warning. 'Perhaps you should stay away longer.'

Jamie raised his eyebrows. 'Really?'

He nodded.

'Would that be . . . advice?'

'I'm just saying . . . think about it.'

Jamie closed the door again. He smiled. 'Have you heard something?'

'No. But you can't go on with this for ever—they'll get you sooner or later. It could be sooner.'

'Ah,' he said. 'Well, I suppose so.' He was still smiling. 'But I take precautions you know. Someone does quite well out of making sure I don't have an unpleasant surprise early one morning. It's one of those tiresome business expenses.'

'Whoever it is could still let you down.'

'He could. But he won't. You have to trust people.' He was completely relaxed.

The phone was ringing as he put the key in the door of his own flat. It was Antonia. 'You've heard,' he said.

'I had a message from Newth. I've been trying to get you ever since. Where have you been?'

'I had things to tie up. I'm sorry I missed you this morning—you weren't around when I left.' Before she could speak again, he went on, 'I want you to know that I've not misled you on anything. Anything.'

She was silent.

'I suppose Newth told you about the heroin . . .'

'Yes.'

'It wasn't mine, I knew nothing about it. At first I assumed it must have been left by Gail. But it was Chinese heroin—it wasn't pure, it had been cut with something else. The person who was supplying Gail gave her only pure heroin. I checked that this morning.'

'But if *she* didn't leave it in your bathroom, who did?'

'It must have been planted. My neighbour found a man in the lobby outside our two flats on Friday. She thought he might have come out of mine. I'm convinced now there's a connection with my being followed again towards the end of last week.'

'Have you told Mansell this?'

'No, I wasn't certain until after I'd left him. But even if he believed me, I'm not sure it would make that much difference now. The fact I never volunteered that I was once on heroin is going to be treated as sufficient reason by itself for applying the chop.'

'You volunteered it to *me*. Didn't you tell Mansell that?'

'No.'

'Why not?'

He hesitated. 'I didn't want to drag you into it. Anyway

200

they might have taken a poor view of the fact that you hadn't passed it on.'

Her voice became decidedly cool. 'Just leave me to look after myself. I've been waiting to see Mansell to get all the facts but he's been tied up since I got back to the office. When I do, I shall tell him what you told me. Also that if you say the heroin isn't yours, I take your word for it.'

Before he could reply, she went on, 'We ought to talk about what you do next to get to the bottom of this. Come and have supper tonight.'

She was the one friend at court he had; but he still didn't want her going out on a limb for him. 'I'd rather not involve you if there's a risk—'

'Shut up,' she said, 'Just shut up and say when you'll come.'

The apartment in Little Venice was one of three converted out of a mid-Victorian house that was not quite facing the canal. It seemed to have left no particular impression on him from his previous visit. Now, wandering about the living room while Antonia was in the kitchen, he decided that it fitted her to perfection. The room was cool and high-ceilinged, with white-painted, folding shutters to close out the night. Modern, mostly Italian furniture was grouped in pools of light. Elsewhere, the emptiness of the shadowed corners seemed a touch austere. But the arrangement of roses on a coffee table beside the fireplace was as vivid and crisply elegant as she always seemed to him.

When she came back he was gazing at a photograph of the same man as the one on her desk at the Bureau. 'Your husband?'

'Yes. He was a test pilot.'

'Do you ever think of remarrying?'

'Not lately.' She began putting mats and cutlery on a dining table.

'Why not?' He was conscious of being on the edge of discourtesy; but curiosity drove him on.

'I find things in myself now that probably wouldn't do much for a marriage.'

He persisted. 'You mean your career . . .?'

She shook her head and looked at him mockingly. 'Just things.'

She gave him a bottle of wine to open. She wasn't going to be drawn. Perhaps she had simply stopped liking men; but he didn't get that feeling.

During the meal she told him about her conversation with Mansell. 'He still likes you. If we could prove the heroin was planted I think he'd be on your side. Tell me more about the man your neighbour saw.'

'When she challenged him, he said he was calling on behalf of the First Church of the Holy Crucifixion. He had some pamphlets but she didn't find him very convincing. Because she was suspicious she took the registration number of the car he drove off in.' He extracted from his notecase the note Gwen had made. 'I wondered if you'd mind putting through a trace to find out the owner?'

'Did she describe him?'

'A cockney—medium height, dark, bad breath.'

She put the note away in her handbag. 'Does he sound like any of the people you saw following you?'

'Not much.'

She was frowning. 'You started being followed at almost the same time you began looking for Lauren Giordano. It could be coincidence—or not. Then you're mugged. Nothing's taken, but the passes that say who you are and where you work seem to have been looked at. When you come back from your leave in Gloucestershire you find you're being followed again. But of course it may never have stopped. You could simply have failed to notice it in the meantime.

'The people following you find out about Gail when you go to see her in hospital. From there you call on a man who deals in heroin. For anyone wanting to do you harm as quickly as possible, planting the heroin in your bathroom and then tipping off Antrim about it was an obvious next move. But who wants you out of the way so badly?'

He stared at the wall behind her head. 'There's something that doesn't fit in all that. I came to the conclusion that the mugging must have been the work of Garcia Fernandes or some friends of his who were here for the ETA operation Rivers was on tenterhooks about. When I was making enquiries to try to find Lauren I asked in the Basque restaurant in Camden Town for news of *either Luis or Garcia Fernandes. And* I left my name and telephone number. If it got to Garcia's ears that a stranger was sniffing about for him as he was about to set up some secret operation, he'd want to find out who was taking the interest. The man who followed me almost as far as the Bureau the morning of the day I was mugged *could* have been a Basque from his appearance.'

'So what isn't fitting?'

'The man behind me when I visited Gail in hospital wasn't any kind of Spaniard, I'm sure of that. Furthermore, I don't see a Basque terrorist successfully convincing Gwen that he's a cockney.'

'You're saying that two different sets of people have been interested in you . . .'

'It looks like it.'

She brooded, crumbling bread in her fingers. 'Would you agree to take the advice of somebody who could be a very good ally? He used to be an Assistant Director in the Bureau until he retired a few years ago. His name is Ludo Fender. He has the shrewdest brain of anybody I know.'

He tried to compose his features in a polite expression. Fender might be the Wizard of Oz but it was difficult to imagine what he would have to contribute. 'I appreciate—' he began, but she cut him short. 'Believe me, with Ludo on your side, it's going to be a lot better.'

'How is he to be convinced he ought to *be* on my side?'

'I shall tell him. After all, you convinced me.' She made it sound very simple.

'I'm not sure how I did that.'

'Perhaps I just can't stand the thought of having to pick up the loose ends you left in the Beynon case.'

She didn't intend him to get the idea that she was over fond.

They spent the rest of the meal going over the day's events without any flashes of enlightenment breaking in. Towards the end he said, 'One of the not-so-minor things that bugs me is the thought of somebody else following up Boyd's story and discovering whether I was right about Giordano.'

'Perhaps it'll wait until your suspension's lifted and you're back in the office again.'

She was trying to buoy him up. He shook his head. 'I don't see Rylance allowing himself to be kept hanging about. He'll already have been on to Antrim asking what progress I've made. I wonder how my non-availability has been explained.'

She remained silent but looking sympathetic. He guessed she thought he wasn't getting his priorities right.

Before he left she asked about Gail. It reminded him that he'd forgotten to return the house keys; the weekend already seemed several years back. He placed them on the table and told her she was in the clinic by now.

'You think she's made the commitment?'

He pushed away the thought of the packet he'd found in the lining of the handbag. 'Yes.'

'Is the treatment tough?'

'Not as nasty as the propaganda makes out. You feel lousy for a fortnight but it passes. That's only withdrawl of course. Staying off is the real trick.'

'She has you now. That should give her the motivation she needs, if anything will.'

He nodded. He had to believe it.

'And you have her.' She was watching his face closely. 'It's what you truly want, isn't it?'

'It's what I want,' he said.

After this hideous day, it was the one thing left to feel confident about.

# XX

EGERTON watched as the fingers with a final jerk reached their objective to grasp the glass of whisky on the bedside table. The operation had begun with a grunting lunge that threatened the seams of the pyjama jacket. Between two buttons a lozenge of dazzling white skin swelled and strained, then subsided. It had been like a mountain in movement, he thought, almost a geological event. 'I do most humbly apologize for receiving you like this,' Fender said, not for the first time.

In fact, he had greeted them, dressed in a blue towelling gown, at the door of his cottage. Hard-soled slippers had slapped against the uncarpeted floor of oak as, snuffling and wheezing, he had led them to a table where their supper awaited. He had told Antonia on the telephone that he hoped they would excuse the discourtesy of his remaining in bed; he had been laid low, it seemed, either by flu or an autumn cold of monstrous virulence. The Woman—an anonymous daily slave—would see they were admitted and shown the supper prepared for them.

Having opened the door, however, he showed no immediate sign of returning upstairs; nor was The Woman visible. He had lumbered about, indicating the whereabouts of supplementary supplies and possible refinements of their comfort, if they were so inclined. Towards Antonia his manner had been a shy but watchful concern to which she responded gently. Egerton he had greeted with an extravagant warmth as though anyone who accompanied her could not have too much of his esteem; but the eyes, brown and sombre, studied him each time he spoke with a brooding kind of concentration. Finally he had withdrawn aloft, taking with him the notes he had asked Egerton to bring, describing his experiences of being followed and what Mansell had said at the interview.

The meal was cold chicken with a respectably prepared salad and a bottle of Sancerre. By the time they followed Fender to the bedroom, carrying coffee, the world had become a better place than it had seemed driving through London's southern entrails to this Sussex village at the height of the evening rush hour. The room was low-ceilinged, a crooked place of beam and plaster walls and waxed floorboards. On a beam opposite the bed was a crucifix. The only other adornment for the walls of the room was oddly out of keeping with everything else, a group of brightly coloured Indian miniatures in which martial and erotic events took turns.

In a double bed, supported by a triangular padded object and pillows, Fender lay waiting in flannelette pyjamas, ready to hold court. On one side was the table with his medicine, a bottle of Chivas Regal; on the other, down against the wall, a hillock of used tissues was not quite concealed by a chair. Now that Egerton could study him in the light of the bedside lamp, he looked younger than he had expected. The cheeks were smooth, even rosy; the short black hair, cut like a schoolboy's, had no trace of grey in it. Since leaving them to their supper, he had brushed the hair so that it gleamed smoothly. But the sheer size of him was what held the eye. Within and at the margins of the pyjamas, flesh swelled in a gently heaving mass. He was a hippopotamus of a man.

He welcomed them again as though they had just arrived. When they were seated, he smiled benignly at Egerton. 'So you've been addicted to heroin, Egerton.' He said it baldly without changing his expression. 'I believe you're the first addict I've met. Knowingly that is.'

'I'm not an addict. I was once. But not now.'

206

'I understood that the latest medical view was that once established the condition was permanent. Have I got it wrong?'

'Some doctors—not all—take that view. I don't. I know I'm not an addict any more.'

Fender nodded politely. 'Where did you start?'

'At Oxford.'

'Tell me why. Were you led into it by others?'

He felt resentment growing inside him. He had not expected an interrogation about the past, at least not in such uncompromising terms. It was as if Fender were provoking him in order to study his reactions.

'I don't think I was led. It was simply that people I admired were already taking heroin. That made it a social thing. I suppose the element of risk appealed as well. Then, unfortunately, someone I knew—the person in the photograph that Mansell had—became a supplier. He was a very efficient one. It was even quite cheap through him.' He shrugged. 'I don't suggest any of those were good reasons. But that's how it happened.'

'You must surely have thought about the dangers at some time?'

'I suppose so. But I was quite sure *I* wasn't the type to get addicted. I saw myself as giving it up after I left university.'

'But you didn't . . .'

'When I came down from Oxford I took a job in a merchant bank. I discovered, or thought I discovered, that I could function better if I took a little. After a while it became quite a lot, particularly in money terms. For that and other reasons, I decided to make a break from London. Some friends from Oxford who also took heroin were there and I thought that if I didn't see them, I'd find it easier to taper off. I went to stay with a cousin in New York which turned out to be not a very bright idea. Things got worse not better. Then I had a crisis one night that made me decide I had to get treated and I went into a clinic my cousin knew about. When I was cured I came back to

England and answered an advertisement to join the Bureau.'

'One *can* be sure one is cured, can one?' Fender said. His tone was casual.

'You know whether you're really going to stop, or whether, deep down, you're keeping the door open. At least I did.'

'So you feel you have freed yourself from the past?'

'I feel it's behind me. I hope others will too.'

Fender said, 'Of course, some would say that is impossible. The past is always there a prison house on our backs.'

'Do *you* say that?'

'On the whole, yes.'

He had had enough. 'Well, that part of my past is *not* a prison house. It's gone. I *know* I won't take heroin again. I loathe everything about drugs. If you find my word so hard to accept, it seems pointless continuing with this meeting.'

Antonia was looking embarrassed. Fender gazed meekly into his whisky. 'You mustn't mind my exploring a little. I find the facts interesting. As to the reality of your word, if Mrs Strachan believes in it, as she tells me she does, I am not likely to take a different view.'

Fender was allowing his glass to nestle in the ledge of linen formed by the upper part of his belly. He lifted his gaze. There was no longer any sign of the snuffles and vague infirmity with which he had greeted them. 'So our problem is to discover who has taken advantage of this background to create the means to have you removed from the Bureau.'

Twenty-five minutes had passed since they had entered the bedroom and only now did he show signs of getting down to what mattered.

'Somebody wishes you ill.'

'Clearly.'

'Who are your enemies?'

'I don't know of anybody who would think it worthwhile doing this to me.'

'Then we should perhaps look at the cases you have been

208

recently handling in the Bureau. There can't be many since you've been there so short a time.'

Antonia said, 'There's been only one where an individual knows that he's about to be prosecuted largely as a consequence of the investigation Mark carried out. A man named Beynon was successful in corrupting several very senior people in the Property Services Agency. Mark interviewed him without disclosing he was an official and bluffed sufficient facts out of him to get the case on its feet. We know Beynon is extremely sore. But he must also know that getting Mark sacked can't change things now.'

'Revenge is still a consolation of sorts.'

Egerton shook his head. 'Beynon might pay somebody to beat me up. That flashed through my mind when I was being mugged outside my flat. But he wouldn't bother with subtleties like planting heroin in the bathroom.'

'What about the drugs world—does anyone there hold a grudge against you?'

'I don't believe so. I wasn't a part of it to the extent of getting involved with the criminal side. The friend I had at university was the only person I ever obtained heroin from in this country.'

'He is . . . still a friend, is he?'

He hesitated. 'I find it difficult to think of him in any other way.'

There was a brief silence. 'Forgive me for saying this,' Fender said slowly, 'but since by your own account you loathe the whole world of drug addiction, how do you reconcile thinking of a man who deals in heroin as a friend? Shouldn't you be doing all you can to get him prosecuted?'

He gazed at the mound of tissues beneath the chair, searching for the words to explain what he felt about Jamie.

'First of all you have to know I owe it to Jamie—his name is Jamie Buchanan—that I'm still alive. In our first year at Oxford, we went river swimming together. Some maniac had dumped a lump of reinforced concrete in the water. Several of the metal rods were sticking upwards out of the river bed. I must have dived into one of them, the point went through my side. I couldn't pull myself away and lost consciousness. Jamie somehow got me free but I know he nearly passed out in the process.'

He moistened his lips. 'All right—now he's dealing in heroin, on quite a big scale probably. People become addicts because of what he supplies. I know as well as anybody that's a terrible thing. But they *are* doing it *to themselves*—as I knew I was all the time I was acquiring the habit. When I think of Jamie I remember not only that he saved my life, but how kind he was. You have to understand that about him too. He was the most *uncalculating* friend. If one went to him for help, he always gave it. I know he has hardly any moral sense. But he doesn't *push* drugs, or even talk much about them. He just gives people what they say they want. That's how he began at Oxford. He enjoyed the risks involved in getting hold of heroin and the status it gave him. He reckoned those he supplied should accept responsibility for their own actions—they knew what they were doing. If you condemn his attitude you also have to condemn the tobacco companies and everybody who supplies liquor.'

Fender said coldly, 'I regard that as sophistry.'

Egerton shrugged. 'You asked why I think of him as a friend. That's my explanation.'

'He's certainly no friend to society.' Fender was looking towards Antonia. Her face was impassive. Neither of them had been the smallest bit impressed.

Egerton drank the dregs of his coffee and put the cup down. 'My father once told me a story I often remember. At university he had a friend who shared his distaste for the Franco side in the Spanish Civil War which was on at the time. One day the friend said that if my father really wanted to give practical help to the Spanish government and all it was fighting for, he'd introduce him to somebody else at university whom he named. My father didn't take up the offer. Years later he heard the name again. The person concerned had died but was referred to in Parliament as having been a Communist spy. My father's friend who had

210

become a fairly senior politician said in a television discussion my father watched the same evening that although he and the spy must have been contemporaries at university, he'd never actually known him.

'My father had to decide what he should do. One part of him said he should go to the security people and report what the politician had said years ago. Another part remembered the politician as the most admirable person he had known in those days. He had thought of him as his truest friend.'

'So what did your father do?' Fender asked.

'He did nothing.'

In the High Street outside, a truck thundered by, shaking the windows. Fender said heavily, 'We must all act as our conscience dictates.'

'I realize my father may have been wrong. But I understand how he felt.'

Silence took root now that the truck had gone. At last Fender said, 'Well . . .' as though he was turning a page. He wasn't going to reveal his judgement of the story. 'Perhaps we should move on.' He picked up Egerton's notes from where they lay on the counterpane. 'In describing the surveillance of which you've been aware you speak of an intervening trip overseas. What was this trip?'

'I was trying to locate someone whose family were anxious about her.'

'Were you doing this as a personal favour to the family or what?'

'I was instructed by the Director to look for her. It was the stepdaughter of a Minister.'

Fender raised his eyebrows and swivelled his gaze towards Antonia. 'The Bureau now undertakes searching for missing persons, does it? Antrim *is* spreading his wings.' The touch of sarcasm was unmistakeable.

She shook her head. 'This was something exceptional. Mark can give you the facts if you think you should know about it.'

He adopted a spuriously tentative expression. 'Perhaps it would be *just* worthwhile.'

When Egerton had finished, he let his head fall back against the pillows. All traces of the cold or flu or whatever he'd been suffering from had now entirely gone. He presented the appearance of someone who had enjoyed a very agreeable meal. 'Fascinating,' he said, 'Quite fascinating.'

He smiled at Antonia. She smiled back. Her smile seemed to Egerton to be a blend of affection and faint exasperation. Between them, he sensed a bond amounting to more than the relationship of people who had worked together. Not physical, surely, he thought, studying the gross figure humped beneath the sheets. Yet, in their glances, there was an intimacy that made him uncertain. During the time he had hovered about the supper table, Fender had touched her hair with the tips of his fingers, making some remark about the effect of the light upon it; then he had clasped his hands together and looked away quickly.

'I imagine Antrim will not have felt too displeased at having obliged Rylance so efficiently,' Fender said.

She remained silent.

'No doubt he makes himself very visible about Whitehall these days.'

She shrugged. She wasn't rising to his fly. He went on enjoying his thoughts for another few moments then sighed as though regretting the necessity of returning to the problem in hand.

'So . . . from what you said on the telephone, the enquiry about the gentleman with the religious tracts has not been productive.'

'We established easily enough the registered owner of the car. His name's Frederick Agar. However when Mark went this afternoon to look at the address in Shoreditch he'd given when he licensed it, he found the building was demolished six months ago. People in the neighbourhood didn't remember much about him. They thought he worked as a bookmaker's clerk.'

'What about his description?'

'Agar's a cockney all right. The rest of the description *could* fit the man who was seen, but not too well.'

'Shoreditch,' Fender said, 'Edward IV's mistress, Jane Shore, is supposed to have died in a ditch there. Hence the name. Unfortunately, like most stories of that kind, it happens to be untrue. She was however a remarkable woman.'

His remarks, inconsequential and casually delivered, were clearly a form of interval music while his brain concentrated on something else. He addressed Antonia again.

'Does Seagram still grace the Metropolitan Police?'

'Yes, he's a Commander now.'

'*Is* he? That could be very convenient. An admirable police officer.' Fender launched into an account, apparently for Egerton's benefit, of his past relationship with Seagram, of one-time conflict giving way to something more profitable to both parties. At the end he said, 'This evidence of being followed—your notes imply it didn't continue during your overseas trip. Why?'

'I saw no signs of it.'

'But were you actually looking out for surveillance?'

He had to admit he wasn't.

'Were there empty seats on the plane to Majorca?'

'I seem to remember one or two.'

'So anyone following you to Heathrow, would not have had difficulty in catching the same plane . . .'

'I suppose not.'

'What about the occasion you went to the girl's apartment in Nice?'

'I went by taxi. But I do remember looking back when it dropped me. The road was empty. I don't see how there could have been anybody on my tail that night.'

Fender lay back against the pillows and closed his eyes. They sat in silence. There was nothing to be done except hope he was thinking rather than dozing. Finally he sat up and smiled politely at them both. 'Well, I suppose you'll be wanting to get off back to London. Aided by your excellent notes, Egerton, I shall now give some thought to all this.' It seemed that the audience was over.

Fender put on the towelling robe and accompanied them to the street door. As he stood watching Egerton unlock the Mini, a cat arrived from out of the shadows to brush against his calves. He lowered himself gingerly to stroke it. 'This is General Tarragon. We are close neighbours. We have many chats. I hope he will join us when you next come.' He was looking towards Antonia as he spoke.

There was frost on the windscreen of the car. 'Shouldn't you be back in bed?' Egerton asked. 'The air's chilly.'

Fender shook his head. 'Don't worry about me.' His features were reporting noble self-sacrifice. 'I shall be in touch again through Mrs Strachan. If my old colleague, Antrim, issues an invitation to resign, whether or not accompanied by money, please consult me before agreeing. In the meantime, try not to get despondent. This is only the beginning.' He stood back to wave them away. General Tarragon was already waiting impatiently in the doorway of the cottage.

On the road north, Egerton said, 'He seems to be doing his best to go down with pneumonia.'

Antonia was lighting a cigarette. 'Ludo is as well or as ill as the occasion demands.'

'I hope he's going to be well in that case.'

'My guess is that he'll be *very* well.'

'I still don't altogether see what he can contribute. The main hope seemed to lie in finding Agar. That looks as though it could prove impossible. Apart from which, the description of Agar I got from neighbours doesn't match at all well with the man Gwen saw. So where does that leave us? He's not going to get anything from my notes.'

He was conscious that he sounded graceless. He owed her something better than that. 'Sorry, you really think he'll pull something out, do you?'

'If anyone can help, Ludo will. He'd have been Director

of the Bureau if there hadn't been all sorts of manoeuvring against him.'

'Wasn't he popular?'

'Not really. I'm afraid his nicknames weren't very affectionate. Sideways Ludo was one. But mostly it was the Black Pope.'

'I can imagine him in a cassock.'

'When we were in Rome last year, I knew that was where he really belonged.' She smiled.

'I thought the case you had together was in Canada?'

She was gazing into the night, her hair hanging loose and wanton against the cheekbone. He could understand Fender being tempted to touch it. 'That was earlier. He came back to the Bureau to do a special investigation which involved going to Rome. He had a bone to pick with the Pope.' She was still smiling. 'I'll tell you about it one day.'

The feeling that there had been something special between her and Fender amounted now to a conviction. It was faintly repellent. Had she a taste for fat elderly men? In that case, why didn't she simply up sticks from Little Venice and go and live with Fender in his gingerbread cottage?

'How does he spend his time now he's retired?'

'He's a great reader. He's also a butterfly buff. And I imagine he keeps the correspondence columns of *The Tablet* well supplied. What's wrong with the Catholic Church is probably his favourite subject.'

'He's against it . . .?'

'No, he just feels he ought to be running it.'

They had reached a point on the A21 where the lights of Tonbridge glimmered like a thousand orange stars over to their right. The road ahead was empty of traffic. He opened the throttle of the Mini. There was nothing to do except hope she was right about Fender. Beside him she was stubbing out the cigarette. 'Anyway, with Ludo in action, at least you won't be bored,' she said. It seemed he might have to be content with that.

# XXI

HE woke early from a dreamless sleep. Something awaited, he thought, something to be done. When memory came slouching back, he realized the opposite was true. His only lead to the person who might have planted the heroin had run into the sand, or very nearly. He could in theory make a round of every bookmaker within a ten mile radius of where Agar had had his address, to ask if they had news; he could tackle people in shops and the local post office; he could drink with all the barmaids in Shoreditch in the hope that one knew him. But it was difficult to believe that any of that would have a practical result—certainly not in the time scale he must reckon with: the breathing space before suspension was turned into dismissal could scarcely amount to longer than a week. And all the time the melancholy suspicion hardened, that Gwen had misread the registration number of the yellow car and the man pretending to be from the First Church of the Holy Crucifixion had not been Agar at all.

That left, as his remaining hope, the unknown quantity of Fender, who had been induced to take an interest solely on account of some unimaginable past relationship with Antonia. Whether Fender's help would amount to more than a spot of intellectual dowsing, in between feuding with the Catholic Church and poring over his butterfly collection remained to be seen. Only the mention of Seagram, the old acquaintance at Scotland Yard, raised hope that something more than cerebration was contemplated.

He lay inert contemplating the cracks in the ceiling

above his bed until the telephone bell roused him. It was a little after eight o'clock. He put on his dresing gown and went to the hall. Judging by past form he would now be greeted by the insistent tones of Rylance's voice, once more engaged in stirring into activity those appointed to do his bidding. There would be a grim satisfaction in telling him that he was off the case, off every case for that matter; if Rylance would like some different answer, he could speak to Antrim about it. But when he picked up the phone, it was a wrong number.

His thoughts turned to Gail. He had no news since dropping her at Paddington station early on Monday morning. He couldn't even be sure she'd arrived at the clinic. He had promised not to call her first; but that, he told himself, didn't exclude asking the clinic for news.

He dialled the number. Somebody said in moderately reassuring tones that she was perfectly all right, just a bit rough for the moment, but that was to be expected. No, she wouldn't feel like coming to the phone. He asked for her to be given his love and the voice said, yes of course, and would he remember for the future the morning wasn't a convenient time for calls.

He had done nothing else, had not even shaved when Clayton rang from the Yard. 'Your office said they didn't know when you were going to be back. I hope you're not sick?'

'Just a few days off,' he said.

'I asked for your home number since you said that enquiry was urgent.'

He managed to summon interest into his voice.

'There's nothing against Giordano, the FBI says he's got a clean record. In fact he's just been nominated for a Presidential Commission on Relations between Organized Crime and the Film Industry which must mean he's rated *respectable*. Catini, as I told you, is a different story but West didn't have a lot to add to what I mentioned.'

'Did he know of any relationship between Catini and Giordano?'

'If he does, he's not saying. He was a bit evasive on Catini. I don't know why. Anyway the general picture's clear enough—Catini runs a sizeable piece of the drugs action round Marseilles and Nice, working in with one of the local gangs. It's unusual for a foreigner to get big in that scene because the Frog competition doesn't like it. But he pays top prices for the stuff and has export arrangements they can't match so he's become accepted.'

'The name of the leader of the local gang—have you got that?'

He heard paper being turned over. 'Yes. He's a guy called Baptiste, Raoul Baptiste.'

The old envelope on which he had scribbled his notes after the talk with Boyd in Epping, was still in his pocket and he fished it out. But he didn't really need to check, the name had stayed in his mind: it was Baptiste's gang the man identified by Boyd had belonged to.

The link between what had happened in the apartment and Sam Giordano could hardly be doubted now. Even if he was to be denied the chance of pinning it on Giordano, somebody else, briefed with the knowledge he now had, would be able to do that. Meanwhile the Rylances needed to be told the facts, though they might not be pleasant for Evelyn to face.

Her voice answered almost at once when he dialled the private number; she must have been sitting at her desk.

'Mrs Rylance,' he said. 'This is Mark Egerton.'

There was a pause before she answered. 'Yes.'

'I would like to see you or Mr Rylance about Lauren's death. I have some information—'

She cut in. 'Mr Egerton, should I be talking to you?'

'What?'

'I've been told you're off work.'

'I'm not working in my department at present but—'

'Your Director told my husband that he'd had to suspend you from duty. It's not my business what you've done but I guess it's pretty serious. Since you're no longer working for us, why are you calling me?'

'You should be aware there's a connection between the thugs who killed your daughter and somebody well known to you. If I could call on you—'

'Who is this somebody?'

'Your former husband.'

'*Sam*!?'

'Yes. I'm sorry but—'

He heard a noise that hovered uncertainly between astonishment and annoyance. 'Mr Egerton, he and I may have had our differences but if you think that means I can be sold any crappy story—'

'It's not a story. As I told the Secretary of State when I last saw him—'

'What you told my husband didn't sound as though it was going to add up to sense. But we agreed it ought to be followed up and that you could do that. Then we heard that you were suspended so we decided to employ a private investigator who operates in Nice. Presumably he'll tell us if there's anything in what this screwy author and you have been saying.'

He swallowed back anger. 'If you won't listen to me at least let me give your new investigator the facts I've got.'

He could tell that behind impatience she was forcing herself to think about it. Eventually she said, 'All right, if he isn't satisfied from his own enquiries that it's all moonshine, he'll talk to you. That is, if your Director OKs it.'

'Wouldn't it be better if—'

'I've given you my answer, Mr Egerton. I haven't anything more to say except I don't expect you to ring this number again. Is that clear?'

He stood listening to the dialling tone for perhaps half a minute after she had disconnected, torn between frustration and fury. She didn't give a damn what had happened to Lauren and why. All she cared about was that a potential embarrassment on the way to becoming the hostess at No. 10 no longer existed.

Somehow the day passed. His mood was slipping into the despondency against which Fender had uttered his unctuous warning. The next morning despondency was still there but beneath his sloth a vein of energy began unexpectedly to throb. Before it faded, he went out in search of paint to obliterate the primrose emulsion with which his predecessor had covered the bathroom walls. This time nobody bothered to pick up his trail, either on his way to the shops or coming back. He was definitely not of interest any more.

The sun was full on the lake as he turned into Prince of Wales Drive again. He crossed to the park. A flotilla of ducks sailed up and down as though offering a performance. Seated on a bench he reviewed the events of recent weeks, hoping that, like the splash and glitter as one of the ducks took wing, a clue to why he had been framed would surface in his mind. But nothing came.

He washed down the bathroom walls then made himself a mushroom omelette before going back to try out the paint. His spirits lifted a little. Only once, gazing at the cabinet where the heroin had been planted did the black dogs come racing back.

The bathroom was finished and he had started on the kitchen when news of a sort arrived via a call from Antonia.

'Ludo's in town. He'd like to see you at his club tomorrow afternoon. Two fifteen. Ask for him at the porter's desk.' She sounded rather tense.

'Will you be there as well?'

'No, I'll already have seen him—he's staying overnight at my flat. Incidentally he'll have read the file on Beynon, also your reports on the interviews you had when you were looking for Lauren and on what happened subsequently. I expect he'll have some questions to ask.'

'You're showing him the office files?'

'Yes.'

He didn't attempt to keep the surprise out of his voice. 'That's . . . all right, is it? I mean—'

She interrupted him. 'He asked for them and I decided that he was only going to be in a position to help you properly if he knew everything you'd been doing lately.'

He could understand why she sounded tense. Fender might have been an Assistant Director in the Bureau once but that didn't entitle him to see current files. She would surely be in trouble if it became known she had taken them out of the office for him to read.

'Has he come up with any ideas?'

'He's found out something that might prove useful—we can't be sure yet. I expect he'll tell you about it, if he's feeling communicative.'

'You think he might *not* be?'

She laughed shortly. 'You don't know him very well yet. Incidentally he asked if you could find out the name of the club in London which Catini is supposed to own.'

'I'll ring Clayton. Anything else?'

'I don't think so. What are you doing with yourself?'

When he told her about his internal decoration programme, she said, 'The trouble with painting is it leaves the mind free to chew the cud. You sound rather mouldy to me. After you've spoken to Clayton, take yourself out for a change of scene. There must be a film somewhere you'd like to see.' She was being firm in a friendly way.

Before she rang off, she said, 'Don't be late for Ludo, he gets scratchy if people aren't on time.' An echo came back: she had spoken almost those words about her lunch date when they had been talking in the Bureau on the day he had had his appointment with Rylance at the House of Commons. So one mystery was solved. Fender had been the notional uncle pacing the hall of his club, impatient no doubt for the chance to touch her hair with his finger tips and imagine more.

He picked up the phone again and rang Clayton at the Yard. His sergeant said he was out and wouldn't be returning before close of play. He promised to get him to call back the next morning. Returning to the kitchen and staring at the expanse of unwashed wall that awaited attention, he decided that Antonia had been right, absolutely right. He showered and changed and took himself to a cinema. Afterwards he went to a restaurant and ate well, on the basis that if he was really going to be out of a job and broke, it might be no bad thing to notch up a meal worth remembering.

It was nine o'clock and the wind blowing off the Thames was turning chilly when he got back to Prince of Wales Drive. He had closed the entrance door to the flat and taken off his coat when he registered that the table lamp in the sitting room was alight. He went in. Seated in the armchairs, their gaze lifted towards him with expressions of solemn but watchful politeness, were two men, dark and thickset. He judged them to be in their middle thirties. One held in front of him a cigarette which he had apparently been about to light. They might have been sitting in their favourite bar, observing the arrival of a stranger.

The man holding the cigarette said, 'Mr Egerton, I hope you will forgive us coming inside to wait for your return. The heater in our car has broken and we did not know when you would come back. I assure you nothing has been disturbed.'

His English was heavily accented and he spoke slowly. While he was saying his piece the other man had risen and moved behind Egerton to close the door into the hall. When he had done so, he stayed there.

'Do you always break in when you're visiting people?'

'We did not have to break in, Mr Egerton.' The man held up some keys.

He stared at them. But it wasn't hard to work out. 'I suppose those are duplicates you took when you mugged me.'

The man looked apologetic. 'I regret very much that occurred. I was not responsible. At the time some friends were anxious for the safety of another friend. The enquiries they had been told you were making appeared to them a threat which they needed to investigate. That was done rather clumsily. I hope you will accept our apologies.' His manner was one of grave courtesy overlaying a relentless determination to control all aspects of the situation. He placed the keys on the coffee table beside him. 'Let me now surrender these and assure you that you will not experience any further annoyance.'

Egerton looked behind him. The other man remained beside the door. To get past him and out of the room before the first could lend him assistance was clearly impossible. He thought of shouting. But Gwen was still away. Whether his voice would be heard in any of the other flats seemed doubtful.

The man with the cigarette said, 'Some colleagues of ours in France have been talking with a Mr Boyd who writes books and has an apartment in Nice. Mr Boyd suggested you might have some information of interest to us.'

He waited.

'You were in Nice recently?'

'Yes.'

'You told Mr Boyd you had been sent to find the American woman, Lauren Giordano?'

'Yes, her parents were worried about her.'

'You also had an interest in Señor Garcia Fernandes' brother, Luis?'

'Only as her companion. I thought I might trace her through him.'

'And that is the reason why you were asking about both Garcia and Luis in London?'

'Yes.'

The man with the cigarette spoke to the other in what Egerton assumed was Basque. He was explaining something—perhaps what Egerton had been saying. The other man's replies were monosyllabic and grudging. Eventually he spread out his hands as though in resigned deference.

The first man looked down at the cigarette still unlit between his fingers. He lifted it in Egerton's direction, seeking leave before he snapped open a lighter. 'That explains something that was puzzling to us, particularly when we learned which department you belonged to.' He blew smoke in front of him, slowly and evenly.

223

'Mr Boyd believes you know the identity of the Americans who visited Señor Luis Fernandes two days before he was murdered.'

'I have no certain knowledge, only a suspicion about the identity of one of them. Why should that interest *you*?'

'Anyone who may have been concerned in Señor Fernandes' murder is of interest.'

'To you personally?'

'Not to me, no. But his brother is naturally very anxious to know who was responsible for his death.'

So this wasn't Garcia himself. Not unless some elaborate deception was being practised.

'Then your colleagues in Nice should be looking for the men who did the actual killing. Boyd believed he recognized one in the police photographs he was shown.'

'Unfortunately that man as well as his companion have disappeared from Nice.'

'Why not ask the leader of the gang they belonged to? His name is Raoul Baptiste.'

The man smiled sardonically. 'Monsieur Baptiste does not make himself very available.' He rose and fetched an ashtray from the other side of the room. Within the limits he had set for the meeting his manners were faultless. 'If you would now tell us who you believe the Americans *might* have been, we can leave you in peace, Mr Egerton.'

He could refuse. Presumably, although perhaps not certainly, they would become rough. What he had to decide was whether there was any point in refusing. The information was of no use to himself. Nor was there cause to hold it as an exclusive titbit for the Rylances' French investigator, assuming he ever made contact. And Luis Fernandes' brother had more right than most to know who could have been behind the killings.

The man smoked and waited patiently as though aware there must be considerations demanding attention, if only to meet the requirements of face. Egerton said, 'All I can tell you is that Miss Giordano's father, a film producer, was in Nice at the time. He was staying with another American named Catini who has a Mafia background and is close to Raoul Baptiste.'

'Why should he have wished to harm either his daughter or Señor Fernandes?'

'I doubt if he intended them physical harm. My guess is that what happened was unexpected. The men were trying to recover something she had taken from her father. The killings occurred because they were interrupted. Although they were employed by him, he can't have intended *that*.'

The man was too polite to appear openly sceptical. He simply rounded his lips for a moment before drawing on the cigarette again. 'Can you tell me where the father is now?'

'When I last heard, he was staying at the Excelsior Hotel in Rome.'

The other looked down at the carpet. He was thinking it through, taking all the time in the world. Then he stood up. 'Thank you, you've been very helpful.' He moved towards the door. 'I hope you will once more accept our apologies for having disturbed you.'

'Before you go, I'd like you to answer one or two questions of mine.'

The man stopped and inclined his head. 'Of course. How can I help you?'

'You were having me followed shortly before I was mugged outside this block . . .'

'Yes.'

'Were you doing it again last week?'

The man raised his eyebrows. 'Why should we follow you once we had established who you were and decided you were not a threat?'

'You swear to that?'

'If you wish, I will swear.'

'The second question is—did you plant anything in my apartment?'

He had to explain what he meant. The man looked baffled, then laughed. 'For what reason?'

'To harm me—by then telling my department.'

'Why should we wish to harm you? You are only a

government official dealing with matters that are not our concern. We have no quarrel with you or the British government.'

He could have been lying. But his manner, slightly condescending, carried conviction. As he went through the door on the heels of the other man, he turned to give a formal nod of farewell.

From the window Egerton watched to see if they had parked their car outside. But they were too professional for that. He just caught their movement in the street lights as they walked briskly towards Prince Albert Bridge.

# XXII

HE found Fender's club in a corner of St James's Square. A haunt of old India hands, Antonia had told him; if he ever invites you for a meal, ask for the curry. Curry lunches and recumbent afternoons in the days of the Raj had perhaps been Fender's downfall, he reflected, the explanation for that monstrous girth.

A porter took him to a room overlooking the square. Beside flasks of coffee, a regiment of cups stood in close order. Beyond was the predictable panorama of armchairs and oil paintings; in the chairs men slept or offered slivers of conversation across their newspapers.

The porter pointed towards the fireplace. Gently heaving, like a great ship at anchor, Fender dozed in one of the larger chairs. Today he wore a crumpled grey flannel suit and a check shirt, its collar points curving limply outwards from a stringy tie. On his lap was a newspaper folded at the lead story. The heading read NEW BISHOP HAD YOUTHFUL CONVICTION FOR IMPORTUNING: NO. 10 KNEW. A SPECIAL GLOBE REPORT.

He seemed oblivious to the world about him, yet he could not have been completely asleep. Opening his eyes in the exact moment Egerton bent forward to whisper, Fender said with elaborate warmth, 'Egerton! How *very* nice to see you!' He struggled to his feet with an appearance of urgency; but it was only for the purpose of making a theatrical gesture towards a chair he wished Egerton to draw up beside his own. 'A glass of port? Coffee? No?' He sank back, shaking his head at a waiter who was discreetly hovering. 'And *how* are you?'

'Fine.'

'What have you been doing with yourself?'

'I'm in the middle of decorating my flat—following your advice not to get despondent.'

'Splendid.' Fender accepted from him the newspaper that had fallen to the carpet during his eruption from the chair. Tapping the lead story with a plump finger he said, 'Have you read this stuff?'

'No.'

'I trust you never sink to becoming an investigative reporter.'

'You don't like journalists . . .'

'Devourers of living flesh,' he said grimly. He threw the newspaper on the table beside him. There seemed a strong likelihood they were about to ride off in a totally irrelevant direction.

'Antonia said you'd discovered something.'

'We have some way to go of course. But I am a little encouraged.' Fender took from the side pocket of his jacket a notebook and began to turn the pages. They were covered in writing that was surprisingly neat for a man who could appear so clumsy.

'I enjoyed reading the reports of your efforts in the Beynon affair and also over the unfortunate Miss Giordano. There are one or two small things that are not yet entirely clear to me. Perhaps you'll be so good as to answer a few questions.'

The light in the square outside had begun to fade before he put his head back against the chair with an air of moderate satisfaction. They had covered, or so it seemed to Egerton, not only every smallest action he had taken over Beynon and Lauren, but also the suspicions, hopes and misgivings that had accompanied each. Fender's approach appeared to be omnivorous. By the end, it was difficult to believe that his mind retained a capacity to distinguish between what might be relevant and what certainly wasn't.

He was gazing at the ceiling. 'I take it there have been no new developments?'

228

'Just a couple of callers last night I wouldn't care to have as enemies.' He described the visit by the two Basques.

'So you are now satisfied that those who were following you last week and who can be assumed to have obtained the photograph of you with—' Fender paused for a moment, pursing his lips over a choice of words '—your friend, the dealer in heroin, were quite separate from these Basques— nothing to do with them in fact?'

'Yes.'

'Excellent.' He offered no explanation why he found the answer satisfying. His manner of speaking even allowed for the possibility that he disagreed with the conclusion.

'Did you by any chance manage to acquire the information I asked Mrs Strachan to mention to you?'

'The name of the club is the Medmenham. It's aimed at the very big gamblers and occupies a house on Chichester Hill in Mayfair. On paper the club's owned and run by a man who used to be in the Life Guards. Catini is the real power behind the scenes. He operates, according to Clayton, through a Maltese who acts as manager.'

'Does he indeed?' Fender resumed his study of the cornice above him as though it had struck him as having an unusually pleasing character. A waiter appeared at his side to announce there was a telephone call for him. He glowered at the interruption. 'From whom?'

'A lady.'

'A *lady*?'

'Yes, sir.'

He stared at the waiter as if suspecting him of deliberate fabrication, then struggled reluctantly to his feet. 'I suppose it could be The Woman wanting to know when I'll be back and what she's to do about the milkman or something equally trivial.'

When he returned, his mood had mellowed again. 'Tea, I think,' he said and ordered it, demanding anchovy paste with four rounds of buttered toast and attributing the volume of the requirement to Egerton without even a glance in his direction. As the waiter moved off, he said,

'Did that distinguished, erstwhile captain of industry, our Secretary of State for Defence, give you tea when you called on him at the House of Commons?'

'No, it was rather late for that.'

'And how did you find him?'

'I'm sorry . . .?'

'How do you rate him?'

'Since he's the first Minister I've ever met, I have no basis for comparison. He seemed fairly formidable.'

'And Mrs Rylance . . .?'

He shrugged. 'Attractive, ambitious, tough.'

'According to the press she intends to be a Prime Minister's wife.'

'I can imagine it.'

'American wives of politicians,' Fender murmured. 'Always *especially* energetic in my experience. The challenge to liven the old world up . . .' They seemed to be drifting off down another byway that had taken his fancy but he collected himself. 'Where were we?'

'I'd just told you about the Medmenham Club.'

'Yes, indeed. As I'd rather hoped that fitted intriguingly with something I learned yesterday.' He took out his notebook again. 'Since your pursuit of Agar had run into the ground, I thought we might look from another angle at the visitor who was observed by your neighbour. I asked Seagram, whom I think I mentioned the other night is an old acquaintance, if there was any trace in the Yard's *modus operandi* records of a housebreaker who, when challenged, claimed to be canvassing for the First Church of the Holy Crucifixion or something similar. This produced a direct hit in the shape of James "Holy" Coleman, occupation listed as "general trader"—always an interesting description I find. Coleman's physical appearance as quoted by Seagram was remarkably near to that provided by your neighbour.'

'Does he own a yellow car?'

'It's not known that he does. However, I think we should regard the car as unimportant. Coleman may well be prudent enough not to use his own when out on serious business.'

'Did Seagram have Coleman's current address?'

'No, nor do the police in Shoreditch where, like Agar, he seems normally to have his being. But Seagram arranged for an enquiry to be put out in an effort to trace him.'

He cursed under his breath. 'If it doesn't produce the answer we're stuck again.'

'Not quite. Seagram was good enough to read to me from what is now called a print-out—' Fender's lip curled in profound distaste '—the paragraph in which Associates of the subject are listed. These included, as somebody for whom Coleman is suspected of performing occasional commissions, the name of Anthony Boffa. Does that mean anything to you?'

'No.'

Fender raised his eyebrows, like a schoolmaster seeking acknowledgement of dereliction. 'I fear you failed to press Chief Superintendent Clayton for all the useful information he had about the Medmenham club. Anthony Boffa who is Maltese also happens to be the club's manager.' It was delivered as a reproof. All the same, it was the first good news of the day.

The waiter had arrived with tea. Egerton waited impatiently while Fender groped in his trouser pockets for coins. As the waiter moved away, he said, 'So, if, as seems certain, Coleman planted the heroin, we have a direct line back to Catini?'

'Yes.'

'Which can only mean that Giordano asked Catini's help in getting me run out of my job in the Bureau. But what would have caused him to do that? He didn't know I suspected him of having anything to do with Lauren's death. At the time I was being followed and photographed I'd told nobody apart from Antonia.'

'You did however mention to Rylance Boyd's story of the two Americans he heard with Lauren Giordano. It would have been odd if he had not told his wife.'

231

'You're suggesting she would have passed it on to Giordano . . .'

'Since he was the girl's father, wouldn't that have been natural—some news about mysterious visitors threatening her shortly before she was murdered?'

He nodded slowly. 'It *would* fit.'

Fender took his third piece of toast. 'As you say, it fits. However there is rather more to it.'

'More?'

'Does nothing else occur to you?'

'Not at present.'

'Ah.' Fender was savouring both the toast and the opportunity to be maddening in more or less equal measure. 'Well, I do have some advantage over you. Let me explain. When it still seemed possible that you had been followed by only one set of people both before and after your trip abroad, I asked Mrs Strachan to have a check made on the passenger manifests of the plane that took you to Palma—you'll remember telling me it was only partly full—and also the plane on which you flew back to this country from Nice. It seemed worth discovering if there was someone who had stayed on your tail throughout, in which case his or her name would have shown up on both manifests. Mrs Strachan telephoned me with the answer a few minutes ago.'

'And *was* there anybody?'

'No. It was of course a long shot. However Mrs Strachan has the invaluable quality of knowing when to interpret instructions flexibly. She decided in addition to check the manifests for flights from Nice to this country on the evening of the killings and also the following day. These produced no name of anyone who had travelled with you to Palma. But they did yield a most interesting passenger.'

Fender wiped his fingers on a fairly grey handkerchief. He was facing the fact that he must finally make an end of his game. Lifting his gaze reluctantly to Egerton's face, he said, 'The person in question was Evelyn Rylance.'

About them the armchairs had emptied of all except a

few ancient sleepers, dreaming of the road to Katmandu. Fender said, 'Let us construct a theory and see if it stands up. We begin with the premise that the Americans threatening Lauren Giordano in that apartment were her father and Mrs Rylance. It's true that in his account of what he overheard Boyd didn't suggest one of the Americans could have been a woman. But you mentioned in your notes that Mrs Rylance had an unusually deep voice for a woman. Given the fact that Boyd found almost everything that was said inaudible, I fancy he could easily have made a false assumption about the sex of the person with Giordano. We believe they were there not out of anxiety for their daughter because she had run off with a Spaniard with terrorist connections but because she had in her possession something of vital concern to them both, possibly taken from Giordano's house in Beverly Hills when Lauren was staying with him during the summer.

'After the private detective fails to find her, Evelyn Rylance presses her husband to use the official machine. No doubt she suffers from the usual misapprehensions about police computers chattering omnisciently to each other all over Europe. Rylance of course faced the problem of justifying a request to use official resources in what was essentially a private matter. Fortunately he discovered something about Fernandes' background which persuaded him that the public interest was involved and that he could approach your Director with perfect propriety.'

Egerton shook his head. 'I'm absolutely sure he made up the story that he'd been told Luis Fernandes was a terrorist.'

'Quite possibly,' Fender said evenly. 'One must accept that to a politician with a wife on his back it would have appeared a moderately white lie. What mattered was that your Director on hearing the story at once offered his help. As I would expect of him.' He allowed himself a brief, ambiguous smile and began to fill a pipe with tobacco.

'At any rate, you undertook the search for Lauren and succeeded where the detective had failed. The outcome of

233

your efforts was obviously a great relief to Evelyn Rylance. We can assume that when the news reached her, she telephoned Giordano in Rome to meet her in Nice the following day. While there Giordano stays with the Mafia man, Catini. Perhaps Mrs Rylance does also—we don't know that. Next day they call on Lauren but fail to persuade her into giving up what they want. So they turn to Catini for the services of some local thugs who will extract it from her by force if necessary.'

The smell of latakia mixture entered Egerton's nostrils as Fender lit the pipe. 'But things start going wrong.'

'Badly wrong. Boyd's well-meaning intervention leads to the deaths of both Lauren and Fernandes. The thugs are sent off into hiding for a while. The risk remains that a thorough investigation will eventually establish the involvement of Giordano and Evelyn Rylance. But the police for whatever reason—perhaps Catini has influence in that quarter—come out with the statement that the killings were political. Boyd's belief that he has identified one of the killers as a local crook is quietly ignored. Paris is no doubt obliged to the police for providing further ammunition for the French Prime Minister to use when he goes to Madrid to protest about the Spaniards allowing their internal political problems to litter French soil with bodies. Catini and his gangleader friend, Baptiste, are no doubt equally obliged. And Giordano and Evelyn Rylance breathe freely again.'

Egerton closed his eyes. A vision had come into his head of a pistol butt smashing down on Lauren's head as she tried to reach Boyd and the open door of the apartment. 'And Rylance—how much of all this did *he* know?'

Fender lifted the massive shoulders and let them fall with a sigh. 'Perhaps everything, perhaps nothing. Evelyn may have kept it all from him, including the true reasons why she was so anxious to have Lauren traced.'

'I wonder what they were.'

'It's irrelevant for present purposes. But suppose Lauren had taken possession of evidence of a discreditable episode

234

in the lives of Giordano and Evelyn Rylance when they were married—something that she had always kept from Rylance himself.'

'Do you suppose the thugs got it back for her when they searched the apartment?'

'If they didn't, it was a terrible exercise in futility.'

They sat in silence except for the steady snoring of the man seated on the other side of the fireplace. 'It's bizarre,' Egerton said.

'But wholly feasible. When Evelyn returns from making arrangements for Lauren's body to be transported, Rylance mentions that you are full of a curious story of two Americans who were threatening Lauren in her apartment before she was murdered. He says you already have some enquiries under way and hope to be given authority to make more. Clearly this constitutes a threat. The only way of nipping danger in the bud is to remove you from where you will otherwise continue to make mischief. I think it likely that she then telephones Giordano who decides they had better ask Catini's assistance once more. Catini says he has just the man in London to take care of things. Enter Anthony Boffa, the manager of the Medmenham club who is told he must either find or manufacture some dirt about you as quickly as possible. He has you followed and his watchers come back with news of your visit to Miss Henderson in hospital where she is recovering from a heroin overdose and a photograph that turns out to be of you on very friendly terms with a heroin dealer. By itself the meeting in the photograph may be capable of being shown by you as having an innocent explanation. So a small packet of heroin is planted in your bathroom and the anonymous communication which your Director couldn't possibly ignore is delivered to him on the back of the photograph.'

Fender put down his pipe. 'Do you agree?'

It seemed convincing enough. 'I think so. But how do we set about proving it?'

'How indeed?' He looked more solemn. 'We badly need

Seagram to come up with Coleman's whereabouts so that we can question him.'

'He'd just refuse to talk, surely? As would Anthony Boffa if we went to the Medmenham club and tackled him head on. Why should either of them incriminate themselves?'

Fender sighed. He knew it was the truth but was reluctant to acknowledge it. 'What one would dearly like of course would be the opportunity to look through Mrs Rylance's personal effects—her desk, handbag and so on. I can't believe there wouldn't be some small scrap to establish a connection with either Catini or Boffa.'

'How would we use it, if we had it?'

'I'm not sure. You would at least have a story with sufficient backing to make your Director pause over dismissing you.' He shook his head. 'We are drifting into the realms of fantasy. Even if you had Coleman's talents as a housebreaker, you would be hard put to get inside the Rylance house unobserved, given the existence of servants and no doubt a permanent police guard outside.'

Fender's expression was becoming morose. A terrible flatness consumed Egerton. 'I can think of nothing—' he began, and stopped abruptly.

Fender looked up. 'What is it?'

'There *is* a way in which I might get in.'

'Do you mean you could break in?'

'No, with the help of someone living in the house.'

'Why should anyone want to do that for you?'

He shrugged. 'She wouldn't *want* to. But I'm in a position to, as it were, lean on her. At least I think I am.' He paused to collect his thoughts. 'When I first visited the Rylances' house in Chester Square, the police were due to call in connection with an investigation into leakages in the *Globe* about GOLIATH, the new weapons system. Perhaps you read about them . . .'

'I noticed there had been a row in the House of Commons on the subject.'

'The police had decided, after drawing a blank in Rylance's department and elsewhere that since Rylance had once worked at home on papers from which the leakages could have come, they ought to look at the security arrangments there. Rylance's daughter by his first marriage, Camilla, met me when I arrived and assumed I was a police officer who'd come about this. She told me she'd seen a man with binoculars in the apartment block behind the house and asked if it would be technically possible for someone in the block to take photographs of papers on the desk in Rylance's study. She said she hadn't put the possibility to Rylance or her stepmother because of embarrassment arising from the fact that they failed to make any use of curtains which Rylance's security people had specified.

'I told the police without saying where I'd got the information. They decided the photography *would* have been technically possible. They also discovered there was a likely candidate in the block behind. As far as I know, they're still investigating this chap, trying to establish some link with the *Globe*.'

Fender's fingers were working impatiently on the leather arm of his chair. 'I don't see quite—'

'I didn't think much more about the business until last weekend when I read that a man named Simon Bowe had landed the job of running the gossip column on the *Globe*. It's one of the highest paid columnist posts in Fleet Street and represented a pretty spectacular jump from his previous one. It so happened that I'd seen Camilla in Bowe's company on two occasions and it was obvious that they were very close.'

'You believe the girl took notes of material she saw in her father's study and gave them to this man . . .'

'I can't be *sure* of it. But I think that when she bumped into me at the house she was in a panic about the police's decision to explore the possibility that the leakages had been through someone there. She hit on the idea of diverting attention by telling a perfectly true story about the man with the binoculars in the block behind and the net curtains not being used properly.'

237

'Have the leakages continued?'

'Not as far as I know. I imagine she's too scared to provide Bowe with any more material. In which case the editor of the *Globe* is going to be disappointed. I imagine that in giving Bowe his columnist job he was not uninfluenced by his apparent ability to contribute stories out of the Ministry of Defence for the news pages.'

'Have you told the police what you now suspect to be the true story?'

'Not yet. I'd forgotten about it until a few moments ago.'

'I see,' Fender said. He was staring into space and beginning to look more cheerful. 'A very reasonable oversight in the circumstances. Also, one from which it would be remiss not to take advantage.'

'I can't be one hundred per cent sure my suspicions are right.'

'No doubt a few well-judged words with the girl will put the question beyond doubt.'

'I ought to stop the police wasting their time on a false trail.'

'Your hold on the girl may be the only way of establishing facts to show you have been the victim of a cruel conspiracy.'

When Egerton remained silent, Fender said briskly, 'Moral dilemmas are invariably tiresome to resolve. However, as your adviser and one familiar with all that is at stake, I shall take the matter out of your hands. You will not tell the police. You will instead seek to use this knowledge for the purpose of getting the girl to act in your interests. All we now have to decide is how *best* to use her.'

He waved a pudgy hand at a waiter to take away the tea tray and sat forward. Some trick of the light as he moved gave him the appearance of actually growing in size. 'I think we may at last be in business.'

Egerton was soaking paint brushes when Antonia rang. 'How did you get on?' she asked.

'Well, for better or for worse, we have a plan. I hestitate

238

to tell you what it is. I'm not sure you'd want to hear anyway.'

'He rang me before taking his train back to Sussex. He didn't say much but sounded pleased with things. I promised to pass on a couple of questions he failed to ask you. Did you note the licence plate of the car that met Giordano at Nice airport?'

'It didn't even occur to me to *try* to see it. I had no reason to then.'

'He thought there was a chance—it's the sort of thing he would have done.'

'But we know Giordano stayed with Catini anyway.'

She adopted a soothing tone. 'You have to understand that Ludo likes to have twice as many links in a chain of evidence as anybody else.'

He grunted. 'What was the other question?'

'Who was David?'

'What David?'

'The person mentioned in the letter from Lauren which you saw and photographed at Jacqueline's house in Deya.'

He failed to swallow back his irritation. 'How does he expect me to know that? There didn't seem to be any David hanging about there. Does he think he has to know everything about *everything*?'

'Keep your wig on,' she said. 'And the answer is usually "yes".' He heard her laugh. 'Remember what I told you.'

'I'm sorry I sounded rude. What was it you told me?'

'That with Ludo in play, at least you wouldn't be bored. You're not bored, are you?'

'No,' he said meekly. 'I'm not bored. Baffled, but not bored.'

# XXIII

A maid answered when he called the Rylance house. He asked for Camilla to be told there was a serious development in the matter she had reported to him a week or two back.

A satisfactory note of anxiety sounded in her voice when it came on the line. 'That story you gave me,' he said. 'We have some fresh information which makes it look pretty funny. Not to say misleading.'

She didn't speak.

'Did you really believe it would do more than buy time?'

She was still silent. He was sure now he had been right. 'You'd better come and talk it over. I'm preparing a report. What goes into it depends on how cooperative you are over something I want. Are you going to be cooperative or do I have to make all this official?'

'Do you mean only you know so far?'

'So far.'

He let her mull over the implications of that before he went on. 'In the circumstances I'm prepared to talk about this with you away from the office. You can come to my flat if you like.'

He could tell she was trying to guess what was going to be the price—money or sex or a combination of both. 'You won't get another chance.'

'Where do you live?' she asked. He gave directions and then told her if she spoke to anyone else beforehand, he was going to know about it. She swore solemnly she wouldn't tell a soul.

She arrived inside thirty minutes, her eyes wide, the mouth ready to tremble. Although she must have moved fast, she had taken trouble with her appearance before she left; under her velvet jacket a white silk blouse had its upper buttons invitingly out of action.

She started on her mitigation even before they were seated. 'I'm desperately sorry about the story I told you. It was terribly wrong of me I know. You see I was in a complete panic. I imagined everyone in the house was going to be asked questions and Slade the butler would remember seeing me come out of Pa's study one night when I was supposed to be changing in my room.'

'Did Bowe ask you to do it?'

'No.' She was twisting her hands in her lap. 'He was quite glad of course to have the stuff but it wasn't his idea in the first place. It began as a bit of a lark. And he was so keen to get taken on by a Fleet Street paper I thought it might give him the boost he needed.'

'You must have known you were committing a criminial offence.'

'It was only the one time.' She gazed at him pathetically. 'I never did it again, I swear.'

'The trouble is that you made it worse by trying to mislead us.'

She started to cry but not uncontrollably; she wasn't going to ruin her appearance in case the deal included him taking her to bed, and tears might put him off. He waited until she stopped. 'I'm prepared not to pass on this information to anyone else, in return for certain cooperation on your part. I can't guarantee somebody like Superintendent Clayton won't find out by other means in which event what he does will be out of my hands. It's just that he won't hear of it from me. Is that clear?'

It was beginning to dawn on her that it wasn't going to be the sexual option after all. 'What do I have to do?'

After he had explained to her, at first it seemed he was not going to carry the day. She stared mutely, just shaking her head. She was hoping to convey it was all beyond her

241

powers, bound to fail through some crass blunder on her part. When he refused to buy that, she fell back on the awfulness of engaging in such dishonesty. He smiled grimly. 'Copying your father's secret papers for your boyfriend to peddle to the press wasn't dishonest . . .?'

She looked sulky. 'That was different. I wasn't letting him do what he liked in the house.'

'I'm not interested in the house—just one room.'

When at last she accepted that he wasn't to be budged, she said, 'What will you be looking for?'

'Nothing that affects you or that you need to know about.'

'Is it something against my father?'

'No. At least not directly. I'm only interested in your stepmother.'

She grimaced. 'All right.'

Before she left he made her repeat back to him his instructions. She did so impatiently, anxious to get away. As soon as she had gone, he was attacked by misgivings. For the moment she was plainly too frightened to double-cross him. But once she had had time to think over the deal, would she resile? She could decide that the best course was to own up to Rylance about everything. She might reason that Pa would find it politically inconvenient if she was prosecuted and that he would surely have the clout to ensure that any proceedings against her were killed. Therefore all she would really have to weather would be his annoyance. It might be considerable but it wouldn't last for ever.

Fender pooh-poohed his anxieties when he reported them later in the day. 'The incentive to keep you on her side is very strong. And I don't imagine her stepmother evokes protective feeling in her. In any case the risk has to be accepted, we have no choice. Relax and be patient. If good music interests you, there is an Elgar concert on the radio tonight which I recommend as therapy.'

Egerton gritted his teeth. 'Meanwhile, what shall I do about the Bureau? It's nearly a week since Mansell had me in. He said that if I wanted to make a submission—'

'Send him a note straight away, saying that you have important enquiries in train that you are confident will prove that the heroin was planted. You expect to report the outcome in a few days. Don't go into more detail.'

It sounded sense. He typed a letter out and took it round to Somerset Square himself to be sure it got there. The receptionist gave him a puzzled look as he handed it in but he didn't give her time to ask questions.

A weekend crawled by with a single bright moment when Gail's voice came through from Devon as he was beginning to think he'd never last the evening without a drink. He could hear conversation in the background; presumably she was ringing from a common room or the hall of the clinic.

She began so softly he could hardly catch the words. 'They told me about your calls.'

'How do you feel?' he asked.

'*Marvellous* . . . well, not exactly. But it seems marvellous by comparison with the last few days. They say I'm over the withdrawal bit. Apparently I've been quicker than most.'

'What do you do all day?'

'I've only been out of bed since yesterday so I'm not into the routine yet. There seems to be some sort of therapy going on most of the time. I'm also allowed out for walks.' He heard a ghost of the old laugh. 'I went into a coffee bar today and felt tremendously daring. It's rather like being back at school.'

'So now you've changed your mind.'

'About what?'

'About not wanting me to come to see you.'

She paused before replying but he guessed it was only a gesture towards her earlier mood. 'You *could* come next weekend—if you really want to.'

'Why not before?'

'What about your work?' She sounded puzzled. He would have to tell her some time what had happened, but now wasn't the moment. 'I can fix things for more or less

243

any day,' he said grandly. It wasn't quite true bearing in mind the call he was awaiting from Camilla; that was something else he could hardly explain now.

They agreed finally that she would telephone him again on the Tuesday. He asked about the others in the clinic and she talked in the old jokey way, her voice growing stronger. But suddenly she said, 'I hated you for a while yesterday.'

'Why?'

'I looked in the lining of my handbag.'

'I see.'

'It *was* you who took the smack, wasn't it?'

'Yes.'

'At first I thought it must have been the staff here. Then I remembered I'd vaguely looked for it on the train coming here and couldn't feel it.'

He wanted to ask her *why* she'd looked. Instead he said, 'I'm sorry I didn't tell you. But why had you kept it?'

'I had a plan. I was going to wait for the really bad moment, the just-one-more-time moment. Then, I told myself, I'd get the packet out and watch myself flush it down the loo.'

'Was that what you were doing when you looked for it yesterday?'

'No. I just happened to notice when I was trying to mend my zip.'

When he didn't say anything, she went on, 'You believe me, don't you?'

'I have to,' he said. It sounded bad. His voice lifted. 'Darling, what I mean is—I trust you. So I have to believe you.'

He thought for a few moments that he had spoiled everything. But when she came back she told him she loved him.

Monday brought bills, a delivery of the builder's weapons for tackling the damp rot and a message from Mansell's secretary. The message was tantalizingly uninformative: he was invited to call on Mansell at three o'clock. Her voice remained carefully neutral throughout the exchange. No doubt it was part of her special talent, concealing from those she summoned any hint of the climate that awaited them.

He applied polish to his shoes and chose a decent shirt to wear before he set out—not for Mansell's benefit but his own. If he was going to find himself walking the plank, it would not be looking like a slob.

Mansell's welcome was ominously genial. He guided Egerton to the sofa in front of the bookcase and sat beside him. He spoke of the weather, announced that his daughter was also moving to a flat in Prince of Wales Drive, enquired about the best route from Twickenham when he and his spouse wished to visit their offspring. In the middle of it all, the secretary appeared to place a tray of coffee and digestive biscuits in front of them.

So he was definitely out. These preliminaries were all part of pentothal time, the happy hour before the knife was produced. His temporizing note hadn't worked. As Mansell paused to stir his coffee, Egerton said, 'If you don't mind, perhaps we could get to my position.'

'Yes!' said Mansell. He made the word sound as though he wanted nothing more than to be obliging. 'I've talked to the Director about the report which was prepared for him. I've also shown him the intriguing note you sent me. He was of course very interested that you believe you will be able at some time to prove the heroin in your bathroom was planted by someone anxious to get you dismissed.'

'Not just "at some time"—very soon. I now know the identity of a person with a criminal record who was seen by my neighbour near the door of my flat the afternoon when I believe the heroin was planted.'

'Who is this person?'

'His name is Coleman. He's known to the police as a housebreaker.'

'Have you located him?'

'He's disappeared from his address.'

'So he can't be interviewed . . .'

'Not at present. But I'm hoping soon to have evidence

linking him with another person who's behind all this.'

'And the name of that person is—?'

'If I tell you now you'd refuse to accept it. I need a little more time to get the proof.'

Mansell said, 'I see,' as though he absolutely understood and felt immeasurably sympathetic. 'Naturally I shall be very interested to hear that information in due course. However I have to tell you that a more general point has weighed very heavily with the Director.' He cleared his throat, 'I'm sure you recognize how essential it is for employees of this department to be free from associations that create suspicion.'

'I've explained why I went to see Buchanan. Apart from—'

'It's not only Buchanan I'm thinking of. You also have as a close friend, Miss Gail Henderson, whom you acknowledge to be a drug addict.'

'She's stopped. In fact she's under treatment in a clinic now.'

'And is it your intention to live with her afterwards?'

'Yes, I want to marry her.'

'I'm sure that's all admirable. I hope things will work out as you want. But you must admit you face us with an unfortunate picture. It would certainly be better if you had never involved yourself with drugs, or others who take them, in the first place.'

'I accept that. But I'm no longer involved with drug-taking myself and I've told you I never will be again. Is something that came to an end by my own act before I joined the Bureau to be held permanently against me?'

'Elsewhere I'm sure no problem need arise. But you must face the fact that the Bureau is a very sensitive department. We cannot afford to take risks, the public would not approve if we did. I'm bound to tell you that in your own interest I think the time has come when you should consider the advantages of a mutually agreed resignation. That way I can arrange for the terms of your departure to be generous. There would be a substantial gratuity and

246

naturally I would do all I could to help you to find other work. Perhaps a return to merchant banking—'

'I want to stay in the Bureau.'

He was surprised to hear the vehemence in his own voice. He had been vaguely conscious, as the Beynon case progressed, and more especially after that three hour interview with Beynon when he had got the disclosures Antonia and everyone else had never believed he would, that something about the work had begun to grip him. Working with Antonia had turned out to be his happiest time since leaving Oxford. To give it up had become unthinkable in the moment Mansell had proposed it.

Mansell was saying, 'As far as your work is concerned you can expect an excellent reference. A fresh start—'

'I still want to stay. I'd like to make my case to the Director personally.'

'I don't see—'

'I need only a little more time in which to establish how and why I was set up with that packet of heroin. I believe when all the circumstances are known, it'll be seen that nothing justifies asking for my resignation.'

'Do I draw the inference that someone in the Bureau set you up?'

'No.'

'Then who?'

'You'd tell me I was mad if I gave you the name. I won't do that until I've got the evidence. But that could come any day.'

Mansell stood up. He didn't look particularly sceptical or even unsympathetic, just tired. He went back to his desk and let his eyes fall on a file. It was obvious he wasn't reading, he had just decided he would be happier like that.

'I believe the Director can't refuse to see me.'

Mansell sighed. 'If you insist, of course I'll try to arrange something. He's extremely busy this week. You may have to wait a few days.'

'I accept that.' He might have added, the longer the better.

'Your suspension will remain in force meanwhile and of course you'll continue to receive pay. Afterwards ...' Mansell was making clear how he saw afterwards.

Antonia's door was open. She beckoned him in. 'How did you get on?'

'They want me to resign. The note I sent didn't work. If I go quietly there'll be what Mansell calls a substantial gratuity and help in finding a new job. If I don't accept—well, that wasn't spelled out but I can guess.'

'What did *you* say?'

'I asked for an interview with Antrim and for more time in which to make enquiries. I said I believed I knew who was behind the planting but he'd have to wait for the name until I had the proof.'

'Is he going to arrange the interview?'

'Yes.'

She pondered. 'If we don't get the evidence before that and Antrim refuses to wait longer you ought to have a case against him in law. He'd be denying you natural justice.'

'Is that really a starter?'

'Probably. You can argue almost anything about dismissal is a denial of natural justice. Anyway Kendick as Legal Adviser is bound to get the willies and tell Antrim he'd better think again.'

He guessed she was engaged in an effort to keep his spirits up. He tried and failed to look convinced. With a touch of impatience she said, 'Don't assume the worst until it happens. While you're waiting for Camilla Rylance to say the coast's clear for action, there's something else you can be doing.'

He raised his eyebrows.

'This morning I looked through your reports of interviews with people who had known Lauren. There's one person you never got to although Lauren was actually living with her when she went off with Fernandes. Lisa Husak—she was away in Singapore. With any luck she's now back. Let's assume the worst and you fail to get proof

248

of a link between Evelyn Rylance and Catini. The single
key to your achieving control over the present situation
may lie *in discovering what Evelyn and Giordano went to get from
Lauren.* They failed. How do we know the thugs they
employed and who killed her didn't also fail? And isn't it at
least possible that Lauren dropped some hint to the person
who seems to have been her closest friend that would lead
you to it?'

'And then?'

'Your next move would depend on what it turned out to
be.'

There was something in the idea but he didn't care to let
her know how little he thought it was. 'I could try ringing
her sometime.'

She pointed to her phone. 'Try now.' She watched,
unsmiling, until he picked it up.

There was no reply from Lisa Husak's home number. He
got through to Victor Crispin, sounding as delighted as
ever to be distracted from work: Lisa *was* back, he confirmed, but off somewhere else soon; he read out her office
number from his diary.

He just caught her. A distracted voice announced that it
was on its way to Edinburgh in ten minutes and wouldn't
be back before the end of the week. When he said he wanted
to tell her, as Lauren's closest friend, something important
about her death, her tone changed. 'Can't you tell me now?'

'No, it's too delicate for the phone.'

Slightly to his surprise, she was hooked at once. For a
moment he had the impression she was even thinking of
postponing the Edinburgh trip. Finally they agreed he
would call at her flat for a drink on Saturday evening when
she was due back.

He replaced the receiver and told Antonia. She grimaced
at the delay but then shook her head. 'Still . . . it's worth
doing.'

He rose. 'I'd better get back in case Camilla Rylance
calls.' As he went out, he was conscious he must have
appeared dreary and undeserving. The fact was his hope

had begun to leak away. He was quite sure Camilla wasn't going to call anyway.

He was wrong. She came through as he was trying to decide whether frying eggs would be less trouble than scrambling them. She declared in sullen tones that the coast at Chester Square was clear for action. Rylance was in Aldershot for the night attending an Army function. Evelyn had left for dinner with friends; afterwards she was going to a charity film première. Hope began to trickle back. 'What is she wearing?' he asked.

'Wearing . . .?'

'Yes, has she gone in a formal evening dress?'

'Yes.'

'So she's carrying only a purse—a small bag, anyway . . .'

Puzzlement was struggling through the sullenness. 'I expect so, I didn't notice. Why—?'

'Never mind. Are you now the only person in the house?'

'Slade, the butler and his wife are in the basement flat. They're off duty and won't come up again. There's no one else here.'

Conditions sounded as good as they were ever likely to be. 'I'll be round in fifteen minutes,' he said.

She hadn't bothered with dressing to please him this time. The jeans did nothing for the puppy fat and her hair needed washing. He told her to go and watch TV and he'd let her know when he was leaving.

Evelyn's study-cum-dressing-room-cum-health-laboratory had presumably been tidied by her maid after she had left for the evening. A chair was still positioned where she would have taken her evening boost of negative ions but no clothing lay scattered about and the papers beside the typewriter on the desk were neatly piled and clipped.

He went first to the handbag on her dressing table but it proved a disappointment. He had hoped he would find inside her diary with an entry pointing to contact with Catini or Boffa or at least containing the Medmenham Club's telephone number. There was no diary. Presumably it was small enough to fit easily into her evening purse and she was one of those women who couldn't bear to be without it.

He transferred his attention to the papers on the desk. They were all innocuous, mostly concerned with do-gooding events she had attended or was invited for in the future. One clip contained political briefing sheets, another the minutes of a society for the parents of handicapped children of which she seemed to be a patron. There was also a booklet on local traditions and country dialect in Rylance's constituency. Evelyn wasn't going to fall short as a politician's wife through want of hard graft at the coal face.

He abandoned the desk top with a sinking heart and went to work on the drawers. This time he struck lucky; it wasn't pure gold but something approaching it. Hiding beneath a desk diary and a vitamin company's catalogue was a plain envelope, containing several photographs. The star in every one was the same. He saw himself walking, standing, talking, even calling a taxi. They had been taken, he deduced, in the days leading up to the weekend with Gail in Shropshire. He was alone in only one, taken as he summoned a cab after his visit to Gail in hospital. The others showed him with another person—with Foxall, of the Bureau's Finance Division, as they entered a pub for a lunchtime sandwich, with Celia French, encountered on a corner of George Street having been last seen in a Tokyo swimming pool nine years ago, even with the unknown Arab who had buttonholed him with a request for guidance on how to get to Soho.

Hand-written notes on the back of the photographs gave identifying details of the people he had been with. Foxall was correctly described, Celia had presumably been followed home since they noted both her name and her address in Regents Park and said what her husband did for a living. Only the Arab had defeated the watchers who had worked alongside the photographer; perhaps their attention had wavered while he was weaving his way through the peep shows.

The last photograph of all had obviously been the prize.

It was a duplicate of the one Mansell had produced on the morning he had been suspended. The inscription said, 'The person Egerton is in conversation with is a member of the club and known to me. He deals in heroin. Also known to the police.'

It would have been nice to have had a signature under the inscription, or even just the initials 'A.B.'. But that was being greedy.

He pocketed the photographs and checked the other drawers, including a locked one which he had to fiddle open with his penknife; but there was nothing else of interest. Downstairs he found Camilla slumped in front of a TV panel game and drinking brandy.

'I'm leaving now.'

She gazed up at him bleakly and without a word walked across the hall towards the street door.

He had half-turned away to pick up his top coat from a chair, when he heard the door open. It was not until he looked towards Camilla again that he discovered she was still a few feet away from it and that it had been opened from the outside with a key. Advancing into the hall, elegant as ever in a three-quarter mink coat, a flame silk dress sweeping the marble beneath her feet, was Evelyn Rylance.

Her gaze was momentarily cast down while she returned the key to her purse: she hadn't yet seen him. Ashen-faced, Camilla was watching her as she passed. 'I thought you were going—'

Evelyn said brusquely, 'I decided to cut the première. There's a bomb scare at the cinema, God knows when they'll open the doors. Anyway I'm out riding early tomorrow.'

Her gaze finally lifted and she saw Egerton. She frowned in disbelief. 'What the hell are you doing here?'

There was nothing for it but to bluff his way out. 'I called hoping you'd spare me a few minutes.'

'I thought I made it clear I had nothing to say to you.'

'I felt you didn't quite understand—'

She had already turned to open the street door. 'Get out. Or do I have to tell the policeman outside to remove you?'

He was happy to oblige. Passing Camilla he shot her a last glance. She was still white with shock and had begun to say something to Evelyn about not realizing she wouldn't want . . . Evelyn's eyes remained fixed on him. He wished them both goodnight.

Outside the policeman was stamping his feet against the cold. As Egerton passed him, he said, 'Air's treacherous tonight, sir.' And it was.

# XXIV

W HEN he rang Fender to report, the voice at the other end was blurred and indistinct. Either he had been asleep or the Chivas Regal was doing active service. He quickly sharpened however when Egerton described the photographs. He asked about the handwriting in the notes.

'Looks like a man's. Nothing unusual.'

'Boffa's, do you suppose?'

'The mention of the club certainly suggests that.'

Words of satisfaction were coming from Fender when Egerton heard a crash; apparently he had dropped the receiver in his enthusiasm. When at last he was back on the line, he spoke as though victory was in the bag.

Egerton said, 'I feel uneasy.'

'Why?'

'Evelyn must have found my explanation for being in the house pretty odd. I suppose Camilla will back it up to protect herself. But if Evelyn really grills her, she'll get to the truth.'

'Let her. *We* have the photographs—that's all that matters. We can now show that at the very least she's been privy to the surveillance on you. What we need next is a specimen of Boffa's handwriting to compare with the writing on the back of the photographs. Then the linkage will be complete.'

'How do you suggest we get that?'

'Didn't you tell me the Medmenham is a gaming club?'

'Yes.'

'Then I fancy I know someone who should be in a

254

position to help, bearing in mind that Boffa is the manager. Unfortunately, I'm off tomorrow to Bristol to spend the night with a fellow lepidopterist but I shall telephone this person from there in order not to lose any time.'

'So when should we meet?'

'I suggest I come to your flat at eleven o'clock on Wednesday morning. If I get an early train from Bristol that should give me the opportunity to call on my friend beforehand. We can then discuss how you present this fascinating evidence to your Director. He should find it a bracing challenge, deciding how to handle the story in Whitehall.' He gave a satisfied grunt. When he took down directions for getting to Egerton's flat, he said, 'Prince of Wales Drive! How interesting! Has that become a good address these days?' He enjoyed a sly gibe, when elated.

His morale rose steadily throughout Tuesday. He even found affection for Fender beginning to take root. Antonia had been right: he was a redoubtable ally. If he now came up with a sample of Boffa's handwriting to clinch the source of the photographs, it was inconceivable that Antrim wouldn't accept he was in the clear. He told himself that after all he might be sitting behind prosecuting counsel, as the Bureau's representative, when Beynon stood trial at the Old Bailey.

Nine o'clock came. Gail had still not telephoned as she had promised. He was sure she wouldn't have forgotten and wondered if this meant a setback. But it seemed unlikely. He made himself supper, trying to decide how much longer to wait before calling the clinic. He felt a surge of relief when the bell finally rang. But the voice at the other end was unfamiliar.

'Egerton?'

'Yes.'

'I've got somebody here you know.' It was a man; the tone was casual, almost jokey. 'She's going to say a few words, aren't you darling?'

There were muffled, unrecognizable noises. Then Gail spoke. 'Mark, is that you?'

255

'Yes, what the hell's happening?'

'I don't know. I thought you did.'

He still half-believed it was some stupid joke, high jinks amongst the others at the clinic perhaps. 'Where are you?'

She began, 'They won't tell me. I think—' Then her voice faded, as though the headset had been removed.

The man was back again. 'Egerton, listen carefully because I shan't say this more than once. Your girlfriend is a guest of ours. She'll be all right as long as you do exactly as you're told. Have you got that much?'

'*Who are you?*'

'All you need to know is that we collected her while she was taking a little walk this afternoon. The reason is that you've been naughty, Egerton. You've been taking other people's property. That's *very* bad.'

Light had begun to dawn. He felt too sick to speak. The man said, 'I'm giving you a chance to put things right. You're going to bring those photographs to me. If you do that, my friend here *may* be persuaded to keep his works in their little box.'

'What works?'

'He thinks your girl hasn't been having too much fun in that clinic. So he's arranging to put things right. One word from me and she'll be back on the stuff in a really big way. You'll like that, won't you darling?'

His voice receded for a moment then returned. 'She's not too sure she wants it, Egerton. But she'll soon get used to the old buzz again. My friend thinks about half a gram would be right tonight. He'll get her up to a gram a day, maybe two, pretty soon. She's going to have a really good time. He says that by the time he's finished with her, she won't want to bother with any more clinics.'

The man paused. 'On the other hand, I might ask him to leave her alone. It all depends on you. I get the photos, you get the girl—as she is. Is it a deal? Or does he make with the needle?'

He closed his eyes to shut it all out. But there was no escape that way.

'I'm not waiting any more,' the man said.

'All right. Just don't touch her.'

The voice became lighter, even encouraging. 'That's a good boy. Listen. There's a gate leading into Regents Park from the Outer Circle opposite Ulster Terrace. Be there tomorrow morning at nine o'clock with the photographs. And alone. Somebody will contact you.'

'I'm not handing them over unless you let her go at the same time. And I want to speak to her again.'

When he heard Gail's voice, he said, 'I have some photographs these people want. But they're going to free you if I hand them over tomorrow morning. There's no need to worry. Just don't let them give you any shots.'

The man cut in before she could answer. 'She's got that, Egerton. One more thing—we'll be checking the neighbourhood. If you thought of having the law about the place, forget it.' The receiver went dead.

Somehow the night passed. He dreaded the telephone ringing again in case it turned out to be Fender or Antonia calling him. He rated it good fortune of a sort that he couldn't ring either of them: Antonia he knew was in Dublin on a case until the morning while Fender was off with his butterfly friend. If they made contact with *him*, he would have to be frank about what he'd agreed to. But there were no more calls.

At twenty to nine, he drove the Mini up Park Square West and left it on the Outer Circle, a dozen yards from the gate the man had specified. At this end the park was mostly open ground given over to hockey pitches. A few people were walking dogs. The occasional jogger panted by. In a children's playground an Indian child was trying to persuade its *ayah* to sit on a swing and be pushed. Under a sky of shifting grey masses he tried to compose himself for waiting.

Nine o'clock arrived, then nine fifteen. Nothing happened. He studied cars parked nearby but none were occupied. Those that passed him seemed bound for innocent business elsewhere. He wondered if this might all be a cruel charade.

From the direction of the Marylebone Road, a boy of eleven or twelve was approaching on a BMX bike. He seemed solely intent on demonstrating what the bike could do to anyone who cared to watch. But by Egerton he reared it to a halt and looked up impassively. 'Mr Egerton?'

'Yes.'

The boy held his hand out. There was a note in it. 'Walk north until you're stopped,' it said.

'Who gave you this?'

The boy swung the handlebars and bounced the bike round. 'A chap,' he said. He returned the way he had come, his attention once more devoted to the ways of avoiding a natural progression.

Egerton entered the park and walked past the playground, past the hockey pitches, the dog strollers, three men raking leaves into piles for collection by a cage truck that hovered in the distance. Nobody showed the smallest disposition to stop him until he reached the gate leading out to Chester Road. Suddenly a balding man in a camel coat and blue-lensed spectacles was beside him. Like the boy he also held a hand out but this one was empty. 'Let's have them,' he said.

Egerton shook his head. 'First I see her.'

The man nodded over his shoulder. On the curve of the road, towards Queen Mary's Gardens, two figures, a man and a girl, stood beside a blue Granada; the man was holding the girl by the shoulders in what could have been an affectionate embrace. They were just near enough for Egerton to make out Gail's features.

'Get on with it,' said the man. 'We're not hanging about.'

When Egerton produced the photographs, he checked them carefully then stepped back and lifted an arm towards the Granada. The engine must have been running because it began to swing away from the kerb before the man with

Gail had released her in order to climb in. It paused to give the camel-coated one a more dignified entry. Then it was away again.

Gail seemed rooted to the spot where she had been made to stand. As Egerton reached her, she began to sway, shivering. He held her until he felt her body steady, then pulled his head back to study her. She looked drained but unharmed. 'The car's about ten minutes walk away,' he said, 'Can you make it?'

She nodded silently.

Halfway back to the Mini, she stopped him. Reaching up, she kissed his mouth but still didn't speak. The men were loading leaves into the truck now; one winked at Egerton.

'Did they touch you?'

'No.'

'Or give you any idea who they were?'

'None.'

He persisted. 'Did you hear them use names to each other?'

She shook her head. 'Once when we were driving to London, after they'd picked me up, the man in the camel coat ordered the driver to stop at a telephone box because he wanted to tell—' she made a slurred sound '—they'd got me. But I couldn't catch the word.'

'Might it have been Tony? Or Boffa?'

'I just don't know.'

He gritted his teeth. 'What about the house? Could you find it again?'

'Not really. It was somewhere in central London, I suppose, because it didn't take more than twenty minutes this morning to bring me here. They made me lie on the floor of the car all the way—the same yesterday evening when we reached the Cromwell Road. It was a house with an inside garage. I never saw the street.' She looked up, sensing his frustration. 'Sorry.'

He shook his head. 'It was just a slim hope.'

They had arrived at the gate where he had waited earlier.

259

As they crossed to the Mini, she said, 'Was what happened connected with your work?'

'In a way.'

'So they were blackmailing you into giving back some evidence you'd collected . . .'

He nodded.

'Couldn't you have told the police so that they'd be waiting?'

'There were complications. It wasn't official evidence. It all had to do with *me*. Somebody has been trying to get me sacked from the Bureau. The photographs would have been helpful towards proving that—proving I'd been framed.'

There was a little colour in her cheeks now. 'But who would *want* to get you sacked?'

'If you're sitting comfortably,' he said, 'I'll tell you.'

As he parked in Prince of Wales Drive, he saw Fender's mountainous shape impatiently shifting from side to side in the entrance to the apartment block. He was dressed in a belted overcoat and woollen muffler. On his head was a battered homburg, presumably a relic of Whitehall days, brought out for forays into the metropolis.

Egerton guided Gail towards him. 'I'm sorry to have kept you waiting. Could I introduce Gail Henderson?'

Fender raised the homburg and gave a little bow. 'Ludovic Fender. How very nice to meet you, Miss Henderson.' If he felt surprise that he was being confronted with someone he had been told was in a Devon clinic, he gave no hint of it. He turned to Egerton. 'Is Miss Henderson familiar with the matter in hand?'

'I've been telling her.'

'Then I suggest we go and consider our next move. I've collected from a good friend who works with the Gaming Board a form which Anthony Boffa completed in his own handwriting as manager of the Medmenham Club. I fancy we shall now be able to make an encouraging comparison.'

He smiled avuncularly at Gail, inviting her to share in the idea of a pleasure in store.

Egerton took out his key. If Fender was going to blow his top, as well he might, it had better be indoors. 'I'm afraid I have some disappointing news.'

# <u>XX</u>V

F ENDER lifted a hand and fluttered it; a gold signet ring winked at Egerton in the light from the gas fire. As a gesture of reassurance, nothing could have been less convincing.

'Please don't think I'm concerned to reproach you. Given your anxiety for Miss Henderson's well-being, I perfectly understand you felt bound to cooperate.'

But of course he *didn't* understand. Wedged in the larger of the two armchairs, his fingernails picking morosely at loose threads of fabric, he gazed into the fire and contrived to convey that he had been personally robbed.

His post mortem on the surrender of the photographs had gone on relentlessly from the moment they entered the flat. He hadn't after all blown his top, instead had moved from scarcely contained incredulity into an icy interrogation that was only now petering out in general gloom. Gail, attacked by dizziness, had gone to lie on Egerton's bed. Her place had been taken in the last twenty minutes by Antonia, summoned from her office desk almost as soon as she got in from Dublin by a telephone call from Fender. Her questions had been few and she had avoided comment. Egerton guessed she had decided the best way of moving to a more constructive phase was to let Fender work his irritation out.

They sat in uneasy silence. Antonia eventually rose and crossed to the window to gaze across Battersea Park. 'It was appalling luck Evelyn Rylance came back when she did.'

Fender said shortly, 'I accept that.'

She gave Egerton a brief smile. 'What do you think happened after you left the house?'

He guessed she was trying to move the focus away from himself. 'She must have decided Camilla was looking shifty and got the truth out of her. Then she searched her desk to see if anything was missing.'

'. . . And phoned Boffa for help.'

'Yes. I wonder why he didn't simply send some heavies round to take the photographs by force.'

'Perhaps after what happened in Nice, Evelyn said it had to be a different approach.' She turned to Fender. 'Isn't it quite likely that the man in the camel coat *was* Boffa? If we could get a photograph and both Mark and Gail can confirm it was, we should be able—'

'It wasn't Boffa. I saw a photograph of him this morning in the Gaming Board's file for the Medmenham Club. He bears no resemblance to their description. I wouldn't in any case have expected Boffa to risk his own neck in such an operation.'

'Even without that, surely Antrim will see—'

'When it comes to the important questions, at whose request, and why, the heroin was planted in Egerton's flat, we lack a vital link in the evidence. Given the status of our adversary and Egerton's unfortunate past, we need considerably more than we now have before doing battle.' Even to Antonia, he wasn't bothering to wrap up his responses with the usual flummery.

'So what do we do?'

He began the maddening ritual of filling his pipe. 'I confess I see this as a serious reverse.'

'Perhaps Seagram will come up with Coleman's whereabouts.'

'Unfortunately, that's unlikely. He spoke to me on Monday. According to informants in Shoreditch, Coleman has gone abroad. I fear we have to assume that he's taking a winter holiday at Mrs Rylance's expense at whichever foreign playground the British criminal fraternity now favours after the Costa del Sol.' He was taking pleasure in being negative.

'What about Giordano?' Egerton asked. When Fender raised his eyebrows, he went on, 'If he were suddenly confronted with our knowledge, not only that he was in Nice at the time of the killings but was actually staying with a man linked to the gang the killers belonged to, we might bluff something out of him we could use as a lever in dealing with Evelyn.'

'You're suggesting a visit to Rome?'

It had already begun to seem absurd. He shrugged.

Astonishingly Fender was playing with the thought. 'I suppose there's a small chance. I wonder . . .'

Antonia's expression became flinty. She took a cigarette out of her handbag. 'Even you, Ludo, wouldn't trick Giordano into saying anything remotely incriminating. You know that.'

He looked up at her mildly. 'You think so?' Seeing the cigarette in her hand, he rose with a surprisingly swift movement to strike one of his matches for her, then hovered attentively until satisfied further ministrations were unnecessary. As he slotted himself back into the armchair, he said, 'Well, perhaps not. We need to take a little time for reflection. If we're to regain our advantage, we may have to change direction and go back to the mysterious something that took them both to Nice.'

They were almost the words Antonia had used two days before. She said, 'That's the reason Mark is going to talk to Lisa Husak on Saturday.'

Fender frowned. Egerton realized they had forgotten to tell him. After hearing the details he expressed grudging approval. It was clearly irritating him that he had not had the idea first. 'No doubt you'll let me know the outcome,' he said stiffly. 'When you have a moment.'

Struggling to his feet, he looked about him in a helpless way until his eye lit upon his overcoat and hat. 'If you'll forgive me, I shall go away and brood.'

Egerton helped him into the coat. 'There's nothing else you think we should be doing?'

'No, what the situation now calls for is properly directed thought.' He paused at the door of the flat. 'It would be prudent, I suggest, if you took rather special care during the next few days. We don't want you run down by a car or removed from circulation by other means before we have decided our next move. The opposition may conclude that, after all, it would be safer with you out of the way. Mrs Rylance is a bold risk taker and Boffa obviously well able to organize strong arm operations. Also I recommend that Miss Henderson does not return to the clinic just yet. She shouldn't stay here either. I would be delighted to have her as a guest in my cottage but I fear that might not be very attractive to her.'

'I can take her down to Gloucestershire to stay with my sister.'

'Very well.' He was perhaps a little disappointed his half-offer had not been taken up. 'Make sure you're not followed.'

When he returned from finding a taxi for Fender, Antonia was emerging from the bedroom, having said goodbye to Gail. 'I noticed you looked disappoving when I spoke about the possibility of confronting Giordano. I realize it was a pretty desperate idea.'

She shook her head. 'It's just that we don't want Ludo pushing off to Rome. He'd love the excuse. If I believed in reincarnation, I'd say one of his lives was spent in the Vatican, probably working for the Inquisition.' She stubbed out her cigarette. 'I imagine Giordano would have to be a rack and thumbscrew job.'

He went down into Prince of Wales Drive again and flagged a taxi for her. 'Is he really going to come up with an answer now, do you suppose? Time's getting short.'

'Ludo doesn't accept defeat. Ever.' She squeezed his arm briefly as she climbed into the cab. 'Anyway, how do you know you're not going to dig something out of Lisa Husak?' She was still working on his morale.


Lisa was rather as he had imagined her, dark and shapeless
265

and restless-eyes. She wore ethnic jewellery that chattered when she gestured which was often. He put her at about thirty-five, a moderate spare-ribber.

'Lauren never mentioned you,' she said.

'I met her for the first time when I went to Nice.'

She sat opposite him, sipping a large whisky thoughtfully. 'How did that happen?'

'We were in the same restaurant. She borrowed my copy of *The Times*. Then she and Fernandes asked me to have dinner with them.'

'So this was just before they were killed?'

'Less than a week. Afterwards I talked to a writer who had the apartment next door to theirs. He told me things that made nonsense of the police version of events.'

He gave her Boyd's story just as he had got it from him, but added nothing about Giordano or the Rylances. She was visibly shaken.

'And you believe the Americans he heard had some part in it all, that they employed the thugs?'

'I'm sure of it.'

'So it was criminal, not political?'

'Yes.'

She shook her head. 'But she was the last person to get caught up with criminals. I really can't imagine anyone wanting to harm her. She was terribly nice, terribly idealistic—everything I imagine her mother isn't.'

'Do you know her mother?'

'No, but Lauren talked about her. Her mother's obviously dead in any moral sense. What Lauren cared about meant nothing to her. She just believes in manipulating people for her own ends.'

'Were you and Lauren very close?'

She looked away from him. 'I suppose so. We cared about the same things. Like the peace movement.'

Several centuries had gone by since he had sat, dripping rain onto a schoolroom desk, and heard that from the pure-hearted Flora. He said, 'A girl she used to know at the school where she worked in Chelsea told me Lauren felt

266

that to achieve something really big for peace would be the most satisfying thing in the world.'

'She was one of those people who are prepared to go out on a limb for it.'

'Do you mean by taking personal risks?'

'In a way.'

Something in her tone made him pursue it. 'Was Lauren doing something *dangerous*—something that could explain her murder?'

She laughed. 'No, no, not dangerous. What she was involved in could have been *embarrassing* if it became known. But it wasn't dangerous.' She laughed again and thrust her hand through her hair. A dozen or more charms, trinkets and other gewgaws caught the light.

'It would have been embarrassing because of who her stepfather was, I suppose.'

Her expression remained watchful. 'She told you, did she?'

It would be a very small lie. 'Yes. She explained it made life quite difficult for her at times.'

She was studying him closely but he could tell she was impressed he had been on those terms. She went to get herself a refill of whisky. 'She was usually cagey about it with others. She couldn't afford the risk of it reaching the press. I knew of course. But none of the other people in ANWA knew.'

When he frowned she said, 'Don't tell me *you've* never heard of ANWA?'

'Should I have done?'

She shook her head in resignation. 'I suppose it's not surprising, the papers and television give all the publicity to CND as though we didn't exist. ANWA is the Anti-Nuclear Weapons Alliance. Cross-party—no publicity-hunting politicians, no pop stars, no priests prancing about in cassocks, just serious people who work in areas where they can exercise influence. Quite a few are government officials. We even have a soldier or two. We intend to change things from the inside.

'I introduced Lauren to ANWA. She became a very enthusiastic supporter. One day after we'd been to a meeting at which opposition to GOLIATH was being discussed and one of the scientist members had described the effect of a single missile on a large town, she suddenly said she believed she could do something really big for ANWA. She believed her stepfather could be argued out of ratifying the proposal to buy GOLIATH.'

He shook his head, smiling.

'Don't smile. *I* didn't believe her at first. She wouldn't explain either. A few weeks later when I realized she was deadly serious, I asked her to tell me how. She explained that the key lay with someone called David who shared our views. David was going to convince her stepfather that he'd got things wrong. That whatever the military might say, GOLIATH wasn't necessary to an effective defence strategy over the next ten years and could actually make our situation more dangerous. She never gave me a hint as to who this mysterious David was but I came to the conclusion it must be some influential scientist in the Ministry who feels the way we do about nuclear weapons but has to play his cards very carefully not to get thrown out.'

'One man couldn't be confident of swinging the issue on a thing like that.'

'I was just as sceptical. But then it was announced, out of the blue, that Rylance had set up a special committee to report on possible alternatives to GOLIATH. I began to think there was something in what Lauren had said. Of course I looked to see if there was a "David" on the committee. But there isn't.'

'It's still very difficult to believe.'

'Whoever he is, she had great confidence in him. Whenever we read the leakages in the *Globe* and about the arguments going on in the Ministry, she used to say, "Don't worry, it's all irrelevant. He'll kill it in the end, you'll see".'

Somehow the mystery of David had to tie in with Evelyn's anxiety to trace Lauren. 'Did Lauren tell you she was leaving England? And why? It seems to me that if we knew the reasons, we might be closer to discovering what led to her murder.'

Lisa lit a cigarette; she drew the smoke in as though it had to reach every corner of her being if it was to do its stuff. 'She told me nothing. I was shattered when it happened. She left no address, just a note saying I was not to worry, there were reasons why she and Luis had to take off and she'd write. There was a postcard from Geneva later, saying they were moving to Spain in the autumn and she'd let me know where at the time. Incidentally she added a postscript to that card: "Promise about GOLIATH still stands!" I went off to Singapore on a job not knowing what to think. The next thing was reading about her death in a newspaper on the plane that brought me back here.' She took in another lethal dose from the cigarette. 'Until you told me about the Americans, I'd supposed it was because she'd got caught up through Luis in some Basque feud.'

He watched her move to the window. She was trying not to let him see that she was blinking as she spoke. 'About those Americans—do you think it possible they were connected with the company that manufactures GOLIATH? That somehow they'd picked up a hint she was saying that she *knew* the deal was going to be dropped and were trying to find out what was behind it? These big companies stop at nothing.'

He guessed she would be hot on conspiracy theories to explain what went on in the armaments business. She was silent for a while, then swung round.

'Do you know the awful thought I sometimes had? I liked Lauren enormously, she was one of the most sincere and *good* persons I've ever known. But she was very intense, obsessive at times. She could become almost irrational when she cared about things deeply. When she talked about David and what he was going to do, I wondered once or twice whether she was fantasizing the whole thing because she so desperately wanted to *achieve* something for

ANWA. Did she perhaps know that her stepfather was likely to cancel the bloody thing for quite different reasons, like cost?'

'You thought that David perhaps didn't exist . . .'

'I don't like to say it but—yes.'

He shook his head. 'There's definitely a "David". Her sister, Jacqueline, knows him. I've no idea who he is but he exists all right.'

He thought she might ask when he'd talked to Jacqueline but she didn't. He went on, 'Anyway, we'll know Rylance's decision quite soon. Yesterday's *Times* said he'd made his mind up and was going to put it to the Cabinet soon. They seem to think the deal will go through.'

She came to sit down again. 'I saw that. I hope to God they're wrong.' She looked into her whisky. 'Of course even if they *are* wrong and it's dropped, in a few months' time there'll be talk of something equally ghastly. The military people won't rest until they've got the same toys as the Big Boys have.'

He smiled. 'If you're such a pessimist, why bother to belong to ANWA?'

'Because if there's a chance that people will listen and be influenced, you have to take it. I sometimes think it's about as unlikely as my premium bonds winning me more than peanuts. But just as I keep looking in the papers for my bond number, I have to stay with the anti-nuclear campaign. You've got to keep hoping.' She grimaced, then laughed. He decided that when she wasn't shaking her beads about, he quite liked her.

Before he left she said, 'If it wasn't a political killing or skullduggery by the manufacturers of GOLIATH what else could explain what happened? As I told you, she'd never have been mixed up in anything criminal. So what was the reason?'

'Fear,' he said. 'She'd got some people very frightened. Of that I'm sure. But about what, I don't yet know.'

He was halfway back to his flat when he decided to turn

north again in the hope of finding Antonia home. She opened the door wearing a shirt and jeans and nothing on her feet. Her hair was caught back in the neck with a rubber band. She looked younger and more vulnerable than the person he knew in the Bureau. 'Come in,' she said, 'you don't know just how welcome you are.'

He followed her into the living room. The smell of beeswax rose to his nostrils: he had interrupted a housecleaning session. She waved him to a chair and sank down opposite. 'I was afraid there was never going to be an excuse to stop.' She looked about her grimly. 'I hate housework. But I inherited a guilt complex from my mother. The marks of the prison house on my back, Ludo would no doubt say.'

He smiled. It seemed a very long time since they had listened to Fender pontificate about never escaping from the past. 'I thought you'd like to hear what I learned from Lisa Husak. It was quite interesting, although I'm not sure it gets us anywhere.'

She listened impassively to his account. At the end she said, 'It gets us *this* far—we need to find David. Either directly or through Evelyn he seems to have a hold over Rylance. If we knew what that hold was, we might be able to start calling the tune.'

'You don't buy the theory that he's a Ministry of Defence scientist?'

She shook her head. 'Far more likely he has nothing to do with Whitehall. He knows something very damaging about the Rylances and Giordano and for reasons of his own he was allowing Lauren to use that knowledge as blackmail to turn Rylance round on GOLIATH. The Committee was a stalling device while Rylance tried to get off the hook.'

She was silent for a moment, then jumped to her feet. 'We'd better put this to Ludo. Have you heard from him?'

'Not a word.'

She swore with unexpected pungency. 'What *is* he up to? I tried to raise him yesterday.'

'Perhaps he slipped away to Rome after all.'

She groaned, went to the phone behind his chair and dialled. Her expression became grim again as she waited then suddenly changed. She said sharply, 'Ludo, where have you *been*? I've been trying to contact you for ages. Mark has some information from Lisa Husak you ought to hear.'

She held the headset away from her ear so that Egerton could catch Fender's responses. He was asking what the information was.

'We think the key to the whole thing could be David, the person Lauren referred to in her letter to Jacqueline. David has, or had, an armlock on the Rylances and presumably Giordano as well.'

He couldn't hear Fender's reply. Antonia was frowning. 'Somehow we have to locate him,' she said.

'Fortunately that's not necessary.'

'What?'

'I said it's not necessary.'

'Why not?'

This time Fender's voice came to him clearly. The tone was triumphant. 'David happens to be here.'

# XXVI

ALTHOUGH the sun was back to encourage Sunday joyriders, the morning traffic south from London had been light. They arrived at Fender's cottage ahead of the time he had suggested. When they rang the bell, there was no reply.

'Church,' Antonia said. She shook her head as Egerton glanced enquiringly up at the spire opposite where he had parked the Mini. 'The other team play there. Ludo answers for his sins further on.' She was pointing along the High Street.

Trying to imagine Fender at confession was an interesting challenge. Would he even squeeze into the box? In the list of the week's misdemeanours, want of frankness would rate fairly high. About the mysterious David, after announcing the previous evening that he was actually present in the house, he had declined to say a word more, pretending to fears that the conversation would be picked up. He had instead summoned them to his presence.

They looked about them, irresolute, considering whether to kill time with exploration of the lanes that ran between the houses. Gazing up at lattice windows and tile-hung facades, Egerton said, 'Isn't this rather quiet for him? He can't spend all his days looking for butterflies and writing letters to the *Tablet*. I don't see him as a golfer somehow. Wouldn't you suppose he'd get very bored?'

'Ludo's never bored. He adjusts to the environment in which he finds himself. He imposes his imagination on it.'

He thought of Lisa Husak's misgivings about Lauren. 'Another fantasist?' he said. He was hoping to provoke her.

If she guessed his purpose, she wasn't letting it show. 'No, it's just that the essence of things is never commonplace for him. His mind can always discover something fresh. That's what makes him a marvellous companion when he's on form.'

Once more, he found himself wondering if there had been, perhaps still was, a physical bond. The picture it produced in his mind's eye was grotesque. Yet nothing he could associate with *her* deserved that description.

'The really sad thing about Ludo,' she said, 'is that he's so alone. To be able to share what he feels and sees—he needs that more than most people.'

'When did his wife die?'

'Nearly thirty years ago. They were living in India. He lost her and the baby she was having on the same day. It devastated him, locked him up.'

'He could have remarried.'

'I suppose so. But for a long time he's been convinced his appearance makes him some sort of a monster. Apart from which he's maddening of course. Most women would feel that taking him on was likely to be hell.' She smiled. 'And they'd be right.'

She lifted an arm suddenly. In the distance, on the other side of the High Street, Fender had become visible. He walked with a curious sideways gait, the trunk turned slightly towards the shop fronts as he passed them. On his head, instead of the battered homburg, was a handsome fur hat.

When he recognized them, he quickened his pace. He was breathing hard as he reached where they were standing.

'My profound apologies.'

'We were early,' Egerton said.

'Ah. . .' His eyes searched Antonia's face. 'Are you sure you're not chilled?'

She shook her head. 'I like your hat.'

He touched it so that the angle became more rakish. 'A Christmas present from my sister-in-law. She has an unnatural passion for my ears and worries that frostbite will carry them off.' He was trying to make her smile.

Leading them into the cottage, he made small talk about the village while he brewed coffee. In the sitting room they looked at him expectantly. 'So . . .?' Antonia said.

He smiled inscrutably. 'Yes?'

'David . . . you said he was here last night.'

'Yes.'

'But no longer apparently.'

'Wrong,' he said. Moving to a table on which stood a video player that had not been visible on their previous visit, he picked up a cassette.

'This is David.'

He watched smugly as they stared. 'A codename, you see, not a person. It was Lauren's private joke. A codename to smite a codename, one might say. She believed, not without reason, it was going to stop GOLIATH.'

He turned the cassette over in his hands, as though it were some curious, faintly amusing artefact, for which he had just been informed of a use. 'Actually I fancy the name *wasn't* a joke. Lauren was, after all, a rather serious girl. She preferred her friend, Lisa Husak, to believe there really was a person named David who was going to argue Rylance out of buying GOLIATH. That presented a more respectable version of what she was doing. The reality was rather shaming: pure blackmail, albeit on an elevated level. She was saying that unless a decision against GOLIATH *was* taken, the cassette would find its way to—' Fender paused. 'Well, I'm not sure exactly what she would have threatened.'

'To a newspaper?'

'That seems the most likely recipient. One of the guardians of our liberty.' He smiled sardonically.

'So the cassette contains something very damaging to the Rylances?' Egerton said.

'Very.'

'But where did *you* get it?'

'From the sister, Jacqueline, of course.'

'You've been to Deya since we saw you?'

'Two days ago. A very charming place I thought.' He paused again, enjoying the expressions on their faces.

'Does that mean Jacqueline was also part of the campaign against GOLIATH?' Antonia asked.

'No, Jacqueline didn't appear to me to hold any views on whether or not the British should protect themselves with nuclear weapons. She doesn't intend to come back here anyway. She does however dislike her mother and stepfather very much and was quite happy to be a part of anything to discomfort them. Lauren had become anxious for the safety of the cassette after the burglary Crispin told Egerton about. She suspected that the break-in was an attempt to recover it and I fancy she was right. One of the reasons she told none of her friends where she had gone with Fernandes was her fear there'd be another attempt before the decision about GOLIATH had been taken. According to Jacqueline she had evidence that Evelyn had employed a private investigator. This prompted her to make the trip to Deya and ask Jacqueline to look after the cassette.'

Antonia had lit a cigarette. Egerton could see that she was trying to control a growing impatience. 'Ludo, if we're to make sense of this, don't you think you should explain what persuaded you to visit Jacqueline in the first place? You didn't even raise it as a possibility when we last saw you.'

Fender seemed mildly chastened. 'It occurred to me only on the train coming back here that day. I was reading a newspaper article about GOLIATH—what good value for money it was as a deterrent, how accurate, and so on— obviously planted by supporters anxious at the possibility of it not being bought. I started reflecting on how unfortunate it was to have given it a codename like GOLIATH. Everybody knows, after all, that GOLIATH was brought down by David with no more than a sling and a few stones. That reminded me of the other David who cropped up in Egerton's enquires. Suddenly that odd sentence in

Lauren's letter to Jacqueline became significant in the context of her interest in the peace movement. Quite a lot would begin to make sense if "David" was a thing and not a person and being used to shoot GOLIATH down, so to speak. It explained what had happened in Nice—the threats to Lauren, the ransacking of the apartment after she'd been killed. It also fitted in with the way the decision over buying GOLIATH had been postponed.'

'So you went to Deya on no more than a theory?'

'I found it seductive. If I was right, it might be used to turn events in our favour. And there was in any case nothing else to pursue.'

She shook her head, marvelling. Fender held out a plate of digestive biscuits. 'When I met Jacqueline, I confess I felt misgiving. Acting as sleeping partner with her sister in a campaign to influence the United Kingdom's weapons policy seemed an unlikely role for her. However, since I'd gone that far, I clearly had to press on.'

'You asked her *outright*?'

'No, I engaged in a trifling deception. I told her I had become associated with Lauren in the anti-nuclear weapons campaign, in fact that I occupied a rather senior position in the STOP GOLIATH movement. I showed her the newspaper article in favour of GOLIATH and said there were ominous signs that Rylance was again being argued round into buying it. Lauren had told me about "David" and said that if anything happened to her, I might have to visit Jacqueline to get "David" and revive the threat to use him. I believed the moment for that had arrived.'

He was trying, unsuccessfully, not to look pleased with himself. 'Most of the conversation took place over a meal in a restaurant some way up the coast from where she lives. The taxi was inordinately expensive but she'd insisted there were no satisfactory places to eat in Deya.' He compressed his lips briefly. 'Striking woman though she is, she would not be my first choice as dinner companion. We arrived back at her cottage in Deya around one in the morning by which time she was fairly drunk. She'd made no direct

277

response to my enquiry for David. On the other hand her manner had convinced me I was on the right track.'

Fender sighed. Egerton tried to picture the scene but the images refused to oblige. Presumably she had remembered to put on her pants this time. Had she invited him to bed? How had he responded?

'What happened next?'

'She insisted on our sharing another bottle of wine and talked endlessly about the unspeakable behaviour of everyone in Deya. I came to the conclusion I was not going to get anything out of her, that night anyway. But then things improved.' He took a digestive biscuit and looked sideways at a shaft of sunlight. It was almost as though he was inviting them to press him. He nibbled the biscuit reflectively. 'In the end she simply went to a drawer and brought out the cassette. I had it firmly in my head that "David" must be a file of papers filched from Giordano's house and disclosing crooked deals in which he and Rylance had been involved when Rylance was still running his computer business. However, I accepted the cassette with, I hope, suitable aplomb. She said I could have it if I would give my solemn assurance it would only be used in the campaign to stop GOLIATH and would then be destroyed. Of course I agreed.'

Reluctant admiration succeeded distaste in Egerton's thoughts. He was, after all, in no position to criticize. *He* had photographed Jacqueline's correspondence while she slept, after lying about his reasons for being in Deya. In worming into her confidence and securing the cassette with a fraudulent promise, Fender had behaved no worse.

As though he had been reading his thoughts, Fender said, 'A regrettable deceit, I fear. But I think you'll agree I had very little choice if I was to gain her confidence.' He spread his hands wide.

Antonia had risen to pick up the cassette. She said briskly, 'Well, it's done. Now you've whetted our appetites, perhaps we can see the thing.'

Fender examined his finger nails. 'You may prefer not to.

278

That is, while I need Egerton to view it in order to tell me if the assumptions I have made about people's identities are correct, you could really spare yourself the trouble. You once asked me to show you round the village. I should be delighted—'

'But I *want* to see it. Is there any reason why I shouldn't?'

Fender was looking acutely uncomfortable. 'It's rather—distasteful. I would prefer—'

She was staring at him in amused disbelief. 'Are you saying after I've driven fifty miles to find out who "David" is, *that he's not fit for my eyes?*'

'I simply feel you will find it distasteful,' he repeated stiffly. He rose to his feet and made an elaborate business of collecting the coffee cups. 'However, if you insist . . .' He gestured towards the video player. 'I imagine Egerton knows how to work this thing. I had to hire it from a shop along the street when I returned from Majorca yesterday. Meanwhile I shall make more coffee.'

He skulked in the kitchen throughout the playing of the cassette. After such a build-up, Egerton had expected a diet strong enough to turn the stomach. But it was relatively mild: he had been at parties at Oxford where people would have begun to jeer. There was no violence, no perversion, only the most conventional sort of titilation. In the centre of an extravagantly furnished room, two women and two men performed a series of sexual acts on what looked like a suede-covered mattress. The camera seemed to have been located at ceiling level or just below. Now and then it shifted from the couplings to probe the audience for reactions worthy of note. There were perhaps thirty people in all, mostly in evening dress. Moving behind those who were seated, and occasionally bending over to whisper in a host-like fashion, was Sam Giordano. His paunch was hardly noticeable and there was plenty of hair on his head: the event must have taken place a few years back. Evelyn Rylance was on a sofa beside a small, grey-faced man in gold-rimmed spectacles. The man's arm was stretched along the back of the sofa, so that the fingers rested at the

279

point of her bare shoulder. His manner towards the spectacle at their feet was largely phlegmatic but once the camera caught him making an exhortation towards the performers. Throwing back her head, Evelyn squeezed his thigh and laughed.

Towards the end the camera reached a tall figure standing a little apart from most of the audience. He was observing conscientiously but without apparent animation. It was Rylance, being British.

The picture faded. At exactly that moment, a church bell began to toll along the street outside. The incongruity of the sounds in relation to what had gone before offered a sudden comic relief. Egerton had avoided glancing at Antonia while the cassette was playing. He turned, smiling.

At some point she had lit a cigarette. She was frowning as though puzzled. Catching his smile, she returned it, then glanced towards the window. 'Do you suppose Ludo's ringing that bell as a sort of exorcism?'

Before he could reply Fender reappeared, bearing the fresh coffee. Perhaps he had been listening at the door to discover when it would be safe to return. He put down the tray. 'So you see,' he said unnecessarily.

'We imagined it was you ringing the bell,' she said. 'To dispel impure thoughts.'

He grunted.

'I'm sorry you thought I ought not to see it. Parts were quite pretty.' She was provoking him.

He gazed at her sombrely. 'Do you not find that sort of thing uncivilized?'

When she simply smiled, he went on, 'Quite soon we shall have a world in which nothing is left except sensation. Feeling, sentiment, will have been eliminated. They are after all tiresome, making demands that can seriously interfere with the pursuit of money and power. Pure sensation will be as far as people care to go. Sensation is safe. Like electricity it can be switched on and off at will.'

She was studying his face as he spoke, her eyebrows

raised slightly. 'You're exaggerating, Ludo. As you well know.'

He looked mournful but resigned. At some point in their acquaintance, it seemed, she had acquired the licence to tease him.

He seated himself and began speaking again in a more matter-of-fact voice. 'I don't know whether you share my impression but I conclude that was filmed at some party in Beverly Hills while Giordano and Evelyn Rylance were still married.' He glanced in Egerton's direction. 'You noted in one of your reports you'd been told Rylance stayed with them occasionally before he became a Minister.'

'Yes.'

'I take it the man strutting about in the background is Giordano.'

'Yes, he carries more weight these days but I imagine he would have looked like that ten years ago.'

'Rylance of course could be seen towards the end. Did you recognize anyone else, apart from Evelyn?'

'One or two of the faces were familiar from films. Otherwise, no.'

Antonia leaned back in her chair and looked at the ceiling. 'So now tell us the rest of the story, Ludo.'

'How do you mean?'

'I mean that while I accept the cassette could be a source of embarrassment to the Rylances if it found its way to a newspaper, it wouldn't be an absolute disaster. After all, they're not performing *themselves*. The idea of that, by itself, constituting a credible basis for blackmail to get GOLIATH stopped, simply won't wash. As to Giordano, what possible harm could come to him from it? Beverly Hills isn't Budleigh Salterton. Is he going to care at all if some columnist could prove he'd had a sex show at one of his parties?'

'You'll remember that according to the information Clayton supplied, he has just been nominated for a Presidential Commission on the Film Industry.'

281

She scoffed. 'And *that* would have got him thrown off it!?'

Fender was watching her face as she spoke. When she lowered her gaze until it was level with his eyes, he smiled in a placatory way. Reaching inside his jacket, he said, 'I confess there *is* a little more.' He drew from an envelope a sheet of paper with a press cutting attached.

'When you established that Evelyn had also been in Nice at the critical time, I thought it would be sensible to carry out some research into her background. Reference books are unhelpful on the subject. *Who's Who* confines itself to mentioning her previous married name, nothing about her parents and so on. I therefore telephoned an old friend from the New York Police Department who now runs an enquiry agency. This letter giving the results of his research was waiting for me when I got back from Deya.'

He put on his reading glasses. 'Evelyn's family tree is of considerable interest. She was born Evelyn Grace Brodsky, the daughter of a delicatessen proprietor, Peter Brodsky and his wife, Anna. They lived in Los Angeles until Evelyn was four when her father died in an automobile accident. Anna was ill at the time and no doubt things would have been pretty bleak had she not come from the sort of family which rallies round in such circumstances. It was a family of Italian stock. The name was Catini.'

He paused to look at them both over his spectacles. Antonia had turned her head to gaze out of the window while she listened; presumably she was signalling to him that she didn't intend to respond any more until he'd come completely clean.

'Anna Brodsky,' he went on, 'had a brother named Frank Catini who was becoming an important figure in organized crime on the West Coast. Frank set Anna and Evelyn up in a decent house in San Francisco and paid for Evelyn's schooling. She was his favourite niece and at one time she was going to marry the *capo* in his Mafia family but the man concerned got himself shot. After that she went off to be an air hostess and eventually married Giordano.'

Fender detached the press cutting from the letter. 'That's

all my friend's report tells us. It doesn't say whether Evelyn and Frank Catini stayed in touch. But of course we know they did.'

He handed to Egerton the press cutting. It was an item about a political fund-raising dinner. A photograph at the head of the story showed a congressman giving a handsome smile to the camera. Next to him, modestly leaning back to leave the glory to the politician was a small bespectacled man. The caption said that Mr Frank Catini, President of Catini Enterprises, had acted as host at the dinner for Congressman Monciano. 'Do you recognize him?' Fender asked.

It was the grey-faced man who had been seated next to Evelyn on the video.

Antonia had turned to look over Egerton's shoulder. 'So *that's* what really mattered about the cassette—not the entertainment but the company.'

'Yes. If the press were put in a position to make that connection, Rylance's political career would of course be finished. Even in today's climate a Cabinet Minister with a wife whose uncle is in the Mafia would not have total appeal.'

'And Giordano?'

'Suppose he was once involved in helping Catini to launder Mafia money through the medium of his film production companies, I could imagine that exposure of the relationship just when the Presidential Commission is about to sit would be very unwelcome.'

Egerton said, 'This explains a remark Clayton made which I didn't note down at the time. He commented that his FBI contact had seemed evasive when talking about Catini. That could have been because he knew of the family relationship with Evelyn.'

Fender shrugged. 'No doubt people in Washington sucked their teeth and then decided that United States' interests were best served by not mentioning the fact. After all the day might dawn when Washington would wish to apply a little moral pressure of its own on Rylance.'

A noise came from the window overlooking the garden. The cat Fender had introduced on the first occasion they had visited the cottage was standing erect on its hindlegs demanding admission. Its expression as it looked from Antonia to Egerton was one of astonished outrage at this evidence of intrusion.

'Rylance,' Fender said, rising to admit the cat, 'remains the one major enigma in all this. Did he *know* what was going on? It's tempting to assume he knew everything. But there's no evidence establishing it. That he was responding to pressure by hesitating over GOLIATH doesn't necessarily mean Lauren was threatening him with the cassette.'

When Egerton frowned he went on, 'Lauren may have dealt throughout with her mother—made her threat solely to her. She knew her mother was capable of influencing Rylance if she needed to. The political writers frequently tell us he makes no major decision without consulting her first. While that may be exaggerated, I have no doubt there's a kernel of truth there.'

'Are you suggesting that Rylance doesn't even know about Catini and his relationship to Evelyn?'

'It's possible. One can't assume he did from the evidence of the cassette—the man on the sofa may never have been introduced to him. And when Evelyn married him she could well have decided it would benefit no one, least of all herself, to reveal she had an uncle who was an important Mafioso. Then out of the blue, years later, disaster threatens. Lauren tells her she's brought the video back from her trip to Sam Giordano's home in Beverly Hills and intends to let the press have it unless Evelyn persuades him to abandon the idea of GOLIATH. Evelyn has no choice but to go to work on Rylance, aiming to get him to prepare for a dignified U-turn by appointing a committee from which he can be sure of getting the sort of answer he wants. She also sets about enlisting help through Catini to have Lauren separated from the video as quickly as possible.

'The burglary of Lisa Husak's flat was an attempt that failed. Then Lauren, guessing what mother is up to, disappears with Fernandes. Evelyn becomes very worried indeed. She persuades Rylance to employ the private investigator, Ingalls, to find her and, when he doesn't succeed, to make use of the official machine. Things look up after *you* find Lauren but only for a while. The bungled operation by the thugs in Nice not only fails to recover the cassette but results in the deaths of Lauren and Fernandes with all the consequent risks of what a police investigation may uncover. In fact the local police, with or without some backstairs encouragement from Catini or his friend Baptiste, give no trouble. But *you* do: the hired hand starts asking awkward questions. From then on, Evelyn is engaged in damage limitation, trying to stop you getting to the bottom of it all.'

'For the theory to hold water that Rylance was ignorant of what Evelyn and Giordano were doing you have to assume he knew nothing of her trip to Nice.'

'But that *is* possible. If you remember, Rylance was on an official visit to Washington when she went. He told you that she'd been staying with friends in Ireland during his absence. He may not have learned the truth.'

Antonia said, 'It's an interesting theory, Ludo. But do we need to go into that ourselves? Our objective is to get Mark cleared and reinstated in his job.'

'I'm absolutely with you.' The tone was one of over-elaborate warmth: he was preparing for a sideways shift. 'I was simply facing the fact that how the evidence is handled is also important in a wider sense. If we hand over the cassette and other information to Antrim now there is virtual certainty that we shall have condemned to obloquy or worse, a man who *may* be guilty of no more than paying undue attention to his wife's views on defence matters.'

'Good enough reasons for you, surely,' she said.

He shook his head. 'I do feel a moral obligation to discover the truth about Rylance's complicity or lack of it before Egerton reports these facts.'

She gazed grimly into the fireplace as though they had reached a situation all too familiar to her. 'What you're trying to say is that you're determined to confront Rylance first.'

He adopted a studiously bland expression. 'I think I must.'

'When?'

Fender glanced at his watch. 'In just over three and a half hours I hope. That is, if you and Egerton will be so kind as to give me a lift to London.' He fingered the side of his chair. He was not oblivious to the frostiness of her expression. 'Last night I established that the Rylances were spending the weekend in their Chester Square house. After some difficulty I managed to get through on the telephone directly to Rylance. I explained that although my name would not be known to him, his stepdaughter, Lauren, had taken certain steps before her death which had resulted in my having been entrusted with a sealed video cassette. I had been given to understand that it was of great importance to him personally. I would like to see him and would of course bring the cassette along. Rylance expressed himself mystified. He said his wife was far more likely to know about the matter than he was. He asked me to hold on while he spoke to her.

'After a fairly long pause he came on the phone again. He said his wife knew all about the video, it was of great sentimental value.' Fender allowed himself a crooked smile. 'He asked when they could get it from me. I explained that I would be in London today and it would be convenient for me to meet him at the Connaught Hotel at four o'clock. He was rather put out that I insisted on seeing him personally and wouldn't leave the cassette at Chester Square. Eventually he agreed to come to the Connaught.'

'You don't surely envisage letting him have the cassette?'

He laughed, at ease now that he had shown his hand at last. 'Certainly not. I shall use the occasion to get at the truth about his own involvement. If I conclude that Rylance was a party to all that went on, I shall tell him that he has no alternative but to telephone the PM in my hearing and announce his decision to resign from office. If I believe he wasn't, I shall say his only chance of avoiding public scandal is to make an immediate break with his unspeakably odious wife. At the same time he must inform Antrim of her responsibility for the wicked attempt to destroy Egerton's career and reputation.'

He sat back clasping his hands over his paunch. 'I now intend to take you both to lunch. Forgive me while I telephone for a table.'

When he had lumbered out into the hall, Egerton raised his eyebrows at Antonia. She had lost some of the sparkiness she had shown earlier. 'Is it really going to work?'

'Time for prayer,' she said.

# XXVII

PARKED on the other side of Carlos Place from the Connaught, they watched uneasily as the light faded. On the way to London, Fender had yielded to their argument that while the confrontation with Rylance could hardly put him in danger inside the hotel, it would be sensible to have them at hand. Now nearly forty minutes had passed since they had dropped him and there was still no sign of Rylance arriving.

From the direction of Grosvenor Square came a small band of demonstrators, abandoning a vigil outside the United States Embassy. Their banners, still held aloft, denounced the evil of American weaponry on British soil. The largest read BRITAIN SAYS NO TO GOLIATH.

The demonstrators were weary yet still dogged in their determination to press the case on any natives they passed. A chauffeur, stretching his legs beside a Granada parked at the hotel's entrance, had a leaflet thrust into his hand. He glanced impassively at the text then balled it up and tossed it into the ragged column.

Antonia lit a cigarette. 'I meant to ask what news you had of Gail.'

'I phoned her last night. She sounded fine.'

'Is she staying on with your sister?'

'She may do. Joanna thinks it would be better than the clinic now. Joanna's very down to earth. She could be right.'

'Isn't it a risk?'

He shrugged. 'It so happens Joanna's GP has experience in drugs cases. And Gail's happy with her.'

'How do you feel about it yourself?'

'I think,' he said and paused. He hadn't wanted to face that. But suddenly he knew he felt differently now; his fingers weren't crossed any more. 'I think she's going to be all right.'

The chauffeur had begun polishing the Granada's paintwork. Beyond him, in the shop windows of Mount Street, perfections of ornament and furniture beckoned. Antonia said, 'Ludo will be fuming.'

Egerton glanced at his watch. 'Do you suppose Rylance decided it was a trap?'

'It's possible.'

He was gritting his teeth. 'I don't want to sound ungrateful but don't you find it annoying that he'd made the arrangement before we'd even arrived—and then didn't tell us for over an hour?'

'I warned you that he was infuriating. He's used to having his own way. Being frank and straightforward is very difficult for him. When he's like that, you have to remember his other side.'

Presumably she was on about Fender's sensibility again. It was useless to reply that he'd seen nothing of it. Whatever she'd discovered behind that devious, faintly menacing manner had disarmed her. She had been recruited to his camp and nothing was going to change that.

'Here he comes,' she said suddenly. He followed her gaze. Fender was emerging from the hotel entrance, buttoning his overcoat. Crossing to the Mini with a surprising burst of speed, he lowered himself into the passenger seat beside Egerton.

'As you will have seen, Rylance didn't appear. I have this minute telephoned his house. The call was answered by a police officer who was very persistent in trying to extract my identity and would answer none of my questions. Something has happened. We'd better drive to Chester Square.'

Egerton swung the Mini round to head for Park Lane. His headlights, crossing the front of the Granada, fell on the occupants. The chauffeur had abandoned his polishing and was back behind the wheel. Beside him sat a burly figure who looked familiar.

At the South Audley Street lights, where he had stood watching Sally Kirkwood strike out unsteadily for St John's Wood, he made the connection. The man had been Gail's minder at the meeting in Regents Park.

The west side of Chester Square had been sealed off completely. White tape stretched across all the access roads. Behind the tape quantities of police stood to prevent cars and pedestrians from entering. He finally found kerb space in Elizabeth Street. Abandoning the car, they returned to the square on foot.

At first the crowd of watchers proved too dense for them to be able to see anything. Fender, thrusting forward as relentlessly as a tank finally managed to get a view point. When Egerton joined him, his gaze was fixed on a gap between the trees where the Rylance house stood. Along the frontage were several police cars, a fire engine and a mobile crane. He glanced at Fender's face. His expression conveyed a curious mixture of recognition and disbelief. 'What is it?' Egerton asked.

Fender seemed for a moment or two not to have heard the question, his lips moving soundlessly. Then he pointed. A spotlight was being trained from the fire engine onto the façade of the house next to Rylance's. Abruptly brought into sharp relief where it lay across the portico was the twisted shell of a white Jaguar car. Along its side panels a frieze of small Union Jacks could be seen.

Another police car had driven up behind them and was waiting for a way to be cleared so that it could enter the square. As the car moved on, Egerton saw Antonia straighten. She had been talking to one of the car's occupants.

When she rejoined them, she said, 'That was Dick Moseley, the head of the Anti Terrorist Squad. Before he was appointed this year, he was on fraud cases. I used to see him a good deal.'

'Did you get any news?'

'He had only the bare facts. He'd just been summoned from a police seminar at Bramshill. The car is Evelyn Rylance's. It blew up as she tried to drive it away about an hour and a half ago. Rylance seems to have been standing by the car, talking to her, when it happened. She was killed instantly, Rylance himself is in hospital in a critical condition. There are two other casualties who haven't been identified.'

'Presumably his people on the spot have more details.'

'Moseley agreed I could hear their story. I had to twist his arm so I don't think he'd be amused if we all went. Why don't you and Mark wait in the car? I'll be back as soon as I can.'

Fender was grimacing. As when Egerton had told him the fate of the photographs, he had the appearance of being personally affronted by events. But he couldn't justify arguing with her. He managed a nod of acknowledgment, raised the battered homburg, which had been substituted for the fur hat before setting out for London, and grimly led the way back to the Mini.

While she was gone, he talked hardly at all, answering remarks from Egerton with monosyllables. Most of the time he spent in a dirge-like humming from which melancholy snatches of Elgar surfaced. It suggested a spasmodic, weaving process of thought. But he was keeping the results to himself.

He sat up briskly when Antonia reappeared. 'So what have you to tell us?'

Her expression held a hint of triumph. 'I was in time to hear the Rylances' maid give her story to Moseley. Apparently she saw most of what happened.' She was looking at some notes she had scribbled on an envelope. 'Perhaps the most interesting thing was her description of one of the two unidentified casualties in a car parked immediately behind the Jaguar. A man in a camel coat and blue-lensed spectacles.'

Fender folded his arms. 'We are all attention.'

It seemed that the two men had arrived at the Rylance house in the middle of the afternoon. While one remained in the car, camel coat had rung the bell. Since Slade the butler was off duty, the maid answered it. He had obviously been expected since before she could ask his name Evelyn appeared in the hall. She had taken him away to the drawing room where Rylance was.

After about three quarters of an hour, during which camel coat had made a call from the telephone lobby at the back of the hall, they had all emerged. Rylance and Evelyn in the maid's opinion were very tense. Evelyn called for her coat. When the maid brought it, Rylance was expressing doubts about a decision against his accompanying her. Evelyn made some remark to the effect that since they agreed the whole thing might be a trap, it was better for him not to be involved.

They had gone out of the house, still talking, and crossed to Evelyn's car. Camel coat had joined his companion in the car parked behind. Leaving the door ajar for Rylance, the maid had then walked across the hall to the staircase. At that moment an explosion had occurred which had thrown her to the floor.

Antonia replaced the envelope in her bag. 'That was all the maid could say. It was a car bomb of course. It could have been attached to the Jaguar several days before because Evelyn hadn't used it for about a week.'

'Did no one else drive it? Not even Rylance himself?'

'No, it was strictly for Evelyn's personal use.'

'Is there any more news about Rylance?'

'Moseley had a message as I was leaving. He'd just died on the operating table. The other two are not so badly injured and are expected to survive. They're still finding pieces of Evelyn on the front of the house.'

Fender's lips moved in what looked like a silent oath. Antonia glanced at him coolly. 'Moseley thinks this could be the first shot in an IRA pre-Christmas campaign. They know an active service unit is in London with orders to mount some spectaculars.'

'*He believes this is an IRA operation!?*' His eyebrows had lifted extravagantly.

'Subject to no surprises coming out of the forensic evidence, yes.'

'I hope he displayed greater penetration when he was dealing with frauds.'

'Why do you say that?'

He made a noise through his nose, intended to convey contempt. 'Could anyone of intelligence really suppose the IRA would set out to murder the *American-born* wife of a politician here? They really must be given *some* credit for political wisdom! Rylance would have been a very reasonable target. But the bomb wasn't aimed at him. It was meant to kill her.' He glanced at Egerton. 'I don't think there can be any serious doubt who *was* responsible for this.'

'Luis Fernandes' brother?'

'I would say so—or friends of his. After they had got Giordano's name from you, they no doubt paid him a visit and established Evelyn Rylance's part in organizing the operation in Nice. She has just paid the price for that. A simple matter of retribution in Garcia's eyes no doubt.'

'But what about Giordano? If you are right, once they had extracted the facts they would have killed *him* as they've now killed her. There's been nothing pointing to it in the press although to have had time to set up tonight's operation, they must have talked to him several days ago. How do you explain that?'

'A good point,' Fender said kindly. He was recovering from his earlier disappointment. 'Of course we may yet hear he *has* come to an unhappy end. If we don't, it can only mean he succeeded in convincing Garcia or his friends that he was not a party to the plot which led to the death of Luis.'

'Are you saying it wasn't Giordano Boyd heard threatening Lauren?'

'No, that *was* Giordano. But it has always seemed odd that, as you learned from his assistant on the telephone, he left Nice to return to Rome *before* the killings took place.'

'So what do you now believe?'

'That when he and Evelyn failed to move Lauren with their threats, he left Evelyn to decide with Catini what was to be done next.'

'And she asked Catini to drum up the two thugs . . .'

'That is my conclusion. In addition, contrary to our previous assumptions, I do not now think the killings were unintended. I believe that even if the thugs had recovered the cassette from Lauren, they would still have murdered her and Fernandes, *because that was what Evelyn asked for.* She realized any lesser course would be too dangerous. Lauren *might* have given no further trouble, although she had shown herself to be very determined in her campaign to stop GOLIATH. But Luis was much too formidable to leave alive. Once force had been used to recover the cassette he could certainly be expected to retaliate robustly.'

An ambulance passed them from the direction of Chester Square. Presumably it was carrying what remained of Evelyn. 'And Rylance?' Antonia said. 'Did he know everything?'

'Whether he was in on the whole thing from the beginning, we shall never know now. I would guess Evelyn left him in the dark until quite late in the affair. But by this afternoon he was aware of what was at stake. Otherwise he wouldn't have been taking part in the conference with Boffa's lieutenant. After my call this morning there was obviously a discussion between Rylance and Evelyn about the possibility of a trap—the maid's evidence points to that. I might have discovered the significance of the cassette and be planning to use it for blackmail as Lauren did. So Boffa was contacted. He sent round camel coat to discuss what should be done if all didn't go well at the Connaught. I imagine the call the maid reported being made from the lobby in the hall was a message summoning the other two heavies you identified outside the Connaught to go there and wait. If Evelyn's persuasion and or bribery had not succeeded in separating me from the cassette by the time I left the hotel, I conclude I should then have received other attentions.'

Fender glanced at his watch and sighed. 'There is obviously no point in remaining here. Perhaps we might adjourn to more comfortable surroundings to consider your next move.'

Egerton switched on the ignition. 'We could have a drink at my flat, then go round the corner to a restaurant I know.'

'Splendid.' Fender began to look cheerful at the prospect of refuelling and even hummed a few bars of Mozart. On the way down Sloane Street, he said, 'You will have a powerful story to tell Antrim. I wish very much that I could be there.'

'Is that impossible?'

'Unfortunately, yes. It would be very counter-productive to your cause for him to learn I had been advising you and giving a small amount of assistance. It would also reveal that Mrs Strachan had introduced you to me.' He smiled briefly. 'That would never do.'

'But how shall I account for the help you've given?'

'I shall provide you with the cassette, also the press cutting that identifies Catini. You can say that you obtained both during your enquiries, together with details of Mrs Rylance's travel back from Nice at the critical time. I suggest you say that the relationships between Catini, Boffa and the man who planted the heroin, Coleman, can all be confirmed by reference to police records. He can hardly fail to be impressed by your efforts.'

'He *could* be impressed without necessarily wanting to keep me in the Bureau.'

'Reflecting on what you know, he will certainly not want you *outside* it. If it came to notice in certain quarters of Whitehall that he had not only accepted a private commission from Rylance to search for his stepdaughter but had continued using official resources after learning Rylance had lied when offering his reason for the request, the consequences would be disagreeable. Of course you mustn't interpret what I say as a personal criticism of your

Director.' He smiled wolfishly. 'I am simply stating a fact.'

'But none of that would come out unless I disclosed it.'

They were halted by the traffic lights at the junction with Pimlico Road. In the window of a television shop beside them, perhaps thirty sets offered their silent images to the night.

'These things have a curious way of becoming known,' Fender said. He turned his face towards the shop window. To fathom what was in his mind, to make out the thought that lay behind the words and then the inner thoughts beyond, was like trying to assimilate at one and the same time what each of the images was saying.

Leading the way up the stairs to his flat, Egerton was conscious of a stirring in his spirits. It was not that Fender had convinced him that Antrim would actually want him back. He had been living a nightmare that had begun to fade.

The phone rang as he was pouring their whiskies. It was the first call for days he had answered without any sense of foreboding. A woman spoke. 'Mr Egerton?'

'Yes.'

'Please forgive me for troubling you. We haven't met.' The voice was very quiet. He detected a Scots accent.

'My name is Janet Buchanan. I believe you're a friend of my son.'

He searched his mind. 'I am?'

'Yes. Jamie Buchanan.'

Suddenly the wind was up again, the dogs whimpering, the bats everywhere in the rafters. 'I see. How—'

'Jamie gave me your number. He said if I could speak to you, you would explain some things.'

'Where is Jamie?'

'He was arrested this morning. Apparently he and a business associate were met by the police when they landed at an airfield in Buckinghamshire. It was a private plane owned by the other man. They had been on a business trip, Jamie told me, when I was allowed to see him for a few minutes this afternoon. I believe it had to do with drugs.'

'They were carrying drugs?'

'So I understand.' Her voice wavered for a few seconds. She sounded drained. 'I hope I'm not disturbing you at an inconvenient time.'

So Jamie's arrangement with whoever was supposed to forewarn him hadn't worked. People could let you down, however well you paid them.

'I'm very sorry,' he said.

'Jamie wanted me to know that whatever the police might say he'd never encouraged anyone to take drugs. He just supplied them to people who asked for them. He thought that if I understood the difference I wouldn't think so badly of him. Of course he doesn't realize my feelings are regardless—' Her voice broke. 'He's really a very kind boy,' she said.

'I know.'

'He told me you knew him as well as anybody did. If he's prosecuted as does seem probable, I wondered if you'd be willing to speak for him. It would perhaps make a difference to the way he's treated by the court.'

'Did he say he wanted me to do that?'

'No. He only said *I* might feel happier if I talked to you. He thought you would help me to understand.'

After a few seconds he realized she had begun to weep.

When he returned to the sitting room, he saw that some part of the conversation had registered with them. Their expressions were polite but enquiring. He sat down and glanced at Fender. 'I remember you once spoke of one's past being a prison house from which one couldn't escape. It sounded excessively gloomy to me at the time. But you had a point.'

'What has happened?'

He explained.

'I've promised to go and see her now. She's in his flat in Portland Place, sounding very alone and bewildered. Perhaps you'll forgive me not joining you for a meal.'

His cheek was twitching. He smiled apologetically. 'I

think this kills the idea of trying to stay in the Bureau. I hope you won't think me ungrateful for the efforts you've made if I just resign.'

'Why should you do that?' Fender asked.

'Even I accept it's no joke for the Bureau if one of its staff testifies on behalf of a drugs dealer. My own history would have to come out.'

'There is no obligation on you to testify.'

'I feel there is. I have to speak up for him.'

'Then you must put the facts squarely to Antrim. You feel you have a moral obligation to testify. I hope he would recognize he has no less of an obligation to stand by you as one of his employees.'

'In his shoes, would you go on employing me?'

Fender gazed at the ceiling, assembling careful words. 'It is only human to hope that one's integrity will be taken for granted by the world and never put to the test. I should not welcome the challenge. In my darker moments I might hope that you would come to me and say that after all you wished passionately to join the Forestry Commission and needed only a testimony of your competence. I confess too that some of your views and attitudes are alien to me. But, yes, I *would* go on employing you. To have fought and overcome drug addiction is no small thing. Others have weakness no less inimical to character but cloak them successfully. I would not want a Bureau staffed only by reformed sinners of course. But, even less would I want one that contained only plaster saints and timid virgins.'

He lowered his gaze and settled into his chair more comfortably. 'Moreover, there is a reason additional to those I have already given you why your Director will no doubt prefer to avoid the consequences of discharging you. I conclude from certain observations made to Mrs Strachan by Mansell that enquiries into your associations at university which might well have militated against your recruitment to the Bureau were omitted. This resulted from Antrim's decision that he wanted no delay in acquiring your services. Very understandable, I'm sure. But investigation of this whole business would no doubt highlight a decision which would be rather difficult to defend.'

Fender's expression invited seemly satisfaction at this thought. When Egerton did not respond, he adopted an air of impatience that was only partly calculated. 'What is wrong with your generation? Is a post in which you serve the public interest not worth fighting for? Once, when I was young, it would have seemed a great prize. Imagine being doomed to one of those innumerable occupations which are either parasitical or absurd or both.' He fluttered his fingers contemptuously. 'Speculators, Parliamentary lobbyists, Euro-MPs!' For some reason he had let investigative journalists off this time.

He was conscious of Antonia watching him closely. 'I *will* think it over carefully of course.'

'So I would hope,' she said.

'Perhaps I could drop you both off at the restaurant on my way to Mrs Buchanan.'

She drained her glass and stood up, still looking sombre. He knew that if he didn't make a fight to stay in the Bureau, she would have no more time for him. Neither would Fender. But that would be easier to bear.

When they arrived at the restaurant, she said, 'Speak to me before you go to Antrim.' He hesitated and she went on fiercely, '*Mark!*'

'I promise,' he said. Her determination irked. Yet at the same time, he was warmed. He looked at each of them in turn. 'I haven't said how grateful I am to you for believing in me. Whatever happens, I'll never forget that.'

As he watched them cross the pavement, he saw Fender reach out as though to guide Antonia through the restaurant door, then withdraw his hand suddenly. The audacity of the gesture had overwhelmed him. She must somehow have been aware of the movement. She glanced up at his face with an expression that was at once ironical and tender. Then she put her own hand on his forearm and kept it there.

He wondered if they would go back to her flat later.

Sunday night trains to Fender's part of East Sussex were no doubt few and far between. She would perhaps invite him to stay. And then? He guessed they had a prison house of their own that neither, in the final analysis would choose to be without. An alliance, almost impossible to believe in, he thought, pulling into the traffic and heading for Portland Place. But, there it was. They were a match.